THE LOCK-EATER

THE
LOCK-EATER

ZACK LORAN CLARK

Dial Books for Young Readers

DIAL BOOKS FOR YOUNG READERS
An imprint of Penguin Random House LLC, New York

First published in the United States of America by Dial Books for Young Readers,
an imprint of Penguin Random House LLC, 2022

Visit us online at penguinrandomhouse.com.

Library of Congress Cataloging-in-Publication Data is available.

Book manufactured in Canada

ISBN 9781984816887

1 3 5 7 9 10 8 6 4 2

FRI

Design by Cerise Steel
Text set in Tisa Pro

For the Brooklyn Wizards:

Nick & Andrew, Billy & Nico, Jack & Seth, Laura & Sarah.

I'm so grateful to have you all in my life.

THE
LOCK-EATER

CHAPTER 1

NEARLY everyone at the Merrytrails Orphanage for Girls agreed: Abraxas was not a good cat.

He was stubborn and hateful, which wasn't itself unusual in cats, and didn't even *necessarily* preclude a cat from goodness. Plenty of the girls' favorite stories featured cats who were notorious grumps, and yet they maintained a certain charisma.

But Abraxas was also unsightly. Again, ugly cats were commonplace in the streets of Crossport, and the girls loved them all the same. Some were rakish toms, riddled with the scars of their many cat duels. Some were misshapen but sweet, with smooshed-in faces and warbling cries that softened even the most callous hearts.

Abraxas was neither. Where he *had* fur, it was a vague sort of gray. His stomach was completely bald, and one white eye had a milky quality to it. And he *stunk*, noxious from the pearly globs of wetness Mrs. Harbargain fed him twice a day.

All of this might have been perfectly fine if Abraxas had at least been entertaining. But the orphanage's pet cat was sedentary during the day, hissing at any of the girls who came too close.

Little Mariana Porch had once dared to bring a broom

handle within a few inches of his face, dangling a feather in the manner she'd seen two rich children in town do, playing with their gorgeous Siamese. She'd hoped to entice Abraxas into doing something silly. Both broom and Mariana still bore the scars from that unfortunate day.

But what made the cat truly *not good* was what happened after lights-out. Because at night, Abraxas finally came alive. He stalked the halls of the orphanage like a wraith, yowling and scratching ceaselessly at every door and window he could reach.

Mrs. Harbargain slept like a stone. Her room was nestled all the way at the bottom of the tall house, while Abraxas was locked into the upper floor hallway. She never heard the cat's nightly pandemoniums, and waved away the girls' complaints as whining—even as the upstairs doors were thinned away one claw-size notch at a time.

It was on just one such a night that Melanie Gate decided she'd had enough.

"Where are you going?" whispered Jane Alley. Melanie could just see her friend's light brown face hovering from the top bunk beside her own, her large eyes wide and worried.

Jane was agonizingly shy—the sort of girl who hid away from her own nameday parties. That she'd spoken up at all meant she'd sensed Melanie was about to do something particularly audacious.

Jane always seemed to know. Sometimes even before Melanie herself.

Outside the dormitory, Abraxas yowled. He was rattling the hall window with his paws, as if playing a glass drum.

"I can't stand it anymore," Melanie said, shuffling to the edge of her bed and lowering herself gently to the floor below. Her face was pale and irritated as she glimpsed it in the room's small mirror. "I haven't slept more than ten hours all week."

Sun-mi Churchyard's bunk was just below Melanie's. She pushed a lock of dark hair from her eyes. "But what are you going to do?" she asked, sitting up as Melanie slid her feet into her slippers. They were donations from the wealthy families during the last Night of Gold festival, addressed: *To the Poor, Sweet Orphans. With Affection & Heartache.*

"He wants out so badly," Melanie said primly. "I'm going to give him what he wants."

Across the room, Agatha Chickencoop laughed. She brushed a tangle of russet curls from her tawny freckled face to better smirk at Melanie. "Mrs. Harbargain locked all the doors and windows. If they're open, she'll know it was you, lock-eater. You'll get punished."

By now, all the girls were sitting up in their beds and watching Melanie as she marched toward the dormitory door in her nightgown and slippers.

"There's more than one way to open a window," Melanie declared. "One of these days, Abraxas is bound to rattle the glass just a *bit* too hard." She revealed the weighty fire iron that she'd smuggled beneath her bedspread, and a chorus of gasps filled the room.

"Don't!" little Mariana squeaked.

"Oh, Mrs. Harbargain will be so mad," said Baruti Harbor. She pulled her favorite blue blanket around her until it nearly covered her dark brown face and eyes.

Melanie reached the door and whirled around, brandishing the iron. Just outside, Abraxas had broken into a wailing aria. His voice was like a mournful young soprano with a rock in her mouth, trapped inside a bucket.

"Mad is what *we'll* be if we don't get some sleep," Melanie said. "They'll have to rename this place the Merrytrails Asylum for Cat Killers. Listen to him," she added, "he wants out as much as we want him gone. I'm striking a blow for liberty."

Abraxas had begun drumming against the windowpane again, providing Melanie's revolution with a jangling anthem.

"Can I at least count on you not to tell?" Melanie asked. "Harbargain can't punish *all* of us." Melanie's eyes slowly scanned the dormitory, falling on each of her friends in turn. "I'm doing this for everyone," she said.

There was a long moment of not-quite silence. Then a timid voice called out. "I won't tell," said Jane.

"Me neither," Agatha announced boldly.

One by one, the girls agreed.

Melanie beamed at them. She nodded, then turned and faced the locked dormitory door. She placed her hand on the knob and there was a genial, mechanical noise. Pins and springs slipped helpfully out of the way. Then Melanie twisted the knob, fire iron in hand, and the door creaked open. She stepped alone into the hall.

Melanie Gate had always been good at opening things. Doors, windows—places of passage just welcomed her. Locks malfunctioned when she needed to get by in a hurry. In the springtime, windows that had been rusted shut for years would lurch open with clouds of auburn flakes.

As a very young girl, Melanie would sometimes be found wandering the lower floors of the house, exploring after lights-out. Though Mrs. Harbargain had always carefully locked both the door to the girls' dormitory and the one leading downstairs, she'd invariably discover them wide-open the next morning. After a few near escapes by Abraxas, Melanie was finally broken of this habit through a week of missed desserts.

But the strange skill went back as far as infancy. Like all the foundling girls at Merrytrails, Melanie had been named after the place she was discovered. As Mrs. Harbargain told it, a pair of city guards had been strolling past Crossport's South Gate during their evening rounds. The gate was fastened shut and locked, as it was every night.

Just when they'd passed by, however, the guards heard a horrific clamor behind them. They spun around to discover that the enormous South Gate was cracked open, as if it had never been bolted closed. Only the enchantments of the city's aldermages kept the ponderous doors from swinging completely wide. And there, wedged between them, was a very determined toddler with chestnut curls trying to pull herself through the gap and into the city.

Melanie was promptly deposited at the orphanage. She had

nothing but her first name, her clothes, and a single token—an embroidered cloth decorated with a field of flowers. Pointed rooftops protruded from the bulbs, and above it all looped the words: *Kinderbloom! The Garden Village*.

Mrs. Harbargain sometimes called her *uncanny*, and Agatha said she was a "lock-eater." But Melanie didn't *eat* anything. She simply asked doors to open and they agreed. To her, opening doors seemed perfectly natural. After all, that's what they were *for*, wasn't it? It was really all very polite.

None of the other girls minded. Not even Agatha, really. Every orphan at Merrytrails had her own traits and skills. Agatha was a brilliant actress. Well, she was dramatic, anyway. Little Mariana could charm the stripes off a bee. Helen Stables claimed to have a way with horses, though the girls had never put this to a test.

Each could be expected to help the others when needed, using their particular talents for the good of all. Now was simply one of those times.

Melanie stared out into the hall, which had gone suddenly, shockingly quiet. She glanced to the window, where a keen yellow eye watched her back.

"All right, cat," Melanie said. "The council of orphans has heard your demands. I'm here to set you free."

"*Maow*," Abraxas replied skeptically.

"Well, you didn't leave us much choice, did you?"

Melanie waved the poker around as she approached the window at the end of the hallway, shooing the old cat. She knew better than to attempt this within striking distance of his claws. Abraxas hissed at her, but he slunk away, watching her with his gleaming good eye from a few feet down.

Melanie turned her attention to the window. It was a large and cheerful casement, and very sunny in the morning. A wide sill lay beneath on which rested a small pretty vase full of small pretty flowers. She set these on the floor for now.

Outside, the moon was high: a shining fingernail. Much of the city was dark, though the magical toverlichts kept the wide avenues lit for the town watch. Melanie could just make out the empire's three-eyed flag waving from the roofs of the nearby buildings. Beyond them were the harbor and the three city gates. The North Gate led to Ultrest, the empire's capital city, where the king lived. The East Gate was sometimes called the Prisoner's Gate because it fed out to the Donjon, a court and prison system so sprawling, it was a city in its own right. Melanie could actually see the South Gate now, towering in the distance. And beyond it . . . ? An ache. A tug.

Melanie had been at Merrytrails for as long as she could remember, and more than anything, she wanted to see the *world*.

Her very favorite books in the orphanage's meager library were The Misadventures of Misty Steppe, a collection of heart-pounding tales starring an audacious explorer. Misty got into all sorts of trouble, but each time she'd find her way out again through gumption and good humor.

Melanie and Jane had read the books countless times,

Melanie sometimes starting again just as she turned the last page, while Jane dreamed up Misty stories of her own. Drawings of the young woman covered Melanie's notebooks, and were tacked to her bedpost. If she closed her eyes, she could clearly picture Misty's face. She felt *that* real.

Melanie wasn't the sort of orphan to pine over lost parents or mysterious origins. She was an ambitious girl, with a gaze set forward rather than back. Misty was all the role model she needed.

And how she *longed* for an adventure of her own, just like Misty. Melanie spent practically every waking moment—and often her sleeping ones—pining for what waited beyond the city. The desire for freedom shaped her dreams, sending her climbing snowy mountains and trekking through dark forests on a nightly basis.

Now, behind her, Abraxas called out an impatient "*Maow.*"

Melanie shook her head. She needed to focus. "Just lining up the strike," she said. "No need for salty language." She raised the fire iron high over her head.

Melanie took a brief moment to consider the consequences of her next action:

Was freedom truly prudent for a cat as old and half-blind as Abraxas?

Wouldn't Mrs. Harbargain mourn his disappearance?

Was it actually true that the matron couldn't punish *all* the girls, if she believed they were conspiring against her?

Considerations so made, Melanie swung the iron bar.

A loud peal brought her up short. It was one of the city bells, tolling from the palace, its voice high and clear. Melanie let out a little gasp. She lowered the fire iron, waiting.

After a moment, a second bell tolled, this one warbling, nervous.

Lights began to brighten in the windows of the houses outside. The bells never rang this late, not unless something dire was happening. Melanie heard shouts from the street below. Boots pounded against cobblestones. Several guardsmen flashed briefly in and out of view, running toward the castle.

The structure loomed in the distance, towering over the other buildings. Its brilliant red roof was discernable even in the darkness, lit as it was by its own magical beacons. The rolling ocean was just to the castle's west, and the city docks, glimmering faintly under the moon.

A third bell rang. Its voice was grim and final. Two bells meant an emergency, but three meant a death. Someone important had just perished.

Melanie stood there a moment, unsure how to proceed. Even if she still freed Abraxas tonight, the girls would get no sleep. She and the others would be up for hours, guessing at who had died and what it might mean for the city. For the thaumacracy, even. Three bells meant the world outside was about to change.

Melanie placed her hand to the glass, and wished desperately that the world was open to her.

It was a brief wish, but a strong one, and it passed right

through her hand where she'd pressed it against the window. The window heard her, and it did its very best to grant such a potent wish. It helpfully exploded.

But it wasn't just the window. Melanie's wish must have passed through the entire orphanage, because right at that moment, every door, window, hatch, and chimney—every opening that connected to the outside—blasted outward with showers of wood, stone, and glass.

Melanie heard the girls in the dormitory scream as their windows burst apart. She even heard Mrs. Harbargain wailing from downstairs. She felt the crisp night air breezing in through the ruined window and took a step back, nearly stepping on Abraxas, who was himself breezing by in the opposite direction.

The cat leaped up onto the sill, unconcerned by the many shards of broken glass that glittered there.

"Wait—" was all Melanie had time to say. Then the old cat was gone, without even a backward glance.

Melanie stared out the window, her mouth hanging open. Behind her, the stair door crashed open, and Mrs. Harbargain charged, screaming, into the hall.

CHAPTER 2

MELANIE was grounded and given double chores for a month, and she was permanently banned from stepping within three feet of a door or window without Mrs. Harbargain there to supervise. It was a very tedious month, which won't be detailed here. Only two things of any importance happened during that time.

First, Mrs. Harbargain and the girls held a fundraiser to repair the doors, windows, and chimney of the orphanage. They sold pies, each masterfully prepared by Sun-mi. (Mrs. Harbargain *had* attempted one to start, but after opening the oven door to a scorched and smoking blister, bleeding raspberry goo from its wounds, she ceded the baking to the expert.)

Meanwhile, Melanie cleaned, and the other girls were forbidden from helping her.

Second, Melanie learned that it was the High Enchanter who had died. Zerend the Red, the Third Eye of the Empire, had been assassinated. His laboratory in the palace was burned to a black and smoking crater.

Melanie knew little of the man, beyond that he was the most important wizard in the thaumacracy. In depictions of him, he always had a trim, dark beard. The High Enchanter led the empire's magical branch of government, the source of its military might. Zerend the Red had a reputation as a stern genius, though Melanie assumed all witches and wizards were likely geniuses, and at least a *little* stuffy.

Devastating magic had been brought to bear against Zerend, and there was no doubt who was responsible—only the Ley Coven could have triggered such a spell. They were a cult of far-flung mages, the thaumacracy's most potent enemies, led by a frightfully powerful witch known as the Hexe of the South.

Riquem, the new High Enchanter, was now calling for war.

Melanie thought the idea of a wizard war was very exciting. It was all just like a story! She'd been right, of course. The world was about to change.

That was all that happened in that month, however.

CHAPTER 3

WELL, perhaps one more thing.

While she finished scrubbing the kitchen floors one night after everyone had gone to bed, Melanie heard a muffled ringing noise coming from somewhere in the house. She took little notice of it. She completed her final chore for the day, then blew out the kitchen lamp and padded quietly to the stairs.

As her foot landed on the first step, however, she heard the sound again, but clearer and closer. Melanie realized it wasn't a ringing sound at all. It was a voice—weeping—and it was coming from Mrs. Harbargain's room.

Melanie lingered on that step for a long time, just staring at the matron's door. Then she trudged miserably up to bed.

No one saw any sign of Abraxas.

CHAPTER 4

IT was raining the night the traveler arrived. A storm had blown in from the Aederian Sea, then dawdled to enjoy its evening in the port city. Melanie and the girls were downstairs, listening to the drone of the rain from the cozy warmth of the orphanage's parlor. A fire murmured companionably in the hearth.

The windows and doors had all been repaired. Merrytrails was whole once again, but the other girls whispered that the pie sales weren't nearly enough to cover the cost. Sun-mi said that Mrs. Harbargain had stopped at a usurer's when they went out for groceries. When the matron finally exited the building and hurried Sun-mi along, her face was stony and gray.

"What's a user?" little Mariana asked in a whisper.

"A *usurer* is a sort of banker," Baruti said. Of all the girls, Baruti was by far the smartest. She never forgot a piece of trivia, and she could multiply and divide fractions as easily as she could tie her shoe. Perhaps easier. "They loan money, but you have to pay back more than you borrowed."

"*Much* more," Agatha said ominously, chewing on a fuzzy curl of hair. "And if you can't pay, they send large men to beat you and take your valuables." Agatha had always been a bit theatrical, but Baruti didn't disagree with her. In fact, she nodded grimly.

Melanie glanced now to Mrs. Harbargain's doorway. Beyond, dim lamplight indicated that the matron was inside, but no sounds or movement had come from the door for hours. Melanie curled her legs into her chest, hugging her knees tightly.

"It's all my fault," she said.

"No it isn't!" little Mariana quickly assured her.

"Yes, it is," Agatha corrected.

Melanie frowned, turning to the window. Rain licked the surface like a kitten lapping at cream. "I'm sorry, everyone," she said. "I only meant to help, but I've ruined everything, haven't I?"

Even Agatha's face softened now. The rest of the girls all watched Melanie, the parlor blanketed by the trill of the downpour. Jane didn't speak—she never spoke much—but scooted closer, taking Melanie's hand in hers. For Melanie, it was enough. Her friend's steady support soothed.

Until, that is, the front door boomed with three forceful knocks.

Mariana yelped, falling into Agatha's arms and hiding her face. One by one, the girls stood and stared at the door. None of them ventured any closer.

"Who would be out in this storm?" Agatha asked.

"It's the user!" Mariana squeaked from her armpit.

There was a groan and a creak from Mrs. Harbargain's room. Slowly, her door inched open, and the matron's worried face appeared, tight with dread. She edged out of the room. Harbargain said nothing to the girls, keeping her eyes forward. She approached the front door warily, as if it were a stray dog.

Mrs. Harbargain's hand trembled as she took hold of the latch and budged it open. Outside, a tall figure loomed in the doorway, concealed beneath a sodden cloak. A cold wind blew in with the figure's arrival, rustling Melanie's hair. She shivered and crossed her arms.

Little Mariana whimpered, her bronze arms still clinging to Agatha.

The figure remained perfectly still. Their posture was rigid, despite the rain and chill. Melanie couldn't make out any features beneath the cloak.

"Can I help you?" Mrs. Harbargain asked tentatively.

"This one hopes so." The figure spoke with a clear, genteel voice, which echoed as if from within a metal helmet.

Was it one of the city guards? Some mercenary clad in armor who'd come to rough up the orphanage? Melanie had assumed by the stranger's size that it must have been a man, but the voice was indeterminate: a tinny alto. "This one is here on an errand," the figure continued. "It is a task of great importance."

"This . . . one?" Harbargain appeared puzzled, then her eyes brightened with recognition. The tightness fell away from her face, replaced by a look of wonder.

"You're a wizard's clockwork servant! What do they call you things? A gearling!"

The stranger nodded slightly, and the heavy hood fell from its head. All the girls gasped as one. The figure's face was smooth and featureless, except for two glowing white dots that shone out from beneath a metal grille, emulating a pair of wide, unblinking eyes. In place of a mouth, a plate covered the lower half of its face, ridged in the center and decorated with lovely swirling flourishes, clearly engraved by a master's hand.

It was strange and wonderful and completely unlike anything Melanie had ever seen. Rain now pelted the figure's head, water coursing down the engravings in thin streams. It didn't seem to notice.

"Is this one permitted inside?" the gearling queried in a deferential tone. "This one found a small creature huddled outside the door. It does not appear to enjoy the rain."

"Creature . . . ?" Harbargain asked, disoriented.

The gearling's arm rose out from beneath its cloak with an audible whir of machinery. There, clawing and biting at its metal hand, was Abraxas.

The rain had not helped the cat's ugliness. His scant fur coat was sodden and matted, resulting in Abraxas somehow appearing both skeletal and swollen at the same time. His good eye bulged with rage.

"This one tried to carry it gently. The creature did not appear to enjoy that, either."

"Abraxas!" Harbargain wailed. She reached her arms out and cradled the drenched cat, and to Melanie's continued bewilderment, he acquiesced. Abraxas released his frantic grip on the gearling's arm, settling into the matron's embrace with a tolerating "*Maow*."

"Thank you! Oh, thank you!" Harbargain gasped. "I'd thought my poor Abraxas was dead for sure. Helen, fetch some towels, would you please? Come in, traveler. Melanie will take that drenched cloak of yours and set it by the fire. Would you like some—oh, I don't suppose you *would* drink tea, would you?"

"This one neither eats nor drinks." The gearling stepped forward into the parlor and Harbargain shut the door behind it. The room immediately felt several degrees warmer. Helen hurried off to gather towels from the linen pantry.

Melanie moved hesitantly toward the clockwork figure, as she'd been told. It was at least six feet tall and stood perfectly motionless in the foyer, dripping sheets of water onto the stone floor. As Melanie arrived at the gearling's side, its face turned suddenly with that odd mechanical whir. The two bright globes watched her from behind their metal grating.

Melanie stopped short, but the figure remained still and said nothing. It gazed impassively as she finally worked up the courage to stretch up and shift the cloak from its shoulders. Revealed from beneath the dark fabric, honey-colored metal gleamed golden in the firelight. The gearling's body was like the finest suit of armor Melanie had ever seen. Engravings similar to the ones on its mask covered the plates, looping into meandering patterns across its entire figure. But even at a glance Melanie could tell this was no armor a human would ever wear. The proportions were all strange; the limbs were too long for a person, and its legs bent at a backward angle.

She'd heard the aldermages in the palace had clockwork servants, of course, but had never actually seen one in person. And wizards had all sorts of strange servants, if every story was to be believed. Animals and spirits and dragons. Even demons.

Melanie carried the cloak gingerly to the hearth and laid it on the hot stone, feeling the gearling's glowing eyes on her the whole time. Once Helen had arrived with the towels, Mrs. Harbargain instructed the girls to dry the clockwork visitor—*"Carefully,* mind you!"—as she dabbed the bedraggled Abraxas herself.

Once everyone was good and dry, Harbargain finally seemed to remember that the gearling had come with a purpose.

"How can I help you, traveler? Er . . . do you have a *name*? Something your master or mistress calls you?"

There was a long pause, in which it almost seemed the gearling was brooding over the question. "You may continue to call this one Traveler, if it pleases you," it answered finally.

Harbargain nodded slowly. "Very well. *Traveler* it is. What brings you to our orphanage?"

"This one represents the interests of the powerful witch . . . Felidae Seagreen," the gearling said. "This one has come in her stead, but she would prefer to speak for herself."

The clockwork figure raised one of its metallic hands, and Melanie saw that a crystal orb had been embedded into its palm. Slowly, the orb began to shine with a glittery blue sheen, and then to glow outright. Light poured upward from the crystal like a drop of ink spilled into clear water. The girls all squealed and chattered excitedly at the sight of wizardly magic, but Mrs. Harbargain shushed them before they could get too agitated.

The liquid light coagulated, pooling into a vague triangular shape. Then the fog shifted into focus, and the tiny image of a wizened old woman floated in the air before them. She was exactly as Melanie pictured a witch *would* look, based on the Misty Steppe stories, with a flowing green cloak, a pointed hat, and a plump, pleasant, olive-toned face. She even carried a broom in one hand and leaned heavily against it, like a walking staff.

The miniature glowing woman cleared her throat. Her voice sounded small and far away. "Ah, hello there. I am the Witch Felidae. I'm pleased that my servant has made it to you safely. You see, I find myself in need of an assistant—a living one, that is. I was hoping to take on one of your fine girls as my ward and apprentice. I'm afraid I'm not getting any younger, and could use a bright young helper to aid me in my work. She'll be well cared for, of course. Afforded an education and every possible luxury a child could want. The only caveat is that I'm in rather desperate need. As you can see, I can't make the trip myself— even walking has become burdensome in my dotage. So I must request that the girl accompany my servant *tonight*, before the South Gate closes. I live in a little cottage just a few miles down from the city. The journey shouldn't be too taxing for a sprightly youngster."

The witch paused, and silence filled the parlor.

Melanie and the other girls all looked at one another with identical shocked expressions.

A witch's apprentice? Truly?

"What a surprising proposition," Mrs. Harbargain said slowly. "No doubt any of my girls would be lucky for such an opportunity, Mistress Felidae. But I'm afraid I can't just allow them to go wandering into the night unsupervised, without following the proper procedures. You understand that there are *some* scoundrels out there who might take advantage of my laxness."

"Oh, I certainly understand," the tiny witch replied cheerfully. "Your prudence credits the fine home you've created for them. The safety of your girls is obviously of utmost importance. Only . . . I'm in a bit of a bind myself. It's *also* of utmost importance that my new assistant arrives right away. My last apprentice resigned abruptly due to family illness, you see. The whole clan struck by foxpox—so sad. And now my roof is leaking in the storm! The South Gate closes within the hour. Perhaps we could see to the official paperwork tomorrow? I'll have your girl post it first thing—she'll need to be literate, of course. She'll also include a handwritten letter, just so you know she's safe and happy."

This all sounded very reasonable to Melanie, but Mrs. Harbargain sat up straighter in her chair. She shifted Abraxas's weight from one leg to the other. The cat growled irritably, settling into his new position. Harbargain's eyes took on a hard, skeptical gleam that Melanie knew well.

"I'm afraid that's not going to be possible," the matron said.

"These girls are my charges, you see. I've made it my duty to ensure the safety of every home that welcomes them through its doors. My apologies, Mistress Felidae."

The only sounds for a long moment were the pops and cracks of the fireplace, and the hum of the rain.

"Ah, how unfortunate," the witch finally replied. "Then perhaps I've deprived myself of my servant for nothing. Thank you for your time." The image of the witch flickered for a moment: a candle set beside an open window. Then it reasserted itself. "Oh, but before we go," Felidae said, "do you mind if I ask a question?"

"Ask whatever you'd like," said Harbargain.

"I've heard that Merrytrails had a run of bad luck recently. A good deal of repair work was needed. Work like that must have been very expensive."

Now Melanie bristled. All the girls cast wary glances at one another.

"This is true," Harbargain replied slowly. "But it's not a question."

"Perhaps if I were willing to make a donation to Merrytrails, it would help convince you of my good intentions? A sum considerably larger than the usual adoption fees. My servant is carrying a pouch of coins in its cloak. If you'd be willing to delay the formal paperwork—by just a day, mind you—then the pouch is yours. You'll want to count it yourself, but I think you'll find there's enough to cover the expenses and more."

Every eye turned toward the hearth, where the gearling's

wet cloak still steamed beside the crackling fire. There *did* appear to be a large bulge sewn into the right side of the fabric. When Melanie finally glanced back to Harbargain, she saw the tightness had returned to the matron's face.

"That is a . . . a very generous offer," Harbargain said.

"Merely a sign of good faith. The work you do here is so important. If you'd be willing to show me this kindness in my time of need, the least *I* could do is return the favor."

Mrs. Harbargain chewed her lip, sagging into her seat as if a great weight had suddenly been added to her shoulders. "And you say you'd get the papers to me first thing? Have the girl write us and let us know she's safe and cared for?"

"It will be her cardinal priority, once she arrives." The tiny witch bowed as low as was possible while still clutching her broom.

"Very well," the matron sighed. "Perhaps . . . perhaps this once we can show a little lenience." Harbargain frowned. Her fingers kneaded the top of Abraxas's head, molding his face into a contorted series of scowls. "What sort of girl are you looking to adopt, then? All of the children can read and write, though the older ones are more proficient. Jane is very quiet and tidy; you'd hardly notice she's there. Sun-mi is a masterful cook, and she often prepares meals for the whole house. Baruti has a way with numbers and an adroit grip of history. I had a mind to set her on the house's finances next year, but she might be better suited to your purposes."

Each name the matron spoke stirred panicked looks from

the girls. For the first time, Melanie began to understand that one of her friends would be leaving forever that night, disappearing into the storm with all the suddenness of a clap of thunder.

Girls had left Merrytrails before, of course, but usually they were the young ones—and there was always time for proper goodbyes. Plus, the orphans who were adopted often stayed in Crossport. Whoever went with the clockwork servant would be leaving through the South Gate, trudging through rain and wind toward a new life beyond the city's walls. As much as she longed to see the world, Melanie didn't begrudge the girl her journey.

It didn't occur to her that she might be chosen. Girls like Melanie weren't usually the sort to get adopted. She was brash and loud—overexcitable and, by some people's measure, under-feminine. And things just seemed to get *complicated* in her presence. Melanie assumed that she was too strange to find a home, which was perfectly fine with her. As far as she could tell, parents were quite the opposite of freedom and adventure. They were rules and expectations and itchy, restrictive clothes.

A witch, however . . . that *was* something different, wasn't it?

The small glowing woman scanned the faces of the foundlings around her. Melanie sat a bit straighter without realizing it.

"They sound delightful," Felidae said. "What a difficult choice. No doubt they'd *all* make fine apprentices. I wonder, however, if you have any girls who've already shown a bit of eerie aptitude, if you catch my meaning. Who are canny in the uncanny? Credibly incredible? A girl who can't seem to help but attract strangeness, like unspooled yarn attracts snags. Magic has a way of twisting up around those with a talent, you see."

It was only the briefest of looks. Mrs. Harbargain's eyes flicked in Melanie's direction, and then back to the image of the witch. It was less than an instant, but it was enough. The small woman turned, her tiny, luminous gaze falling on Melanie. Melanie noticed that the glowing eyes of the clockwork servant were also upon her, and she shrank back. The other girls whispered as Felidae took her in.

"What's your name, then?" the witch asked.

"Melanie Gate, mistress," Melanie answered in a small voice.

"Most of the girls arrived knowing only their first names," Mrs. Harbargain interjected softly. "Or had them written in the apology notes left with them. Their surnames are meant to be temporary. She would be free to take yours once you've adopted her, if you chose." The matron's eyes were wet as she watched Melanie. Her gaze was almost tender. It was then that Melanie understood her fate was decided.

"Gate," Felidae said. "How serendipitous."

The tiny witch's floating image bounced excitedly in place. "Yes, I believe this will do nicely. Melanie, pack your things, dear. You're off to become a witch."

CHAPTER 5

THE second time the front door opened that night, Melanie felt the force of the storm hit her like a solid surface. Rain lashed her face, even shielded with a heavy hood. In an act of shocking generosity, Mrs. Harbargain had given Melanie her own wool traveling cloak, which now hung nearly to the girl's feet.

"Every adventurer needs a cloak," the woman had said, her eyes brimming.

Melanie carried her small bag of belongings beneath it, pressing it tightly to her chest.

Felidae's cottage was southeast of the city, tucked cozily between the imperial highways. "I just know you'll love it," she'd told Melanie with a hint of mischief.

Once the negotiations were completed, the witch had bid the girls farewell, disappearing in a swirl of smoke and leaving Melanie in the care of her clockwork servant. The gearling stood outside the doorway now, watching impassively. Its own cloak—having finally dried beside the fire—was once again soaked. Two unsettling dots of light shone out from beneath its hood, giving the figure the appearance of a spirit from a haunted tale.

The other girls were all gathered around the doorway. Many were sniffling and wiping their eyes. Little Mariana wept openly, her arms now wrapped around Sun-mi. One by one the girls hugged Melanie and said goodbye. They wished her safe journeys, and happy tomorrows, and made her promise to return someday and show off her fabulous spells and fairy servants. Mariana peeled herself away from Sun-mi long enough to leap into Melanie's arms, and Melanie nearly broke into tears herself then. She kissed Mariana's hair and assured her that she'd write the girls. Every day, if she had time. Then Agatha gently pried Mariana away.

"Take care out there, lock-eater," she said with surprising warmth. "Don't . . . Just don't forget us."

Jane was the last of the girls to say goodbye. She took Melanie's hands in her own, her eyes full of some unfathomable feeling.

"Oh, Jane . . ." Melanie breathed. She didn't trust herself to say more. A pang of guilt speared her. How could she be leaving her very dearest friend who, just an hour ago, held Melanie's hand and comforted her? What would Jane do without her? Retreat further into herself? And what would Melanie do without Jane?

"I'll see you again," Melanie finally rasped.

Jane nodded, tears now falling from her eyes. "If you don't, I'll come find you. No magic will keep me away." She pulled Melanie into a lung-crushing hug.

Mrs. Harbargain's embrace was even tighter. Melanie

couldn't remember the last time the matron had hugged her so. She let herself sink into the woman's arms. Her eyes began to burn and she nearly choked on a sob.

"*Melanie*," Harbargain whispered. Her voice was quiet, barely audible beneath the noise of the rain, even with her mouth pressed so close to Melanie's ear. But the matron's tone was urgent. "If anything is improper with this Felidae Seagreen—anything at all—you must *immediately* alert us in your letter. Simply write 'Give my love to Abraxas' and I'll know that you need help. I'll petition the city guard—the aldermages if I have to—and we will find you, I swear. 'Give my love to Abraxas.' Don't forget."

"The South Gate closes in ten minutes." The clockwork servant's voice rang out like a bell from behind Melanie, causing her and Mrs. Harbargain to jump apart.

"Yes, of course," the matron said. She nervously straightened her dress. "You're a special girl, Melanie. I always knew you were. I know I'm not your . . . Well, I've tried to be a . . . Oh, take care, my little wonder."

And then, before she was ready, before she could do more than nod at Harbargain and wave to the girls, Melanie found herself outside in the pouring rain. The door to Merrytrails banged firmly shut behind her.

"Haste is necessary," the gearling said. "Can you move quickly?"

Melanie nodded, her mind numb with cold and addled by the abruptness of it all. She'd longed for adventure, but *this* . . . It was all happening so fast.

"Follow this one."

She did. The gearling moved with inhuman grace, its long legs loping across the cobbled streets. Melanie hustled after it, then broke into a jog when she realized she was still falling behind. Even beneath her cloak, her fingers pricked from the chill, and the sideways angle of the rain made it hard to see. The city's toverlichts were shining. Their blue brilliance flooded through the downpour, giving Crossport the appearance of a city underwater.

It seemed like both an eternity before they reached the South Gate and far too soon. The glittering brass structure bulwarked the southern outlet to the Zeestraat, the westernmost of the empire's great roads. Technically the road ran right through Crossport—the city was named for its enviable position as the crossing point of the Zeestraat and the Wonderstraat. Travelers looking to journey up or down the coast had to pass through its famously gigantic gates and into the city itself.

But the gates were closed every night, magically sealing until the next dawn. Anyone caught in or out would need to wait to get through.

The night bell tolled just as Melanie arrived. Two guards were pressed bodily against the heavy doors, pushing them shut for the evening. Both had the three-eyed symbol of the empire emblazoned on their armor. One guard caught sight of the gearling, just as the looming figure drew close. He shrieked in surprise, jumping nearly a foot into the air. Melanie knew the feeling.

The second guard was a bit bolder. He pulled his sword free

of its scabbard and held it shakily out in front of him. "Who's there?" he shouted over the rain.

The gearling stopped in place, standing suddenly still. As Melanie caught up, it hadn't yet answered the guard.

"What's going on here?" the first one demanded. He too pulled his sword free now, aiming it at the gearling. "The gate's closed for the night. You'll have to find shelter somewhere else."

Melanie glanced up at the clockwork servant. It remained silent. Then, slowly, it turned its face toward her. Both guards followed its gaze, their eyes landing on Melanie.

"I . . ." Melanie was at a loss. Shouldn't the witch's servant explain the situation? She wasn't even an apprentice yet! But the hard faces of the guards told her that someone would need to speak, and the gearling didn't seem like it had any intention of doing so.

"Please, we must get through," Melanie said. "I'm—I'm a witch's apprentice. And it's very important that we return tonight."

"A witch's apprentice?" The first guard, the one who'd jumped at the sight of the gearling, nodded toward the stooped figure. "Who's this, then? And what's wrong with his eyes?"

"It's not a he," Melanie answered unsurely. "It's my mistress's clockwork servant."

Now the guards' curiosity seemed to overtake their fear. They squinted through the rain at the gearling.

"So it is!" the second guard exclaimed with a note of

fascination. "I've seen these things before. The High Enchanter has an army of them at the palace. They walk and talk like people. You could even have a civil conversation with one. 'How's the weather, then?' 'Oh, very fine, indeed!' But it's all brainless imitation. Just spells and metal."

"Brainless is claiming *this* weather's fine," the first guard grumbled.

"They don't even have real voices," the second continued. He stepped right up to the gearling now, and was squinting at its face beneath the hood. "What you're hearing is just steam and ensorcellment! Like drawing a smile on a kettle and naming it Junior."

The clockwork servant shifted slightly, turning its face toward the guards. The second guard flinched, then laughed nervously and backed away. "Creepy things, though."

"Who's this mistress you're apprenticed to?" the first guard asked, turning his attention back to Melanie. He'd sheathed his sword, but his posture was still stiff and anxious. He narrowed his eyes at her. "Not the Hexe of the South, I hope."

"Felidae Seagreen," she answered. "In a cottage just a few miles from here."

The two guards turned to each other.

"Ever heard of her?" the second asked.

The first shook his head. "*You're* the expert on magicked kettles, all of a sudden."

The second guard frowned, his eyes sliding slowly from Melanie to the gearling and back again. "What's your name?"

"Melanie."

"Melanie . . . ?"

"Gate."

The first guard had a nice chuckle at that, glancing at the imposing entranceway behind them. "And how old are you, Melanie Gate?"

"I . . . I'm not sure. I'm a foundling."

"'A foundling,' she says." The second guard chewed his lip and let out a sigh. "Listen, Melanie, things are about to get dicey for magic types in Crossport," he said. "That assistant of Zerend's—Requiem or whatever—has been promoted to High Enchanter. And he's on the warpath. He's after the Hexe of the South, sure, but word has it he means to stamp out *all* of the Ley Coven before he's done. And the king agrees. You're too young to remember the last Wizard War, but they're ugly things to get swept up in." He nodded to the gap between the gate's doors. "Go on. Tell your mistress that if she's wise, this will be your last visit to Crossport for a while."

Melanie nodded, just hoping that the rain hid whatever dismal expression she was making. Her life had changed so suddenly. Doors were closing behind her, and the farther she walked, the more likely it seemed that even she wouldn't be able to open them again.

The guards waved them toward the gap in the gate, stepping aside as the gearling passed. It slid between the doors like a cat, disappearing quickly outside. Melanie followed with one quick glance back at the frowning soldiers.

Beyond was open road. A grand stone trail, the Wonderstraat, disappeared behind a black curtain of rain. The gearling turned its head toward the sky, still dimly illuminated by the two toverlichts bracketing the gate like flickering parentheses.

The ponderous doors boomed closed behind them. A sizzle of magical residuum filled the air.

They were locked out.

The gearling's two illuminated eyes sputtered. Blinked? Rain coursed down its metal visor.

Then its posture suddenly slumped with a whir, arms hanging forward. It let out what could only be described as a long, metallic *sigh*.

Melanie and the other Merrytrails girls sometimes struck this very pose after the open-house days, when they greeted prospective parents. Their bodies taut from a day full of rigid curtsies and dementedly delightful smiles, some simply collapsed to the floorboards. Indeed, they too made that same weary sighing noise, after the front door had been firmly shut.

It was a startlingly human gesture, and it sent a cold shiver up Melanie's back that was far worse than the rain.

The gearling turned its gaze to the sealed gate, then back onto her. The two glowing motes *blinked* again.

"Well . . ." the automaton said, with an unmistakable note of relief. "*That* was rather close, wasn't it?" The eerie gentility was gone from its echoed voice. This was *not* the mindless gearling that had visited the orphanage. Melanie had the sudden impression of an actor shedding a role the moment the curtain closed.

"I spent every coin I had," it continued, "but I made it out." Then it raised its hands at Melanie's expression. "Oh. Please don't—"

Melanie couldn't hear the rest. She'd already begun to scream.

CHAPTER 6

HEAVY rain has a way of nipping the faces of those who run through it, like tiny pinches from grown-ups' fingers squeezing at one's cheeks.

The rain pelted and pinched Melanie's face now as she dashed across the slippery road, screaming as she went.

The blue glow of the toverlichts faded quickly behind the veil of storm. Melanie's steps became less sure, but she kept running. She wasn't really thinking so much as acting—a common criticism of Mrs. Harbargain's. Melanie thought of the matron wrapping her up in her own warm cloak just moments ago. She whimpered and ran faster.

Perhaps it will come as little surprise that she slipped.

Melanie's ankle lurched beneath her, her foot skidding across the rain-slick road. The angle of the pinches changed suddenly, rain now prodding her face with full force. Then—a great, jolting quake as her back slammed onto stone.

Bright lights flashed across her vision, shimmering prettily. Melanie tried to breathe, panicking momentarily as she realized she couldn't. With some effort, she sucked in a braying gasp of air.

Her butt really, *really* hurt.

In her discomfort, she'd nearly forgotten all about the rain until it suddenly stopped. The pretty lights faded from her vision—all except two.

The gearling gazed down at her, its lamp-like eyes blinking curiously.

"Are you all right?"

Melanie scrambled—not quite up, but backward-ish, into the mud just off the paved road. The torrent of rain returned. She noticed a transparent . . . thing? bubble? umbrella? . . . floating above the gearling and primly diverting the rain from its head.

"Now you're all *dirty!*" the automaton said, appalled. "And after your matron gave you that nice cloak." It tutted—*tutted!*—from within its mask, the noise ringing against the metal.

Melanie just stared for a moment. "What?" she finally managed, before her throat closed around the word.

One of the gearling's glowing eyes contracted, giving it a skeptical expression like a raised eyebrow. "Perhaps I should have gone with Baruti after all. You don't *seem* especially bright."

Melanie tried again. "What's . . . going on?"

The automaton sighed. It took a meek step forward, raising its elegant hands in a pacifying gesture. "That's what I'm trying to explain, if you'll let me.

"I promise I won't hurt you, Melanie," it added. "On the contrary, I rather desperately need your help."

The gearling held out its right hand, where the orb at its center shivered with watery light. Melanie gasped as a bubble of clear air expanded above her, sloshing the rain over its side and away. The edges of the bubble wobbled cheerily as it rotated. "But perhaps you'd like to get out of the mud first?" it asked.

She *would*, in fact. Melanie rose, her hands squelching as she pushed herself to her feet. She took a small step forward, onto the stone bricks, but stopped there, keeping her distance from the . . . the, uh . . .

"What are you?" she asked, because she felt this was perhaps the most pressing of her many questions. It was clear that the gearling had faked at being one thing, when in reality it was something else. Melanie had no experience with magical automatons from which to draw a reference, but the deceit spoke of a cunning that it was *not supposed to possess*.

To her continued surprise, the gearling appeared momentarily offended. It paused a moment, leaning backward. "I don't completely know how to answer that," it said with a note of distress. "Beyond telling you that I am *who*, not a what. I'm me. I awoke several weeks ago in what appeared to be a magician's laboratory. There were dead aldermages all around me. And fire. A great deal of fire, in fact. At the time, I was dazed. I remember moving, leaving a large building. And then I was wandering the streets of Crossport and people were looking at me rather aghast. I caught a glimpse of myself in a window, and I understood why."

Melanie shook her head. This was all too much. All too strange. "You woke up with no memories?"

"Not exactly," the gearling said. "I know things about the

world, and the city. I know what an orphan is, and a gate guard. I know there's a village five miles east of here named Hamlen, where most of the shepherds have gone from rearing sheep to breeding battle gryphons, because war earns more coin than wooly blankets. And I have an encyclopedic knowledge of magic: more than enough to know that I'm a thaumaturgically animated clockwork retainer. Colloquially called a gearling."

Its head tilted, buzzing with that ever-present whir. "I also know that never, in the history of empire wizardry, has a gearling been created that was sentient. I should not exist."

This last statement was the sad, clear note in an otherwise confounding song. Melanie recognized it instantly. Nearly all the foundlings had, at some point or another, wondered at the *whys* of their existence. Of their futures. But Melanie and the girls had each other in these moments, to talk through the bothersome thoughts.

Who did the gearling have?

Once again, her feet moved without her thinking, this time striding forward. The bubble umbrella shifted with her, locked in her orbit like a personal moon. Melanie took the automaton's gleaming metal hand in hers. It was very cold.

"Yes, you should," she said. "Exist, I mean."

The gearling's gaze shifted down to their cradled palms. For a long tick, there were only the sounds of the rain.

"Melanie, you seem like a good person," it said finally. Those two glowing motes rose again, meeting her eyes. How strange it was, making eye contact with dots of light. Yet Melanie could *feel* the gaze peering out at her from behind the automaton's visor. She took a step back. She felt for the gearling, yes, but could she trust it?

"I'd like to make you an offer," it declared, regaining some of its height. "I wasn't lying when I said I needed an apprentice. A rogue gearling won't last long wandering the thaumacracy alone. If I mean to evade the attention of the aldermages, then I'll need a . . . chaperone."

Chaperone? Melanie balked. Chaperones were grown-ups— adults who guided children across the street and through the Museum of Thaumaturgical Philosophy and who said things like, *Don't you dare eat that off the floor, Melanie Gate*.

"But I'm a kid," Melanie said. "A foundling."

The gearling nodded slowly. "Perhaps . . ." it said. "Or perhaps not. Perhaps you are the stupendous magical prodigy Lady Porta the Periwinkle, on a tour of all the cultural centers of the empire. From the chateau of Princess-Electa Maximillia, to the palace of the Archistaff himself, you've *wowed* the elite with your precocious talents." Here the automaton's hands whirred in a theatrical flourish. "Touring prodigies aren't so rare a thing. Who could forget the famous *wonderkind* Asmodeus Boneblack?"

Who indeed? Melanie didn't have the heart to say she'd never heard the name, much less forgotten it. Instead, she gave the gearling a doubtful look. "What's *periwinkle*?"

"It's a sort of purplish blue. Ambitious empire magicians like to associate themselves with colors when they register with the census. So they're easier to remember."

"Could I be pink?"

Traveler clanged out a laugh. "Only if you mean to challenge Zaubermeister Ferdinand for the right to the color! No, broad colors like pink, blue, or white are highly prized titles. We're not quite ready for a contest of that kind. Best to use something obscure and specific. Something non-threatening."

"What about green?"

The gearling sighed, though Melanie doubted it had any breath to expel. "We can discuss it later. What I'm offering you tonight is *freedom*. Tour the empire with me. Let's find our places in this world. And if we can't find them, why, then we'll *make* them. You and I want the same things, Melanie—I can see it!"

The gearling's proposal pulled at something deep within Melanie's chest, a longing that had been strung so tight, it now threatened to snap. Was this truly possible?

"I don't know the first thing about magic," she said. "How am I supposed to fool people into believing I'm some kind of genius?"

"It's all about confidence," said the gearling. "I'll teach you the basics as we go, while I pose as *your* clockwork servant. What you can't do, I will. With a bit of misdirection, no one need know I'm performing the real spellcraft." The automaton's glowing eyes widened, the lights beyond the grille burning brighter.

Melanie frowned. She realized that the rain had let up, pacified to a drizzle. Clouds still churned in the sky above them, but she no longer quite felt like she was drowning.

"And what if I say no?" Her voice was tense. Only after she'd asked the question did she realize how important it was. The gearling claimed it offered freedom, but in Melanie's limited experience as both a child and an orphan, *freedom* was just a temporarily longer leash. Like the automaton itself had said, there were always chaperones.

Was it offering her the freedom to refuse?

The gearling's eyes dimmed back to their normal brightness. Its armored shoulders slumped. "Then I'll leave you in peace. You can return through the gate at dawn and resume life at Merrytrails. I . . . just hope you'll keep my precarious situation a secret. Say Felidae dismissed you. I'll have to trust you. You aren't a prisoner, Melanie."

And with this answer, the thread of longing inside her broke.

"I'll do it," Melanie said.

"Oh, thank goodness!" the gearling hollered, flinging up its hands. "I honestly don't know *what* I would have done if you'd said no. Thrown myself off a mountain or something."

This seemed a tad dramatic to Melanie. Already she was second-guessing her decision.

"What should I call you?" she asked. "Do you have a name?"

"You know, I honestly rather like Traveler! It's aspirational. One day I'll have to thank Mrs. Harbargain for the idea." The gearling began pacing around, stretching its arms and legs. Was stretching actually useful for it? Or was it a habit it had picked up watching the people of Crossport? Melanie wondered if she'd ever get used to how strangely human the automaton seemed.

"All right . . . Traveler," she said. "And . . . well, pardon me if this is rude, but are you a boy or a girl gearling?"

Traveler raised a finger to its mask, tapping contemplatively where a human's lips might be. "Ah! Hm. I honestly hadn't thought of it," the gearling said. "Must I be one or the other?"

Melanie shook her head. "Not at all. Harle, the baker's apprentice Mrs. Harbargain buys our bread from, goes by *they*."

"Still, it seems very *human*."

"Which you . . . don't consider yourself to be?"

"Oh, not at all! There's a difference between humans and *people*, you know. Humans are bipedal primates. A person is more difficult to define, but let's start by saying it's a thinking individual. I consider myself a proud member of the second category, but merely a baffled witness to the first."

The gearling stopped pacing for the first time since Melanie had agreed to the journey, turning toward her with a whir. "Very well. Let's go with *he* for now. May I change my mind later?"

"Sure!" Melanie said with a laugh. "Some people do."

Traveler stood straight, those two eyes blinking at Melanie. She felt strangely self-conscious under the gearling's scrutiny. "Traveler . . ." he said, "Gearling wizard. Voice for the voiceless. It has a nice ring, don't you think?"

Melanie nodded, breaking into a smile. Traveler was strange, so foreign to her life at Merrytrails. Whatever he was, she no longer had any doubt that this *was* a person, at least. But a person still figuring himself out. Melanie had never met anyone like him. Apparently no one had.

She glanced down the Wonderstraat. The stone trail led away into the grassy distance, a tartan of gray and green shadow. "Where should we go first? We promised Mrs. Harbargain I'd write her tomorrow morning."

Traveler turned his head, following her gaze. "Hamlen, the village I mentioned, is the closest stop. On a bright, sunny day, it would take us between three and five hours to walk. In pitch-black, with the Wonderstraat likely flooded in spots, it might take us ten. Or even twenty, if the flooding is as bad as I fear."

"*Twenty* hours!" Melanie blurted. "We'll never get the letter to Mrs. Harbargain in time! What if she alerts the city guard, and they start searching the roads for a girl and a gearling? We'll be caught before we begin!"

Traveler chuckled, the noise echoing inside his mask with a tinny ring. "Melanie, don't forget, I'm a *magician*. And tonight begins your very first lesson. We're going to *ride* to Hamlen."

CHAPTER 7

"**WHAT** exactly will we be riding?" Melanie asked. She gazed up and down the misty Wonderstraat, and across the peaty grasslands that clung to the road like meat to a bone. There were no horses. No carriages. Not a single soul or vehicle that she could spy.

The gearling meant to cast a *spell*, then?

Melanie wondered if Traveler could summon fabulous beasts to his side, as the stories described witches and wizards doing. "A . . . a dragon?" she guessed nervously. "Oh—a *unicorn!*"

Traveler laughed again. "That would certainly make an impression, wouldn't it? But dragons and unicorns are a bit advanced for the moment. Not to mention expensive. No, our mounts are already here, loyally serving us even now." One of Traveler's eyes fizzed, darkening briefly.

"Was that a wink?"

"I'm working on it," the gearling said, a touch defensively. "At any rate . . ." He deftly unbuckled his cloak, billowing it out with a twirl. "Behold! My faithful steed."

Melanie grimaced. "We'll be riding your coat?"

"It's more of a mantle—and only *I'll* be riding mine—but yes! A frugal witch doesn't require ostentatious frippery to get around. All she needs is a trusty cloak and a bit of imagination." Traveler held his free hand over the sodden rain cloak. The crystal in his palm illuminated. He let go of the fabric, which billowed gently to the ground.

Except.

It didn't.

The cloak stopped midair, as if settling across a bowed figure. Then the figure raised its head and the fabric draped, veiling a long, equine muzzle.

A horse. There was a *horse* just beneath! But there couldn't be. The cloak gave a little whinny. The earth thudded with the sound of a hoofbeat, though Melanie could see no legs extending beyond the edges of the fabric. She knelt down and gasped as she spotted the outline of a horseshoe imprinted in the mud.

"There's a good cloak," Traveler said, scratching the fabric behind the ear. It snorted and reared an invisible leg up, apparent only by the billowing cloth. "I suppose we should name you too, now. Any thoughts, Melanie?"

Melanie had exactly no thoughts. She stared at the hovering cloak in openmouthed awe.

"Perhaps later," Traveler stage-whispered to it. "After we've all settled a bit." Then the gearling cheerfully regarded Melanie. "Now it's your turn, my young apprentice. Craft yourself a steed worthy of a prodigy. I just know you'll make something spectacular!"

"Y-you want me to do magic?" Melanie sputtered. "I told you—I don't know how!"

"Not to worry. It's quite straightforward. I'll teach you the basics, so long as you promise me one thing."

"What's that?" Melanie asked.

The gearling's cheerful voice lowered, his posture sinking with it. "Never use your magic to intentionally harm others. I'm serious about this. War magic is . . . cruel. Abominably cruel. Witches and wizards are capable of producing miracles. We can do so much good with our gifts. To turn them into weapons is profane."

Melanie frowned, unbalanced by Traveler's sudden shift in tone. So the gearling was a pacifist? She knew from Misty Steppe—*The Plight of the Penitent Pirate*—that *pacifist* was the name for people who refused to fight. "What if we need to defend ourselves?" she asked. "You heard the guards. The Hexe of the South *killed* the High Enchanter. If others use magic as a weapon against us, why—I mean, shouldn't we fight back?"

"Shield or disarm first," Traveler said, sinking to one knee to look Melanie in the eye. "There are countless charms of protection. And if that fails, flee. This is my only requirement, Melanie. I'm not a killer, and I won't teach you to be one."

Melanie nodded. The conversation had taken a grave turn. Still, it wasn't as if she intended to hurt anyone, let alone kill them. As long as they stayed away from the coming war, it had no reason to ever come up. "All right," she said. "I agree."

And so unfolded Melanie's first lesson on the fundamentals of magic.

Traveler had been truthful. It was *not* a long explanation, or a particularly complicated one. In fact, as Melanie listened with dawning comprehension, she quickly realized the truth that wizards kept politely obscured: Practically anyone could do magic. Once you grasped the basics, it all made perfect sense.

The gearling nodded, apparently satisfied with her expression. "I can see you understand already. Just be mindful, Melanie. Magic is easy to learn, but difficult to master. Even simple spells can be dangerous. But I'm sure you'll have little trouble with this task! Oh, I'm practically rattling with excitement to see what you'll conjure."

Melanie felt a bit rattled herself. She undid the clasp of Mrs. Harbargain's cloak, holding it in front of her as Traveler had done. She immediately missed its warmth as the cold night air, still wet with the storm, crept into her clothes.

"Like this?" she asked. She lifted her palm over the cloak.

"That's the way! Now just do as I taught you."

Melanie pondered the gearling's lesson. Her nervous stomach bobbed. She took a deep breath, then attempted to re-create the process she'd just witnessed.

Traveler watched all the while, providing helpful commentary as she worked.

"Remember to twist the bit there. Twistier!

"Oops, better catch that before it flies away.

"Well—ha!—there's a rather interesting way of doing that. But it worked!

"Oh, don't look so terrified. The spell will notice!

"And what's the *final* ingredient? Love! Think of something that warms your chest. Put some real feeling into it."

Melanie pictured Merrytrails. She remembered the girls crowded around the doorway as she stepped into the storm. She thought of the nameday parties Mrs. Harbargain had thrown for them, celebrating their arrivals at the orphanage, since none of the girls knew their actual birthdays. Sun-mi baked cakes, except during her own nameday when the girls and Mrs. Harbargain worked together to produce a misshapen block of hardened flour—frosted with sloppy messages of love.

Agatha insisted on performing plays for her namedays, and always cast herself as the lead. (This year, Melanie had been instructed to play a goat, though she'd really elevated the role by chewing on Agatha's dress. Until Mrs. Harbargain noticed and told her to stop.) Jane, meanwhile, had seemed so mortified by the extra attention that they'd started slipping her notes, instead of the usual morning serenade.

And Melanie? Her throat clenched as she remembered her last party. The girls had all written brand-new Misty Steppe stories and compiled them into a manuscript, presenting it with her cake. Jane's was the best—a swashbuckling drama full of tragedy and triumph. But Melanie had cherished every one, even Mariana's half-finished yarn about a rabbit seeking carrots for lunch that somehow digressed into a request for extra cake.

Melanie realized only now that she'd left the document back in Crossport.

A current of sensation pricked at her nerves, traveling up and out of her extended fingertips.

"Now," Traveler said gently, sensing she was ready, "let it go."

Melanie released the cloak.

Being shorter than the gearling's, Melanie's cape had less far to fall. In fact, it billowed up in places, the fabric ballooning as it filled with air. A shape moiled beneath the mantle, muscles stretching and legs kicking. The hood elongated into a muzzle.

Then an elegant neck rose up. Two large ears jutted into the fabric of the hood, flicking back and forth curiously. The creature raised its head and let out a triumphant—

Well. The noise that trumpeted across the plain was perhaps best described as a honk. Melanie had never heard anything like it from a horse, at least. And Helen Stables always said horses *neighed* or *whinnied*.

"A donkey!" Traveler exclaimed delightedly. "Very sturdy creatures. And smart too. If you lead a donkey to water, I assure you it'd drink."

Traveler patted the hollow flank. "Not this one, though."

Melanie cautiously raised her hand. The cloak leaned its head into her palm, honking again. "I think it likes me."

"I'm not surprised in the slightest," the gearling said warmly. "Only . . . Melanie, do you mind if I make one small adjustment to the spell? You've done everything perfectly, don't worry. It's as beautiful a transanimation as there ever was."

"You won't hurt the donkey?"

"Technically there's no donkey to hurt, but I assure you she'll be fine."

Melanie gazed from Traveler back to the cloak. Her first spell, and it had actually worked! Melanie had coaxed a cape into becoming a donkey, like some kind of fairy-tale god-mother. "All right," Melanie acquiesced. "As long as it doesn't hurt her."

Traveler placed his palm to the spot where the donkey's forehead would be, right on the hood. The cloak went still at his touch. Light spilled out from beneath the gearling's hand, then darkened. As Traveler withdrew, the cloth began to billow. A small tear rent the fabric, right at the center of the forehead. And from this tear, a delicately twisted horn emerged, spiraling into a spectacular point before it finally stopped. The horn was shiny as a pearl, and its ridges were lined with glittering threads of gold.

"*Unicorn* . . ." Melanie whispered in amazement.

"I think that's as fine a name as any," Traveler said. "Now. Shall we ride our new mounts to town?"

CHAPTER 8

THE ride down the Wonderstraat was cold and dark. Melanie stroked Unicorn behind her ears the whole way, the scratchy wool cloak letting out little honks of pleasure as they went.

If Melanie had the time for rumination, she might have wondered upon the strange turn her life had taken. In just the last several hours, so many impossible things had come to be. Then they'd plodded cheerfully ahead without a second thought as to their own impossibility.

Melanie *didn't* have time for such considerations, though. Not with Traveler chattering at her side, asking her questions about her new prodigy persona, Lady Porta the Periwinkle. The gearling said it would help if she felt a sense of ownership for the character. So he tested her as they went, having her make up likes and dislikes for Lady Porta.

"Character traits," the gearling said, "are essential. How does Lady Porta view the world around her? What does she *want*? These are what truly make a role come alive."

"Can she be like Misty Steppe?"

"Who?"

Melanie launched into an explanation of her favorite

heroine. Her talents and foibles. Her grand escapes. The time she accidentally stowed away on a pirate ship bound for haunted seas, then wound up captaining its crew against ghostly buccaneers. She explained how she and Jane would spend *hours* inventing new stories for the character. Well, Jane made the best stories—like this one where Misty traveled into a mirror world, where all her friends were *bad* and her former villains were heroes. But Melanie accompanied them with pictures.

"I like your enthusiasm," the gearling said, interrupting Melanie as she simulated the sounds of steel clashing against spectral cutlasses. "But perhaps we should start smaller than mirror worlds and ghost pirates . . . leave Lady Porta *some* adventures to come."

Traveler glanced at her. "Tell me, Melanie, how much do you know about the Aederian Thaumacracy? Did Mrs. Harbargain teach you civics at Merrytrails?"

Melanie nodded hesitantly. Civics *and* history, though she'd never been as apt a student as Baruti or Jane.

"Let's quiz you, then. What do the three eyes on the empire's flag represent?"

Luckily, this was an easy one. The flag was everywhere in Crossport, and even little Mariana could recite the symbols from memory. Melanie pictured it now: three eyes staring out of a white background, all topped by a golden crown. One eye was blue, one brown, and the last a vivid red.

Three eyes to watch over the world, as the empire motto said.

"The blue eye is the king," she began. "He's the First Eye

of the Empire. The brown Second Eye represents the Prime Minister, who writes laws and judges criminals. And the *Third Eye of the Empire* is the High Enchanter and his aldermages. They're why it's called a thaumacracy. *Thauma* means magic, like in *thaumaturgy*. And *-cracy* means a kind of government. Zerend the Red used to be High Enchanter, but he died. Now it's someone new—a man named Riquem."

This last one was easiest of all, as Crossport was the official seat of the aldermages. They lived up in the red-roofed city palace. Melanie had never seen one in person, but she took pride in knowing her city housed such important figures. Or at least she *had*.

But as soon as she said the names Zerend and Riquem, the gearling seemed to buzz in his seat. His relaxed posture went taut.

"Is something wrong?"

Traveler shook his head. "It's nothing. Just a momentary confusion." He turned back to her. "And what does *Lady Porta* think of the thaumacracy?" he asked. "Of the three eyes, constantly watching?"

Melanie tilted her head at this strange question. "Proud? Everyone's proud of the empire. Adults don't like it if you aren't."

She turned to Traveler to see if she'd answered right, but the gearling didn't comment. He merely gazed at her for a moment, his glowing motes bright and unfathomable.

Then he switched topics, asking her to name three more character traits—two truths and a lie.

The more he prodded, the less confident Melanie felt in their plan.

"How am I supposed to know all this?" she groaned. "Fancy courts and magical tutors . . . The only time I met a noblewoman, it turned out to be a very realistic mannequin."

"Not to worry," Traveler said brightly from atop his mount— he had eventually named the cloak Vagabond. "Children are still children—even the geniuses. You're indulged a degree of flightiness."

Melanie rolled her eyes. Technically, Traveler was younger than she was, but he certainly talked like a grown-up.

The gearling whirred his visor toward her. "And I'll always be with you, helping to fill in the gaps where needed. I've got a special spell just for the job." Traveler's right eye fizzed again. He really was terrible at winking.

Still, for the first time since accepting the offer, Melanie felt her anxiety beginning to disperse. She was riding down a path that led to any number of marvelous possibilities.

What a change, in just a handful of hours.

Back in Crossport, the rain had receded, but the sky was still a brindle of churning clouds.

In the quiet left behind the storm, a lone figure approached the door to the Merrytrails Orphanage for Girls. His youthful face was pale beneath the blue hues of the city's toverlichts, his gaze wide and curious.

He was a thin, unassuming man. He wore a plain imperial uniform: slacks, a crisp white shirt, a crimson vest. Beyond two small ruby earrings, his only ornamentation was the intricate piece of armor fastened over his left arm: A golden pauldron led to an armpiece led to a glittering gauntlet.

It looked almost like the arm of a gearling, complete with a crystal embedded into its palm. But this armor had been fashioned for a human wearer.

The man raised his unadorned fist and knocked gently upon the door, each rap as soft as an apology. After several moments, a bewildered face peered out. The mistress of the orphanage, still in her nightgown. She was a dowdy woman, her face pale in the blue light. Early sixties, by the look of her. Her gray hair had been pulled hurriedly into a bun.

"Mrs. Esther Harbargain?" the man greeted her in a soft tenor. "I'm terribly sorry for disturbing you at this hour, but I'm here on an urgent mission. I hope you can help me."

The woman took one look at his armored hand and her face blanched. The man noted her expression grimly. She recognized the design. So it *had* been here.

"Is this about Melanie?" the matron asked. "Is . . . is she all right?"

"Melanie . . ." the man repeated thoughtfully.

Melanie Gate. It was the name the gate guards had given him too. A young girl accompanied by a rogue imperial gearling, who claimed she was on her way to apprentice to a nearby witch. The witch had been a fabrication, of course. There was no Felidae Seagreen registered in the Imperial Census of Spellwrights.

If his hunch was correct—if this bizarre fluke of magic was even possible—then he would need to move quickly now.

"She's in grave danger," he said softly. "Mrs. Harbargain, my name is Riquem. I'm the new High Enchanter . . . the Third Eye of the Empire."

Behind him, Riquem heard a cacophony of clockwork as his gearlings sprang into motion. Dots of light emerged from the shadows of the street, each pair shaded behind an emotionless metal mask. He'd brought two dozen along, just in case the rogue machine was here. He would need to take it down quickly, after all.

In a moment's time, a legion of automatons surrounded the orphanage.

The look of fear on the matron's face melted into wonder for a moment, and then to a much deeper, darker kind of fear.

Good, thought Riquem the Red.

"Perhaps we could speak inside?" he asked, raising his hands in a soothing gesture. "I'm afraid things have become complicated for this . . . Melanie Gate."

CHAPTER 9

THEY arrived in Hamlen with the sun. Light the color of Crossport's fruit stalls spilled into the sky—reds, oranges, and yellows, all crisp and delicious.

Or perhaps Melanie was just hungry.

She was certainly *tired*. She didn't think she'd ever been more tired than this moment, after the night's parade of shocks and surprises. And here she was now, riding an animated cloak, one more curiosity for the parade. Still, she had a giddy, fizzy sort of energy. She'd stayed up *all night*. Outdoors! And this morning was the first test of Traveler's plan: the debut of Lady Porta the Periwinkle.

"Remember," the gearling was saying, "to have *fun* with it. That's also essential. You don't want to get caught playing a dour char—".

A shadow passed over them, a dark streak across the grass that was quickly followed by two more. Melanie looked up in time to see a trio of white-winged shapes gliding high above, streaking toward the southern horizon. Even from this far away, she could sense they were enormous, with gorgeous wings that reflected the dawn light like molten gold.

A moment later, the cry reached her. A piercing screech echoed across the cliffs.

Unicorn honked anxiously beneath Melanie. She placed a steadying hand behind the cloak's horn.

"Were those . . . ?" she began. "They looked too big to be birds."

Traveler watched the sky as the winged figures wheeled away. "Gryphons," he confirmed. "The new pride of Hamlen." He added this last part with a wistful note. "Once, these grasslands would have been teeming with shepherds grazing their sheep. Now they've gone fallow."

Melanie gazed across the windswept cliff, surrounded by ancient, snow-topped mountains like white-haired elders. All along the road, thick grass billowed in the breeze. And beneath her, Unicorn billowed too, her cloak flapping cheerily.

They continued on, though Melanie kept an eye toward the sky the rest of the way.

Hamlen appeared first in the form of a giant, spinning plus-sign, tucked into the mountainside like an enormous pinwheel.

"The village windmill," Traveler offered. "It pumps water through the rock, and pulverizes the grain that feeds the aerie."

"The . . . aerie?" Melanie asked.

"It means a home for birds. Though, as you noted, the gryphons are not normal birds."

Melanie spotted round buildings curving up from the earth, encircled by a humble stone fence on three sides. The mountainside that bordered the village on the fourth side was steep as a wall and pocked with shallow clefts—along with one *very* large one. Squinting, Melanie could just made out pale puffs of color in the recesses. Were those the gryphons in their nests? Then Hamlen quite literally hung in the aerie's shadow. Melanie wondered if the villagers ever feared the gryphons.

She also wondered what had happened to all those sheep.

Curiosity mingled with dread. Melanie had never witnessed a live gryphon before, though she'd seen illustrations in the orphanage's secondhand books. They were eagles that had been magically crossed with lions, to become a creature more terrifying than either.

The breeze shifted, positioning Melanie and Traveler downwind of the village. With it came a putrid, metallic scent— rotten meat and rust. Melanie squinted upward again, even as she squeezed her nostrils closed between her fingers. She could just make out the rivulets of white dung that trailed down the mountainside beneath all those nests.

Suddenly, Abraxas's comparatively mild odors seemed almost agreeable. At least *he* had stuck to the small box of ash and sand that Mrs. Harbargain cleaned daily.

Traveler didn't seem to notice the smell. The gearling turned his eyes to Melanie. "From here on, we should stay in character. Are you ready?"

In fact, Melanie found she was *restless* to begin. A young heroine in disguise, journeying across the empire in the secret care of a magical companion? This was the adventure she'd been *dreaming* of at Merrytrails—

Though perhaps it smelled a bit worse than in her imagination.

"Of course," she said. Then she tilted her chin up at an imperious angle. It seemed the sort of pose a prodigy might strike.

The gearling nodded. "Nicely done." He leaped easily from the back of his mount, and with no more than a curl of his wrists, whisked the fabric theatrically into the air. Vagabond's horselike mien disappeared instantly, the cloak settling over Traveler's shoulders.

"I'll take it on foot from here. Don't worry, Melanie. However different I seem, I'm still me. And I'll be with you the whole time."

Melanie scrunched her nose in feigned confusion. "Who's *Melanie*?"

Traveler laughed, his eyes tilting into a mirthful angle.

Then they suddenly dimmed. The dots of light grew round and vacant. His casual posture straightened, arms falling to his sides. Melanie fought to keep the surprise from her face, but the effect was utterly unnerving.

Back was the eerie gearling who'd arrived at Merrytrails the night before.

They pressed forward.

A pinkish boy who couldn't have been older than little Mariana Porch was picking flowers just outside the village gate. He caught sight of Melanie approaching on her floating cloak, flanked by the lumbering gearling, and froze in place. His eyes bulged so comically that Melanie nearly burst out laughing. Once she was sure he was in earshot, Melanie called out, doing her best imitation of the rich girls she'd observed ordering sugary fritters in the market.

Character trait: Lady Porta doesn't ask. She insists.

"You there!" she said. "Alert the innkeeper that a great witch is paying call. I'll need a bed and refreshments waiting, along with a pot of ink, a pen, and several pages of paper."

To Melanie's delight, the boy leaped up immediately. "Yes, Miss Witch! Right away!" Then he scrambled through the gate and sprinted full-speed into the village.

"That was *fun*," Melanie said under her breath. Traveler didn't respond. The gearling kept his vague eyes forward.

It wasn't long before more village children arrived, nearly a dozen in total. The girls all wore lacy caps with patchwork skirts and white aprons, while the boys were dressed in breeches and wide, colorful suspenders. They looked like something out of a storybook, or a pamphlet celebrating the thaumacracy's bright future, all rosy-cheeked and sun-kissed. Some were almost as old as Melanie herself. She had to swallow down the creeping anxiety that they'd immediately see through her act, recognizing her for the penniless foundling she was.

Most of the children kept their distance, though the oldest boy stepped forward to the gate, greeting her with a raised hand.

"Welcome to Hamlen, Miss Witch!" he said formally. "Do you need a stable for your . . . your, uh . . . ?"

Melanie smirked. She patted Unicorn on her side and the cloak came to a stop. Then she dipped slightly for Melanie to dismount. Not quite daring enough to attempt Traveler's sweeping showman's flourish, Melanie instead lifted the mantle primly into the air, whereupon the fabric deflated into a normal cloak. She did note, however, that the *horn* remained, still extending jauntily from the hood.

The children just beyond the gate all gasped, some of the younger ones breaking into excited chatter. Melanie felt a flush of pride.

"That won't be necessary," she said.

The oldest boy found his voice first. "I'm Dieter. I can lead you to the inn now, if you like. Katzy runs it for her father."

Melanie smiled, but kept her eyes relaxed, her expression almost bored. "And I . . ." —she drew the pause out for dramatic effect—"am Lady Porta the Periwinkle, *child* prodigy. I'm on my *third* tour of the Aederian Thaumacracy. This is my clockwork servant. We've *just* arrived from the house of Ultra-Wizard Karl the Blue-with-Little-Flecks-of-Gold-in-It, where I performed *many* magical tricks."

Was this too much information? The children seemed impressed, at least. They all gaped, whispering and covering their mouths in amazement. "I don't require an escort," she added. "Though perhaps you could point the way."

Dieter indicated one of the overturned-bowl buildings peeking out from between the others. The rest of the children jostled to either side of the stone road, leaving a wide gap for Melanie and Traveler to pass.

As she strode forward, Melanie stroked the cloak now hanging from her arm, right along the base of its horn. She heard a faint sound that might have been her stomach growling, or might have been Unicorn honking in approval.

CHAPTER 10

THE innkeeper was a cat.

Not a four-legged housecat like Abraxas, of course. Rather, she was one of the catfolk—the kassipoi—who hailed from the thaumacracy's frigid northern territories.

It had taken all Melanie's willpower to keep her jaw shut when she first entered the inn and found two large green eyes staring at her from within a red-furred face. The kassipoi's vertical pupils dilated in the sunlight from the open door.

Character trait: Lady Porta is not a sheltered bumpkin. She's met all sorts of interesting people.

So, Melanie had simply smiled politely, forcing her eyes to wander the tiny inn instead of sticking to its innkeeper.

"Hello!" she said. "I sent a boy ahead. Is my room prepared?"

Katzy, as the children had called her, blinked at Melanie, but said nothing at first. Instead, she regarded Melanie with a look of such potent skepticism, it could only have been borne by a member of the feline family.

Sheltered as Merrytrails may have been, Crossport was still a bustling trade capital, and Melanie had occasionally seen some of the empire's nonhuman citizens in the city market: the feline kassipoi; the amphibious grouille. Once even a jaro, the nomadic birdfolk from the far south. Melanie had never had a chance to truly interact with these rare visitors to the city, however.

Katzy looked small compared to the kassipoi Melanie had seen in Crossport. A girl, then, like her? Or perhaps a teenager. She wore a plain dress and apron, though she'd forgone the lacy bonnet the other girls wore, likely because of her wide, pointed ears.

"And who did you say you were again?" The kassipoi's voice fluttered as she finally spoke, every word a purr.

Melanie felt her lazy smile tightening.

"Lady Porta," she offered. "The . . . Periwinkle."

"I've never heard of you."

"Well, that's—quite a surprise! Considering I am so very famous!"

Behind Melanie, Traveler stood unhelpfully silent. The children of Hamlen, having followed them inside, were literally bouncing off the walls of the tiny hostelry. Melanie caught sight of the young boy from the gate—the one who had been picking flowers—spiritedly inserting the blossoms into his nose.

Beyond the chaos of the village children, the inn itself was a calm, lovely place. A skylight in the roof brightened the small, circular receiving room. Leafy plants hung from the ceiling, and a basin had been set beside the desk filled with clear drinking water. A ladle rested invitingly against its rim.

Katzy tilted her head. Behind the counter, Melanie caught

the flick of a ginger tail. "And you're some kind of witch, then? The aldermages who come are all apefolk like yourself, though usually older. You're a young one? A kitten?"

"Precisely!" Melanie said. "Like a kitten! I'm a prodigy, you see. The most talented young magician of my age." She leaned in conspiratorially. "But don't tell Agatha Pondscum I said that." The name had just sprung to Melanie's lips, but it felt right. Improvisation was quite fun! "Agatha is *very* jealous, you see. Always considered me her rival, the poor deluded thing."

"And what can you *do* with your magic?"

Melanie smiled dashingly. In the Misty Steppe stories, the potential of magic was nearly limitless, though in function it usually just made exciting narrative nuisances for Misty to get swept up in.

"Oh, I can do all sorts of things. Bless your babes or strike your fools with muteness . . . or vice versa! Once I banished a *demon* that was terrifying an orphanage every night. The little darlings were *ever* so grateful; they rewarded me with—"

Melanie heard a whirr just behind her as Traveler turned his head toward the innkeeper. "This one's mistress is especially talented at household spells. Her magic can turn cooking and cleaning into the work of a moment."

The children scampering over chairs and climbing up the curtains all quieted at Traveler's pronouncement. Clearly the gearling would draw attention with his every move. No wonder he so rarely spoke.

Katzy turned toward the automaton as well, studying him.

"Well, you have a gearling, at least. Only see those with the aldermages from Crossport. Household spells, hm?" She made a thoughtful sound like heavy pebbles grinding together. "It would be useful to have a witch as a servant."

"S-servant?" Melanie grimaced before she could stop herself.

Katzy nodded, her eyes flashing in the morning light. "With the adults all working in the aerie, it's up to the older kittens to take care of Hamlen during the day." The kassipoi sighed—it came out as a breathy yowl. "We have an important guest staying in the private suite," she said. "I could use some help taking care of the place before he returns. I'll write up a list of chores. If you and your gearling really can finish them quickly, then you're welcome here, witch-kitten. I'll accept it as payment for your stay."

Another blur of tail whipped by behind the young innkeeper. She watched Melanie expectantly.

Well, this wasn't quite the glamorous life that Melanie had expected of a prodigy, but they'd found a bed for the night. And she was no stranger to a little housework. Perhaps with magic, the chores really would fly by.

"I *suppose* it would be a small thing to help you," Melanie said magnanimously. "Seeing as I am so very talented at magical spells."

Katzy's slitted pupils sharpened. "I like you, Lady Porta," she purred. "You're strange."

Melanie felt the tension leave her shoulders like a cloak slipping away. She gave the kassipoi a swashbuckling smile, posing with a hand on her hip.

"As I said," the innkeeper continued, "the private suite is reserved, but the public beds are yours. There's paper and a quill inside the room. I'll head to the kitchen now and make you a plate." Katzy's eyes rose, taking in the other children behind Melanie, who'd by now resumed their feverish fidgeting. "Scamper, kittens! Take your naughtiness outside where it belongs!"

The Hamlen children all groaned. "We want to see a trick!" one demanded.

"Make her do *magic!*"

Now Katzy's eyes flashed briefly back to Melanie.

"Don't worry, kittens. I intend to do just that."

Melanie gently shut the door behind her, then leaned against it with a sigh. The bedroom was almost like her own in Merrytrails—a public sleeping space with six beds set into two neat rows. The shared privy was just outside, connected to the receiving room.

Thankfully, the inn was empty.

"I'd say that went rather well!" Traveler chirped from beside one of the beds. The gearling was back to his usual effusive self, his posture loose and lightsome.

"It got us in, at least," she agreed. "And the food smelled delicious. I can't believe I'm staying at a real countryside inn! It's *just* like an adventure story." She tossed her cloak toward a free bed, and for a moment the horn rose into the air, the fabric trotting forward. Then Unicorn settled into a corner of the mattress, her horn dipped contentedly, and she became an empty cloak once more.

Melanie grinned. "I'd better write to Harbargain now, and complete the adoption paperwork. Katzy says the courier to Crossport usually arrives after breakfast." Melanie realized with a clang of guilt that this meant she'd have to lie to Mrs. Harbargain—and Jane and the others as a result.

She'd never lied to Jane before. The two were always honest with each other, even when Jane had broccoli in her teeth, or when Melanie's own, made-up Misty Steppe stories trailed off with no clear ending. Jane could often sense the truth in Melanie before Melanie even spoke.

Still, the clarion of her excitement was so much LOUDER than the guilt. Melanie would make it up to Jane and the others someday. Perhaps she'd bring them treasure from her adventures.

She moved to a small writing table, set away from the beds. A heavily annotated guest book lay on top, along with a pen and several sheets of blank paper. Melanie sat before the table.

She began penning her letter, listening as Traveler hummed cheerfully from the bed.

Then she noticed a stack of travel brochures occupying a small corner of the desk. Each was neatly illustrated in a bright, cheerful style. Melanie paused and picked up the stack, paging through advertisements for the most exciting travel destinations in the empire.

Ski the pristine slopes of the Albes! one read. *Or settle in with your sweetheart and a cup of cocoa* ♥

In the second, a handsome human family, all skin tones of brown and bronze and burnished sand, rode on horseback, outlined within a golden circle. *How do you reach the Imperial Capital of Ultrest? Just follow the Wonderstraat—straight toward the rising sun!*

There was even one for Crossport: *Magic Metropolis of the Coast! Seat of the Mystical Third Eye!*

Melanie flipped to the last advertisement, then let out a little gasp. Her hand slipped, splattering ink across the letter she'd just begun writing.

Pointed roofs. A field of flowers.

Kinderbloom! The Garden Village.

Melanie dropped the sheet, then turned and dug frantically through her small bag of belongings.

Behind her, she heard a whir of movement. Traveler had paused his humming. "Is everything all right?" he asked.

Melanie didn't answer. She pulled a piece of cloth from her pack, then laid it down on the desk.

The same. They were the same. Except the brochure had another line just below the first. . . .

A charming sanctuary at the edge of the empire.

Traveler arrived behind her, gazing down at the brochure.

"Kinderbloom . . ." he said. There was a curious echo of uncertainty in his metallic voice. "Huh."

"I had this cloth with me as a baby," Melanie muttered. She swallowed, then turned toward the gearling. "Traveler, can we go there?"

Melanie was surprised by the cant of the gearling's glowing

eyes. The lights were muddy and thin, as if their brightness had turned inward.

"I don't think that's wise," he said.

She frowned at this unexpected answer. "Why not?" Short as the question was, she couldn't hide the intensity in it.

The gearling took a step back. "Kinderbloom is one of the last outposts of thaumacratic territory before . . . well, before open land gives way to the Zwarte Woud. The domain of the Hexe of the South."

Melanie sucked in a gulp of air and nearly choked on it. "The witch who *killed Zerend the High Enchanter*?!" she blurted.

"Quiet, now. We don't want Katzy hearing us." The gearling placed his hands on his metallic hips. "But, yes. It's best we avoid the border between territories. We want to keep *away* from the coming conflict, remember?"

Melanie frowned. "Do you know much about the Hexe of the South?" she asked. "Is she a very bad person?"

"My memories tell me she is indeed," Traveler began thoughtfully. "An ancient tyrant and a powerful dark sorceress, kept alive by her magic for hundreds of years. She lives in the Zwarte Woud—the Black Forest—and never leaves. Instead, she sends spirits out to do her bidding."

"Why did she kill the Third Eye?" Melanie asked. "Were they enemies?"

Traveler hesitated, then shook his head. "They definitely weren't friends. But the Ley Coven uses a different kind of magic from ours. As far as I know, it's the only thing that binds them. They belong to no nation, and are ruled instead by a council of eight 'wardens' who lead through the Old Ways. Alfrynd, Seidrman of the North, the Suneater. Fabiola, Mambo of the West, the Sea Cleric. And of course, the Hexe of the South, the Conjurer. There are others too. Their magic comes from the wild places of the world, far from civilization, and is passed along strictly tended bloodlines. For thousands of years, theirs was the only arcane knowledge that existed, hoarded away in the world's most secret places."

The gearling lifted a hand, where a spinning globule appeared in his palm, shimmering like a soap bubble. "Then thaumaturgy arrived—a new kind of spellwork that *anyone* could learn, no matter their lineage. It was quite the upset for the Ley Coven. Those early days of magical discovery were heady times, full of radicals and renegades. The two schools, if you could call them that, have been in conflict ever since."

Melanie narrowed her eyes. Something about this wasn't sitting right with her.

"You said your *memories* tell you the Hexe is bad," she said. "But how do you *know*? Have you ever actually met her?"

"I was right about Hamlen, wasn't I?"

"But *how*?" Melanie frowned. "Where do your memories come from?"

The gearling was silent for a stretch. His glowing eyes sloped to an uncertain angle. He closed his hand into a fist and the bubble popped. "I'm . . . not sure. I don't remember a time before I awoke. Perhaps I came here once as a wizard's gearling? Or maybe the spell that created me imbued me with knowledge of magic and history."

"Can spells do that? Make you know things?"

"Divination magic can impart truths, but not whole encyclo-pedias' worth. And usually it's all a bit theatrical, to be honest: a cryptic vision delivered by a skull or some such." The doubt-ful cant of the gearling's eyes eased. "A question for another day. As is all this talk of Kinderbloom."

Traveler loped back toward the bed with a wave. "There's miles yet to cover before it's even a possibility." The gearling collapsed into the mattress with a metallic clamor, splaying his arms out behind him in a pose of utter relaxation. "You're on a grand adventure, right? Just like Misty Stoop."

"*Steppe*. Misty Steppe," Melanie corrected.

"Exactly. Try to *enjoy* it a little before jumping headlong into a conflict. . . . I wonder if someone around here has an oil can."

Melanie gazed back down at the brochure on the desk, run-ning her fingers over the field of flowers. Traveler was right, of course. This journey *was* everything she'd ever wanted. But she also had the nagging sense the gearling was using that to steer her.

Melanie wasn't about to fret over it. The idea of the sad little foundling pining over her lost mommy had never much appealed. She was stouthearted, like Misty Steppe. Was she curious about her origins? Sure . . . but in her mind, it was just one more mystery to add to a world already brimming with them.

She reached for the wooden pen and vial of ink, setting the brochures—and Kinderbloom—aside for the moment. There were chores yet to do, and a letter to write. All part of the exciting life of a magical prodigy. As Melanie continued scribbling her note to Mrs. Harbargain, she thought absently about the matron's offer—of the secret phrase she should write if she was in trouble and needed saving.

Give my love to Abraxas.

Melanie was fine, of course. Though Harbargain had been right to mistrust the situation, Melanie was here of her own accord. The phrase wouldn't be needed.

Still, she silently committed the words to memory.

Dear *Mrs. Harbarn.*

Dear Mrs. Harbargain,

We've just arrived at the Witch Felidae's home, and I'm ever so happy! Felidae is a kind old woman, though perhaps a bit too carefree for her circumstances. I can certainly see why she needs help! I know it's only been a day, but I've already learned a bit of magic! I'm very excited to show you and the others at Merrytrails when I can.

Tell everyone I already miss them terribly. Please, especially, give Jane a hug. I hope she's all right, and I'll write again soon. I'm on a grand adventure, but for now, my thoughts are still of home.

Your friend,
Melanie Gate

CHAPTER 11

KATZY provided a *substantial* list of chores.

There was the dusting and sweeping of the entire downstairs, and linens to be changed and washed. Katzy even expected Melanie to prepare the afternoon tea! All the while, the kassipoi would be upstairs, turning down the private suite for the inn's prestigious guest.

Melanie suspected the young innkeeper had loaded her up with a season's worth of troublesome chores. She handed the list to Traveler with a grunt. "I don't suppose magic really can make all *this* the work of a moment?"

The gearling read slowly through, his glowing eyes climbing down the page as if descending a particularly rickety ladder. Even *that* took longer than a moment.

"Perhaps a *couple*," he admitted.

Melanie sighed, falling back onto her bed.

"We can make a game of it," Traveler said. "Whoever finishes their tasks first wins?"

Melanie sighed again. "We played those kinds of games at Merrytrails. They weren't very fun."

"Ah," said the gearling, "but you've never played them with me before. I'm *very* competitive, you know. Or at least I think I am." Traveler edged the door open, peering out into the receiving room. Seeing the space was clear, he slipped through the doorway. "On your mark . . ." he whispered as he went. "Get se-e-et . . ."

He gently closed the door behind him.

Melanie just lay there a moment, summoning the will to rise. Housework, on her first day as a prestigious, prodigious witch! And she'd only just finished her month of double chores at Merrytrails. Finally, with a grunt, she pushed herself up and shuffled to the door.

"All right, Traveler," Melanie said as she opened it. "You're on—"

And she gasped.

The room had come alive.

An old broom seesawed through the air, sweeping the last remnants of dust out of the inn's front doorway. Meanwhile, Melanie's empty breakfast dishes dawdled toward the kitchen like messy children toward a bath.

Through the window, Melanie saw bedsheets marching themselves to a metal tub filled with soap and water. Each dived with exaggerated athleticism into the tub, scrubbed itself against the washboard, then emerged fresh and clean to make room for the next.

Melanie heard a kettle going off in the kitchen, the whistle high and cheerful. A moment later, it quieted all on its own.

"Melanie," Traveler said, "would you put that duster back in the closet?"

She turned to find a feather duster floating just next to her, weightless as a dandelion seed. Melanie took hold of the handle and walked it to the cupboard, setting it on the shelf inside.

"Ah, bother," Traveler said. "You're done! It looks like you won after all." The gearling winked, his eye fizzing playfully. "I'll get you next time. Now . . . while these finish, I have an errand for us to run."

Even growing up in an orphanage, Melanie could sense that Hamlen was what Mrs. Harbargain would have called *provincial*. Which was a sort-of-mean way of saying *small*.

Nestled into the feet of the Albes Mountains, the village was made up of gray stone buildings with pale thatched roofs, mimicking the shapes of the mountains themselves. A stone pathway snaked chaotically through the town, bending suddenly toward points of interest before it veered away in other directions.

The village was pressed against the steepest wall of the mountains, for shelter against the wind. A squat stone wall ran along the other three sides, the implication of a boundary against the endless grasslands beyond.

The storm was gone—no trace of it remained in the bright blue sky—and wind rustled the steppe outside Hamlen like a green sea. It was almost too warm for a cloak, but Melanie couldn't bear to part with Unicorn quite yet.

She found the place utterly wonderful. Whereas Crossport's streets were set into rigid squares, carefully designed to organize a city packed full of people and buildings and *stuff*, Hamlen seemed to have no plan at all. She took a deep breath, tasting air that was clear of the city's haze, smells Melanie hadn't even realized were a constant in her life.

"What's this errand?" she asked. Melanie couldn't imagine what the gearling meant to accomplish here.

"I was thinking about Katzy's skeptical welcome," Traveler said. "And that perhaps it was a matter of personal presentation." Traveler's neck whirred as he glanced around the town. "There! Perfect."

Melanie followed Traveler's gaze to a small brick rotunda with lace curtains in the windows. A sign hung above the door, reading in neat block letters: SEW FAR, SEW GOOD. A tailor's shop. Out front, a dress form displayed a lovely sundress.

"Personal presentation?" she echoed thickly.

"You need a new look. Something befitting a prodigy. Come along. We're going shopping."

"Traveler," Melanie sighed, "we don't have any *money* for clothes."

"My, you humans are obsessed with money." A buzzing sound of disapproval emanated from the gearling's mask. "Fashion isn't about exchanging little metal coins, Melanie. It's about *aspiration*. About *passion*. About connecting with a *style* to discover who you are."

Melanie looked down at her modest dress. Like all the foundlings at Merrytrails, her wardrobe was made up of donations and hand-me-downs. Still, what Traveler described sounded an awful lot like window-shopping. Melanie already had plenty of experience looking at things she couldn't have.

She glanced to the gearling and his armored body. The carved panes of metal were beautiful, but he wore no clothing beyond his tattered cloak, now back at the inn. What sort of clothes sparked *passions* and *aspirations* in a living automaton? Perhaps this little detour wasn't just for her, then.

"All right," she said. "You've convinced me. Porta the Periwinkle shall grace this *charming* boutique with her presence."

Traveler folded in a stiff bow, and the two headed into the shop.

The inside of Sew Far, Sew Good was a panoply of color. Fabrics of every kind draped across the walls, climbing up ladders and dress forms to better display themselves. A whole wall was occupied by wool yarn—tightly spun balls of fluff, arranged in a colorful spectrum.

A shopgirl sat behind the counter. She looked much like the other village children with pale pink skin, but unlike the plainer uniforms, she wore a chaotic mash of hues and patterns. Her dress was composed of several splashy prints all sewn together—each brighter and busier than the last.

Even her *hair* was colorful, shining with streaks of pink, blue, and green all woven into a motley braid.

She was the most intriguing person Melanie had ever seen.

The girl glanced up at the sound of the door, but as she took in the stranger and her gearling, the practiced saleswoman's smile that had been spreading collapsed. Both she and Melanie just stared at each other for a long, quiet beat until Melanie looked away, cheeks hot.

"Oh! I'm so sorry," the girl said, shaking her head. "How can I help you, Miss . . . ?"

"Mela—*I mean Porta!*"

Melanie was so flummoxed, she'd nearly used her real name! What was wrong with her? She'd spoken to a kassipoi for the first time today—had just witnessed chores cheerfully tending to themselves—and yet it was this shopgirl who threw her off balance.

She adjusted her dress and took a deep breath.

Character trait: Lady Porta never loses her balance.

"My name is Lady Porta the Periwinkle, and this my gearling servant. I'm a traveling witch and a prodigy, which means a *very* talented ki—uhh, young woman."

The shopgirl nodded. "Yes, I . . . my brother tried to tell me there was a visitor, but he wasn't making any sense. He kept talking about armor. I thought he meant a knight had come through." Her eyes traveled from Melanie to Traveler and back again.

The girl tugged at her lustrous braid. "Well, you're welcome to look around! And I'd be happy to take your measurements if you need anything custom-fit."

Melanie felt her face warm. *Gosh, she's pretty.*

I'll take your word for it, Traveler's voice blared through her thoughts, clear as if he were speaking. *She seems fascinated by you too, don't you think?*

At the sound of the gearling's voice in her head, Melanie screamed.

She spun around in a wild circle, her foot kicking out from

under her and forcing her to grab at a besuited mannequin just to keep from landing on her face. Still, she nearly slid to the floor anyway—taking the dummy with her—until Traveler grabbed Unicorn and steadied her long enough to regain her balance. The cloak shifted unhappily on Melanie's back.

Revised character trait: Lady Porta occasionally loses her balance.

"This one advises its mistress to be careful," the gearling said.

Ah, sorry about that, Traveler's voice echoed again. It skipped across her mind like a stone across water. *This is the spell I mentioned earlier! It's called the Gossip's Friend charm. Useful, isn't it? After Katzy, I thought we should be able to communicate in secret. Perhaps . . . perhaps I should have warned you. Anyway, just think in my direction, and I'll be able to hear you.*

"Are you all right?" The shopgirl had rushed from behind the counter to Melanie's side. She wasn't *smirking*, per se, but she hovered just at the threshold.

TRAVELER! Melanie thought as loudly as she could in the gearling's direction. *DO NOT READ MY THOUGHTS WITHOUT PERMISSION!*

"Yes!" she squealed. "Yes, I'm *ever* so sorry. I thought I saw a spider! But it was just—a very skinny mouse!"

"Well, we'd better find it, then," the girl said as she righted the mannequin. "I'll offer the poor thing a home-cooked meal."

Now she was definitely smirking.

"Or it could have been a piece of fuzz," Melanie mumbled.

She adjusted her dress, putting on the most dignified expression she could muster. "I seem to be fine. No need to worry, Miss . . . ah, sorry. What *was* your name, then?"

The shopgirl dipped into a curtsy. "Livia. And your dance partner here is Lord Backstitch." Livia took the hand of the mannequin and twirled into his arms. She was so graceful. Melanie wondered if they had dance classes in a town as small as Hamlen.

"You . . . named the mannequin?" Melanie asked.

"Oh, I've named all of them!" the girl chirped. "Colonel Darning, Madam Crossgrain. It really is very boring here! Especially with the adults all up in the aerie."

Melanie frowned. "*Every* grown-up in Hamlen tends to the gryphons?"

Livia nodded glumly. "The money helps the village. The gryphons are difficult to rear, but just one sells for a whole year's worth of what the shepherds used to bring in. And with the empire going to war against the Hexe of the South, Mother says the aerie can hardly keep up with demand."

"Have you seen them?" Melanie asked. "The . . . the gryphons?"

Livia shook her head, wrapping her arms around herself. "Only from below, when they're out flying. Parno rides them, but . . . I don't know if I could work up the nerve."

Parno! Traveler's soundless voice echoed with surprise. Melanie noticed the gearling's eyes brighten. *I recognize that name. There's something important about him. Oh but what is it?*

"Who's this Parno?" Melanie asked.

Livia grimaced, as if accidentally having chewed the bitter seed in an orange slice. "He's the empire's gryphon buyer. A wizard, like you. He even has a gearling."

Oh no . . . Traveler said. *That's where I know the name—Parno Fabrillo is an imperial aldermage!*

The shopgirl shrugged. "Usually he stays at Katzy's when he's not up in the aerie. I'm surprised you haven't run into him yet."

Melanie, once we're done here, we should leave Hamlen immediately.

Leave?! Melanie exclaimed silently at the gearling. *But we got just here!*

Empire aldermages are not to be trifled with. We're not ready for that kind of scrutiny.

"Is everything all right, Lady Porta?" Livia asked. "You look faint. Maybe *you* could use a meal. I have some cookies in the back?"

Melanie heard a whir and felt a soft weight settle upon her shoulder. Five metal fingers squeezed gently. "This one's mistress was forced to journey through the storm," Traveler said in his polite, emotionless brogue. "She endured a most draining night."

Livia's gaze softened, moving from Melanie to the gearling. "It almost sounds like it cares about you," she said. "Are your parents aldermages? Did they make this automaton to travel with you?"

"No," Melanie said somberly. "I don't have any parents. I'm just a . . . a magical genius." She shook Traveler's hand from her shoulder with a sigh.

Livia grimaced. She seemed about to say she was sorry—or offer any of the other awkward condolences people made to orphans—so Melanie cut her off. "Cookies would be wonderful," she said. "And . . . do you have anything in periwinkle? It's my favorite color."

Apparently, she thought.

It's really nice! You'll see.

"Periwinkle?" Livia repeated thoughtfully. "Well, there's . . . hmm. Heh. I have one garment in your size, but . . . Well, let's just see what you think. I'll be right back!"

The girl rushed through the rear of the shop and past a breezy white curtain, leaving Melanie and Traveler alone.

I don't want to go yet, Melanie grumped. *I like it here. The village is pretty and . . . and I haven't even had a chance to sleep!*

Melanie . . .

First Kinderbloom and now this! You said I'd always have a choice.

You do, Traveler responded. *But we have our safety to consider. What do you think will happen if an aldermage deems you suspicious? You don't understand what they're capable of.*

And you do?

Melanie could even hear the gearling sighing through the magic of the charm. He sounded exasperated, but also a bit sad.

After a moment, he spoke again in a low murmur. *There are*

evil people in the world, he said, *for whom hurting a child means very little. Often those people wield more power than is right. Trust me when I say the aldermages are dangerous. Perhaps just as dangerous as the Hexe of the South.*

"Fine," Melanie said dismally. "We can go. As long as we head to Kinder—"

"What's that?" Livia called from the back.

Oh fudge nugget, she'd been speaking aloud!

"Nothing!" Melanie and Traveler both spouted at once.

Livia arched an eyebrow as she emerged from the back. Draped across one arm was a garment bag, while the other balanced a tray set with a kettle, two cups, and a mountain of scrumptious-looking cookies. She set the tray down on the store's countertop. "I have this coat, but . . . well, take a look." Livia pulled the bag away, and Melanie let out a little gasp.

It was *wonderful.*

The coat was trim and dashing, with golden buttons and pure white cuffs, all embellished by a lattice of lovely black trim. It was an exquisite blue color, almost purple, which gave it a playful, flashy attitude. Tiny embroidered stars decorated the fabric.

The coat was very clearly made as part of a boy's ensemble. Melanie had never wanted something more in her whole life.

"Periwinkle . . ." she whispered to herself.

I told you! Such a pleasant color.

Livia smiled impishly at Melanie's expression. "It looks like it might actually fit you."

"I *love* it!" Melanie blurted.

Livia laughed, her cheeks reddening slightly. "Then let's try it on! I'm sure we have some breeches and a vest to go with it." She giggled, then rushed to retrieve them from the back.

The coat fit like a dream—a hypnotic vision of stars emerging at eventide. Melanie admired her reflection in the mirror, this dashing figure clothed in twilight. She knew little of wizards and prodigies, but in that moment, in that outfit, she finally felt she could understand a bit of the exuberance Traveler seemed to exude at every moment.

"Well!" Livia said, after she'd applied the last stitch. "I don't know whether to call you beautiful or handsome, Lady Porta. In any case, it suits you."

Melanie felt her face heat. A pretty older girl had just complimented her and it felt . . . strange. And exciting. And a little mortifying too.

"Th-thanks," Melanie stammered, quickly averting her eyes from Livia to the mirror. Until she remembered the truth of her situation, and the dreamy, giddy feeling fell away like a fairy godmother's illusion. "But I can't. . . . I don't . . ."

"This one's mistress would be happy to barter for the outfit," Traveler buzzed from behind her. "Many find the services of a spellwright preferable to coin. She is capable of enchantments, charms, glamours, and any manner of thaumaturgic assistance. Though she has a professional policy against curses."

Livia considered the idea, her eyes bright. "A magic spell? I wouldn't even know what to ask for. I read once about a witch who spun straw into golden thread. But surely that's impossible?"

Possible, but impractical, Traveler muttered invisibly. *The spell alone would take months to craft, and we'd need the true name of either a gnome or djinn.*

Then what should I offer? Melanie asked. She made a great show of thinking the question over, pinching her chin between her fingers and scratching her head. *She makes such beautiful clothes. Is there some kind of sewing charm?*

Oh, how about self-sewing needles! the gearling suggested. *The enchantment is easy. We'll just need a few earthworms and a handful of soil.*

Melanie relayed the difficulties with golden thread—she could have sworn she saw Traveler wince at her pronunciation of *Jim*—and offered Livia a set of enchanted needles. The girl enthusiastically agreed. She went to fetch the earthworms from outside, pretending to roll up her invisible sleeves when Melanie offered to do it herself.

"No way am I letting Hamlen's first ever visiting prodigy dig through the dirt," Livia said with a grin. "Plus, I know exactly where to find them in Old Franke's garden. I won't be a moment."

While she waited, Melanie studied herself in the mirror. The coat was truly a thing of wonder. She'd heard countless stories, of course, of children who came into possession of magic garments of all kinds—coats, and hats, and sparkling slippers—either through inheritance or good deeds or just dumb luck. Wearing this coat covered in shimmering embroidered stars, Melanie couldn't help but imagine herself in just such a tale.

In the reflection behind her, she noticed Traveler shift slightly. The gearling's eyes fell to the countertop, where a matching pointed hat lay drooped on the counter, instantly recognizable as a wizard's cap. Melanie hadn't yet added it to the outfit.

"Traveler," she said. "Would you bring me that hat?"

The gearling moved smoothly, scooping it up by the brim and carrying it over. Melanie took the hat from his hands, then reached up and laid it gently atop Traveler's head.

"Very dashing." Livia giggled as she reentered the shop with a pail full of worms and soil. "Now it matches you."

Very dashing indeed, Melanie thought at Traveler. She stepped aside, letting him get a look at himself in the mirror.

For a moment, the gearling's glowing eyes expanded, the motes brightening like lanterns fed more oil. Then Traveler caught himself. He blinked, and the motes returned to their vague, expressionless configuration.

I love it, Traveler said.

When it was time to cast the spell, Traveler silently instructed Melanie on what to do. She took five worms and a bit of soil in one hand, then five needles and five different fibers in the other—a snip each of cotton, wool, linen, leather, and even silk.

It's sympathetic magic, Traveler told her. *Like makes like. Use what you've learned so far in animating Unicorn. We want the needles to be as at home in these fabrics as a worm is to soil.*

Melanie closed her eyes and summoned up her lesson from the previous night. Even without seeing her, she could feel Livia watching with rapt interest.

And don't forget the final ingredient, Traveler's voice echoed.

Love, Melanie remembered.

Perhaps it was the tea and snacks, but Melanie's mind wandered to her cooking duties with Sun-mi and Agatha at Merrytrails. Sun-mi was as close to a chef as the orphanage had—she always prepared the most sumptuous hens and creamy, flavorful soups. Agatha, ever the actress, entertained them while they worked by imitating the pompous grown-ups who visited the orphanage. Once, Sun-mi had laughed so much that she accidentally added sugar to the stew instead of salt, much to Mariana's deli—

Uh, yes, that too. Traveler's spectral voice dispersed the memory. *But in this case, I meant the* final, final *ingredient: showmanship. Do something magicky.*

Um . . . like what?

Recite an incantation. Or wail and sing. Something with a little pizzazz.

Melanie cleared her throat, searching for an idea. She remembered a rhyme that the girls at Merrytrails sometimes recited to each other before bed. She lowered her voice, chanting with what she hoped was a mysterious air.

"Keep you safe, my precious souls, until the dawn's reviving toll. And if you fart while night's still deep, keep it quiet—for I'm asleep."

There was silence.

Melanie peeked her eye open, to find Livia was watching her with a baffled smile.

Then she felt a sharp sting in her hand. Melanie opened her eyes, turning her palm over. She nearly gasped at the sight of five needles wriggling like tiny silver snakes across the creases in her hand.

Livia *did* gasp.

"Look at them!" she said. "They're moving on their own!" She held out a bowl and Melanie dropped the needles and bits of cloth into it, careful to avoid any more stings. Then she set the earthworms back into the pail. Suddenly Melanie felt very tired—heavy and hollow, like a draped coat.

Traveler buzzed sympathetically in her ear. *That's two amazing feats of magic without so much as a good night's sleep. I'd say you've earned a rest, my industrious apprentice. Let's head back to Katzy's. Perhaps . . . perhaps there's time for a brief nap, before we go.*

Melanie nodded. "I'm . . . I'm afraid I'm *rather* sleepy," she said as grandly as she could. "But thank you again for the clothes. Especially the coat. It's the most . . . It's truly lovely."

Livia smiled. "It was my pleasure." Two dots of color appeared on the girl's cheeks. "Do you . . . would you come by again, while you're in town? I've enjoyed meeting you, Lady Porta. Very much."

Despite her exhaustion, a thrill of *something* shivered

through Melanie. The feeling was taut and musical, like a harp string being plucked.

"Definitely," she said, feeling her own face split into a ridiculous grin.

Character trait: Lady Porta likes Livia.

Very much.

The walk back to the inn felt twice as long. Perhaps it was. Melanie's feet dragged the whole way, her earlier exuberance spent in casting the needle spell. Now the twisted path felt cumbersome. The late afternoon sun had slipped behind the cliff, throwing them into shadow.

Still, she was elated. She'd helped a clever, funny, fascinating girl with her magic, and earned a chic new look in the process. Melanie couldn't quite believe her luck.

Traveler? she thought. She received no reply. That inner, fizzing voice was gone.

Melanie tried again, this time aloud. "Traveler? If we can speak without speaking, why don't we do it all the time?"

"Gossip, while fun, can eventually turn wearying," Traveler replied, his voice low. "The same is true of the charm. The Gossip's Friend requires a modicum of concentration at all times. Imagine rubbing your belly and patting your head through that entire encounter. Pat your belly once, or forget to tap your head, and the magic sputters out."

Melanie, who had never been able to perform that trick at the best of times, nodded sagely.

When they arrived at the inn, Traveler stepped ahead, pulling the door open for Melanie as a true servant might. She stepped through, happiness and exhaustion blending into a warm, dreamy haze, which snapped away as soon as she saw the figures standing inside.

A well-built, gray-haired man in a crisp red uniform leaned against Katzy's desk, inspecting the broom that Traveler had animated with magic. He looked even older than Mrs. Harbargain, though Melanie couldn't be sure, what with the thick beard covering his pale white face. The broom was attempting to escape his grip, its bristles reaching plaintively toward a last lingering pile of dust near the door.

The man caught sight of Melanie and quirked a single brow. Beside him were two other figures—one small and one large. The smaller was a boy no older than Melanie herself, with olive-tan skin. His uniform was similar to the man's, though much simpler.

The larger figure was a gearling.

It looked exactly like Traveler, but the metal that made up its body was copper-red instead of Traveler's brassy yellow.

All three surrounded Katzy, who was fairly cowering behind the desk.

The man tightened his grip on the broom handle, and suddenly the inn was buzzing with a pulsating, unpleasant thrum. When it passed, Melanie saw the broom's bristles sag. It fell inert.

The man let go, and the broom dropped to the floor with a clatter.

He took a step forward. "And you must be the *prodigy* I've heard so much about."

CHAPTER 12

MELANIE froze, feeling her eyes grow wide.

The uniformed man's mouth pulled into a smirk. His gaze traveled downward; Melanie got the distinct impression he was combing her for weaknesses. When he spoke, she discovered she was right. "Perhaps not so gifted after all, if you can't tell the difference between a boy's coat and a girl's."

Behind the man, the boy snickered.

Traveler, what do I do? Melanie quested for the gearling, desperate to hear its reassuring voice in her thoughts. Her mind was utterly quiet.

"Well, what's your name, girl?" the man demanded. "And how exactly did you come into the possession of an imperial gearling?"

"L-Lady . . ." Melanie licked her lips, summoning every scrap of courage she'd ever possessed, and perhaps borrowing a bit of Agatha's. "I'm Lady Porta the Periwinkle," she said firmly. "And I don't believe that's any of your business, Mister . . . ?"

The smirk on the man's face tightened into something worse. Something angrier. "We have ways of identifying stolen property, girl. But you won't like the methods. Only an aldermage can license a clockwork retainer to its operator. That thing may follow you around, but without the imprinting spell, it isn't *truly* yours." The smirk was back, the man's blue eyes shining with gleeful malice. "So I'll ask you one last time. Where. Did you get. This gearling?"

Behind the desk, Melanie saw Katzy shift nervously. The kassipoi's fur was stiff with worry. "Please . . ." the innkeeper muttered in a small, fearful rumble. "Just answer the aldermage's questions, Lady Porta."

Melanie narrowed her eyes on the man. "No," she said. "Because that's not. Your. Concern."

The boy behind the aldermage gasped softly, and the man's bearded face split into a wide, frightening smile. His teeth were disturbingly white. He looked like he'd just been given permission to sink into a meal.

The aldermage lifted a small rod from his leather satchel— some kind of red crystal with golden filigree—and raised it into the air.

His gaze shifted behind Melanie: to Traveler. "Retainer, by the authority of the Third Eye of the Empire, I command you to subdue this girl." As soon as he'd finished speaking, the crystal began to glow bright red. A shrill, tinny noise—almost too high to hear—chimed through the inn.

Behind the aldermage, the copper gearling's eyes glowed red, the motes bloodying to the same hue as the rod. Its body curled, legs shifting as if ready to pounce. Melanie felt gooseflesh rising along the back of her neck. So that was some kind of . . . gearling control wand? Could that . . . ? Could he . . . ?

Slowly, she turned toward Traveler, terrified of what she'd find looming behind her.

But unlike the other gearling, Traveler's eyes were their usual clear, white orbs.

"This one serves the Lady Porta," his voice stated flatly. "And will defend her to the best of its ability."

Melanie glanced back to the aldermage, grinning. Relief washed over her like a warm bath.

The man's eyes widened, his smile dropping almost comically fast. Slowly, he lowered the rod, and the bloody glow faded from the stone.

"It seems you're licensed after all," he muttered. "Why didn't you simply say so?"

Melanie shrugged. "I'm a very *private* person," she drawled. "Which is difficult, as I'm also very famous. I like to keep *some* things to myself."

The aldermage quirked a brow, but let the issue go. "I'm Associate Aldermage Parno Fabrillo," he said, biting off the words. "Behind me is my apprentice, Adrianus. Lady . . . Periwinkle, you said? What an eccentric color you've taken. What brings you to Hamlen?"

"Just a rest stop on my journeys, visiting the *fanciest* noble houses of the empire."

"Indeed? Have you been to the court of Princess-Electa Maximillia?"

Melanie cleared her throat. Her nerves were returning, burdened by exhaustion. Probably best not to lie now, in case he had some insider's knowledge. "I don't believe I have. Yet!"

"Jonkeer van Stravern has a lodge to the north. He hunts this time of year. You've been there, surely?"

"Oh, I can't recall. You see, I've been riding *all* night, and—"

"Shame. There hasn't been a *wonderkind* in the area since Boneblack." Parno frowned, those cruel blue eyes scrutinizing her again. "Tonight you'll show me your act. If you impress me, perhaps I'll set up some introductions. I *may* even be able to put a word in with Riquem the Red, the new High Enchanter."

At the mention of the High Enchanter's name, Melanie felt Traveler shift subtly behind her.

"I can't promise anything, of course," Parno continued. "With the war effort now underway. But a bright young mage of the empire—in gender-appropriate clothing—*would* be an effective morale booster. Our current stock of apprentices . . . well . . ."

Parno shrugged and raised his hands—*What can you do?*—while the boy behind him flushed.

"Adrianus here certainly *tries*," Parno continued. "Adrianus, prepare the suite for Lady Porta's demonstration." The aldermage smirked. "My apprentice is no *wonderkind*—far from it—but he's capable enough to arrange a simple thaumaturgic circle. Usually." Parno chuckled as his apprentice glanced miserably down at his own red shoes. "Well, I'm off to the aerie. Depending on your performance, perhaps you'll see it tomorrow."

Melanie's head was spinning as the aldermage left the inn. Parno spoke so quickly, and said so much—most of it laced with tiny, stinging insults. She could hardly keep up. Just as she was realizing that he'd arranged for her to *perform magic* in front of him, the man was already out the door. It thunked shut behind him.

Melanie glanced toward Adrianus, the young apprentice he'd left behind. The boy's tan brow was furrowed as he watched the door. He glanced briefly toward Melanie, and she gave him an encouraging smile.

"Is he always like that?" she asked.

Adrianus just glared at her. His expression boiled with hate.

The boy turned and stomped up the stairs.

"I'm terribly sorry," Katzy said as she ushered Melanie into the bedroom, balancing a pot of tea on a tray. "I had no idea Parno would be returning so early. Or that he would be so unfriendly to you! I swear I'll never understand you wizards."

Melanie trudged into the room, her eyelids heavy. She only barely registered that the innkeeper was apologizing. Traveler followed behind the two, pausing to wait silently beside the door.

"That's . . . quite all right," Melanie said groggily as she sat on the bed. With the excitement of Parno's confrontation now passed, it felt as if Melanie were sinking into herself. The outside world became muffled and unclear. "As I am *in fact* a prodigy and my gearling *is*"—oh, what was the term Parno had used?—"*licensed* to me, everything will be absolutely *fine*." Melanie yawned, a noiseless yowl that gripped her whole body, unfurling her arms like billowing flags. "After a nap."

Katzy nodded, her fur settling a degree. "I'll leave you to your rest. Thank you, witch-kitten, for your help. And . . . and be careful around Parno."

As the kassipoi left the room, she paused a moment, peeking her shiny yellow eyes back through the opening. "I like your coat," she said shyly. Then she shut the door behind her.

Melanie listened as the innkeeper's feet receded, quiet as fog.

She sighed. "Should we escape now?" she asked. "Or wait a few minutes so he's farther away?"

The gearling shook his visor. "It's too late," Traveler said. "If we run, it will only confirm that something's amiss. We'll have the entire thaumacracy after us by nightfall."

"But how am I supposed to fool an aldermage?" Melanie dropped her face into her hands.

To her surprise, the gearling chuckled warmly. Melanie gazed back up at him.

"Melanie, you already *have*," the gearling gushed. "You were incredible! You defied Parno, and then he *thanked you for it* by offering you the chance to perform. I never would have believed it if I hadn't been standing right there!"

Melanie felt her face flush a bit at that. But exhaustion still tugged at her. It was an effort just to sit up. "I'm so tired," she said. "I don't think I can learn any new spells by tonight."

"Leave the magic to me," Traveler said. "This is exactly why we're partners. We help each other. Get some sleep."

Melanie's head had found her pillow by the time she answered. "Thanks . . ." she murmured. She reached absently across the bed, searching for Jane's hand across their bunks like she always did when it was time for lights-out. Then she remembered. A twinge of loneliness accompanied her into sleep.

A moment later, someone gently laid a blanket over her, tucking her in.

"Don't worry, Melanie," Traveler's voice buzzed in her ear. "When you wake, the world will be right."

CHAPTER 13

THE messenger arrived in the afternoon.

Jane was crowded with the other girls in a clump in the parlor, anxiously watching the gearlings stalk through the orphanage, the automatons trailed by a furious Abraxas. Every few moments, a tinkling crash could be heard from upstairs—the noise of *something* shattering as they searched the building—followed by an indignant feline yowl.

Little Mariana flinched every time, the younger girl's arms wrapped around Helen. It had been a sleepless night, and everyone was on edge.

At first the rest of the girls had thrilled at the arrival of the High Enchanter. No one at Merrytrails had ever been in the presence of someone so important. But Jane thought having the Third Eye of the Empire trained upon their quiet little home was an uncomfortable sort of scrutiny. She did her best to avoid his gaze.

Riquem the Red sat in the plush chair facing the girls. The seat was usually reserved for Mrs. Harbargain, but she huddled instead with the foundlings on the sofa. The High Enchanter had gently yet persistently questioned them throughout the racket—about the gearling who visited the night before, the witch Felidae Seagreen, and especially about Melanie.

"And what is her connection to the automaton?"

Crash! Maaaaaaaaow!

"I see. Then why was she chosen to accompany it?"

Bam, bam, bam. Bambambambambam!

"Fascinating. And she's always had this . . . talent . . . for opening things?"

Hissssss . . . BOOM!

Riquem was very apologetic about the ruckus. He let the girls sit where they liked, and even convinced Mrs. Harbargain to allow Sun-mi to serve cookies with their tea—though it was not yet even noon!

"I've never been very formal," he said with a wink at Agatha. "It drove the former High Enchanter up the wall. But strange circumstances call for strange breakfasts, wouldn't you say?"

Agatha, ever the flatterer, nodded enthusiastically between mouthfuls. "Feel free to stop by anytime!"

"And what's that *you* have there?"

Jane was so busy trying to disappear from notice that she missed when the High Enchanter noticed her. She gripped the piece of paper she'd been holding, averting her eyes.

"That's Jane," Mariana said. "She and Melanie are best friends." Mariana retrieved a clump of sodden cookie from the bottom of her teacup and deposited it into her mouth. "*Were*," she corrected.

Jane flinched, her eyes lowered. She knew for Melanie, loneliness crept in when she was isolated, whereas for Jane it came in a crush when she was surrounded. Somehow they'd always found a comfortable balance with each other. Now Jane felt the burden of all those eyes on her. She hoped Melanie wasn't feeling equally lonely on her own.

"Indeed?" Riquem said. His gaze too fell to the sheet. He extended his unarmored hand.

The page was one of Melanie's drawings of Misty Steppe, left behind when she'd departed. Perhaps Melanie had never realized it, but her vision of the swashbuckling heroine looked almost like a grown-up version of herself, with curly brown hair and large, expressive eyes. It was the closest thing Jane had to a picture of her friend.

Reluctantly, she handed it over. Riquem gazed down at the image and his brow furrowed. For a moment, it seemed as if he recognized the scratchy figure. Which was impossible, of course.

"It's Misty Steppe . . ." Jane muttered. "From the books."

The High Enchanter returned the paper with a tight smile. "It's very . . . symmetrical!"

Riquem insisted that the curtains stay drawn all through the search, and that the girls remain in the parlor. Under no circumstances was anyone allowed to leave the orphanage.

Only Baruti dared to question him.

"What is this all about?" she asked, once noon had come and gone. Her dark eyes flashed in the gloom. "We've already told you everything we know. You can't just hold us hostage here. We haven't done anything!"

Riquem smiled in response. Though the man had the

friendly air of a permissive uncle, his *smile* was something else. Jane sensed a blistering intensity behind it—a heat strong enough to melt metal.

He lifted his gauntleted hand then, the embedded crystal flickering with an eldritch light reminiscent of the gearling's magic from the night before. Something shivered through the room, causing the empty teacups to skitter chaotically across the tray. The windows all rattled in their casements, the glass splintering into long, spidery cracks. Helen only just saved a ceramic horse from plummeting to the floor.

After a moment, Riquem closed his hand into a fist. The vibration ceased.

"Be quiet," he said mildly.

No one had any questions after that. Baruti sank into the sofa, retreating into its well-worn folds.

The sun had just begun to thin when a knock finally jolted the front door. Mrs. Harbargain rose on instinct, but then gazed nervously to Riquem.

The High Enchanter frowned. "Answer it," he said, "but don't let anyone inside. And do *not* tell them I'm here."

The matron nodded slowly. She edged past his chair—*her* chair—and budged the door open just an inch.

"Could it be Melanie?" Jane whispered, her quiet voice rising hopefully. Her light brown hands clutched the drawing. "Did she come back?"

Sun-mi grimaced. "Let's hope not. For her sake."

Baruti shook her head. "I don't think it's her," she whispered.

She pointed toward the clock. "Look at the time. The post always comes about now."

Agatha nodded. "And Mrs. Harbargain would have given it away. She's the worst liar of us all."

Harbargain soon proved both girls correct. She slipped her hand through the crack in the door and retrieved a single sealed letter. Then her eyes bugged as she looked at the address.

"Th—thank you very much, Jarl!" she stammered loudly enough for the girls to hear. "You have a lovely day, now! Don't get into any *trouble!* Not that you *would*, HA-*HA!* Trouble! *INDEED!*"

She quickly closed the door and put her back to it. Her eyes were glassy as she wandered back to the parlor, clutching the sealed envelope with pale knuckles.

Riquem watched her placidly. He took a sip of his tea. Then he murmured, "Must you make me ask?"

"It's from Melanie," the matron confirmed dismally. "Jarl said that the courier has just arrived from Hamlen."

"Hamlen . . ." Riquem repeated. "Fascinating." He held his armored hand out. "Give it to me."

Harbargain hesitated a moment, then placed the envelope into the open gauntlet. It snapped shut like a jaw full of metal teeth.

Riquem nimbly opened the envelope and unfolded the letter. His eyes scanned it, blinked, then scanned it again. Finally, he lowered the paper to his lap.

The High Enchanter shook his head and sighed. "You wish

to know what this is about?" he muttered. "Very well. I'm afraid that your former ward is in quite a bit of trouble. She absconded with a priceless piece of empire property—one that's in the midst of a dire malfunction. Up to this point, I was willing to give this Melanie Gate the benefit of the doubt. Perhaps some terrible mistake had been made. But this letter has burned my doubts away."

Riquem raised his gauntleted fist, crumpling the note and envelope together. There was another flare of light, and the papers suddenly caught fire, burning illustratively to ash.

Harbargain watched the flames for a quiet moment. Then, something in her gaze hardened.

"You cannot possibly believe that Melanie is some kind of . . . con artist," she said in a low, indignant voice. "She is *a little girl*. Are you insinuating that she contrived to steal an imperial gearling? What's really going on here?"

"Yes!" Sun-mi cheered. "The gearling came to *us*."

"Melanie's a good girl!" shouted Mariana.

"She's *way* too flaky to plan something like that," Agatha added.

Jane also said something supportive, though her voice was drowned out by the others.

Soon, nearly all the girls were shouting—defending Melanie and protesting their treatment.

For their courage, they were once again rewarded with Riquem's scorching smile. He lifted his gauntleted hand, the embedded crystal flickering awake.

The room went quiet again.

"I see you all care very much about your friend," Riquem said. "And it's heartwarming—truly. There's no higher virtue than loyalty. Melanie is lucky to have you."

The High Enchanter lifted his teacup, gazing thoughtfully down at the spinning leaves within.

"Very well..." he said to himself. Then his eyes rose, and back was the cheerful uncle. "Girls," he said, "Madam Harbargain— pack your bags. Enough clothing for several days. Merrytrails is going on a trip."

CHAPTER 14

MELANIE dreamed.

She slipped through a murky passage, hurrying to some-place unknown. Even the passage itself was inexplicable—a hazy crawlspace that bordered reality, but was somewhere else altogether. She wondered idly how she'd crossed into it . . . and how she'd find her way home.

Her body moved, pulled by the same need that had always tugged at her. For adventure. For freedom. For *more*.

There was somewhere she needed to be—and she was very, *very* late.

If every fantastical story is to be believed, then nearly all dreams carry a whiff of prophecy, and should be carefully examined for omens of doom. But the truth is that most dreams are ordinary. Dreams that suggest the future appear so rarely that they may as well be myths.

Which is why it was *very* exciting for Melanie, currently, to be having one.

The passage unbottled, and she found herself standing before a vast wooden table, a slice so round and thick, it might have been cut from a single great tree. There were other figures seated at the table, all speaking in whispers that Melanie couldn't quite make out.

She couldn't see their faces, either. The strangers seemed almost to be made of mist. Or mist enveloped them so snugly, it was like the clothes they wore. Still, she could sense they were not all human. Feline and froglike silhouettes occupied several seats, and one figure sported a long, curved beak.

Melanie approached the table and sat in the lone empty seat. She knew with all the certainly of dream-knowledge that the setting was for her.

There were seven figures in all—eight, including herself—and each was seated equally distant from the next. Before every one of them was an arrangement of silver utensils, a clean white napkin, and an intricate, beautifully crafted plate.

All the plates were different, and each was made of impossible materials. The figure across from Melanie sat before an enormous snowflake, the glasslike dish glittering with cold complexity. Glancing left, Melanie spotted an oyster half-shell topped with a shimmering black pearl, and to her right a miniature storm churned in a silver dish. Its purple-gray clouds occasionally forked with lightning.

Slowly, she thought to look down at her own place setting.

Melanie sat before a black bowl, in which a tangle of plant life had been artfully plated. Moss and vines formed a dense mass, covered by tiny flowers. Their petals opened and closed in unsettling rhythms.

Mist filled the rest of the bowl and now spilled over its edges, dissipating across her lap. Melanie noticed her napkin ring was engraved with a stylized *S*.

It was all so strange. Melanie laughed bewilderedly, and the whispering around the table stopped.

She felt the other presences noticing her then. Eyes that were close, yet also deceptively far away, watched her from north, east, west, northeast and northwest, and southeast and southwest. Some hostile. Others delighted. All curious.

Then a voice from behind her—the first clear voice she'd heard so far:

"Who is sitting in my chair?"

A shadow fell over Melanie, and a warm palm gripped her shoulder.

"*You.*" The word rang out.

Which was when Melanie awoke.

The dusk light that peeked through the window was syrupy and overripe. Melanie squinted her eyes open. Traveler sat upon the bed beside her, his mechanical legs knotted into a seated position. His glowing eyes were totally dark, the mesh that housed them unlit.

But as she roused, so did the gearling. The motes blinked awake, angling toward her.

"Ah," Traveler said. "Good evening. I hope you're feeling better?"

Melanie sat up in her bed. She was still wearing the clothes she'd had on that morning, including the periwinkle coat. Her hair, she assumed, was a mess. She dimly remembered an odd dream she'd had—something about a table full of strange dinner plates—but already it was dissipating.

"I am, thank you." Melanie inclined her head. "Were you sleeping too? Do gearlings need to sleep?"

"No," Traveler said. "At least, I haven't yet. No, I spend most nights watching the stars, wondering what's beyond our world. Imaging the sorts of places the thaumacracy can't build roads to. Today, however, I was preparing for your demonstration with Parno."

It all came back to her in a rush then—the aldermage and his challenge. The heat of her fear burned through the last of her drowsiness.

"Traveler, I—" Melanie's voice hitched. "I don't know if I can do this. It was one thing to ride into town on a cloak and bring some needles to life . . ."

"Don't worry," Traveler said. "I've already cast the necessary spells. Just say three words, and Parno will be met with a demonstration unlike anything he's ever seen before."

Melanie squirmed. "What words?"

Traveler looked somehow pleased. "'Enjoy the show.' *DON'T* say it before you're ready, though. We wouldn't want the enchantment going off before you're in the circle."

Melanie tilted her head, quirking a brow. "Why? What's going to happen?"

Traveler sighed. The noise buzzed in his mask. "Must I spoil it?"

Now Melanie stood. "No more surprises! And no more secret spells."

"Oh, very *well*." The gearling threw his hands up. "I've combined an extraplanar quanta, a spatially localized state, with packets of illusion magic to be deployed at timed intervals. Essentially, I'm going to uncouple the aldermage's suite from time and space. Oh, it's just for a minute, calm *down*. During that period, you'll put on a dazzling show—all light and color, really—and when the last packet finishes, the room will rejoin our universe at the very place and moment we left."

Just this description made Melanie dizzy. "I don't understand," she said. "You can . . . you can *do* all that?"

"Can *I*?" The gearling sounded insulted. "Surely, with enough preparation and a properly prepared thaumaturgic circle. Such circles require rare runechalks to draw, but Parno and that angry little boy have apparently saved us the expense." Traveler shook his head. "I wouldn't allow a less experienced magician to try something on this scale, however. There *are* certain dangers in shaking loose from reality, even for a very short time."

The gearling hopped up from the bed in a swift, graceful movement. "There is one last caveat, however. I'm afraid that we won't be able to communicate in Parno's presence. At all. Not even with the Gossip's Friend."

As this news sunk in, it was like Melanie had come uncoupled from time and space herself. She remembered trying to reach out to Traveler when she first encountered the aldermage, and getting no response. "Why?" she asked.

Traveler's glowing motes flicked in her direction, angling contritely. "Gossip's Friend isn't foolproof. Think of it like an invisible room. Any wizard can listen in, so long as they have their ear to the door. Some aldermages even wear talismans that keep them attuned. It's not safe to use the spell around Parno, or *any* sufficiently powerful magician."

Melanie exhaled, frowning at the door to their room. "Well, what do I do if he asks me a question I can't answer? Or, even worse, asks me to explain the spell?"

"As you so bravely displayed earlier, Melanie, you're under no obligation to tell Parno anything at all. Certainly not the secrets of your craft. In fact . . ." The gearling knelt before her, his glowing eyes watching seriously. "You aren't under any obligation to *stay*, either. I know what I said earlier, but we could still leave right now if you'd like. Perhaps he'd give chase . . . but he might not."

Melanie shook her head. "No," she said. "No, we knew when we started this journey that we'd have to bluff our way through to stay safe. If we can fool Parno, we can fool anyone. Better that than running, and *proving* something's amiss. Besides, he said he'd introduce us to noble houses for our travels."

Traveler gazed at her a moment longer, then nodded. "I agree. And . . . thank you, Melanie. Now, let's go impress that unpleasant man, shall we?"

When Melanie arrived at Parno's suite, the aldermage had already returned from the aerie. Adrianus answered the door, his contempt barely veiled beneath a gauze of politeness. The apprentice showed her into the grander upstairs lodgings without a word.

The private suite was bright and open, with a large bay window that yawned over the town, providing an expansive view of Hamlen and the mountains and fields beyond. Melanie could see why cleaning the space would have kept Katzy so busy. It was the size of the entire downstairs!

Parno was seated in a sumptuous leather chair, his feet planted upon an ottoman.

The central space of the room had been cleared away, and a large, complicated circle was drawn onto the wooden floor with iridescent chalk. It was filled with all sorts of other shapes: stars and triangles and symbols that Melanie had no names for, along with scratchy writing that clung to the edges like magnetized dust. Just staring at it all made her legs wobbly.

Parno nodded approvingly at her interest. "I trust this will suffice?" he said by way of a greeting. "I've looked over the sigils myself, but you'll want to confirm Adrianus's work, of course."

"Of *course*," Melanie said pertly. She circled the circle, making a great show of looking at it all. It's round edge. The round edge over *here*. Once, she glanced furtively toward Traveler, who stood waiting at the entrance of the room, nearby the copper gearling. The two automatons bracketed the entrance of the suite like twin sculptures, though Traveler now donned his big, pointy hat.

The sight of the gearling so flamboyantly decorated soothed Melanie's nerves. She remembered Traveler's advice from the night before: *Have fun with it.*

The gearling's eyes were glowing blanks. If he had opinions about the quality of the thaumaturgic circle, he was unable to share them.

"This will do," Melanie said. She smiled appreciatively at Adrianus, and the boy actually rolled his eyes at her.

"Then let's begin," Parno said, settling further into his chair. "I've had a very busy day and I'm quite fatigued. Apparently, *wandering prodigies* aren't burdened with such problems. You haven't left your room at all, from what my apprentice tells me. Show me the level of *genius* that allows one to repose the day away."

Melanie's face flushed. So Adrianus had been keeping tabs on her? The little creep.

Nevertheless, she took a deep breath and entered the circle, just as she and Traveler had discussed, planting herself at the center. She still remembered the gearling's offer. They could turn around at any time, leaving this horrid man behind them. Traveler's safety was important, but just having the option made her feel a bit more in control.

"*Hours* of work were put into the presentation you're about to see," Melanie informed the man. True, though not by her. "So I *do* hope that you enjoy—"

As soon as Melanie said the first word of the triggering phrase, she felt power swelling out of it. Time seemed to dilate, the world slowing down. Her voice echoed strangely, even in the cozy space.

"—the—"

With the second word, Melanie's fingers began to tingle. Small objects around the room vibrated upon their surfaces, and the glass in the windows rattled gently. All around her feet, the iridescent chalk shimmered with a strange light.

Parno's eyes widened. The aldermage sat up again in his chair.

"—*show*."

Melanie couldn't truly be sure whether *she'd* spoken the last word, or if it had spoken *itself* through her.

The walls and floor of the suite blasted suddenly away, careening into oblivion. They were replaced by a milky field of stars, as bright as daylight. Curiously, all the room's furniture remained in place, as did Melanie, Parno, Adrianus, and the gearlings—each maintaining their original orientations in space.

Melanie only barely stopped herself screaming and stumbling, even knowing it was all light and color, as Traveler had said. She acknowledged a small note of petty satisfaction in seeing Adrianus had done just that. The boy had fallen onto his butt, his eyes goggling.

Though the room had vanished, some invisible floor still supported them. Melanie glanced down to find the magic circle persisted beneath her feet, glittering softly.

Their little diorama screamed through the heavens, past a

molten orb of orange fire so large and bright that Melanie was forced to look away. Then the stars threaded into thin fibers of light as they picked up speed, abandoning the fireball for places more far-flung.

A moment later they shuddered back into stillness, the stars twinkling again as motes of brightness.

Only this time, they circled what appeared to be another *world*.

A great globe of violet smoke turned pleasantly on an oblong axis, surrounded by no fewer than seven multicolored moons.

No, not violet. *Periwinkle*, Melanie realized with glee.

"An illusion . . ." Parno gasped, though his voice sounded unsure. "A—a hallucination . . ."

Melanie was surprised to hear her own voice answer, still echoing with the power it had earlier: "A telescope," she said. "A window."

They descended toward the world, their speed slowing as they plunged into the purple cloudplay. All around them, blue veins of lightning branched beneath the storm that was this world's skin. In the distance, great cyclones twirled together in clusters of a dozen or more, dancers spinning in an unreal ballet.

Melanie could no longer keep the wonder from her face. Her mouth was open in a wide, amazed grin. She only hoped that Parno and Adrianus were similarly enraptured, their attention away from her.

They emerged from the storm as suddenly as they'd arrived,

plumes of purple smoke trailing after them as they broke free. The world beneath them was unlike anything Melanie had ever seen. Toadstools larger than buildings scraped the clouds, their great fibrous stalks bending easily with the winds of this place. Fingers of light pierced the churning skies, illuminating a cosmos of glittering spores that floated through the air. Creatures like shimmering beetles buzzed gracefully across the alien sky, as large and lovely as the fancy carriages of Crossport.

To say this felt like a dreamworld was to understate it. Melanie could never have dreamed such a place.

And then, just as they'd arrived at this unearthly vision, it faded. Shadows crowded along the edges of the view, spilling in like black paint. The clouds and toadstools and intricate insects were overtaken, swallowed by the gloom.

Melanie watched it all go with a bittersweet feeling. Traveler had said the spell would only last about a minute, but it didn't feel like enough. It was a tantalizing demonstration, which she supposed was the idea. Better to leave Parno wanting more.

The blackness completely overtook the view now. Melanie knew that the spell would right itself, returning them to the aldermage's suite at the exact time and place they'd left.

But something strange caught her attention.

An edge of the circle beneath her looked . . . wrong. The cheery iridescent sheen was a rotted green, the chalk burned away like ash.

All around Melanie and the others, the inky blackness curdled to muddy gray.

"What's happening?" Parno asked. His voice echoed into the empty gray field. "Is this part of the show?"

Melanie cast a stray glance toward Traveler. The fearful cant of the gearlings eyes was enough to tell her it wasn't.

Something had gone wrong. *Very* wrong.

Melanie looked down again. More of the circle had eroded now, moldy like bad bread. The corruption spread in expanding clusters, eating through the intricate sigils.

Suddenly, the gray world that surrounded them shook, nearly knocking Melanie from her feet.

"There's something wrong with the circle!" she shouted.

At that, the aldermage leaped from his leather chair, rushing across the emptiness to the chalk drawing. He kneeled down and touched his fingers lightly to the edge of a corrupted section. With a yelp, he pulled them back. Sickly green smoke trailed from his fingertips.

"This has been tampered with," Parno gasped. "A hasping curse. The thaumaturgic circle is locked with you inside. The magic has nowhere to release. It's *consuming* itself."

The aldermage's sharp gaze lanced upward, piercing his apprentice. "Adrianus—what have you *done*?"

Still on his back, the boy looked petrified. His watery eyes were frantic with fear.

"I—I didn't realize!" he sputtered. "I only meant to spoil her spell!"

The gray world rumbled again, more violently this time. Now Melanie was truly thrown from her feet, only barely avoiding one of the necrotic blotches. She heard Parno yell as he went down too.

Traveler launched himself toward the circle, but when he tried to pass beyond its edge, the gearling was buffeted away by an ethereal barrier. He raised the orb at the center of his hand, pointing it down at the chalk line. Light erupted from the crystal's center.

All around Melanie, the symbols glowed more brightly, the iridescence exploding into a panoply of color. But whatever Traveler had hoped to do, it didn't appear to be working. In fact, the corrupted sections began spreading *faster*, rotting with alarming speed.

"You stupid boy!" Parno screeched. "We're in a *pocket dimension!* You've killed us all!"

Melanie looked up from the withering circle to Traveler. The gearling's eyes met hers, dismally dim.

"It's locked . . ." he whispered. "I don't think I can—"

"*Maow.*"

A flash of movement behind the gearling drew Melanie's eye. She let out a small gasp.

Of all the improbable things she had experienced in the past several moments, this, by far, was the most unexpected.

Abraxas watched her from a distance.

The cat was lazing upon his bald stomach, completely at ease. He seemed indifferent to the gray world currently boiling away all around him.

Abraxas's two eyes—one milky, the other yellow—watched her. "*Maow,*" he said again, perhaps a bit more insistently.

The circle is locked.

Locked.

Melanie remembered that night, weeks ago, when she'd released the elderly cat from the dormitory window. She'd used her strange skill that night, to explosive effect.

She looked down at what was left of the rotted circle. Was it possible that her ability would work on something like this too?

"Melanie?" Traveler said, just as she pressed her hand to the shimmering surface.

Hey circle, she thought. *I need you open now. Please.*

Her arm shivered as the request passed between her palm and the illuminated chalk. Its light flickered a moment—the circle understanding—and then it graciously released.

There was a great popping sound, like the loudest balloon in the universe exploding in the quietest room in Merrytrails. The grayness and the circle went with it, tearing instantly to nothing.

And then, Melanie, Traveler, and the others were back in the suite in Hamlen. Melanie searched the room for Abraxas, but there was no sign of the cat. In fact, the only indication that anything had *ever* been amiss was a gentle hissing noise.

Beneath Melanie's feet, the chalk lines of the thaumaturgic circle had burned a smoking imprint into the wood.

Several things happened over the next few moments, which Melanie experienced in a haze. Katzy burst into the room with a yowl, her irises wide with feline excitement. Apparently the loud pop that had accompanied their return was audible even from downstairs.

Parno looked furious. He lunged toward his apprentice and extended his hand, using some sort of hex to hurl the boy backward, pinning him to the wall. Parno demanded to know how Adrianus had corrupted the circle.

Adrianus didn't even attempt to lie. He'd hidden the hasping curse underneath one of the floorboards. The aldermage ripped the board free—Katzy hissing indignantly as he did so—and inspected the sigil painted into the wood. He frowned at the apprentice's work. Then his blue eyes rose.

"Well, at least you drew the seal right," Parno muttered. "I'd have thought even that was beyond you." He tossed the board aside. "But I'm afraid you're in for a world of punishment, my foolish apprentice. Unlike anything you've experienced yet."

Adrianus's eyes widened with fear then. Melanie felt her back go rigid at the sight, her haziness clearing.

"Perhaps . . ." She swallowed, taking a deep breath. "Perhaps some leniency is called for in this *happy* moment. We're safe and sound, after all."

"Only thanks to you, Lady Porta," the aldermage said. "I don't know what you did to break that circle, but if I had my doubts about your genius before, you've dispelled them. I can't apologize enough for this. To recklessly sabotage an empire-trained witch in her casting—Adrianus *must* be dealt with in the very harshest of terms, for his own good." Parno made an expression that Melanie supposed was meant to convey regret. "I take no pleasure in it, I assure you."

She remained unassured. "Then for *my* sake," she said. "Please, I don't wish any more unpleasantness tonight."

The aldermage watched her a moment longer. Melanie couldn't quite read his expression through the beard; she half wondered if he'd attack *her* too. But then Parno waved his hand and Adrianus slumped to the floor with a little gasp. "You are too kind by far, Lady Porta," the man said. It didn't sound like a compliment. "But since you've saved all our lives, I'll honor your request."

He turned to Katzy, who was watching this all with startled fascination. "Would you prepare a bed of straw for my apprentice in the stables? I'm afraid I can't look at him a second longer."

Katzy led Adrianus from the room, muttering vague words of comfort. If the boy was grateful for Melanie's interference, he didn't show it. He kept his eyes on the floor the whole way out. Katzy, however, met Melanie's gaze as she left, nodding appreciatively.

Parno had already turned from the door. He collapsed into his chair with a sigh.

"I must admit that was impressive, Lady Porta," he said. "The illusion was one thing, but your feat with the circle was quite another. I still don't understand how you accomplished it."

The aldermage's fingers tapped lightly at his armrest. Despite his begrudging praise, he seemed discomfited. Or perhaps because of it. "Very well," he said. "I've decided. I'll take you on as my apprentice. You'll have to wear the livery of the aldermages, naturally, but I daresay red is an improvement over periwinkle." Parno chuckled to himself. "War means opportunities for an ambitious wizard—*or witch*—to make a name for themselves. You'll rise quickly, I expect. We both will."

Melanie nearly laughed in the man's face. His *apprentice*? After what she'd just seen?

"Thank you for the offer," Melanie forced out. "But I must decline. I'm a pacifist, you see. I never use my magic to harm others." Melanie glanced toward Traveler, where the gearling stood impassively.

Parno rolled his eyes. "So you're one of those," he muttered. "It's a pretty belief to keep while you're young, I suppose. Riquem once thought as you do, you know. He favored *diplomacy* with the Ley Coven over direct action." The word sounded positively frivolous in the wizard's mouth. "He even led a small wing of reformists for a time. I don't know why Zerend kept the fop around, to be honest, much less named him as his successor. But he's ash now, and Riquem's seen the hard truth: Some attacks simply can't go unanswered. The Hexe will learn the same lesson soon enough."

Melanie swallowed. The Hexe of the South again . . . The name pulled at her, at something closer than memory but less dense. She envisioned an *S*, cast in silver. Felt a weight upon her shoulder.

"Well, anyway," Melanie said, shaking off the odd sense of discomfort. "I'm on my way to Kinderbloom at the present moment. I've always wanted to see the *charming* village."

The aldermage leaned forward. "Kinderbloom . . ." A note of suspicion touched his gaze, then vanished. "In that case, I insist you accompany me to the princess-electa's estate tomorrow. It's just a short journey from there to the garden town. We'll ride by gryphon."

Princess! He was inviting her to meet a *princess*? Two conflicting desires pulled at Melanie. She wanted to visit Kinderbloom, of course, but meeting real-life royalty? Now that was straight out of a Misty Steppe story!

And, as Parno said . . . it *would* be on the way.

Melanie suppressed her rising glee as she drawled, "How *very* kind. I'd be delighted."

Parno waved a hand and looked away; her delight was never in question. "Wear something warm for the aerie. It gets cold a mile up."

Melanie interpreted this as her dismissal, but as she turned to leave—Traveler moving gracefully to stand beside her—the aldermage spoke again.

"It's not your friend, you know."

Melanie turned slowly, frowning at Parno.

"The gearling. I see you looking to it when you feel unsure. And it's not a doll, either, no matter how you dress it up. It's a weapon. The retainers are ensorcelled to protect their operators, and they will do so by utterly destroying *any* perceived danger. Isn't that right, Oh-Two-Nine?"

Melanie jumped when the copper gearling lurched to life. "That's correct, operator," it said. Its pleasant, genteel voice was identical to Traveler's—a fact that filled her with unease.

"You may play at being a pacifist all you like, Lady Porta," Parno continued instructively. "But as long as a tool of war shadows your every step, you'll remain the most well-armed pacifist in the empire."

* * *

Melanie excused herself, and once she and Traveler had made their way back to the bedroom, she gently closed the door, leaning her back against it. Then she slid, inch by inch, to the floor.

"What a—horrid man," she muttered, biting back all the worse words that would have gotten her in trouble at Merrytrails. "Did you *hear* him?"

"Indeed," Traveler said. The gearling placed a hand to his metallic chin. "We'll have to be careful around Parno. He's more observant than I gave him credit for."

"Observant!" Melanie objected. "He called you a tool, Traveler!"

"He also called me a weapon." Traveler tilted his gaze to the window with a whir. The sun had sunk behind the mountain, blanketing the village in purple. "Being a tool isn't such a bad thing. The farmer levers the earth to feed the masses. The poet is a wedge, cracking into language to hunt for deeper meaning. There's pride in being a tool, as long as one has a choice." The gearling turned back to her, his glowing eyes bright and steady. "I choose *not* to be a weapon. And in any case, I'd rather discuss the fascinating event that just took place."

"Which?" Melanie asked tiredly. "That Adrianus tried to sabotage your spell, or that Parno seemed ready to kill him for it?"

"Oh, both were very exciting, to be sure—and that was generous of you to protect the boy. But I was talking about *you*, Melanie. How *did* you release the curse?"

Melanie looked up. The gearling stood over her, his hands

on his hips, watching her with a wide, interested cant to his eyes.

"It's just something I do," she said tentatively. "You asked Mrs. Harbargain if there was a girl who attracted weirdness. Well, I've always been good at opening things. Even very difficult things. Even very difficult things that are *magic*, I guess. But I can't always control it. If I wish too hard, things can get out of hand. That's what happened to Merrytrails." Melanie took a breath. "Agatha calls—*called* me 'lock-eater.' As if I chew up locks and spit them out. I always hated the name. But maybe she was right."

Traveler shook his head. "Well, whatever you choose to call the talent, it was downright masterful. A circle that's gone into a degenerative loop . . . technically it shouldn't be *possible* to unlock. Not until it's eaten itself." The gearling's glowing eyes shifted, the shutters flattening to squint at her. "Have you secretly been a real prodigy this whole time?"

Melanie laughed. "Maybe I am and I didn't know it."

"Lock-eater . . . it's not such a bad name. It sounds powerful."
Character trait: Lady Porta is a—
A . . .

Melanie sighed. "I'd prefer not to eat locks. Just open them."

"Then we'll speak no more of it," Traveler said. "It's all about choice, hm?"

Melanie paused, frowning slightly. "Traveler, did you notice anything strange while we were still trapped in the spell?"

"Stranger than what was currently happening?"

"Like a . . ." Melanie swallowed. "Well, like a cat. Abraxas, to be specific. He's the cat you brought home to Merrytrails."

The gearling's head tilted. "You saw this cat while we were in the pocket dimension?"

Melanie tugged at a bit of her hair. "Maybe? I'm not sure. I thought I did, but then he was gone when we'd returned. There's no way he could have gotten into the spell, is there?"

"It seems unlikely," Traveler buzzed. The gearling brought a hand to his mask, tapping his finger thoughtfully against the metal. "Though cats *are* famously adept as witches' familiars. Tell me more about Abraxas. Does he disappear often? Is he silent and stealthy?"

She thought about it. "Does passing gas count? Though honestly Jane was best at keeping hers silent. Silent but *deadly*."

"I'm getting the impression Merrytrails was a very fragrant orphanage."

"I don't know why people think girls don't fart." Melanie rolled her eyes. "We do."

"A warning I'd take to heart, could I smell. Well, what about his intelligence? Is he cunning? Did you get the sense that he knows more than he lets on?"

"He always knew when his dinner was served. I mean, he *usually* woke up when Mrs. Harbargain set the plate down in front of him."

"Uh . . . huh." The gearling turned, pacing the room with his hands clasped behind his back. "Would you say he's especially captivating, then? That there's just something *special* about him?"

Melanie snorted. "We all more or less agreed that he was very dreary. When he wasn't being actively annoying."

"Melanie, I'm not coming up with the picture of a potent familiar spirit. Perhaps, in all the commotion, you simply imagined something that felt safe. Like when we practice your spellwork."

It was as good an explanation as any. Though when Melanie thought of home, she usually summoned happier subjects— candles illuminating the winter streets during the Night of Gold festival; Helen's horse drawings, tacked to her bed by the dozen; Mariana's vise-like hugs. Or Jane's surprising, bubbly laughter whenever Melanie told a gross joke worthy enough to make her friend erupt.

Abraxas didn't rank high on the list.

"You're probably right," she said. "I should get some rest anyway. Tomorrow will be a big day for us."

The gearling's eyes tilted cheerfully. "I predict many of those ahead for Lady Porta the Periwinkle. You're making quite the name for yourself."

Melanie grinned. "We certainly are."

As Melanie and Traveler readied for the night, neither noticed the figures just outside the window, or the four eyes peering in.

Two belonged to a cat, the others to a boy—a stranger dressed in furs and feathers, his straight hair standing on end.

Nor did they hear as the boy turned toward the cat and whispered, "You're sure it's her?"

The cat's tail flicked. Abraxas let out a definitive "*Maow*."

The boy nodded. "Very well. I'll leave you to it." He glanced away from the window, toward the south and Kinderbloom, where three battle gryphons had disappeared into the horizon just that morning.

CHAPTER 15

MELANIE gripped the rails of the lift. It rocked through the air with a racket of loud, complaining creaks. The sky felt cruelly bright this morning, and the wind shook them with the demented cheerfulness of a dog yanking at a rope toy.

At least Unicorn seemed pleased; the cloak Melanie wore billowed dashingly even when there was no wind.

Below, the thatched roofs of Hamlen crowded against the stark gray mountain, receding as the lift rose. Soon they were little more than tiny bubbles floating in that sea of green grass.

And Livia was among them. Melanie had rushed to the girl's tailor shop before meeting with Parno—just as dawn was breaking—but no one had answered her tentative knocks. Too nervous to wake the whole household, Melanie had settled for leaving a note at the inn saying goodbye and how sorry she was to go. She'd even promised to come back someday soon, blushing furiously as she wrote the words. Katzy had pledged to deliver it first thing.

Parno leaned against the rail, his eyes on the horizon. His thick gray beard billowed in the wind. He'd been strangely muted all morning, and Melanie noticed that he'd left Adrianus behind.

Traveler had donned his hat and his own long cloak, giving him a dramatic, wizardly appearance. Parno had raised an eyebrow when he saw the gearling emerge so besuited, but thankfully refrained from another lecture.

While they rode, Parno explained how the mill powered the lift, among other necessary machines for the aerie. "Hamlen owes the aldermages a great deal," he boasted. "Before the aerie, these people were all backwater shepherds. The fields were absolutely *pocked* with sheep manure."

From what Melanie could see of the passing mountainside, the village had just traded one kind of dung for another. Long trails of white excrement dribbled from the cliffs, like pigeon droppings but a hundred times the volume. It smelled *awful*, like moldering meat and wet metal, and only intensified the higher they went. A wave of nausea made her look away, but that meant she was looking down at the ground far below, equally dizzying. Her eyes settled on the gearlings standing side by side in the lift.

Apart from Traveler's outfit and the different colors of their metal, they were nearly identical. Both stood at attention, their poses perfectly mirrored and their glowing eyes utterly blank.

Melanie desperately wished she and Traveler could communicate using the Gossip's Friend charm. Last night had felt like such a victory, but now in the cold light of morning, with Hamlen disappearing below, she remembered Traveler's warning—that the aldermage was more observant than he let on. She must be on guard with Parno at all times.

"I'm aware that the *youths* of today find it fashionable to skirt the norms of decorum," he said, having apparently changed topics. "But really, if you hope to make a positive impression at court, you should dress like a young *lady*. You don't want people getting the wrong idea."

Melanie fought from rolling her eyes. Whatever ideas Parno thought were wrong, she decided Lady Porta enthusiastically supported them.

The lift lurched, and a large shadow passed overhead.

"Ah, here we are," Parno said. "Be careful getting out. The first step is a tricky one."

Suddenly, the face of the mountain disappeared, and the craggy gray wall bent into a cavern as wide and open as a warehouse. Empire flags fluttered all around the space, many more than in Hamlen itself. Melanie felt their three-eyed gazes settle on her. She remembered Traveler's question on their journey to Hamlen.

And what does Lady Porta think of the thaumacracy? Of the three eyes, constantly watching?

Melanie Gate had never considered it before. But Lady Porta . . . found the gaze unnerving.

Women and men scurried around, hauling square bales of straw, casks filled with grain, and powder-blue eggs so large, it took two grown adults to carry them. Their uniforms were larger versions of the ones worn by the village children, except threadbare and smudged with white gryphon manure.

Likewise, the adults of Hamlen looked worn. Old or young, dark circles ringed every eye.

Nearby, a lift attendant leaned against a mechanical lever

that was connected to an intricate pulley system. He yanked back on it sharply once the lift arrived, and the whole arrangement jerked to a halt. The man hopped off his platform, then cranked another lever attached to a mechanical wheel. A long metal scaffold extended out to meet the car, forming a walkway into the cavern.

Parno threw open the door, barely waiting for the walkway to click into place. "Dozens of tunnels have been carved into the mountainside," he said proudly. "We have enough nests for twenty full-grown war gryphons, not that we've filled them all. It takes three years to fledge the beasts to adulthood. Until then, the young ones nest with their parents."

Melanie toed her way cautiously across the walkway, following behind the aldermage. "How many gryphons do you have now?" she called after him. The cavern was noisy with the sounds of industry—shouts and clangs and thunderous rumbles—along with the roar of the wind.

Behind her, the gearlings stepped onto the bridge. Melanie felt the whole configuration judder under their weight.

Parno seemed unbothered by the movement. He continued without looking back. "Not nearly enough! The empire requires every tool in its arsenal against the Hexe of the South. Zerend's murder was an attack against all of us."

"How many *would* be enough, then?"

Now the aldermage finally paused, turning slightly. The restless eyebrow rose again. "Frankly, I find that question unpatriotic, Lady Porta. One can't put a limit on our security. We're in the midst of a war."

Which seemed a bleak answer to her.

The lift attendant stared at Melanie as she arrived in the wide cavern, and he wasn't the only one. The villagers of Hamlen all glanced her way, their eyes passing suspiciously from Melanie to Traveler. It was just like the flags, she thought. She recalled Traveler's explanation about sympathetic magic. *Like makes like.* Perhaps people were a bit like that too. If the thaumacracy's three-eyed gaze was always searching for enemies, its citizens would naturally follow suit.

One of the grown-ups—a large, pinkish man with thinning hair—approached. He was better dressed than most of the others, his uniform clean and trim. He carried what looked like a black accounting book instead of a heavy load.

"What's this?" the man said. "Master Parno, this is no place for children."

"Calm yourself, Mister Frederick," the aldermage soothed. "We won't be staying long. Lady Porta is a visiting prodigy. I'll be escorting her to Princess-Electa Maximillia's estate, if you would be so kind."

The man's eyes widened. He looked Melanie up and down. "That's Livia's work, yes?" he said. Then his eyes softened a touch. "Well, you've got taste, at least. Looks good on you."

Parno's unctuous smile dropped like a wad of gryphon dung.

Mister Frederick nodded briskly, then waved to a group in the back.

"Prepare the carriage!" he boomed. Melanie flinched. It was a voice well-suited to the noisy atmosphere.

Others carried the order like an echo down to the back of

the hangar. Parno adjusted his shirt while he waited—calmly inspected his watch. Then, a sudden crash.

Melanie heard voices rising in alarm, and an ear-splitting cry. A woman across the cleft began ringing a copper warning bell. At the sound, Hamleners ran for the cavern walls, parting just as a group entered from one of the tunnels. There were six in total, each holding a long pole with a loop of rope at the end. Knotted between them, tangled by the snares, was the most terrifying creature Melanie had ever seen.

Its eye was as big as Abraxas, a sun-yellow orb of pure hatred with a black void at its center. The gryphon towered over its handlers. While the lion and eagle aspects were certainly present, *this* beast was so much larger than she'd imagined either creature could be.

Melanie felt a cold hand grip her shoulder. Traveler slid smoothly forward, interposing himself between her and the animal. Melanie saw that Parno's gearling had done the same.

"Back to the wall!" Frederick barked, and together they edged to the perimeter of the space.

The handlers moved with practiced care, each restraining a particularly dangerous appendage: wings, forward talons, and beak. The last of the six led the team—a burly man with thick biceps—ensnaring the gryphon's neck. They brought it to the edge of the cliff, their movements part dance, part shuffle. Then the leader called an order that Melanie couldn't make out, and all six twisted something within their snares. The ropes released, and the gryphon was freed. The handlers all dove away as it lurched forward.

And Parno moved to intercept it.

The wizard held a glittering object. Melanie couldn't see what was in his hand, but clearly the gryphon could. It crashed to a stop, shrieking. Then, to Melanie's surprise, it went still and quiet. Though the animal had been released from its snares, it wore a collar and a glittering anklet on its right forward talon. Melanie could just see a red leather band peeking from between the gryphon's feathers.

A second team of Hamleners emerged from the back of the hangar, pushing an enormous metallic sphere. They brought it to a stop just behind the gryphon, and one of the attendants slammed down a raised switch.

The sphere came alive.

It whirred like clockwork—*Like a gearling*, Melanie thought with a tightness in her chest—the surface spiraling open in a series of intricate circular movements. So, it was some kind of container? In a moment a passage had formed, revealing an inner room like a noble's palanquin. A set of two plush leather chairs waited invitingly, along with a small army of pillows. There was even enough space for both gearlings to stand unimpeded.

"Ready the jess!"

One of the Hamleners had climbed to the top of the sphere. He yanked a thick glittering chain free of some unseen holster, then tossed a length of it down to a woman waiting just below. She in turn hooked it to the gryphon's anklet, then hurried back from its reach.

Parno strode confidently past the gryphon and into the interior of the sphere. His copper gearling followed behind.

Melanie glanced toward the animal. Though apparently cowed by Parno's magic, the monster's cruel yellow eye still twisted her gut.

"Oh, come *along*, Lady Porta," the aldermage called impatiently. "The beast is subdued . . . for now."

Character trait: Lady Porta is n-not afraid of gryphons.

Melanie took a deep breath and plunged forward, affecting as much indifference as she could. Traveler moved alongside her; the gearling kept himself between her and the gryphon the whole way. Melanie wondered if this was still part of the act. Would Traveler fight if the beast attacked?

They arrived at the sphere, where Traveler gave her his hand to boost her up and inside. The interior was the finest space Melanie had ever been in. Just her chair was a revelation of comfort. She sunk into the mountain of pillows, and only barely restrained herself from mewling in pleasure.

Traveler followed her inside, installing himself beside the copper gearling. Once they were all in place, Parno depressed a second switch installed within the sphere.

The walls of the gyre sprang into motion. Melanie was reminded of the celestial models at the Crossport Museum of Thaumaturgical Philosophy—concentric rings that spun together, mapping the movement of the heavens in shiny brass. After a swirling dance of lattices, the carriage had sealed closed again. There were several windows, however, from which to view the outside. Melanie turned to the nearest one, then yelped.

The gryphon's yellow eye peered back at her.

The creature craned down to the sphere, its predator's gaze trained right on Melanie. It raised its forward claw—the one that the sphere was now chained to—and brought it down upon a handle at the top of the structure. All Melanie felt was the faintest shudder as the entire palanquin was dragged forward by the beast.

"Oh!" she exclaimed. "Oh, no!"

Parno merely chuckled.

Melanie could still see the huge, lumbering shape of the gryphon above them through a porthole in the sphere's ceiling. The muscles of its leonine body rippled overhead as it worked to pull the sphere to the cliff's edge.

Then, before she could process what was coming, it threw itself from the cliff.

Melanie screamed as the gryphon opened its wings. If she'd thought the beast was big before, its full wingspan was truly mammoth. The gryphon lifted into the air with a shriek, moving gracefully upward. One powerful beat of those wings—then two, then three—and they were off. Though the sphere swung tumultuously in the gryphon's taloned grip, the interior of the carriage remained perfectly still. Only the outer layer rotated with its jerky movements.

Melanie whipped around to see the aerie quickly receding behind them. Soon it was nothing but a dark stripe in the mountainside, and Hamlen a scattering of pebbles on the grassland.

"Impressive, isn't it?" Parno said, staring calmly ahead. "The carriage is my own design. It's supported by a bevy of enchantments that offset the weight. Even a gryphon wouldn't be able to ferry two gearlings very far without magical assistance."

"M-most impressive," Melanie managed to grind out through firmly clenched teeth.

"Sit back and relax, my dear. We have quite a journey ahead of us before we reach the princess-electa's estate."

Melanie tried. She sank deeper into her pillowed seat and forced herself to breathe. She imagined Jane was with her, quietly marveling at every detail below, the vast sky all around them. Still, Melanie's heart wouldn't stop racing. They were so high up! And all that protected them from a deadly plummet was the grip of a vicious monster!

Melanie took a deep breath, then a shallow one. In and out. Nice and easy. Eventually, she felt her pulse slow.

Parno glanced toward her and smiled unctuously. "There we are. Perfectly safe. Now, to pass the time, perhaps you'd do me a favor."

The aldermage steepled his hands. "I'd like you to tell me who you really are."

CHAPTER 16

A shadow crossed over Hamlen, just as the village's newest visitors approached the village—seven foundlings and their middle-aged matron, all escorted by the most powerful wizard in the Aederian Thaumacracy.

Jane Alley shielded her amber eyes, glancing upward through the carriage window. She caught the shape of an enormous bird outlined in the morning sun.

Was it carrying something? The bird had shrunk to a dot before she could be sure.

None of the girls had ever left Crossport before, and despite their nerves, they were buzzing with excitement. Even Mariana, who'd had her arms wrapped around Baruti since they left the city, came uncoiled to gaze out the window.

They rode together in a grand coach, pulled by four exquisite horses. Helen Stables had screamed in glee when she saw the team pull up to the orphanage. Only the presence of the gearlings, along with the swift grip of Mrs. Harbargain, had kept her from rushing the animals.

And the gearling presence remained, long after they'd left the city walls. The coach was surrounded by loping metal automatons who kept easy pace with the carriage as they traveled. They now stood at a removed distance, staring implacably ahead.

Behind the coach, a second wheeled wagon had been hitched to the first, though this one held no passengers. Instead, an enormous shape bulged beneath a red tarpaulin emblazoned with the three-eyed symbol of the thaumacracy. None of the girls could get a sense for what the mysterious cargo was, and they didn't dare discuss the matter in front of Riquem.

But it was clearly very big.

The girls were all pressed together around Mrs. Harbargain, so no one would have to sit too near to Riquem. All except Agatha. She'd happily perched beside the Third Eye, chatting companionably with him the whole trip.

"Fascinating! So is the piece attached to your arm, or worn?" She indicated Riquem's gauntlet.

"Worn," he answered gamely. "It's the insignia of the Third Eye of the Empire. Sort of a badge of office. A bit flashy for my taste, but easier than lugging an enormous staff around like they used to. And it comes with some *exhilarating* unique enchantments."

"Like what?"

"State secrets," the High Enchanter said with a wink. "Wouldn't want word getting to the Hexe of the South, now would we?"

Agatha feigned a look of horror and Riquem chuckled.

"Don't worry. We'll get her in the end. And *all* of the Ley Coven. It was Zerend's final wish."

"Were you close with High Enchanter Zerend?" Agatha asked. "Before the attack?"

Real emotion shaded Riquem's easygoing smile then. A distance touched his eyes that Jane couldn't help but notice. He looked sad, and perhaps a bit lost.

"We were," he answered faintly. "But he wasn't the only one who died that night. Some of the thaumacracy's brightest magical minds—my friends and colleagues—were working together when the explosion hit. I was spared only because I'd been running late."

The softness in his brow constricted—a loose knot pulled tight. "The Hexe will pay."

They arrived at the village gate. A horde of children greeted them, returning the girls' gawking with wide-eyed stares of their own. The children all kept far away from the gearlings, except for a single boy in the red uniform of the imperial alder-mages.

Riquem the Red frowned at the boy.

Jane noticed Baruti shooting Agatha a what-are-you-doing glare—but Agatha maintained her inane smile, as if she hadn't seen.

"Wait here," Riquem said. He opened the coach door and jumped gracefully to the ground.

"High Enchanter!" Agatha called after him. "Go easy on Melanie, would you? She really is a good girl."

Riquem smiled kindly back at her. "That all depends on her, I'm afraid . . . But I'll see what I can do." He turned away, and Jane only just noticed the smile wrench into a scowl as he did.

"Where's Parno?" Riquem asked, before he closed the carriage door behind him.

A moment of tense silence hung in the space. Then Agatha's beaming face collapsed.

"Lords and ladies, that man is exhausting," she huffed. "Hopefully that bought Melanie some mercy when she's sent to the Donjon." She frowned coolly at Baruti. "I'm not a *complete* monster."

"IS MELANIE GOING TO *WIZARD JAIL*?!" Mariana cried.

Mrs. Harbargain grimaced. She sat between Baruti and Helen, Abraxas nestled in her lap. It was hard to tell who looked more miserable in that moment—Harbargain or the always-miserable cat.

"I . . ." The matron swallowed. "I'm afraid I don't know any more than you do. Please sit down, Sun-mi. Don't rock the carriage."

The girl had risen from her seat and was gazing away from the town. But Jane's eyes had followed Riquem out the other window.

Whatever conversation he was having had grown serious. The boy in red handed Riquem what looked like a handwritten letter. He kept pointing to the inn, where a kassipoi and a girl dressed in mismatched patterns stood rigidly at the threshold.

"*Hssssss!*" Abraxas suddenly leaped straight up. The cat's good eye was wide, his pupil trained on something far away. He lunged at the carriage window from which Sun-mi was gazing, yowling angrily.

"It can't be," gasped Sun-mi. "Everyone, look!"

All the girls crowded to the left side of the carriage, peering out.

"There!" said Agatha. "Is that . . . ?"

"Impossible," whispered Mrs. Harbargain.

"It's Abraxas!" exclaimed Baruti.

At the edge of the village, standing just outside the tall grass, a cat identical to their own Abraxas leered at the carriage. It had the same dull gray fur and bald stomach, with the same sour expression tugging its face downward. It even had Abraxas's milky eye.

The cat was sitting calmly, watching the cart with benign interest. Then, with a flick of its tail, it turned and disappeared into the grass.

The real Abraxas stayed at the window, hissing and growling, but the girls all sat back in their seats.

"It's a coincidence," suggested Baruti.

"With the same white eye?" Agatha asked heatedly. "What are the chances?"

"But what could it mean?" whispered Jane.

Jane recalled the stories she and Melanie had read of "dubbelgangers"—mysterious lookalike spirits whose appearance foretold a coming doom. Misty Steppe had once met hers in *The Tale of the Terrorizing Twin*, and only managed to escape her evil fate by showing the dubbelganger a reflection of *itself*, thus turning the curse back onto the spirit copy.

Dubbelgangers were made up . . . probably . . . but Jane

couldn't help feeling this was a dire omen. *One* Abraxas was bad enough.

"Quiet, girls," Mrs. Harbargain said, "here he comes." She pulled the cat away from the window as Riquem stalked back to the carriage. Abraxas let out one final hiss, then allowed himself to be deposited onto her lap. "Don't mention the other cat," she added. "It's probably nothing, but—"

The door was yanked open. The High Enchanter's bright expression was like a sunny morning where the curtains are pulled away too quickly—it hurt Jane's eyes just to look at it. The human and kassipoi girls both huddled behind him.

"There's been a detour," Riquem announced. "It seems Melanie has fooled a particularly *lunkheaded* aldermage into believing she's some kind of prodigy. They've already left Hamlen by air, headed for the grouille court. We'll catch up to them via the Wonderstraat. Make room, girls. We're adding more passengers."

The foundlings all gaped at the two Hamleners standing behind Riquem.

"What about their parents?" Mrs. Harbargain protested. "Surely you cannot just kidnap these children from their homes!"

"Not kidnap—conscript. They're being called upon to serve their country. Parno's apprentice Adrianus will inform their parents. These two have witnessed Melanie's little ruse with the gearling firsthand. I . . . may need them."

"*Need* them? For what? This is absurd!"

A beat of silence passed as Riquem narrowed his eyes. "I agree," he said pointedly. "It seems increasingly unlikely that an innocent foundling would have managed to get this far on her own. Things keep looking worse for your Melanie Gate. She's even taken on a fake name: Lady Porta the Periwinkle."

Mrs. Harbargain swallowed. "There's some mistake," she muttered.

"Perhaps," Riquem said. "Or perhaps she's been enticed by the Hexe of the South to join the Ley Coven. Adrianus claimed she had some impressive magical talents. Far beyond what you've mentioned. How well do you really know this girl?"

Riquem waved the two Hamleners into the cart, then pressed in himself. Space that was once ample now felt uncomfortably cramped.

"I'm Mariana," the little girl said to the Hamleners. "Sorry Melanie tricked you. She's not a bad person; she's our friend. That's Baruti and Sun-mi and Helen and Agatha."

"And me," whispered Jane.

"Oh, and Jane. We forget about her sometimes. Sorry, Jane."

The kassipoi's slitted eyes lit upon Agatha. "You . . ." she purred thoughtfully. "Lady Porta mentioned you."

A look of warmth touched Agatha's face as she heard this. "Melanie talked about me?" she said. "That's—"

"Agatha Pondscum, her jealous rival."

"Her *what?*"

Riquem pinched the bridge of his nose as the cart lurched into motion, the gearling driver urging the horses forward.

Through the windows, Jane saw the rest of their automaton escort had also begun to march. The buzzing cacophony of clockwork reminded her of a beehive coming awake.

"High Enchanter," Harbargain pleaded. "I've known Melanie since she was a toddler. There's simply no way that she's behind some . . . nefarious *scheme*."

Riquem sighed. He was quiet for a moment, his eyes wandering over his gauntlet. Then he lowered his armored hand and gazed sadly at the matron. "If your bond really is that close," he began, not unkindly, "then I *implore* you to convince her to surrender. That, Mrs. Harbargain, is why you're all here. To give Melanie a chance."

It was in this moment that Jane Alley knew the High Enchanter was lying.

His calm, sympathetic gaze was nearly perfect in its mimicry of compassion. Nearly.

But Jane Alley was a quiet child. The sort who was easily forgotten. This distance kept her removed from the world, but it also gave her a better vantage from which to observe it. She *saw* people, especially people who, like her, avoided being seen.

Riquem was panicking.

Jane could tell by the way his hands were always moving. By the sudden hardness in his eyes as he glanced out the window. His mind was already far away, chasing an orphan across the countryside.

She didn't know why yet. Surely one foundling didn't merit the Third Eye's personal concern in the middle of wartime, even if she *had* stolen a gearling.

But Riquem was scared of Melanie. So scared that he'd rounded up every person whose path she'd crossed in the last two days, refusing to let them out of his sight.

They were loose ends.

A chill spread over Jane as the gearlings' metallic footfalls rang around their crowded carriage like a net of noise. The other girls were chattering excitedly with the Hamleners, asking about Melanie's new persona, Lady Porta. Livia, the girl with colorful hair and the most bizarre dress Jane had ever seen, answered them readily. Then she responded with a bevy of questions of her own. Mrs. Harbargain stroked Abraxas's ear, which flicked in annoyance.

But none of them understood the truth. They weren't Riquem's guests. They were his captives.

Sometimes when Melanie was restless—or lonely—she was prone to spectacularly rash decisions that landed her in equally spectacular trouble. Like the time Jane had been contagious with foxpox, and Mrs. Harbargain had quarantined her in a makeshift isolation room in the basement. Though the space was dark and musty, Jane had been content with the solitude—and the steady supply books and honeyed milk Harbargain brought to cheer her up.

Melanie had not handled the separation as well. Just as Jane was getting better, Melanie had snuck into the basement to see her, catching the pox and forcing *herself* into quarantine. Jane was touched that her friend had missed her so, but when Jane's recovery forced her woefully back upstairs with the crowd of other girls—and left Melanie fully alone and wretched in the basement—their parting had been doubly miserable.

All because loneliness had prevailed over prudence.

Jane couldn't help but imagine her friend was feeling just as alone right now, with only a mindless gearling for a companion.

Melanie, she wondered. *What have you gotten yourself into?*

CHAPTER 17

WHAT *have I gotten myself into?*

Melanie licked her lips. She looked at Parno. As evenly as she could manage, she said, "You already know who I am: Lady Porta the Periwinkle."

The aldermage's eyes were like tacks pinning her to the seat of the sphere. A mile down, the ground shifted unhurriedly beneath them.

"Your story doesn't add up." Parno tugged at his beard. "Something's off—I can sense it. What's your business in Kinderbloom?"

"I told you, I've always wanted to see the *charming*—"

"You're lying!" The aldermage lost his composure, burying his fist into an unfortunate pillow. "Are you working for the Ley Coven? The Hexe of the South?"

Melanie coughed out a genuine laugh. "I truly *don't* know what you're talking about," she drawled.

"You unlocked a degrading feedback loop. There's no magic in the empire capable of that. So whoever taught you that trick operates outside of thaumacratic society." The aldermage's eyes widened, and his feverish beard-tugging paused. "And I'd be willing to bet that there's no record of a 'Lady Porta' in the Imperial Census of Spellwrights, either."

"Well, then . . ." Melanie said evenly. "You would *lose* that bet."

Though she had no idea what these "imperial senses" were, Melanie could tell she was in trouble. Clearly Parno had a means of testing her story. She fought to remain calm but had never been a good liar under pressure. She wished she had even a scrap of Agatha's composure.

She managed a steadying breath. But the more scrutiny Parno added, the more brittle she felt. She imagined coming clean right there, admitting the whole thing and pleading for mercy, like she had when Mrs. Harbargain sniffed out her forgotten beetle collection.

Then she remembered how Parno had treated Adrianus the previous night when *he* begged. This was not a man with mercy to spare. The only way forward was to keep up the lie.

"Perhaps I'm wrong," Parno said. "Perhaps you really are a *genius* of the highest caliber, a cross-dressing wonderkind who invented a kind of magic that has eluded centuries of empire-trained witches and wizards." The aldermage leaned forward. "But I don't think so," he whispered. "Do you know what the punishment is for impersonating a spellwright, *Lady* Porta? How about for conducting dangerous magic without a thaumaturgic license? Let me give you a hint . . . The Donjon possesses *several* unburnable stakes."

Would—would they really *burn* her? A kid? Melanie

remembered Traveler's warning about the aldermages. That they had no reservations about hurting children.

If only they'd fled when the gearling had suggested it!

Another thought crept upon her, quiet as mist and just as cold: Would he defend her if it came to that? Or would Traveler flee to avoid a fight?

Despite the comfort of the seat, Melanie felt as if she were sitting on broken glass. Every movement seemed dangerous.

"Then again . . ." Parno leaned back, crossing his arms. "Perhaps we could strike a deal. You do something for me, and I let the matter go. The census bureau is never consulted, and you can be on your way."

Melanie frowned. "What deal?" she asked suspiciously.

"A trivial matter for someone with your singular talents," Parno said. "I need you to open a door. That's all. The door is sealed by impregnable magic. It's impossible to open without the princess's personal key. At least I thought so. But the spell is similar to the hasping curse you so easily nullified. You, I think, may actually have a shot at it."

Melanie swallowed her surprise. She'd expected that whatever Parno's request was, it would involve Traveler's magic. But he was interested in *her*? Back at the orphanage, she'd never thought of opening doors as particularly rare or interesting. Compared to the flashy magic Lady Porta had performed for Parno, lock-eating seemed practically humdrum.

But in the end, Melanie Gate was the tool that had caught the aldermage's eye.

It's all about choice, hm?

Melanie wanted to look to Traveler, but the mage was studying her too closely.

"What's inside the door?" she finally asked.

"That"—Parno smiled—"is *not* part of the deal. Just the door itself. In this partnership, the less we both know, the better. Don't you agree?"

Melanie gritted her teeth. Parno was asking her to steal from the princess? She didn't even know the princess!

But what choice did she have? She was trapped with the aldermage in his sphere, hundreds of yards above the ground.

She knew the thaumacracy burned criminal mages sometimes. In Agatha's grisly tellings, it had always seemed a horrific death. Melanie dug her hands into the pillows beneath her to hide her trembling fingers.

And yet . . . curiosity mingled with the dread. An unopenable door, behind which some priceless mystery awaited. A daring heist, and *she* was uniquely vital.

It was just like a story, though with harsher stakes than Misty Steppe might navigate. Melanie couldn't help but wonder what awaited beyond the door. A cursed jewel? The staff of some powerful, long-dead wizard?

"While I don't have *anything* to hide," she said slowly, "I will agree to this deal as a show of my loyalty to the thaumacracy."

Parno rolled his eyes, but she sensed that he was pleased. The mage settled further into his seat, patting at his beard.

"How will I know the door when I see it?" she asked.

"Oh, you'll know. Maximillia makes no effort to hide it.

Quite the contrary—her personal Greenguard patrols the corridor at all hours."

Melanie grimaced. "Then how am I supposed to unlock it?"

"My dear Lady *Periwinkle*, I thought you were a genius." Parno raised his shoulders in an eloquent shrug. "For your sake, I hope you figure it out."

Melanie wasn't sure how much time had passed when she saw the castle erupt from the horizon. It must have been a couple of hours at least, all of it spent in tense silence.

Tense for Melanie, anyway. Parno—his blackmail now complete—seemed utterly relaxed. The aldermage even dozed, producing little gurgling sounds from his open mouth.

Once, Traveler dared to turn toward her, when he was sure Parno was asleep. His eyes dimmed as he leaned forward.

"Melanie, are you sure this is wise?" he asked in a clipped whisper. The hint of judgment in his question was subtle and surprising, like the tang of newly soured milk.

Melanie looked up at him and felt a hollow form in her chest. She thought of Jane's gentle warnings when she was about to do something particularly brash. Somehow this felt worse. Traveler sounded . . . *disappointed* in her. But what choice did she have?

Then, as the copper gearling turned its glowing eyes upon him, Traveler stood back up and went inert. He didn't speak the rest of the ride.

The castle began as a silver sheen against the water. The

gryphon now flew over a vast wetland, with miles of bog visible from either side of the sphere. Melanie could still trace the raised Wonderstraat carving a navigable path through the mire. The wide stone road was the life of the empire; merchants and armies alike used it to navigate the western coast, and the king took great expense keeping it in good repair.

Yet it looked so small and insignificant from above.

Eventually, the sheen in the distance grew a point, then several more. It was like the swamp had grown a gigantic tooth with which to bite the sky. The palanquin shook slightly as the gryphon angled downward, beginning its descent.

The movement roused Parno. His own teeth clacked together as his mouth snapped shut.

"Ah," he said blearily, "and here we are."

The closer they got, the more beautiful the castle became. Great columns of transparent crystal jutted upward, shimmering prettily against the water.

Melanie saw figures waving their arms as they caught notice of the gryphon. Soon the figures came into relief, and she let out a delighted gasp.

Frogfolk! They were visiting the Grouille Principality!

Like the kassipoi, the grouille were one of the empire's non-human races. Melanie thought back to her lessons about the Grand Awakening. Humans had evolved from apes, of course, and kassipoi from wildcats. And the amphibious grouille evolved from an early ancestor to frogs and toads.

Melanie wondered idly if that's what had happened with

Traveler too. Perhaps the gearlings were evolving in a similar manner. It was an interesting idea.

The grouille were a more recent addition to the empire. Melanie didn't remember many details—oh, she wished Baruti were here!—but she knew it had to do with the last Wizard War. And a city? Something to do with a city.

The grouille were clearing a landing area on a stretch of dry dirt. Their shiny skin ranged from blue to green to brown, and they were all dressed smartly in colorful liveries.

The ground rose up to meet the carriage faster than Melanie anticipated. Her expansive view gave way to a telescopic focus on the commotion of the field. Despite her fear of flying and her odious travel mate, Melanie was sad to land. The view from above had been extraordinary.

The palanquin rattled gently as they touched down, then rattled again when the gryphon alighted next to the sphere.

All the grouille attendants hopped back, giving the creature a wide berth. In a moment, Parno had opened the carriage—there was a sizzle of magic as he did—and was standing in front of the beast. Again he held an item toward the creature, but this time Melanie could see what was in his hand.

An eye.

Though it was shaped differently from a human eyeball—with a small, round front and an oblong back—the object was unmistakable. A vivid yellow iris, almost identical to the gryphon's, haloed a black pupil, all of it staring angrily forward.

"Fascinating," Traveler whispered. With Parno's attention

elsewhere, the gearling had turned slightly to watch the show. "An eagle's eye, preserved somehow . . . isotopic solution, maybe? It's an ingenious use of sympathetic magic. Like makes like—use the small to control the large. I wonder what other uses it might have."

The copper gearling angled its head toward Traveler with a whir. Its glowing motes watched vacantly.

"Ah, don't mind me, cousin," Traveler chirped quietly. "Just a little professional curiosity."

Melanie tried to catch Traveler's eye, but both gearlings had returned to their upright positions by the time Parno stuck his head back into the sphere moments later. "Any day now, Lady Porta. The grouilles must have enough time to hood the beast."

Melanie exited the sphere, followed by Traveler and the copper gearling. As she did, another contingent of grouille servants emerged from the front of the castle, hopping quickly toward them.

"Aldermage Parno!" croaked one the servants. His voice was high and gravelly. He stepped ahead of the other two servants, who bowed their heads. "We were not anticipating your arrival today. Welcome to the Chateau de Papillon. To what do we owe this honor?"

"Hello, Bufonis." The wizard smirked. "I've recently met a delightful young witch, Lady Porta the Periwinkle, who it turns out is a traveling prodigy, of all things. Having witnessed her talents firsthand, I immediately thought of the princess-electa. She'll want to be one of the first to see this exceptional child perform."

Bufonis turned to Melanie and bowed so deeply, she was surprised he didn't fall over.

"Welcome, Lady Porta. I am Her Highness's majordomo. No doubt Princess Maximillia will be overjoyed to meet you," he croaked. "And may I add—that's a very fine coat. Very handsome indeed."

"Why, *thank you*, Bufonis! You are *so* kind." Melanie glanced to Parno, and could sense he was tightly holding the reins on a scowl.

"Please, follow me to the receiving room. The staff are preparing private bedchambers for you now."

The grouille lifted a leg and pirouetted around, the other two servants following his movement with perfect synchronization. Each hopped forward, then switched to a long-legged stride.

As they were led into the chateau, Melanie glanced behind her. The servants still maneuvered the addled gryphon, handling it with obvious fear. The beast's fire-yellow eye burned hatefully, blazing straight at Parno.

Then all that heat was smothered beneath a dark black hood.

Princess-Electa Maximillia was perhaps the smallest grouille in the castle. Certainly she was the smallest in the audience chamber. Courtiers, retainers, musicians, and green-clad grouille knights surrounded her, watching Melanie with curious expressions.

All wore jewelry made of glittery insect shells and shimmering wings. To Melanie's left, a lady bore a pendant of ruby-red ladybugs. The pierced ridges of a gentleman behind her dangled with bluebottle flies.

The princess herself was dripping with the most ornate decorations. And she practically swam in her poofy royal garments. An intricate golden tunic covered a rich purple gown that covered most of a luxuriously lacy underskirt—and those were only the parts that Melanie could see.

Melanie felt a bit like an ogre amidst all the finery. She, Parno, and the gearlings looked as if they'd stumbled into the wrong genre of story. The chamber was large and lustrous—every crevice gilded, every color juiced to its brightest. Arches somersaulted across the walls, topped with golden dragonflies. The largest and pointiest of the arches stretched up from behind Maximillia's throne.

The princess was an elderly grouille. What had been bright green skin (based on the many portraits of her that lined the receiving chamber) had lost much of its hue, and the vivid red stripes that once lined her face now more resembled a spicy mustard.

But her eyes were keen as she gazed upon Melanie, the horizontal pupils wide with a girlish excitement.

"Aldermage Parno says you are a prodigy?" she croaked.

"Y-yes, Your Highness," Melanie replied with a deep bow. "My name is Lady Porta the Periwinkle." Her voice carried through the enormous chamber, and she heard her own timidity echoed back at her a dozen times.

"Lady, you say?" The princess squinted thoughtfully at her. "You're a noblewoman, then?"

Character trait: LADY Porta is . . . a noblewoman?!

"Only very, very, *very* distantly," Melanie replied slowly. "I'm . . ." She paused, her voice catching on simulated emotion. Melanie dabbed at her eyes, channeling Agatha's performances for the prospective donors who sometimes visited Merrytrails. "I'm an orphan, you see. All I have to remember my parents by is my *dear* gearling companion."

There was a whir as Traveler raised his hand and settled it on her shoulder. Gasps and *Awws* rang out from among the gathered retainers, and a chorus of sympathetic-sounding ribbits. Melanie doubted Agatha herself could have done better.

"Their last gift to her!"

"Oh, how darling. It's like her own giant doll!"

"See how she's dressed it up? In the hat?"

"It matches her *dashing* coat."

Melanie only just caught Parno rounding out an eye-roll before the aldermage stepped forward. "A touching story," he deadpanned. "But where Lady Porta truly inspires is her magical talent. I've seen her perform firsthand, and it's not to be missed. As an enthusiastic patron of the thaumaturgic arts, I naturally thought of you first."

The princess croaked approvingly. "I once dabbled in sorcery myself," she said to Melanie, "when I was little more than a tadpole. I even called myself *Maximillia the Green*! Cheeky, I know. But then I was forced to give it all up. I'm sure Gilda Green-Grace was relieved to lose her challenger to the color."

The princess winked at Melanie, three sets of membranes fluttering at once.

"Perhaps you could pick it back up again," Melanie said conversationally. "If you love doing magic, you should do it."

It was like a toverlicht had been suddenly snuffed out. The court went quiet, all the gaiety draining from the chamber. The courtiers, seated on either side of the hall in two lines of velvety emerald stools, glanced toward Parno, clutching at necklaces strung with pearly grubs.

"I mean . . ." Melanie cleared her throat. "Shouldn't a princess, of all people, be able to do what she'd like?" Again, she felt like a goon that had wandered into the grouilles' midst. As if her every step—every ungainly word—might shatter something small and precious.

Melanie had little experience reading the expressions of the grouille, but she thought she caught a flicker of amusement in Princess Maximillia's eyes. Amusement . . . and maybe a bit of sadness.

"While she *is* a talented magician," Parno interjected, "the Lady Porta is clearly inexperienced in matters of court. Even wonderkinds, it seems, are better off *seen* than *heard*." Parno knifed Melanie with his glare. She felt a fresh surge of hatred for the man, but managed to secure her tongue before she embarrassed herself further.

"I must respectfully disagree, aldermage."

Melanie glanced toward the princess with surprise. She wasn't the only one. Parno frowned as he turned back toward the grouille royal.

"Children are *meant* to question their elders," the princess said. Her bright yellow eyes sparkled from within the silken cocoon of her outfit. Though her voice was reedy with age, the gleaming arch that towered behind her gave her words a ministerial weight. "Not just to learn, but to challenge what they've learned. Thus, the world grows with them, wouldn't you say?"

"I would not, Your Highness," Parno answered icily.

The princess exhaled in a ponderous croak. "No, I don't suppose you would." Then her eyes shifted to Melanie. "The truth is, Lady Periwinkle, that the moment I became princess-electa of the grouille, I was forbidden to practice magic by thaumacratic law. The Grouille Principality and the Aederian Thaumacracy were not always so . . . cordial. It took a Wizard War to bring us under the sight of your ever-watchful banner."

The princess's webbed fingers emerged briefly from a pouf of fabric. She waved toward the three-eyed flag that was installed at the front of the chamber. It was draped half as high over the grouille's own banner—a pink water lily.

"That," the princess said, "and the annihilation of our capital city."

Lillipeaux.

The name rushed back to Melanie then. The city had once teemed with "evil" ley magics, and was destroyed by the Third Eye—the one who preceded Zerend. Melanie couldn't remember his name. The spell that razed Lillipeaux had cemented the empire's position as the most powerful nation in the world.

At least that's what the orphanage's lone history book had said. Melanie had never thought much on the matter—enough, even, to remember the city's name. Now, surrounded by the downcast eyes of the grouille court, she felt gooseflesh rising.

Gooseflesh . . . and something else. A hot and scalding feeling.

The Wizard War had been a long time ago, but not so long that many grown-ups didn't still remember it. She glanced around at the courtiers lining the chamber, and the servants and musicians and knights behind *them*. How many of the grouille in this room had known people killed in the war? All of them?

The princess issued a doleful croak. "Now the census keeps a tight grip on the number of licensed grouille wizards and witches. Certainly, no heads of state are allowed to practice."

"Perhaps we should shift to more pleasant topics," Parno muttered, tugging at his beard. Melanie couldn't quite imagine the pugnacious aldermage being embarrassed, but this was close. "Politics are so *serious*, wouldn't you say?"

"I would," the princess responded dryly. "How nice to be back in agreement."

Again, she raised her hand. Unlike humans, the grouille had only four knobby fingers, and Princess Maximillia's were each adorned with sparkling rings made of artfully embalmed spiders. "Lady Porta, I would very much like to see your demonstration. We recently added a theater to the East Wing, with a permanent magic circle inlaid into the stage. Will this suffice?"

Melanie wished she could turn to Traveler for guidance. But

even as she had the thought, she remembered the clot of displeasure in the gearling's voice earlier.

Are you sure this is wise?

She'd agreed to steal from these people, whom the aldermages had already taken so much from. The hot feeling inside her flared brighter.

"That will do nicely," she said softly. "Thank you."

"Wonderful. Then you may perform your magic for us this evening, after which we'll retire to the dining room for supper. Would you prefer your soufflé with crickets, or without?"

CHAPTER 18

BUFONIS led them through the West Wing of the chateau, to where the guest bedchambers awaited.

The grouille chateau was easily the largest and most opulent building Melanie had ever been inside. The walls here rivaled the magnificence of the receiving room, papered in the patterns of butterfly wings—iridescent oranges, blues, and greens rose all the way up to a white vaulted ceiling. Crystal chandeliers drooped like enormous hives, a few hanging so low that Melanie could have climbed onto Traveler's shoulders and touched them.

The servant led Melanie and Parno to a wide hallway, which was where Melanie caught her first glimpse of the doorway.

Parno had been right; it was impossible to miss. Twenty feet tall and cast in gold, it was as much a sculpture as an entryway. Countless figures decorated two massive doors, grouille in poses thoughtful, warlike, and some embarrassingly romantic. And filling the space between them was what must have been hundreds of water lilies, each meticulously sculpted.

It was a breathtaking display, all the more so because it sizzled with enchantments so intense that Melanie could feel the magic in her teeth.

Before the doors, two grouille knights stood in glittering emerald armor, each carrying a spear that was easily twice their height.

Melanie couldn't help but imagine what lay beyond such a grand barrier. There was enough gold molded to the doors to feed a city, so its value must be more than just money. She thought of all the tales she knew of priceless treasures— enchanted rings and wish-granting lamps and swords that could only be wielded by the worthy. Whatever was inside *must* be just as exciting.

Would she truly be able to bypass the doors' protections? Melanie had never failed to open something before, but this door hummed with a power that felt . . . different. Almost familiar. It was like a smell she'd encountered before, but couldn't quite place.

"The Lotus Gate," Bufonis croaked gently beside her. "It's older than even this castle." Melanie realized with a start that she'd stopped cold in the hallway, just staring at the door.

"It's incredible," she said.

"Thank you." Bufonis nodded, all his eye-membranes blinking at once. "In many ways, this door is what remains of our culture, after the destruction of Lillipeaux. It houses something very important to our people. The Treaty of Water Lilies, in which the grouille officially joined the empire, was contingent on it remaining in our care."

Melanie could actually feel the blood leaving her face. Parno wanted her help in stealing something so precious to the grouille?

She glanced over her shoulder, to where Traveler stood just behind her.

His glowing motes were vacant as ever, but they were trained on her. Had he been watching her this whole time?

"*Ahem.*" The aldermage's voice echoed from down the hall.

"My apologies, Master Parno," Bufonis croaked. "The young lady took an interest."

Parno cast her the quickest of glances, a look that communicated both a scolding and an appeal for caution. Melanie got the gist. The more she connected herself with the door, the more difficult her job became. And after what Bufonis had just said, it was already feeling difficult enough.

The majordomo hopped ahead to join the aldermage, leaving her treading miserably behind.

Melanie held back a gasp as she entered her private bedchamber, but only just.

It was as big as the whole first floor of Merrytrails, and decorated from floor to ceiling in colorful beetle shells. As Parno was escorted to his own room down the hall, she gently closed the door behind her, taking a moment to drift through the enormous chamber.

It was so much space for just a girl and gearling. Too much. She felt a pang of homesickness for the cozy bedroom she'd shared with her friends, whispering to Jane across the bunks after lights-out, the two of them spinning grand fables for Misty Steppe. Jane always knew when to add a perfect extra twist. She had astonishing depths beneath the placid pool of her quiet, beyond the invisibility she wore close around her like a cloak. Jane devised the most devilish ensorcellments for Misty to resolve—fairy oaths and witches' curses that were unraveled by a single clever flourish of logic. If *their* story had gone another way, Jane could easily be the promising young apprentice Traveler had departed with.

Perhaps she should have been. She might have done a better job of it.

Melanie wondered how her friend was doing. She wished Jane and the others could be here now, that they could see this place and share her adventure. She wished for Jane's calm and insight, and felt suddenly, overwhelmingly adrift.

She could practically see Agatha smirking at Lady Porta's predicament. Baruti would know all sorts of useful facts about the princess and the grouille—perhaps even about the Lotus Gate. Sun-mi would relish the chance to learn grouille cuisine; Melanie had agreed to a small serving of crickets, in case she ever got the chance to tell her about it. And little Mariana would be both delighted by the princess and terrified of her jewelry. The thought brought a sad smile.

Melanie thought of Livia too . . . and the promise Lady Porta had made to visit her in Hamlen again. A promise that was becoming more precarious by the moment. If she didn't help Parno, she might end up in the Donjon—or worse.

But if she *did* help him? Melanie wasn't sure she'd be worthy of Livia's attention then.

Things were moving so fast. For as far back she could

remember, Melanie had wished for adventure—for *change*. Now, as Lady Porta, she had this twisted version of it. But it wasn't like the Misty Steppe books at all, with solutions only marginally more fanciful than the problems they untangled. She ached for something more like her old life.

At last, Melanie turned to where Traveler hovered at the closed door. Though they were alone now, the gearling hadn't relaxed to a more casual pose as he usually would. He stood rigid, his shining eyes unreadable.

"I don't like this any more than you do," Melanie said.

"Are you sure?" the gearling asked softly. She wished he would uncoil, or drop heavily to bed as he had in Hamlen. Instead, Traveler stayed stiff and guarded—his hat casting his face in shadow, so that only his glowing eyes showed. Melanie felt her own eyes fill.

"I had the distinct impression," he continued, "that you were excited out there, looking at the Lotus Gate—and in Parno's flying sphere too."

"That's not fair," Melanie said, her frustration mounting. "Parno threatened my life. I hope you caught *that* bit too."

Traveler raised his palms, as if in surrender.

But he didn't surrender.

"When we started on this journey, I said I'd be a voice for the voiceless. How could I rightly claim that, then help Parno Fabrillo break a decades-old treaty by stealing from the already conquered grouille?"

"Well, how nice that your help isn't needed, then, since *I'm* the one he's blackmailing." Melanie's hurt was simmering into something hotter. "You can just stand around, silently judging me, instead of lifting a finger to stop him."

"What does *that* mean?"

Melanie fumed. The ember of frustration and fear and shame—because that *was* the scorching feeling that'd been forming inside her all day, wasn't it?—now blazed forth.

"Parno is a bully!" she cried. "Worse than a bully; he's threatened to *burn me* at the stake! But he does whatever he wants because no one around here is powerful enough to challenge him. No one except you."

"I told you," Traveler said tightly. "I am not a weapon."

"Well, *he* is. Everyone talks about the evils of ley magic, but from where I'm standing, the aldermages are the real danger. So only they get to use magic to threaten and destroy? And they go completely unchallenged?"

Traveler's glowing eyes narrowed. "You know that's not what I'm saying. I'd prefer it if no one—"

"But that *is* what you're saying, because it's what's happening." Melanie waved her hand toward the door. "They won't even let the *grouille princess* use magic, in case she decides to fight back."

"Is that what this is about?" Traveler said, stepping forward. "You want me to *fight* Parno? To duel the bad wizard in some fabulous lightshow battle? Humans are so obsessed with violence; it's always the first solution you turn to. But battle magic is *dangerous*, Melanie. It's not like something from your stories. The last Wizard War created wastes that will remain uninhabitable for generations. And it wasn't *just* the aldermages who were maiming and killing. The grouille followed the Old Ways; their ley curses could liquefy a person to a puddle of ooze in moments. Right or wrong, good or bad, all it takes is one slip—one hex shot off in anger—to destroy countless lives."

"And what about *my* life?" Melanie felt a tremble growing in her chest. Here was the sharp, angry question that had been stinging her all day like a horsefly. "What if I tell Parno no, and he tries to take me to the Donjon? Will you let him? Will you flee and find some other kid to coax from their home with stories of made-up witches?"

The gearling's eyes dimmed at that. Traveler paused, his silence growing so dense, it became like an answer itself.

Melanie shook her head. "Right now, violence is aimed at *me*. Don't you care?"

Suddenly the door swung open without so much as a knock. Parno stood in the doorway, chewing on the last of some crumbly pastry. The remains of it were littered down his beard. The aldermage took in the scene: Melanie and Traveler facing off, both in poses of frustration.

Traveler snapped to attention, his glowing eyes widening to vacuity.

"What's going on here?" Parno's gaze moved warily from Traveler to Melanie and back again.

She swallowed. "Just . . . just practicing for the presentation. Sometimes I have my gearling run lines with me."

"I don't recall any dialogue."

"Oh, I have many *different* performances," she drawled. "I must keep things fresh, you know. I'm constantly fine-tuning."

Beneath his beard, the aldermage scowled.

"I came to tell you that the plan has changed," he said.

Melanie frowned. "I didn't realize there *was* a plan. I thought I was supposed to figure out how to open the door on my own."

"You are," Parno said. "I can't hold your hand through the entire visit. Especially when you're so set on making a spectacle of yourself. But I didn't anticipate the princess would have you perform this early. I thought we'd have the night, at least." The aldermage shrugged. "I'll sneak away during the show, while most of the court are tucked inside your pocket dimension. The Lotus Gate must be ready for me when I do."

Melanie's mouth fell open. "That means I only have a couple of hours!"

This time Parno didn't even bother to hitch his shoulders. "Then perhaps you should waste less time *running your lines*." The aldermage frowned suspiciously again at Traveler. "I'll leave you to it. Work fast, Lady Porta. Your life depends on it."

The wizard turned and strode through the door, but just before it was closed, he paused. A thoughtful expression crimped his face.

"One more thing," he said. "If you attempt to escape, I *will* find you. And I'll bring the full force of the thaumacracy down upon you."

And with that, Parno was gone.

Melanie stared at the closed door, hopelessness twisting her insides. She wouldn't have believed it possible, but she felt more trapped now than she had in Parno's flying metal sphere.

"Should we run?" she finally asked. Her voice was leaden.

There was a whir as Traveler moved to her. "No," he said with a sigh. "No, Parno is correct. He'd find us. I can shroud against detection spells for a time, but not from the combined forces of the aldermages."

"Then . . . what do I do?"

Melanie could hear the dread thrumming through her own voice. She shut her eyes tightly, fighting against the prickling heat behind her eyelids. She thought of Misty Steppe, and how she might handle a moment like this. Would she cry? No. She'd think of a scrappy, surprising plan.

But Melanie wasn't Misty. And she wasn't Lady Porta, either. Not really. She wasn't a wonderkind; she was a lock-eater. Traveler was the real master. And Melanie was the tool, to be used and discarded by Parno. And maybe by the gearling too.

Traveler sighed. "I view the world through a window, Melanie," he said softly. "Always outside, looking in. Always once-removed from the real conversations taking place. Katzy, Livia, the princess-electa . . . even Parno. *I've* never truly spoken with any of them. You're the only real connection I've ever made."

The gearling kneeled in front of her. Through the grille of his mask, Melanie could see his glowing motes burning. "I'm not a weapon," he said. "Perhaps that makes me a coward and a hypocrite, but all I've ever wanted is a peaceful life. Not to remake empires."

Traveler placed a hand on her shoulder. The cool weight

of it was a comfort. "But I would never abandon you, either, Melanie. *Never*. You saved me."

Melanie rubbed at her eyes. "I don't know what to do," she said. "Helping Parno steal from the grouille is wrong. But if I don't . . ."

A metallic sigh emanated from within Traveler's mask. "We need more information," he said. "Parno refused to tell us what's behind the door. I suggest we see it with our own eyes. Once we know . . . Well, we can decide what to do from there."

"If I open it, though, isn't that giving Parno exactly what he wants?"

"Not necessarily. He won't make his move until the performance, when he's less likely to be seen breaking the Treaty of Water Lilies. Which means we'll have a little time to decide. If we flee before that, or give ourselves up, there's no performance to give him cover. His plan fails."

Melanie nodded, taking a deep breath. "Can you get us past the knights and all the way to the Lotus Gate in less than two hours?"

The gearling's glowing motes took on a mischievous cant. "I can get us there in less than five minutes."

Melanie peered out from the guest quarters. Servants bustled around the castle, hopping from task to task. A pair of green-clad knights passed a group of noblewomen and saluted politely. The chateau teemed with activity.

And now they must try and sneak past it all.

"Are you ready?" Traveler asked from beside her.

Melanie grimaced. No. Not ever. This was wrong. "As I'll ever be," she muttered.

"Then stay close."

The gearling raised a hand, his metallic thumb and middle fingers pressing almost together, as if about to snap. Melanie had just enough time to wonder if metal fingers *could* snap, when Traveler clanged them together.

A high, musical sound resonated from his fingers, small and warbling at first, but then steadier. As the gearling lifted his hand, the note picked up strength, filling the hallway. Traveler quickly took Melanie's hand into his free one. She felt a charged, giddy sensation jolt through her.

The atmosphere within the chateau . . . changed. Colors muted, seeped of their vibrance. The servants bustling around grew sluggish, as if plodding through water. Melanie saw one of the Greenguard turn his head curiously towards the sound. His red eyes widened.

Then they stopped.

Just as everything else in the space had stopped. Figures stood frozen mid-stride, some carrying heavy loads. At the far end of the chamber, a servant had accidentally dropped a teacup, which dangled unsupported in the air with liquid sloshing out. The only noise was the eerily suspended note from Traveler's tuning-fork fingers.

"We only have until the tone ends," Traveler buzzed. For the first time Melanie could remember, the gearling sounded strained. Whatever this spell was, it was difficult to uphold. "Let's hurry."

They moved together, dodging around frozen nobles and through colorless hallways. Melanie caught sight of Parno on their way, the aldermage pointing his finger scoldingly at a servant.

"Hold on," she said. Her voice harmonized strangely with the tone.

Traveler turned. "What is it?"

Melanie reached into the aldermage's coat pocket, the one she'd seen him use twice that day. Her hand closed around something cool and round.

She pulled out the petrified eagle's eye. It was perfectly smooth and surprisingly light. As soon as the eye was settled into her palm, its color returned. The gray iris glaring up at her brightened to brilliant gold.

"Just in case?" she said, smiling at Traveler as she pocketed the item. "If we *do* need to run, maybe this could give us a head start."

"Melanie, I so admire you."

"Compliments later," she said. "Let's hurry."

They hustled past Parno and through several more suspended hallways. Traveler remembered the way, and Melanie was grateful. The sheer size of the chateau confounded her! But soon they'd turned a corner and she caught sight of the door—huge and dark and utterly terrifying, even in the colorless mire of Traveler's spell.

Bufonis was in this hallway, speaking with one of the Greenguard. Melanie felt a flare of fresh shame at seeing the majordomo. Then she noticed something strange.

Bufonis's eyes twitched. Slowly, very slowly, three sets of eyelids slid closed in a torpid blink.

Melanie gasped. "Traveler? I think the spell is wearing off!"

All through the grand hall, knights were shifting, sliding back into time. Melanie could hear the magical note waning. What a moment ago had been a bright, steady hum began to waver and weaken.

They bolted past Bufonis, toward the immense doorway at the great hall's center. A pair of guards stood just past the gate. Their backs were to Melanie and Traveler, but Melanie could see they were coming unstuck from the magic too. One—a tall, blue-skinned grouille with black patches across his snout—was turning. His clay-colored eyes glided watchfully forward. Melanie realized with a jolt that *color* was returning to the chateau.

The Lotus Gate was even more imposing up close—two great gold slabs with intricate handles wrought amid the other writhing shapes. A black keyhole waited between the handles, set deep into the door. She couldn't make out any light within. But Melanie *thought* she could sense a strange aura emanating from inside, even beneath the throbbing enchantments on the door itself.

"Let's see what we're up against," Traveler said. The gearling's eyes flared momentarily and a glowing red rune appeared on the dark metal: a diamond seated upon two legs.

"Ley magic!" Traveler exclaimed. "This is bad. Parno was wrong. The door isn't just locked—it's trapped! There's not enough time to get back to our original positions, much less unravel the spell."

"Ley magic?" Melanie asked. "Maybe I could still try." The burning rune crackled with an odd heat. Melanie couldn't explain why, but the magic radiating from it *did* feel different from what Traveler had taught her. Not evil, though.

She was struck again by the sense of familiarity.

Traveler glanced down at her, his dim eyes flickering with exertion. Clearly, the time-slowing spell was taking its toll on the gearling. The humming from his fingers was almost completely quiet now. "I can't let you risk it," he said finally. "This rune is more than just a lock. I'm sorry, Melanie, but I promise I'll do everything to—"

Melanie sighed. She placed her free hand on the door.

"—Melanie, *no!*"

A hot sensation suddenly gripped her palm, like a burning hand intertwining its fingers with her own. Melanie felt the *anger* of the spell, its indignation at this trespasser. She could sense it traveling up her arm, a prickling, furious heat intent on punishing her transgression.

No, Melanie thought at the spell. *I need you to* open, *please.*

Then, quite agreeably . . . it did.

All that heat and fury pent up in the magic fizzled, replaced by a pleasant coolness that pushed down from Melanie's arm and into the metal. The odd feeling of familiarity was undeniable now. The spell was just like Melanie's own gift for opening things, but inverted. The two forces flowed in conversation, and *she* was the more persuasive voice.

But as she spoke with the spell, Melanie realized it was bigger than it seemed.

No, that wasn't quite right. It wasn't the spell that was big. It was a small part of something *else*. Like a single strand of hair that connected back to—

You.

Melanie gasped. Just as the rune's power dissolved, she brushed against the periphery of an immense and unfathomable presence. And it noticed *her*, as well. Eyes that were not eyes turned toward her. A voice that was not a voice *boomed*—

And then was gone.

Melanie felt an accommodating *click* beneath her palm. The odd, tooth-aching hum of the magic had disappeared. Hand trembling, she released the door. Slowly, ponderously, it slid inward.

Traveler's eyes expanded, his glowing motes brightening. "You . . . dispelled the rune?"

The gearling didn't indulge in his shock for long. He hustled Melanie inside and pushed the door gently closed behind them.

"Hopefully no one noticed us," he muttered. "We should have appeared as a momentary blur to those stuck in time."

The space behind the door was utterly dark. It was a jarring change from the cheery butterfly patterns of the chateau. The only light sources were Traveler's eyes. The two dots blinked down at Melanie from behind their mesh.

"I thought you said no more surprises," the gearling whispered peevishly.

Melanie shrugged, then wondered if Traveler could see it in the dark.

"I had a feeling I could do it."

"A feeling?"

Melanie grimaced, thinking of the odd presence beneath the spell. "Traveler, that rune felt like what I do. Like my . . . ability. And something *saw* me through the magic, right as I was finishing. It spoke to me."

A beat of stunned silence followed as the gearling took this in.

"Well. How deliciously mysterious!" he finally gushed.

"Traveler!"

"*And* very troubling, yes. Clearly there's more to your gift than we realized—and to the Lotus Gate. Ley magic is illegal, especially for the grouille. Why would the thaumacracy turn a blind eye to it here?"

Melanie frowned. "It's not one of those things you just . . . know?"

"Apparently not," the gearling muttered thoughtfully.

"Traveler, I could *feel* the spell whenever we were close to the door," she said. "But now it's gone. What if others can sense that we've broken the rune?"

"*I* didn't feel anything," Traveler said, canting one of his eyes. "But you're right. Swiftness prevails."

They turned together, staring into the blackness beyond.

"Let's see what's got Parno so worked up," the gearling said.

He lifted his palm. A droplet of glowing blue light congealed in the air, like pale milk poured into black tea. With a flick of Traveler's wrist, the toverlicht billowed dreamily down the hall, illuminating an empty corridor as it went.

The hall was made of stone. Shallow trenches of dark water ran the length of it on both sides, reflecting the light.

When it reached the end, the toverlicht paused, hovering before a second, humbler door. This one was made of simple wood and an iron handle, with no lock or keyhole that Melanie could spot.

They walked carefully down the hallway, their footsteps echoing against the stone. Traveler's clockwork body whirred with every tread, but no one seemed to hear them through the heavy metal doors. Soon they'd arrived at the end of the hall.

"I don't sense any more magical traps," Traveler said.

"Me neither," Melanie agreed.

She took the dark iron handle into her palm, but paused and glanced up at the gearling.

Traveler nodded. "I'm with you," he said. "Always."

The door pushed fluidly open. As it did, light spilled out from the other side, filling the hall and overtaking even the glowing toverlicht. Melanie squinted against the sudden brilliance. A muddy shape solidified in the distance, outlined in brightness.

"Oh." Traveler's usually buoyant voice dropped to a dismal whisper. "Oh, no."

It was a pedestal, Melanie realized. And sitting—no,

floating—atop the column hung an eerie, undulating shape. At first the object looked like some kind of sphere, but it didn't hold that form for long. It was constantly changing, its boundaries rippling and re-forming before Melanie's eyes. At its center, a scratchy symbol similar to the one on the door glowed brightly—the only unchanging shape in the mass. Another rune, then. Two parallel vertical lines connected by a downward slash.

"What is it?" Melanie asked.

"A weapon," Traveler said with a metallic sigh. "A very powerful one." The gearling shook his head. "To think the grouille had succeeded in creating it."

"What does it do?"

"During the last Wizard War, there were rumors that the grouille were working a spell to push back the advancing thaumacratic armies, one so devastating, it could destroy a nation, if not the world. They called it Hagalaz."

The gearling spoke slowly. Melanie still half expected the doors of the Lotus Gate to burst open behind them, for Greenguard knights to come rushing in. But if Traveler had been worried about the same thing, it was eclipsed now. His bright eyes were focused on the odd, floating spell.

"I told you that the Hexe of the South's magic is connected to the Old Ways, yes?" he said. "And that her wellspring is something called the ley? The ley is a sort of web that runs through the world, with lines collecting together in places of frightful power. This"—Traveler waved toward the rippling shape of the weapon—"well, think of it as a magical *germ*. If the Old Ways are to be believed, the ley is a living thing, though one far beyond our understanding. Hagalaz is its plague."

Melanie glanced back toward the floating shape. The spell looked almost like an enormous droplet of water; its skin was shiny and translucent. Perhaps it was her imagination, but she felt woozy just standing near it, as if it radiated a noxious power.

She thought of the immense *presence* she'd felt beneath the spell that sealed the Lotus Gate. Traveler had said that it was ley magic too. Could the presence have been . . . ?

"Wouldn't the thaumacracy *want* the ley destroyed?" she asked. "If it's what gives the Ley Coven their magic?"

Traveler took a step back. He brought his hands up, grasping at his hat. "It's more complicated than that. The ley's power is felt *everywhere*. Severed from it, plants would wither. Animals would perish. All life might succumb to the blight."

Gooseflesh exploded along Melanie's arms. Plants and animals? Traveler had said ley magic was in opposition to the thaumacracy, yet it sustained that much?

"Hagalaz is why Lillipeaux was destroyed." The gearling's motes tilted toward the spell. "To prevent its creation. But the grouille already had it, and they never used it. Not even when the aldermages destroyed their capital city. That they haven't says something, but why keep such a dangerous weapon hidden all this time? Why not destroy it?"

"Maybe it *can't* be destroyed," Melanie guessed.

"That is . . . a troubling idea." Traveler's motes sheathed anxiously.

"Traveler, how do you know this?" Melanie asked. "You know what the spell is and what it does, but you didn't know it was here. How is that possible?"

The gearling shook his head. "I don't—" He faltered. When his glowing eyes found hers, Melanie could sense the distress behind them. "As ever, my memory is fitful. A wide chamber, lined with closed doors. But rumors of the grouilles' attempts to create Hagalaz are not uncommon. Those who studied the war—or who lived it—would have heard them. The details of the treaty, however, and what it actually guarded, would be known by very few within the empire. Perhaps only to the three heads of state themselves."

Melanie nodded slowly. She'd never had a head for politics like Baruti, but the pieces *were* clicking into place. If the grouille really did have such a dangerous weapon, and had managed to keep it from the hands of the aldermages, it made sense that the High Enchanter would want to keep that knowledge hidden. It meant the Aederian Thaumacracy was less mighty— and far less secure—than it boasted.

"Melanie, under no circumstances can Parno be allowed near this. Nor any of the aldermages."

Melanie couldn't agree more. But how did they ensure Hagalaz was safe from Parno, now that she'd opened the door for him? If they ran, would the aldermage really just give up on his plan to obtain such a wickedly powerful weapon?

Traveler had been right all along. Though Parno had blackmailed her into it, opening the Lotus Gate was a blunder of the worst possible kind. One that she couldn't just slink away from. Now she had a decision to make.

"I need to tell the princess what he's up to." Melanie swallowed. "No matter the consequences."

Traveler watched her for a moment. "It will be your word against his," he finally said. "And even if Princess Maximillia believes you, the thaumacracy won't. Especially when Parno reveals you aren't who you appear to be. If we had proof he was attempting to break the Treaty of Water Lilies, that would be one thing, but—"

"Proof?" A thought occurred to Melanie—a small caprice, but sharp and clear, like the cheerful first notes of the carols the girls all sang during the Night of Gold festival.

Traveler tilted an eye curiously.

Melanie shook her head. A smile was spreading unbidden across her face. Despite their predicament, a laugh slipped out. It echoed brightly down the dour hall behind them. Was this possible? Perhaps there was more of Misty to her than she realized. "I've got an idea, if you can pull off the magic. But we'll need to hurry. There's lots to do before tonight's performance."

CHAPTER 19

THE theater was an enormous, opulent space, so newly constructed that Melanie could smell the tang of fresh paint coming off the walls. She stood alone in the center of the stage, with Traveler watching from the wings. Beneath her feet, an intricate magic circle was inlaid to the stage floor, carved of glittering agate and outlined in gold.

The theater's seats were filled with spectators. Grouille nobles watched Lady Porta the Periwinkle expectantly, the accumulated susurration washing over her like a bath of whispers. The sight of so many onlookers sent Melanie's heart racing, no matter how she tried to calm herself. Did *all* these people truly live in the chateau?

She located Parno at the rear of the theater, standing with his copper gearling beside the exit. They'd spoken only once since that afternoon. Melanie had been waiting behind the curtain when the aldermage finally found her. He had grabbed her arm and hissed, "Is it done?"

Melanie had nodded balefully at him, unable to restrain her dislike.

"It better be," he whispered. "Remember—if you betray me, I'll make sure you burn for it. One way or another."

Then he exited the stage, scowling at Traveler as he went.

Melanie gazed up toward Princess-Electa Maximillia's private box, where the grouille was installed upon a sumptuous divan, still encased in her frilly cocoon. Bufonis stood beside her, frowning as he conversed with one of the Greenguard.

The princess peered down at the stage, her sharp eyes catching Melanie's.

Melanie took a deep breath.

"Your Highness!" she called, channeling Agatha's easy confidence with everything she had. The murmuring of the audience quieted. When the last few lingering whispers had finished, Melanie lowered her gaze. "Gentlefrogs of the court! What a *marvelous* opportunity this is." She winked playfully. "For *you*." There were croaks of laughter, and just as many offended gasps. Melanie's heart was still racing, but she found herself leaning into the feeling. If the nobles had found *that* scandalous, wait until they saw what came next.

"My name is Lady Porta the Periwinkle. As Associate Aldermage Parno has mentioned, I'm a magical prodigy . . . and I have quite a show for you today. Spells that will deceive and surpr-AEEZ!"

Melanie's voice cracked as she caught sight of a strange pair of eyes in the rear of the theater. It was a gaze unlike any other present—one eye golden yellow, and the other milky white.

Abraxas watched her from above. He was perched unseen atop the theater railing, visible only from the stage. His tail twitched with interest.

What? *How?* Melanie couldn't fathom how the cat had made it here from Hamlen so quickly, much less escaped the notice of the entire chateau staff.

Still, she was already riding this proverbial gryphon. She *had* been since she exited the Lotus Gate, her hands raised in surrender, and turned herself in to the extremely startled Greenguard knights still keeping watch outside.

If Abraxas meant to take the ride with her, then so be it.

The audience laughed again, this time at her expense. Melanie cleared her throat, grinning sheepishly. "Excuse me!" she said. "When puberty calls, it shrieks." Another round of laughter. They were back with her.

At the end of the room, Melanie saw Parno whisper something to his copper gearling.

"Well," Melanie said, "before adolescence interrupts again, let's begin! I *do* hope you all enjoy—"

For the second time, Melanie felt power rippling from her as she began the key phrase. Traveler had worked furiously to finish the spell in time, and even Melanie had pitched in, despite her inexperience, to fine-tune some details.

Time expanded, the theater slowing. Melanie's voice echoed over the audience.

Everyone except Parno. The aldermage had slipped out the door, closing it silently behind him. Only his gearling stayed behind; its glowing motes stared vigilantly forward.

"—the—"

* * *

"—show!"

As Parno closed the door behind him, the theater went suddenly silent. He listened closely. Not one sound issued from the other side. Lady Porta's spell had worked.

The princess's entire court was now locked inside a pocket dimension for the duration of the performance, completely cut off from the world. Only a few straggling Greenguards and servants remained in the halls, but nothing an empire-trained aldermage couldn't handle.

It was time to move.

Parno quickly composed an invisibility charm, drafting it with expert precision. The spell required the relinquishing of a secret, and though Parno was alone, secrets fed to spellwork had a nasty habit of reappearing just when they shouldn't. Magic had an ironic sense of humor, it seemed. Still, he had one that he was all too ready to reveal.

"I'm going to take Hagalaz from these frivolous frogs," his whispered into the shimmering fiber of the spell, "and use it to replace that fop Riquem as High Enchanter."

Once the enchantment was finished, Parno faded from view, his form melting into the yellow beehive wallpaper. Then he hurried down the hallway, only barely heedful of his own clicking steps.

He passed a group of grouille knights, their heads tilting curiously at the sound of unaccompanied footsteps. When crossing a servant loaded with fresh linens, Parno knocked the pile aside impatiently, scattering sheets and pillowcases across the floor.

Finally, he arrived at the Lotus Gate. Greenguards stood on either side of the hallway, but that was the only protection the grouille had elected to provide their hidden weapon. Beyond the rune itself, of course.

Parno sidestepped the knights and entered the hallway. The ease of it delighted him. The grouille had grown so confident in the inviolability of their lock—so sure that their precious treaty would protect them. It must never have occurred to the princess that a truly enterprising wizard might discover her little secret and elect to do something about it.

But this was what separated Parno Fabrillo from Riquem the Red. What made Parno *truly* fit to lead the aldermages. A weapon like Hagalaz belonged in the hands of someone with the will and wisdom to use it strategically.

He paused before the great portal, gazing up at its forbidding metal flowers. Did he experience a moment's hesitation? His actions now would change the course of the thaumacracy.

It had taken years of bribery and blackmail to learn the secret of the Grouille Principality. Parno couldn't imagine why the frogs hadn't unleashed their doomsday spell during the Wizard War when they needed it—or at least threatened to— but their hesitation would be his gain. Hagalaz was the ultimate bargaining chip.

Once he returned to Crossport, he would use it to demand Riquem cede his position. To the aldermages who'd given Zerend the best years of their magical careers, the quibbling coward's rise to power had been a cruel joke. Parno would correct it, and then as High Enchanter, he would use Hagalaz to force the Hexe's surrender, ending her and her barbarous ilk for good.

Parno did not thirst for power. Doubtless some would say so after his coup, but in truth the wizard only wanted prosperity for his nation. The king and prime minister would understand. They *must*. Power was the key that unlocked the gate to peace.

He would be the most well-armed pacifist in the world.

The aldermage shook his head—he was wasting time. He placed his hand cautiously to the door. Nothing. No curse or enchanted lock. True to her word, Lady Porta had stripped the spells away.

He still had no idea how she'd accomplished that trick, but he *would* find out eventually. Parno had no intention of letting such a valuable asset go.

He pushed against the rightmost door and it budged open without a sound. The guards were facing forward, away from the very thing they were protecting. He almost chuckled.

Parno slipped quietly inside.

The hallway within was pitch-black. Parno let the curtain of invisibility fall away, then raised his palm and conjured a watery toverlicht. The wisp swam around his hand in lazy circles. He walked slowly, taking each step carefully in case of magical traps, until he reached the door on the other side. Parno took the handle with his free hand. He was almost there. The power to destroy the Hexe of the South—to bring *true* peace to the empire—must be here.

Parno pulled the handle, and was met with a flood of light.

And . . . whispers?

He blinked against the glare, his eyes slowly adjusting. Voices murmured just out of sight, but the noise felt familiar. It reminded him of . . .

The theater.

Parno gazed down. He was standing on a stage. Beneath his feet, the inlaid thaumaturgic circle glittered prettily. The hallway and the light and the cold stone bricks all burned away, revealing an audience packed full of grouille nobles. They watched him with expressions of horror and rising fury.

He didn't understand. How was he back here?

Then he met the gaze of Lady Porta, standing in the aisle with her ridiculous gearling. A little girl in a boy's coat. She looked so *satisfied*. And then he knew.

Lady Porta the Periwinkle would burn.

Melanie stood in the aisle of the theater, with Traveler positioned behind her. Her face was grave as she frowned at the stage. But inside, her heart was thundering.

The ruse had worked. It had *worked!* Everyone in the theater had seen Parno sneak through what he thought was the Lotus Gate. It was exactly the sort of ridiculous scheme Misty Steppe might have concocted, and it had fooled *an aldermage*.

Now Melanie simply had to finish the epilogue and ride away to her next adventure.

"Aldermage Parno Fabrillo," she drawled. "You attempted to

break the Treaty of Water Lilies by stealing from the grouille. And everyone here has just witnessed you do it."

"This—this isn't possible." The aldermage's eyes were wide with shock. "I left before you even *cast the spell*."

"I cast it the moment you found me backstage," Melanie said. "Only you didn't notice, because nothing had changed. The pocket dimension you entered copied the chateau exactly, down to the Lotus Gate. You were still here the entire time, trapped in the illusion, acting out your theft on stage before an audience shrouded in a silence spell. But we saw everything you did, heard everything you said. It was quite the performance!"

Princess Maximillia called out from her private box. "Lady Porta warned me of your plans. Oh, Parno. This is a *very* serious crime. You've breached the Treaty of Water Lilies. No doubt you thought you'd get away with it, and would perhaps even be *rewarded* when you revealed your ill-gotten prize, despite breaking thaumacratic law." A ruminative croak. "But you didn't."

Parno wasn't looking at the princess, however. His eyes were still on Melanie. If she'd thought the aldermage's glare was like a dagger before, this was a broadsword. Despite her victory, a blade of fear carved through her.

"Lady *Porta* the *Periwinkle* . . ." he spat. "The little deviant. Did you happen to tell the princess that isn't your real name? That you're impersonating an imperial spellwright as an agent of the Hexe of the South?"

There were several nervous croaks from the nobles in audience. Melanie swallowed. She'd anticipated this. Now that Parno was cornered, he'd do everything he could to take her down with him.

"You're trying to distract from your crime," Melanie said evenly.

"Nothing short of the Ley Coven could break that seal. Admit it, girl. Are you the Hexe's apprentice? Is this gearling some kind of . . . *glamoured* elemental?"

"I don't even know what that means!" Melanie shouted.

Parno shook his head. "Very well. Your lies will burn with you."

"Lady Porta is under my protection!" the princess-electa declared.

"No . . ." Parno growled. "She is *not*." He reached into his satchel and pulled out the crystal rod he'd used in Hamlen. The center ignited with red light, and that shrill noise from the inn rang throughout the theater. The assembled nobles clasped their webbed fingers to their heads, croaking in distress.

"Oh-Two-Nine, neutralize the gearling," Parno commanded.

Melanie had just enough time to turn as she heard the whir and heavy footfalls of a giant mechanical body sprinting from the back of the theater. The copper gearling's eyes blazed bloody crimson. "Yes, operator," it said in its cheery alto.

Then it leaped into the air and landed upon Traveler, tearing into the gearling.

Now the nobles really began to panic. They pushed away

from the aisle and toward the theater's sides, hopping over one another in their fear.

"Greenguard!" the princess shrieked. "Stop him!"

Several blurred shapes catapulted from the theater mezzanine. The emerald-clad knights each clutched an enormous spear, using their powerful legs to launch toward Parno like living harpoons.

But the wizard was ready. With a sweep of his hand, the grouille warriors suddenly jerked to a stop in mid-air. They floated weightlessly above the panicked mob.

"Now," Parno said. "Let's see how a *prodigy* handles herself in a real magical duel." The aldermage lifted his hand and Melanie was yanked into the air. Parno contorted his fingers. With a crack of each knuckle, her arms and legs were wrenched apart, restrained by invisible binds.

"Pathetic," the aldermage snarled.

Melanie screamed as the room tilted, the rules of *up* and *down* breaking their promises. Her stomach felt lodged in her throat. "Let me go!" she shouted. "Get away from Trav—!"

Parno scowled, pressing his pointer finger and thumb together and pulling them through the air in a sharp horizontal line. Melanie's voice abruptly vanished. Her fear multiplied. Parno would kill her, and she wouldn't even be able to scream in protest.

"I think you've said enough for today, ley witch," he growled.

"And *I* think you should let my friend go, you witless windbag of a wizard." A new voice rang out—a metallic echo that cut through the noise of the theater.

Parno gasped, his eyes going so wide, Melanie thought he might burst something. Traveler stepped into the fray, the gearling's hat now shredded to ribbons.

Melanie craned her neck against the hold of Parno's magic. The copper gearling was trapped in a floating bubble. It was just like the spell Traveler had used to shield her against the rain. The gearling clawed at its prison, its red eyes bright with demented purpose.

Traveler had stayed to defend her.

But that meant—

"No cruel quip at the ready?" Traveler taunted the alder-mage. "I suspected your imagination might fail you when confronted by a real wizard. It's so much easier to threaten children, isn't it? Well, your inferiority complex is perfectly justified. Now, I'm going to say this one more time: Release. My. Friend."

"Demon!" Parno screamed. He lifted a hand and fire poured from his palm, gushing over the seats like a red tide. The alder-mage had no care for who was in the way: flames flooded forward, instantly setting the seats ablaze. Melanie felt the sudden heat like a bludgeon.

Traveler raised his palms, the embedded crystals flaring with light. The air before them billowed, growing thick and viscous. A curtain of water droplets shimmered, reflecting the light of the blaze, then swelled and hardened into a wall of ice. The flames hit the barrier with a deafening hiss, frost and fire both dying in a war of fevers.

What had been croaks and shouts of fear were now

full-throated screams. Though Traveler had kept the worst of the blast at bay, the theater still burned. Columns of smoke billowed toward the ceiling like gray stage curtains.

"Are you *mad*?" Traveler cried. "There are innocent people in here!"

Parno didn't appear to care. The wizard clapped his hands together and a blinding white light flared between his palms. Rays of uncanny radiance peeked out from his fingers.

Just looking at the light felt *wrong* to Melanie. It had a nauseating, sickly quality that twisted her stomach. Traveler's glowing motes widened with alarm. He stepped toward the aldermage.

"Oh, I know what you are, gearling," Parno said, "but it's not a wizard. You're an outline of a dead man, burned onto metal. You're a spell gone wrong. I will not lose to *you!*"

A spell? What? Despite the chaos, Parno's words tolled through Melanie's mind, as grim and loud as the bells of Crossport.

The radiance between the aldermage's fingers swelled, filling the theater like daylight. Melanie squinted against it, struggling to break free of her magical bonds.

Her . . . her bonds.

Of course.

Melanie summoned her willpower, pouring every last bit of her terror into a single potent request: *Open!*

The magic holding her dissolved immediately, dropping her to the floor.

But that wasn't the only effect. The wish carried through the air, as out of control as Parno's own destructive magic.

It touched the bubble containing the copper gearling, bursting it apart and releasing the automaton. The suspended grouille knights were similarly freed, and went sprawling downward.

But the wish didn't stop there. It passed through the entire chateau, throwing open every door, window, and cage in the enormous, sprawling complex. Bees and beetles were freed from their enclosures, and lidded pots exploded open to liberate the spiders cooking inside.

And in the distance, farther than Melanie could hear, a great shriek rose up, as all the binds holding an enormous gryphon blew uselessly away.

The theater windows had all shattered apart, and sunlight flooded in. Grouille nobles poured out of the now unobstructed exits.

Traveler was in the midst of a complicated spell, the gearling's hands working quickly as he attempted to disrupt the aldermage somehow. He didn't see the copper gearling rising from the ground, its red eyes trained on Traveler's back. He didn't notice the gearling stalk forward and raise its hand, where an embedded crystal of its own flared crimson.

But Melanie did.

She forced herself to her feet, dashing between the gearlings. "Traveler, look out!" Melanie threw herself before the advancing automaton.

"Melanie!"

The gearling barely paused before it snatched her by the throat and lifted her into the air. The strength of its grip was unreal. Cold metal fingers pressed down, cutting her breath. Melanie clawed at its arm, but it was like pulling at a mountain. Her vision went blurry. The gearling's red eyes swam before her.

"MELANIE!"

Whatever Parno was doing, it was getting worse. The revolting light grew brighter, outshining even the sunlight pouring in. Melanie saw her and the copper gearling's shadows stretching across the wall, impossibly long. Her fear seemed to stretch away with them, becoming nonsensical. She thought of Jane, of reaching from their bunks before bedtime, their fingertips straining to touch. Melanie was so tired.

She saw Parno's shadow too—and Traveler's—both made giant in the glare. They all danced across the theater in a dreamy encore performance. Traveler had finished his spell and now held an object aloft—not a circle, but close.

The eagle's eye. When had Traveler taken it from her?

He made a whistling sound now that was eerily like the screech of the gryphon.

Parno gasped. "How did you get that?"

For a moment there was quiet—a delicious quiet that Melanie sank sleepily inside. Then things got *very* noisy.

An explosive *BOOM* shook the whole structure, followed by a great tearing sound, like doomsday clawing its way inside a fortress.

Melanie saw a lumbering darkness fall across the theater as something huge and winged burst through the gaping window. She saw a lion's tail and an eagle's beak, and heard a cry of rage so potent, she was sure the sky itself was screaming. The darkness shifted, stalking across the walls.

"No!" Parno shrilled. "Get back! *Get back!! I am your MASTER!!!*"

The darkness descended upon Parno, swallowing his shadow completely.

Then the light died out, and darkness swallowed her too, and Melanie didn't see anything after that.

CHAPTER 20

JANE pressed her hand against the carriage window, her fingers splayed across the glass as the shadow of the grouille castle fell over them.

It was a clear, cool evening as they pulled into the chateau grounds, flanked on both sides by gearling attendants. The carriage came to a stop before the stables, and as Riquem the Red exited, a number of grouille servants emerged from the entrance to greet him.

Jane watched him frown as he took in the state of the place. As far as she could tell, every window in the building was destroyed, along with most of the doors. Many had been boarded up, but the servants were still actively cleaning the mess. Whatever happened here, it had happened recently.

She felt a fresh eddy of fear for her friend.

Behind Riquem, the girls quickly filed out of the carriage, with Mrs. Harbargain exiting last. It had been a long journey through the marsh, and though the carriage was enormous by any standard, it was still filled with seven fidgety foundlings, two bewildered Hamleners, and their unhappy chaperones. All of the party were in various states of disorder. Agatha's hair stood up on one end, as did Katzy's fur. Livia's braid had come undone, hanging like a loose skein of multicolor yarn. Mrs. Harbargain clutched Abraxas to her chest and the cat simply acquiesced, too exhausted to resist.

Even the Third Eye looked rumpled and tired. The dark lines under Riquem's eyes gave the dapper wizard a haggard air.

Riquem had insisted on stopping as little as possible, so all the girls had full bladders. They gazed at the chateau hopefully, too uncomfortable even to gawk and chatter over the scale of the place and all the grouille hopping about. Mariana bobbed from foot to foot in obvious misery.

The head servant hopped forward to greet Riquem. "High Enchanter," the servant said, sweeping into a dizzying bow. "I am Bufonis, the princess-electa's majordomo. Welcome to the Chateau de Papillon. I apologize for the state of the grounds. As you might have guessed, we've had an eventful few days. I'll have the servants rest your horses and take your carriage to the chaise house. As to your *other* cargo . . ."

Bufonis glanced toward the wagon hitched behind their cart, and the ominous shape that bulged from beneath the bright red tarpaulin.

"Please don't trouble yourselves," Riquem demurred. His smile was cool wind and warm tea. "The gearlings can handle everything."

"It's no trouble at all," Bufonis assured him. "Someone of your station must—"

A fearsome heat ignited behind Riquem's smile—the warm

tea now scalding hot. "Your servants will go nowhere near that wagon," he said. "And they will touch nothing."

Bufonis nodded, his eyelids blinking slowly. "As you say."

Then the Third Eye nodded, back to his genial self. "What's happened here?" he asked, spreading his fingers toward the chateau. "And where is Parno Fabrillo? I was told he was on his way, in the company of a girl and a gearling."

"Yes, well . . ." Bufonis croaked uncomfortably. "Her Highness would prefer to speak of the matter personally. I'm afraid there's been a diplomatic incident involving the Lotus Gate."

Riquem paled. "You *can't* mean to say . . ."

Bufonis bowed again. "Her Highness will explain further."

Riquem brought his gauntleted hand to his face, pinching the bridge of his nose. "Take me to her." At Mariana's squeak of discomfort, he added, "I believe the girls could also use a privy."

As their party all headed for the castle, no one noticed Jane Alley when she straggled behind.

Quiet and unobtrusive, Jane kept out of the way. People thought her unremarkable, but Jane didn't mind. No one truly understood yet. Like their made-up surnames, *Jane Alley* was just a placeholder. A safe space to grow into herself.

And there were many things a person could accomplish from out of the way.

They could watch. And think. And they could even act. And now, with characteristic silence, Jane seized the moment.

She watched the others as they were led away, then shifted back a step toward the covered wagon.

Slowly, she lifted a corner of the covering.

The bulging shape beneath was made of metal, that much she could tell. Its shiny panes were burnished and new—somewhat like a gearling's. Metal, except for three enormous red orbs that stared up at her, reflecting her anxious face. They looked almost like eyes.

Jane had just enough time to see the figure appear behind her reflection before her hand was wrenched upward. She twisted around to stare up into the vacant gaze of an imperial gearling.

"This one warns you not to approach the wagon," the gearling said pleasantly. Behind the grille of its mask, the automaton's own glowing eyes radiated mindless menace. "The consequences will be dire."

"S-sorry!" Jane rasped. "I won't do it again!"

The gearling was silent for a stretch. Then it released her wrist.

It didn't say another word, but the automaton's gaze followed Jane as she hurried after the others. Those two horrible eyes stayed with her long after she was beyond their sight.

Their legs stretched and bladders emptied, the foundlings of Merrytrails were now better able to enjoy the insectoid grandeur of the chateau.

"This place is amazing!" Baruti whispered. "The Chateau de Papillon was meant as a summer home for the grouille royal family, but after the destruction of Lillipeaux during the last

Wizard War, it became their de facto capital. I bet it's even more beautiful when the windows aren't broken."

"And without all the mosquitoes buzzing through them," Sun-mi muttered. She swatted her arm, then grimaced at the spot of blood on her palm.

"I doubt the grouille mind them too much," Baruti said. "They *love* arthropods. As pets, as jewelry, as food—"

"Bugs as FOOD?!" Mariana screeched.

"Bugs . . . as food?" Sun-mi repeated thoughtfully. "I wonder if the princess would let me speak with their chef."

"NOOOO!"

"Shh!" Agatha hushed them, the noise echoing through the long, opulent hall. "Melanie's in enough trouble as it is," she whispered. "We all know who's responsible for the windows."

Livia, trailing behind the Merrytrails girls, perked up at that. "Lady Porta did all this?" she asked. "With her magic?"

Agatha rolled her eyes and Jane chuckled silently to herself. The Hamlen shopgirl had spent half their journey asking all sorts of questions about Melanie. What foods she enjoyed and did she like dogs and how long something called *periwinkle* had been her favorite color. She seemed to really believe that Melanie was some kind of dashing outlaw magician, and couldn't be persuaded otherwise.

But Jane and the others knew this particular flavor of catastrophe all too well.

"For the last time," Agatha said, "Lady Porta isn't her name and she's not a witch. She just opens things—sometimes *too* well. It's why we call her lock-eater."

"No one calls her that but you," Baruti pointed out. "Melanie doesn't like it."

"I don't know what *lock-eater* means," Livia responded with a quirked brow. "But if *this* is it, then it's definitely magic. Powerful magic. Are you so sure Melanie *isn't* a witch?"

Agatha turned to reply, but apparently found she had no words. She and the other girls glanced anxiously at one another.

"You're her best friend, right?" Livia said, turning to Jane. "What do you think?"

"I . . ." Jane faltered, but something in Livia's patient expression urged her on. The girl reminded Jane of Melanie in that way.

"I suppose there isn't any other explanation for it," Jane continued slowly. "A week ago, I wouldn't have called her anything as deliberate as a witch. More like . . . explosively restless."

The other foundlings chuckled and nodded in agreement.

Jane smiled, her cheeks warming. "I guess I always knew Melanie's gift was magical, but what *is* magic, really? It's . . . a lie. A lie so convincing that the universe decides it's true. For Melanie, that means finding closed doors and convincing them they're open." Jane glanced around. "But we all do that in our own ways. Sun-mi gathers ingredients, and enchants them into feasts. Baruti can transmute even the most complex problems into elegant solutions. And I have no doubt Helen's bond with horses is just as pure and powerful as her love for them."

Jane paused a moment, considering. "Lies aren't always

wicked. Like magic, it's in how you use them—to deceive and hurt, or as a way to seek greater truths?"

She looked back at Livia, who was watching her with a wide smile. "And I think I'm starting to see what your magic is," the girl said.

Now Jane's cheeks truly burned. Suddenly *all* the girls were gazing at her with stunned expressions, as if she'd appeared from thin air right into their midst.

"That's the most I've ever heard you speak at once," Sun-mi said, bumping Jane's shoulder affectionately.

They kept quiet the rest of the way. No one wanted to further Melanie's trouble.

Still, it's very difficult to be quiet when faced with a real-life princess. As they entered the elaborate receiving room, little Mariana quickly slapped her hands over her own mouth, keeping whatever excited noises were in there from spilling out.

Princess-Electa Maximillia watched them file inside, nestled within a colorful puff-pastry of lace, silk, and other unidentifiable frippery. Though the grouille was very elderly, her eyes sparkled with obvious intelligence.

"What a charming retinue you've brought with you, Riquem the Red," the princess croaked. "When did it become the fashion for aldermages to travel with troupes of children, I wonder? I hope, for my castle's sake, that none of them are prodigies." But the princess's tone seemed more amused than angry. She studied the assembled group delightedly.

"The girl who arrived with Parno is no prodigy," Riquem answered. "I'm embarrassed to admit that Parno has been duped by a con artist, one who's made off with a piece of thau-macratic property."

"The gearling," the princess said.

Riquem's friendly expression darkened at the word. "Indeed."

Curious, Jane thought.

"Well, now it's my turn to be embarrassed," croaked Maximillia. "Because I'm afraid the girl and her gearling—*your* gearling, apparently—have already left."

Riquem took a step forward, the heat returning to his eyes. "You let them go?"

"I had other pressing matters to attend to," the princess said dryly. "Like the death of Parno Fabrillo at the claws of his own gryphon. And his attempted burglary of the Lotus Gate."

There was a lo-o-o-ong stretch of quiet as Riquem processed this announcement. Mrs. Harbargain and the girls gazed at one another in shock. The aldermage with Melanie had died? And he'd tried to steal something from the princess?

"You're sure?" the Third Eye finally asked.

"I have a castle full of witnesses," the princess said, "beyond my own two eyes, which work perfectly fine. I'm *hoping* you will tell me, High Enchanter, that Parno was acting under his own foolish initiative. Otherwise, this might appear to be a breach of the treaty between our governments."

"I assure you he was," Riquem said quickly. "The aldermages understand the importance of the Treaty of Water Lilies to our political family."

The princess croaked thoughtfully. "Family. What an

interesting word for an empire." Then she waved her own comment away. "Very well. I believe you. And you should know that Parno's gryphon is free, probably eating goats on the mountainsides. I doubt you'll catch it again. My Greenguard managed to shoo it from the chateau grounds before it killed anyone else, but it wasn't easy."

"And the girl?"

"Was instrumental in bringing Parno's treachery to light. Once he was caught, the aldermage became violent. We were lucky the gryphon attacked when it did."

Riquem grimaced. "I meant where has she *gone*? I must insist that you tell me now, Princess-Electa. The gearling she stole is in the midst of a dire magical malfunction. It is extremely dangerous."

The princess croaked a noise that might have been a sigh, if it had come from a human throat. "I'll tell you," she said. "But answer one question for me first, Riquem the Red."

"I will . . . try," the High Enchanter grated. Jane sensed that Riquem was nearing the end of his patience. She wondered if he would try to kidnap the princess now as well, and stuff her into the carriage with them.

If the princess noticed his agitation, she didn't appear to care.

"Why are you going to war with the Hexe of the South?"

The question clearly surprised Riquem. His eyes widened a moment, then cast downward. "She . . . she killed Zerend," he said. For a moment, all the fervency cooled away, revealing a lost-looking man beneath.

"I'd heard that . . . and that you and the former Third Eye were close. Perhaps very close."

Riquem's eyes snapped up, but the princess held out a pacifying hand.

"I only mean that I'm sorry for your loss," she said. "It was an attack on the thaumacracy, true, but surely you felt it more acutely than anyone. I only wonder if you're *sure* it was the Ley Coven who launched the spell. Or if perhaps your grief is leading you into a hasty conflict."

And just like that, the vulnerable young man was gone. Riquem's expression burned again. "I am sure," he said tightly. "And I'm afraid I find this newfound sympathy for the Ley Coven extremely troubling, Princess. The thaumacracy has turned a blind eye to the Lotus Gate, but don't think for a moment that we've forgotten the magic that was used to seal it. I hope the grouille won't be repeating past mistakes."

The princess sighed at that. "We . . . will not," she croaked quietly. "Perhaps you've heard by now that when the Council of Electors convened to choose the new High Enchanter after Zerend's death, I was the lone vote opposing you."

The queen's three sets of eyelids fluttered as she gazed at the aldermage. She didn't sound especially contrite to Jane, even facing the man she'd declared against.

"Perhaps you resent me for it," she continued. "But in truth there was a time when I'd have happily cast my lot with you, Riquem. I remember a bright reformer, a rare voice for restraint among the aldermages. I am sorry for your loss, truly. And believe it when I say I know something of loss myself. I *implore* you not to let it twist you into someone you don't recognize."

Jane watched Riquem as he gazed at the princess-electa, his face working to dam some private flood of emotion. So Maximillia had voted against him. Jane remembered that the princess was among the electing body of the thaumacracy. It was a small concession to the grouille after the Wizard War, as they were no longer allowed a monarch of their own.

Still, despite their differences, her words seemed to have had an effect on Riquem.

After a moment, he cleared his throat, his composure reclaimed. "I will think on what you've said, Your Highness," he muttered. "But now I must insist: the girl. Where. Did. She. Go?"

Princess-Electa Maximillia hesitated, but only for a moment.

Even sharp-eyed Jane Alley couldn't sense this, but Maximillia had liked Lady Porta quite a bit, despite what the girl had done to the chateau. And she was grateful to her for keeping Hagalaz out of the hands of the aldermages, though it clearly cost her a great deal to reveal her little charade. A weapon like Hagalaz was too dangerous to exist, much less be used. But exist it did. The *grouille* had created it without first understanding if they could safely *un*create it—and so the grouille would keep it hidden away forever. This time behind a better lock.

If such a lock was even possible.

It was because of her admiration for Lady Porta that

Maximillia kept the detail of the girl's gearling being alive—truly *alive*—to herself.

Or that Lady Porta had wielded the ley to such explosive effect. Likely the girl herself didn't understand where her power came from. When she'd told the princess that she had dispelled the door's protections—a feat no thaumacratic wizard should have been able to achieve—her answers on how had been vague. It was "just something she did," apparently.

But the princess had studied magic—of *all* kinds—and she recognized the thrill of the ley when she felt it. She was perhaps the only person in the chateau who still did.

Maximillia had the entire grouille people to consider, however. Her duty to her subjects' safety must always come first. So she answered Riquem's question, and she answered it truthfully.

And all Jane could sense was the note of resignation in her in voice as she did.

"Kinderbloom," the princess croaked. "Lady Porta is on her way to the Garden Village."

CHAPTER 21

MELANIE stared over the campfire, into the darkness beyond.

The night clicked and cooed, and the fire replied with its friendly prattle. It was the only conversation taking place in the wide, rocky meadow.

Across the flames, Traveler lay on his side, facing away from her. Melanie remembered the gearling told her he spent his nights watching the stars, wondering what lay beyond the thaumacracy's roads. Was he stargazing now? Or were his glowing motes turned inward, following colder paths?

She scratched absently at Unicorn's horn. The cloak rested its head against her leg.

It had been three days since they'd left Princess Maximillia's chateau. Three days of silence and sorrow from the gearling. Melanie and Traveler had fled quickly after the battle with Parno, especially once they discovered the full destruction that her power had caused. They'd traveled along the Wonderstraat through the swamp, then abandoned the road when they reached solid land. It would be too easy for the aldermages to find them.

Melanie wondered how the grouille were faring now.

Princess Maximillia had seemed dazed and suspicious in the wake of the battle, especially of what appeared to be a fully sentient automaton. The princess had escaped unscathed, though her knights earned a few scrapes from the gryphon before Traveler used the eagle's eye to subdue it. She allowed Melanie and Traveler to leave unimpeded—and even provided them with a bit of food for the journey—under the condition that they never return.

Even three days later, Melanie's injuries still howled from time to time. When she awoke in the theater, dizzy and confused, she'd discovered Traveler kneeling over her, gently coaxing her awake. The twisted scrap of the copper gearling lay several yards away. Its intricate clockwork body was a ruin.

"Did you . . . ?" she'd asked.

"The gryphon," Traveler muttered. "With its operator dead, the gearling was compelled to attack the creature that had killed him. It was a short fight."

Traveler's glowing motes had shifted to the copper gearling then. He stayed like that a moment, holding a hurried vigil for his fallen cousin.

Now, watching as he stared into the dark, Melanie wondered if perhaps Traveler wasn't still keeping one.

A vigil for the gearling, and maybe even a vigil for Parno, killed by Traveler himself.

Yes, the gryphon had ultimately stricken the aldermage down, but Traveler had called it to the theater using a mix of spellwork and the eagle's eye—and he did so knowing what the consequences would be. And this, Melanie knew, was what had ultimately broken the gearling.

I'm not a weapon.

Now he was. And worse yet, he'd used the gryphon as one too. Another living creature, created for war and forced by the gearling to fulfill its cruel destiny.

Melanie had tried to thank him for coming to her aid, had even told the gearling he was a hero. This only seemed to make things worse. Eventually, he asked her to stop.

"I'm sorry, Melanie. I just . . . I can't."

They hadn't spoken since—a full day ago.

Melanie watched the sparks float off the fire, twinkling beautifully before they succumbed to the gloom. She thought of Merrytrails again, and this time the tight grip of heartsickness threatened to shake loose her tears. She could never return now, no matter what she wrote in her letters. The princess had seen Traveler's true nature. Once that news reached the aldermages, it wouldn't take long to connect him with the girl who'd left through the South Gate, the foundling who was off to apprentice to a fabricated witch. The authorities would head straight to Merrytrails—to Jane and Mrs. Harbargain and the others. What would happen to them?

Melanie desperately hoped she hadn't brought the cruel finger of the thaumacracy down upon her home.

"Traveler?" she ventured. In the murk of night, her quiet voice seemed loud as a shout.

There was a soft whir as the gearling turned his head. But he didn't answer her.

"How far is Kinderbloom?" she asked.

"I don't know." The gearling turned his visor back to the darkness.

"I'm cold," she said. "I wish we were somewhere safe."

There was a pause, then Traveler lifted himself up from the ground, his body humming with the sounds of clockwork. "I don't know that safe actually exists, Melanie. I wish it did. I wish I'd never darkened the door of Merrytrails. This is my fault. All of it."

Melanie shook her head, frowning. "Don't," she said. "Don't do that. I made my choices."

"Did you? At every step you've been threatened and coerced into action. Not to mention that you are a *child*."

"And what are *you*, then?"

Traveler looked down at his metal hands, laid atop his metal legs. "I don't know," he rasped. A note of despair echoed through his voice. "A thing? A mistake? A *weapon*? Perhaps I'm all those things."

An outline of a dead man. A spell gone wrong.

Melanie pushed the memory down. This wasn't the time for mysterious accusations. Traveler needed certainty now, not doubts.

"Those are *his* words," she said. "Don't let *Parno* tell you what you are. He never had that right."

"He knew more about me than I know about myself!" The

gearling gestured wildly, throwing his arms into the air. "Or at least he claimed to. And now he's dead and I killed him. What does that make me, if not a killer?"

"My friend!" Melanie shook her head. "My protector! Possibly the protector of the whole world!" Hot tears were now tracking paths down her cheeks. "And what did Parno call me? A deviant? Do you think that's what I am?"

Traveler scoffed. "Of course not."

"I'm a girl in a boy's coat. I've lied and I've stolen, and that was just my first day outside the gate." Melanie sighed. "We're both still figuring out who we are. Don't let the cruelest people you meet decide that for you."

Traveler turned away. Silence flooded back into their campsite, as if it had been waiting just beyond the edges of their conversation. Then, a moment later, the gearling spoke again. "It is a very handsome coat."

Melanie giggled, wiping her eyes. "The handsomest. At Merrytrails . . ." She swallowed. "At Merrytrails, all our clothes were donated. We didn't get to pick our outfits, so we became what other people made us. This coat is the first time I made a choice of my own. I became the adventurer I'd always wanted to be."

"It's all about choice, hm?" Traveler's voice echoed softly.

Melanie rose. She wandered around the crackling fire until she stood over the gearling. Then she plopped down beside him—her injuries shrieking. She ignored their protests.

"You told me you're not here to remake empires," she said.

"That all you want is a peaceful life. But when Parno tried to steal Hagalaz, you didn't run either. You refused to let the aldermages take it. Your choice saved lives, including mine." She smiled sadly at the gearling's wide, glowing eyes. "I *know* what fighting Parno cost you. I know that you're—you're clever and you're curious and you're gentle and kind. And those are my most favorite things about you! But maybe—maybe *justice* is what real peace is built on."

The gearling pondered this for a beat, before finally responding. "The want beneath the want, hm? Perhaps you're right. Perhaps peace built over the suffering of others is just flimsy scaffolding. It still hurts, though. More than anything. I wish I'd found another way."

"I know," Melanie said gently.

Traveler turned to her. His face was as smooth and unchanging as ever, yet she thought she could sense a shift. "And what is it that *you* want, Melanie Gate?" he murmured. "Adventure? You've certainly had plenty of it in just a few days' time. But is there something bigger for you? The want beneath the want?"

Melanie startled at the question. "I'm not sure," she admitted after a moment.

"Well, if you ever figure it out . . ." Traveler said, "you let me know. I'll do everything in my power to help you get it. I owe you that much."

This time when the silence returned, Melanie let it. Above them, the moon was half full, a drowsy, drooping eye. Melanie yawned quietly, letting her weariness shiver through her. It was time she got some sleep. Hopefully they weren't too far from Kinderbloom.

"Maow."

Melanie's eyes shot open. She turned sharply, then caught sight of a squat, pointy-eared figure just beyond the firelight. The figure's tail flicked impatiently.

Abraxas.

Melanie turned to find Traveler's glowing motes were also trained on the cat, wide and bright with surprise.

"You see him?" she asked.

The gearling nodded. "It's the same cat. He must have escaped again, but . . . how?"

Abraxas's response was a second, less tolerant "Maow." The cat stood and turned, then tilted his head back to glare at the two of them. The yellow iris glowed green in the fire.

"Well, that's an invitation to follow if I ever saw one," Traveler said.

Melanie shook her head. This was all too strange. What was Abraxas doing in this wide-open field? And how had he followed them all this way? She stood slowly and Unicorn rose with her, beating her invisible hooves in anticipation of a ride.

Traveler raised his palm and the crystal embedded at the center shimmered with blue light. Their campfire died instantly, blanketing the wide plain in darkness. A moment later, he summoned a pale toverlicht into the air.

But Abraxas had tired of waiting for them. The cat was already padding away across the grass.

* * *

They rode in silence. Their only lights were Traveler's spell and the sleepy moon above. Their only guide was the surliest cat in all of the thaumacracy.

The farther they rode, the more trees appeared. The field became something not a field, but not quite a forest, either. Tall, regal elms formed arches for them to walk beneath, like gates into an invisible city.

"Do you know where he's leading us?" Melanie whispered to Traveler.

The gearling shook his head. His glowing motes were narrow and curious. "I'm not sure . . . but I have an idea."

In the distance, a hill rose into view: a tall, treeless expanse. Beyond it, the sky was finally lightening, dawn unveiling the land. Melanie gasped as she saw the wind ripple across that hill. The bulbs of what must have been a thousand *thousand* tulips waved softly at its touch. Even through the dimness, she could see the exhibition of colors on display. The flowers were grown in wavy rows, creating dreamy paths of color.

Melanie pulled the embroidered cloth from her pack, holding it up to the toverlicht.

The same. It was the same.

"Kinderbloom," Traveler said softly. "The Garden Village."

At the sight of such beauty, Melanie felt something inside her loosen. A tightness deep within her chest uncoiled, inch by precious inch. She thought of Traveler's offer. Of the want beneath the want.

Kinderbloom. A question she'd always claimed she wasn't asking, and yet here she was.

They rode toward the hill, Abraxas disappearing into a forest of tulips. Melanie could only follow the cat by his tail, which flicked back and forth above the bulbs.

They reached the flower line. Above them, the sky was a bashful pink. Unicorn honked contentedly beneath her, and Melanie let out a little laugh of her own. What a lovely sight. She had no idea such beautiful places existed! Melanie turned toward Traveler, a smile playing across her face.

But the gearling didn't appear at ease.

Instead, Traveler leaned forward against Vagabond, his posture tight with alarm. His glowing motes darted quickly from side to side, searching.

"Something's wrong," he said.

Melanie's smile fell; she turned her attention back to the hill's summit.

Now she saw them. Thin lines of smoke rose up from beyond the slope. Two. No, three.

No . . . nearly a dozen.

A faint glow that was not the sunrise now haloed the whispering tulips. It was flickering and orange. The color of fire.

They crested the hill.

And below them were the ruins of Kinderbloom.

CHAPTER 22

"**WHAT** happened here?" Melanie asked in a small voice.

Traveler didn't answer. The gearling had lapsed back into silence, but of a different sort this time.

Once over the hill, the field of tulips ended abruptly at a fiery border. Everything beyond was scorched and black, and somewhere in those ruins were answers Melanie hadn't even known she'd been seeking, burned to ash.

She felt burned out herself—hollow and light, like charcoal. So, this was a Wizard War. *This* was the devastation Traveler had tried to shield her from.

How could anyone use *fire* against *people*? And how many had died?

How?

They rode quietly through the wreckage, giving the still-smoldering buildings a wide berth. Melanie couldn't fathom what the village had looked like before its destruction. Some shapes she recognized as houses and some as trees. Many she wasn't sure. They passed an alarming configuration that appeared to be one great burning husk collapsed upon another. Enormous creatures of some kind? Melanie didn't dare guess at what they might have once been, though a small, scared part of her knew they were about the right size for gryphons.

Abraxas padded ahead. The cat had lost his impatient air. His tail was tucked beneath his stomach.

"Why would the thaumacracy do this?" Melanie asked.

"Not just the thaumacracy." Traveler's metal voice tolled. "There was a battle here recently. A very bad one." The gearling continued to scan their surroundings, his eyes alert. "We shouldn't be here," he said. "There might still be combatants nearby."

"Maow."

Melanie and Traveler both glanced toward Abraxas. The cat blinked slowly, then turned off the main path, toward a partially collapsed building. He slunk beneath a blackened beam, disappearing into the ruin.

Strange, Melanie thought. Abraxas was so animated, so insistent. What had gotten into him?

"We should *go*," Traveler said again. The gearling's voice was raw with real fear. "This feels like a trap. That building could come down at any moment."

"Someone might be hurt inside," Melanie countered softly. "What if they need help?"

"I'm still not sure I'm capable of helping anyone."

"Traveler!" Melanie said, the word part groan and part order.

". . . Oh, very *well*."

Traveler dismounted, and Melanie followed his lead. They

both pulled their cloaks from the air, their invisible mounts deflating. Traveler sent the toverlicht ahead into the ruined building. The watery light scouted their path.

"Stay close," the gearling said.

They followed the cat inside. Melanie had to climb over the collapsed beam, Traveler lending her his arm for support. Their journey inside was a maze of charred obstacles. Melanie never quite felt like she had sure footing, though Traveler moved with his usual easy grace, his long legs bypassing even tall piles of bricks and burned furniture. The gearling's motes shined upward occasionally as he assessed their surroundings.

The dim crackling of the fires outside had abated. The only sounds now were Melanie's breathing and the gentle whir of Traveler's movements—*and* the occasional rain of debris from what was left of the ceiling.

Then, Melanie saw a light. It was strange and flickering, casting shadows in jerky, dancing movements. The light was accompanied by an odd sound—a sort of sizzling hum.

"Is that . . . electricity?" Melanie asked. She knew all about electricity, from a trip she and the other girls had taken to the Crossport Museum of Thaumaturgical Philosophy. They'd watched with awe as the museum's curators threw back a switch on a small brass contraption, and the orb atop it came alive with glowing arcs of miniature lightning. The electricities had inched across the surface like hungry caterpillars.

Traveler didn't answer. He prowled forward, carefully lifting a mostly intact sofa from their path. The gearling revealed a door in the wall just behind it, slightly ajar, from which the light was emanating.

"Be prepared to run," he said. He held his hand up, the embedded orb glowing brightly with some prepared spell. The gearling threw open the door.

Melanie was surprised to see open sky within. A large, circular portion of the roof had collapsed, the thatch having mostly burned away. The room was still surrounded by high walls; it almost looked intact, but for the dawn light peering down.

In the center of the space was a contraption not so different from what Melanie remembered at the museum, only ten times the size. An intricate weave of rods rose to an enormous glass orb, which was topped by an ornamental lightning bolt. It was a lightning rod, though perhaps the most complicated lightning rod ever invented. The structure was turned on its side, where it sizzled with energy, shooting out little tendrils of electricity into the air. A metallic wire ran from the rod, leading to a magic circle very similar to the one Melanie had used just a few days ago.

Inside the circle was a kid.

The boy's eyes rose, glaring hatefully at Melanie and Traveler. The look reminded her so much of Adrianus—Parno's apprentice from Hamlen—that she half expected to see the elder wizard step into the crackling light right then.

But this new boy was not Adrianus. Far from it.

"Get back!" he screamed. "Empire scum! I'll *kill* you if you come a step closer!"

Melanie and Traveler both raised their hands at the same time.

"We're not with the aldermages!" she said.

The boy scowled. He wore a mix of fur and feathers, all enveloped in a lush green cloak. A complicated belt was banded around his waist, covered in charms and pockets that were bursting with what looked like dried herbs and mushrooms. The boy reminded Melanie of the hunters who sometimes came to Crossport to sell pelts in the market, though the charms and herbs gave him a decidedly more mystical air.

It slowly dawned on her that this was a member of the Ley Coven—a sworn enemy of the thaumacracy.

"You can't fool me," he said. "Only Zerend's brood travel with the metal demons."

"That *word* again," Traveler sighed. "Do I really look so diabolical?"

The boy gasped, stumbling backward. The edges of the circle crackled with electricity when he drew near them. "What—what is this? It speaks like a spirit. Or a person."

"He *is* a person," Melanie said. "Just . . . a new *sort* of person. His name is Traveler. And we aren't friends of the empire. In fact, we're on the run from them."

Traveler knelt at the edge of the circle, his glowing eyes taking in the iridescent sigils. "Fascinating," he said. "I'm unfamiliar with this type of trap. They've combined a conductive rod and a thaumaturgical snare. But why?"

"The demon *sounds* like an aldermage," the boy said pointedly.

Melanie heard a *maow* at her feet. She glanced down to find Abraxas lying placidly between her legs. The boy's eyes suddenly widened. His gaze traveled from the cat to Melanie and back again.

"It's *you*," he said in a hushed voice. "I mean . . . you're Melanie."

Melanie frowned. "How do you know my name?"

"The cat told me."

Melanie blinked. And then, when an explanation was still not forthcoming, she blinked again. Finally, she gathered enough mental resources to blurt, "The cat *talked* to you?"

The boy nodded. "We're both servants of the same mistress. I'm an apprentice to the Hexe of the South. The cat . . . has been taken into her service. Just as all wild things fall under her purview."

Melanie's jaw dropped. She glanced down at Abraxas, who had collapsed onto his side, revealing his bald stomach.

What?

The idea that this elderly, pampered house cat was somehow an agent of the most notorious witch beyond the thaumacracy coaxed a delirious giggle. Melanie choked it down, but not before Abraxas turned his head and gave her a surprisingly indignant glare. It was followed shortly by a puff of flatulence.

The boy crossed his arms. "It's not her *most* impressive servant," he conceded. "Nevertheless, it seems this is my mistress's will. My name is Blitz. If you free me, I promise to take you to safety. We're not far from the border."

Melanie's eyes widened. "The border to . . ."

A smile spread across the boy's face. "To the Zwarte Woud. It's my mistress's home, and her seat of power in the ley."

She glanced to Traveler. The gearling still kneeled beside the circle, but his eyes were on her.

"What do you think?" Melanie asked. The news that the Hexe had somehow used Abraxas to lead them here was unnerving enough. This offer was downright suspicious.

Traveler shook his head, the simple gesture setting off a small symphony of clockwork. "Melanie, I'm trying to be open-minded, but what do we really know about the Ley Coven? Just because they're the enemies of the aldermages doesn't mean they're not our enemies too. It doesn't mean they're . . . *good*. The boy may be in there for a reason. Right now, that circle would contain any curses he throws at us. Without it . . . Well, think of the state of the village."

Blitz jerked to the front of the circle, his movement uncannily quick. "This wasn't our fault!" he cried. "Kinderbloom has enjoyed my mistress's beneficence for years! The red wizards discovered we'd come to trade and attacked us. The three-eyed empire have *always* been the aggressors!"

"Is that why she killed Zerend the Red?" Melanie asked.

Blitz emphatically shook his head. "She didn't! The aldermages are lying."

Melanie sighed. What to think? The boy *seemed* honest enough; she got the sense that he at least believed his own claims. But she'd already made so many mistakes, endangered so many lives. Kinderbloom was a smoking ruin. What if this boy had had a hand in that?

Traveler believed the Hexe of the South was evil. That all of the Ley Coven were. But this had never sat quite right with her, and here was a boy claiming the exact opposite was true.

Melanie couldn't deny the tug of curiosity. No, that was too mild a word for it. A real, live ley magician stood before her. He was connected to that enormous presence she'd felt beneath the Lotus Gate.

What was the ley . . . and why did it stir such a powerful feeling inside her?

"I don't know what to do," Melanie whispered, turning back to Traveler. "You said the aldermages would find us eventually."

The gearling lifted a hand to his chin. "I'm surprised they haven't already, to be frank. There must be something slowing them down. But it's only a matter of time."

"Then what choice do we have?"

"There are always choices." Traveler sighed. "Just . . . not always good ones."

"Fine," she said. Melanie bored her eyes into the boy. "You *promise* that you won't hurt us? You or the Hexe?"

The boy nodded. "I give you my word. And if you're hiding from the aldermages, then my mistress's wood is the safest place to be. Not even all the red wizards combined could get inside."

Traveler stood, backing away from the line of sigils. "I can draw the electricity away long enough for you to unlock the circle."

Melanie nodded. She took a deep breath and stepped closer to the edge. This near to it, she could feel the energy coming off the perimeter as a gentle tingling. Her hair began to rise around her head, drifting rebelliously.

"On three," Traveler said. "One, two, th—"

The gearling placed his hand against the lightning rod. There was a deafening *crack* as the energy poured away from the circle and into his metal body. Traveler's eyes glowed brighter and brighter and *brighter*, outshining the watery dawn light. His armor crawled with glowing yellow worms.

Melanie placed her own palm against the edge of the magic circle. *Open*, she thought as delicately as she could, so as to avoid another fiasco like at the chateau. Then she added *Please*, for politeness's sake. The glowing sigils flared, then darkened as the magic left the trap. At the same time, the lightning rod flickered and went out.

The room fell into quiet. The only light was the purple-blue sky overhead.

Periwinkle, Melanie thought a bit sadly. Despite everything, she missed playing the part of Lady Porta. She had been fun.

Melanie blinked against the sudden gloom, willing her eyes to adjust. In a moment, she could see vague shapes, and cast her eyes about the circle.

Blitz was gone.

She gasped. Impossible! How had he gotten past her so quickly? Her eyes darted wildly around the space, but there was no sign of the boy.

"Well, let's get going," the apprentice's voice called cheerily from behind her. Melanie whirled around to see Blitz standing in the doorway, tightening the drawstring around one of his satchels.

"It's still a day's journey to the Zwarte Woud, and I'd like to be far away from here before the aldermages send reinforcements, wouldn't you?"

Melanie frowned. *How...?* She glanced to Traveler, who was also watching the boy with a curious cant to his eyes.

The gearling looked at her, then gave a little shrug. The movement sent off a crackle of static.

CHAPTER 23

THOUGH Blitz had no enchanted mount, the boy also had no trouble keeping up. Melanie wasn't quite sure how he did it. He walked briskly enough, but never seemed to have to truly hustle. Occasionally she lost sight of the ley apprentice, turning away for a moment only to turn back and find him gone—then back a moment later somewhere totally different!

Melanie supposed it was some kind of special ley magic, but the effect was unnerving. She was never exactly sure where Blitz would pop up next.

For the second time in a week, she'd stayed up all night, and as morning bled into afternoon, Melanie felt the familiar cloak of exhaustion settle over her.

Here, Blitz proved to be especially helpful, as the boy talked constantly. Mostly about the Hexe of the South, and her rivalry with Zerend and his cruel aldermages.

"Zerend was always jealous of my mistress," he said. "Her specialty is conjuration, you know. That means she can summon all sorts of incredible spirits and elementals using the ley—and they help her out! But the thaumacracy can't just mine the ley's magic like they do everything else. *Its* power has to be freely given to a trustworthy custodian."

The boy stretched his arms, clearly getting into the lecture. This last bit sounded like he was quoting someone. The Hexe herself?

Melanie frowned, worrying Unicorn's cloth ears between her fingers. "And what happens when the Hexe . . . well, when she retires? Does she have any kids?"

Blitz shook his head, glancing away. "No . . . no children. When the time is right, she'll pass her gifts on to a trusted apprentice."

"Is that you?" Melanie asked.

Blitz cleared his throat. "Perhaps," he said noncommittally. Which seemed a strange answer. How many apprentices did the Hexe have?

Blitz explained that there were eight wardens in total, the leaders of the Ley Coven. Others might make use of the ley's gifts, but *no one* was more powerful than them. Each was named after a cardinal or intercardinal direction, like on a compass, based on their positions in the ley. Though they rarely left their sites of power, they were all connected, and could sense each other if they concentrated. He claimed Fabiola, Mambo of the West, wasn't even on the continent! She lived out in the ocean somewhere, probably alone on an island. Melanie found the idea wonderfully odd.

Traveler found it all fascinating too. Despite his reservations about ley magic, the gearling listened intently. Abraxas had parked himself on Traveler's lap for the journey, and as the gearling conversed he petted the cat, his golden fingers running gently through Abraxas's gray fur.

Another oddity. Abraxas had never been a *cuddly* animal.

Only Mrs. Harbargain could reliably handle the ornery old tom without injury. Still, Melanie was heartened to see her friend distracted from his misery.

"Empire magic is a new invention," Blitz said, "relatively speaking. They call it *civilized* magic, which just means it's messy and selfish. And like every civilization, it will eventually burn out. The Old Ways are eternal."

Traveler tilted his head. "You'd call it selfish? In the thaumacracy, anyone can learn magic, as long as they put in the effort. Is that not fairer than a handful of witch-monarchs hoarding the power of the ley?"

"*Can* anyone do magic?" Blitz asked brightly. "I'd heard the red wizards required their *permission*, which they kept behind a tangled forest of rules."

"As opposed to a literal forest, eh?" Traveler asked, just as good-naturedly.

Melanie couldn't help but smile at this little war of friendly questions. It was interesting to see Traveler's prejudices challenged by an actual ley magician, each claiming the *other's* path was wicked.

Still, she wondered if they'd truly be safe with this boy and his mistress. The aldermages were hardly a better alternative, but that didn't help unclench her jaw.

But as the sun rose higher and the day grew warmer, fatigue weighed like a heavy load. Eventually sensing Melanie slump atop her, Unicorn raised her head and honked. The cloak planted her invisible feet, coming to a halt. Though Melanie urged her on, the donkey refused to budge.

Traveler turned, pulling Vagabond to a stop. In his lap, Abraxas opened his eyes to glower at Melanie. "Ah," the gearling said. "Seems we're past time for a break. Forgive me; I got distracted."

Melanie shook her head. "I think we all did," she said. "I *could* use a rest, though. And a meal. Blitz, I have a little food left over from the grouille. Would you like some?"

"No, thanks." The boy was suddenly beside her, causing Melanie to screech in surprise. She lurched to the right and had to grab handfuls of Unicorn's cloth body to keep from spilling over. Unicorn gave an irritable honk, but stayed stubbornly planted where she was.

Blitz bent over in a side-stretch. He looked as bright and cheerful as ever.

Melanie and Traveler briefly glanced at each other.

"Are you sure?" Melanie asked once she'd composed herself. "You haven't eaten anything all day. When's the last time you were fed?"

Blitz paused his stretching. "Oh!" he said. "Now that you mention it, I suppose I am hungry. I'll just . . . uh . . . eat some food."

Melanie found a soft tuft of grass to sit on while she divvied up what was left of the grouille's stiff, twice-baked bread and cheese. It wasn't much, but it would get them through the day. And at least it wasn't crickets. Melanie had not taken to those, though the chocolate-covered ants were delicious. She handed Blitz his portion, wrapped in a cloth parcel.

The boy looked down at it with not a small amount of unease. He lifted a tiny crumb of cheese, inspecting the morsel. Then he brought it theatrically to his mouth and took a bite, making sure everyone could see his exuberant chewing.

"Mmmm," he said. "Food! I love food."

He was the weirdest boy Melanie had ever met.

"Personally, I've never had a taste for it," Traveler said. The gearling had dismounted Vagabond, and now lowered himself to the grass, carefully depositing Abraxas back into his lap and feeding him little crumbles of cheese. "But while you're having such a marvelously entertaining time engaging with *food*, perhaps you'd answer one more question of mine, Blitz."

"What's it about?" Blitz asked.

"Spirits," said the gearling. "Specifically, I'd like to know what type of spirit *you* are."

Melanie had been midway through gnawing her bread into a swallowable paste, but now her mouth fell open as she turned from Traveler to the apprentice.

Blitz cringed. He stuck out his tongue and let the morsel of cheese he'd just "eaten" fall out. "Was I that obvious?" he asked.

Traveler shook his head, his glowing eyes tilting cheerfully. "Only to a trained eye. We have some experience as con artists ourselves." The gearling turned to Melanie and his right mote fizzed. His winking skills hadn't improved much.

Still, Melanie closed her mouth and nodded knowingly. "We're professionals," she said. "We spotted you a mile away."

The boy sighed. "I suppose you were going to find out

eventually. It's true. I'm not really an apprentice. This is the disguise I use when I leave the forest to conduct my mistress's business. It's not safe to travel in my true form."

"Which is?" Traveler patiently stroked the cat in his lap.

"I'm a lightning elemental, of course. I'm surprised you didn't guess."

"Fascinating!" The gearling's eyes brightened. He leaned forward, squashing Abraxas beneath his armor. The cat scrabbled at him with his paws, and Traveler pulled back, absentmindedly caressing Abraxas's face.

"So *that's* why the lightning rod was connected to the magic circle," he said. "To trap you."

Blitz nodded glumly. Melanie was still having a hard time processing all this. She had no idea what *elementals* were supposed to look like, but the boy in front of her was certainly not it. He appeared so . . . human. Melanie could see the lines in his palms!

"They ambushed us," Blitz said, his voice somber. "The Hexe has been friendly with Kinderbloom for years . . . for generations. A few of the folks there still held to the Old Ways. The thaumacracy used it against us. Or perhaps someone in the village sold us out, hoping to earn those little metal coins humans love." The boy's eyes darkened, clouding with misery. "They learned the true reward for dealing with the red wizards." As Blitz grew more upset, Melanie felt a strange tingling sensation roll across her arms, like when she'd stood beside the electrified circle.

"How many of you were there?" she asked gently.

"A dozen, though not all were elementals like me. There were also gnomes and trolls and goat-riders. A standard procession." Blitz waved his hand, as if this explained any of the baffling words he'd just said. "The mistress's servants always travel in parades, and usually at night, carrying lanterns and glamoured in finery." The boy grimaced. "This was only my second visit since I was conjured."

"You were . . . ?" Melanie frowned.

Blitz nodded. His seriousness lifted as he took in her confusion. It seemed to amuse him. "My mistress captured me one night during a storm, when I was just a minor lightning bolt. She extended my brief life by binding me to the ley." He puffed his chest out proudly. "I'm a walking, talking spell."

Melanie felt a jolt of something like lightning right then, but deeper and more unsettling. It took her a moment to understand why, but Blitz's explanation *disturbed* her.

"But that means you aren't real!" she blurted.

Traveler turned, his bright gaze landing upon Melanie. Was there . . . hurt in his eyes?

Blitz merely rolled *his*. "Because I'm not made of meat, like a human? How boring. Spirits are made of all sorts of exciting things—trees and stones and water. Some are even made of *ideas*. Isn't that *interesting*?"

It was, though Melanie still couldn't get over her strange aversion to the concept. Magic, she'd come to understand, could animate lifeless objects—as with Unicorn and Livia's sewing needles. But the ability to create *true* life was something wholly different. . . . Wasn't it?

Her mind wandered to Traveler, and a small quake of shame rumbled through her. Up to this point, Melanie had always thought of the gearling as real. As a person. And he was! He had emotions and opinions . . . or at least he seemed to. He spoke and reasoned and presented his ideas about the world. He cared for and protected her.

It's all brainless imitation. Just spells and metal.

Melanie remembered the gate guard from her last night in Crossport.

It's not your friend, you know.

Parno's cruel voice whispered in her ear.

I know what you are. You're an outline of a dead man, burned onto metal.

Melanie tried to unhear the words. Perhaps she'd been unhearing them all this time. Just the night before, she'd told Traveler not to listen to Parno! But despite all this, a strange sensation was still crawling up her spine, igniting one vertebra at a time.

You're a spell gone wrong!

She knew this was a betrayal of the deepest kind. But something had taken root within her—a question that she didn't want to ask . . . or answer.

She looked at Blitz and Traveler conversing. The gearling's glowing motes were the very picture of interest and newfound camaraderie. Blitz's skin, which looked so *real*, was in fact just an illusion. Another spell.

She looked at Vagabond and Unicorn, two enchanted cloaks standing in the grass. Shaped like beasts and yet utterly empty.

Magic surrounded her: beings that were animated by forces she barely understood. But were they real, or was it all a performance of reality? Like . . . like a clockwork automaton waving hello.

The thought crept over her, raising the fine hairs on her arms like Blitz's electrical current had a moment ago: If none of this was real . . .

Was Melanie alone right now?

CHAPTER 24

THEY reached the Zwarte Woud just as the sun began to fall.

The journey had brought more trees to the landscape—tall, dark elms that watched Melanie and the others like whispering sentries. But these were nothing compared to the black wall of forest they faced now.

It was a barrier as sure and imposing as the walls of Crossport. At its edge, Melanie could make out the trunks of trees—skinny things that reached up into a shrouded canopy, their tops disappearing above. But just beyond this outermost vegetation, all light vanished behind a shadowy curtain.

Perhaps it was a trick of the setting sun. Melanie squinted, but was unable to see any farther. She imagined eyes peering back from just beyond the line of darkness. She imagined lips breaking open, grinning with white teeth.

But alongside the unease there was a twin sensation—one that seemed to be emanating from the trees themselves. And it was almost worse. Melanie tried to shake it away.

"That's my mistress's magic," Blitz murmured. Melanie glanced to the boy—spirit—and he smiled encouragingly. "That feeling you have? Like the trees are warning you away? It's all part of her enchantment. It's uncomfortable, isn't it?"

Melanie nodded slowly, forcing the muscles in her face to relax. She hadn't realized her brow was furrowed. She'd been biting her lip. "I do feel . . . something."

"It's a sort of magical intimidation," Blitz said. "The red wizards stole something important from my mistress many years ago, and ever since, she's kept the forest doubly warded. But the feeling will pass once we're inside." He tapped his chest. "Even I'm affected, if you can believe it." He glanced curiously toward Traveler. "Do you feel the magic too, as a spirit of metal?"

Traveler blinked in surprise. "What an interesting way of describing me." Then his glowing motes were on the tree line. "I *do* feel the spell . . . though faintly."

Traveler was fascinated by Blitz, Melanie could tell, despite his apprehension for ley magic. He seemed unendingly curious about spirits in general. Luckily, Blitz was all too happy to catalogue their many merits.

Melanie had listened quietly during the journey. She tried to quash the intrusive thoughts that had appeared from nowhere—like the swollen, buzzing flies that materialized every summer—along with the sense of betrayal they brought. But the more the spirit and gearling prodded each other for answers, the more questions she had.

What made a life real? Was it a body? A mind? What was the difference?

If a person was made of conjury and clockwork instead of flesh and blood, what did that *mean*? Parno had called Traveler a spell gone wrong. An outline burned into metal. So was he some kind of illusion of a person? Like the shadows of the battle at the grouille chateau that had danced across the theater walls?

Melanie had never taken well to being alone. It was an itchy, buzzing sort of discomfort that made her want to claw at whatever walls were within reach. Perhaps she and Abraxas had that in common, after all.

Her heart thrummed, no matter how she tried to muffle it.

"Are we . . . are we sure about this?" Melanie asked softly.

Traveler turned to her. His glowing eyes tilted into a configuration of curiosity.

Melanie grimaced. "I just . . . Perhaps it would be best to find a town full of *people* to hide among."

"Hey!" Blitz bristled. "I *am* a person." Again, Melanie felt the air become charged with that tingling sensation. At the boy's feet, Abraxas's fur suddenly stood on end. It seemed to happen whenever the boy was upset. "And I'm doing you a *favor* here."

"Melanie . . ." Traveler's lights dimmed. "Something's wrong. What's this about?" He lowered his voice. "Is it what I said earlier? About the enemies of the aldermages possibly being—" He glanced at Blitz, then leaned closer to her. "I think we should give him a chance."

Melanie clasped her hands into small fists. What *was* it about? It wasn't what Traveler assumed—not exactly. Why, all of a sudden, was she second-guessing things that had seemed so simple before? Traveler was her friend. He had been from the moment they decided to journey together. And Blitz had been nothing but kind so far. He'd even promised them *sanctuary*!

But when she thought of the Hexe—thought of her creating spirits from rocks and lightning bolts and sending them out into the world—it filled her with a deep unease.

It was like with the foxpox, when Melanie had forced herself upon Jane's recovery and nearly exposed the whole house to the illness. If she'd just waited, she'd have seen her friend in days. Instead, her recklessness had kept them apart for even longer.

But her loneliness had felt like a physical force—like a pressure building within her. Melanie *hadn't* been alone, of course, but rather than talking with her other friends about her feelings, she'd bottled them up. Until the strain became too much.

What if she had just spoken out? Leaned on her friends? So much might have been different.

"I'm sorry," Melanie said, shaking her head. "So much has happened. My life . . . everything's changed so quickly." She felt tears prick at her eyes, hot and wet. "I've never seen anyone die before. And I've never had a grown-up try to *kill me*. Last week, my life was simple and steady. Now it's complicated, and the adults—the aldermages—I always thought were supposed to protect us turned out to be *monsters*, and everyone I care about keeps disappearing. And then Blitz said that thing about being a spell and you . . . What if *you* . . . ?"

Traveler kneeled beside her. The gearling's legs clicked and whirred with their intricate mechanical music. "Ask me," he said.

"You're real . . ." Melanie swallowed. "Aren't you?"

She'd said it. The question itself was a betrayal, but she'd spoken it aloud.

Spells could be *dis*pelled. Illusions faded. Shadows vanished under light. What if Traveler disappeared from her life too, at the wave of a wizard's hand? What if he had never truly existed in the first place?

Traveler turned his head. A sigh emanated from within the mask. It sounded just like a human breath.

But gearlings didn't breathe.

"For a time, I wasn't sure," he said quietly. "I doubt, Melanie. I doubt my *own* realness, as silly as it sounds. A talking clockwork person . . . it seems impossible, doesn't it?" The gearling turned back to her. "I wonder sometimes if I'm dreaming. Perhaps this body, this adventure—even *you*—are all going to wash away with the dawn. Or perhaps I'm just an illusion like the one we cast in Hamlen. Maybe everything that's happening now is a fiction penned by someone else, like Misty Steppe. But can I tell you what I've decided?"

Melanie nodded, wiping at her eyes.

"Doubt is good. It proves to me that I'm real. Even if everything else is a lie. Even if this metal body *itself* is a lie. The one thing I know for certain is that I am a thinking, reasoning being. Because I can doubt. You should doubt *everything*."

"Even you?" Melanie asked. "How can I know that your doubts are real, if all I know for certain is *me*?"

The gearling's eyes took on a mirthful angle. "You truly are very bright. That's correct, Melanie, you can't. Not for sure. So, yes, doubt me too. I won't take it personally." The gearling stood. "Still, solipsism is a lonely room to live in forever. Once I knew that I was real, I used it as my path forward. Asked other questions. Made decisions based on my best evidence. And you've taught me with your own doubts too. You challenged me in ways I never would have thought to myself. You were my bridge to the world; what could I call that but a *real* and lively mind? Perhaps my conclusions are wrong. Perhaps the questions themselves are wrong." Traveler raised his arms in a helpless gesture. "I know I'm real. Everything else I must choose to believe."

Melanie nodded, feeling a tightness in her jaw beginning to loosen.

Traveler's motes brightened, shining cheerily from behind their grille. "If all of this is just a dream," he said, "then I'm glad you're in it, Melanie Gate. And who knows? Perhaps when we wake, the world will be right."

Watching all this from the edge of the forest, Blitz burst into laughter.

"All that talking," he whooped, "just to decide . . . *that you exist?* Does everyone in the empire fret over nothing? It's a wonder you get anything done!"

Beside him, Abraxas glared impatiently at Melanie and Traveler. He didn't share Blitz's amusement, but the cat's contempt for their hand-wringing was no less potent.

Blitz shook his head. "I'm telling you, it's *the spell.* It makes you worry over silly things. Once we're inside, it'll fade. You'll see."

Melanie gazed at the tree line, and the wall of darkness beyond. She hoped Blitz was right, but something told her he wasn't. That *other* feeling had taken root in her chest, growing more potent the closer they got to the forest. Melanie hadn't wanted to notice it at first, but now it was undeniable. The feeling was worse than doubt, or exhaustion, or even fear.

It was belonging.

Because Melanie had a different reaction to the power emanating from the trees than what Blitz had described. The forest was just like the grouille's lock. And just like her own ability. It spoke to her, but it wasn't warning her *away* at all.

It welcomed her.

The Zwarte Woud was utterly soundless. The trees all stood straight-backed and tall, their trunks as black as mourners at a funeral. They didn't touch one another, nor rustle in the wind. They simply watched as Melanie, Traveler, and Blitz trod clumsily through their vigil, going the rest of the way on foot.

Melanie had only recently gotten used to the quiet outside the city. At first, it had unnerved her. Crossport was never truly silent, even at its latest hours. With so many people working night shifts, or sailors carousing, or guards patrolling, the city had a steady percussion that beat well into the early morning. Melanie had barely heard it until it wasn't there anymore, replaced only by the wind coming off the mountains.

Now even that was gone. A second, more palpable silence had descended over them, like a held breath.

Traveler conjured a toverlicht. It swam ahead and cast the forest in gentle blue light. Lush moss covered nearly every surface—the earth, the stones, even many of the trees themselves. In some places it looked thick and soft as a carpet. Melanie imagined what it would feel like to curl up on a tuft of the stuff.

But the woods were far too cold for the idea to bring her much comfort. Colder even than the air outside had been. Melanie pulled Unicorn tightly around her. In response, the cloak embraced her in a woolly hug.

Strange mushrooms gathered between the trees—configurations that dotted the moss and climbed up trunks, like fussy children asking to be carried. Their colors astonished Melanie, especially the ones that gave off eerie lights of their own in the glare of the toverlicht.

"Stick to the path," Blitz warned in a whisper.

Melanie glanced around at the trees, as if they might shake their branches disapprovingly at the noise.

The spirit led the way, walking just ahead of Traveler and Melanie. Abraxas padded at his side. The elderly cat charged forward with grumpy determination. Melanie had never seen him so active for so long. It made her strangely suspicious. Could the Hexe's influence really change the cat so?

"We'll be safe in my mistress's glade," Blitz continued, "but the rest of the forest is still wild. Best not to disturb the moss-folk. They're ornery this time of night. And we all know how trolls get if they smell children!"

Melanie and Traveler glanced at each other. From the

confused cant of the gearling's eyes, Melanie gathered that neither of them had any idea how trolls *got*.

Time passed silently, though Melanie couldn't guess how long they journeyed. It might have been minutes or hours. Oddly, she found she didn't mind. The farther they walked, the more her sense of familiarity intensified. Diving into this forest felt a bit like burrowing into a homespun blanket. It even *smelled* familiar—the tangy earth and crisp greenery cloaking her in a feeling of well-being. How could a place so strange and silent speak to her so loudly? She'd never even been to a forest!

Had she?

The want beneath the want.

Melanie had always told herself she didn't care about family or mysterious origins. What she wanted was a life of adventure, like Misty Steppe's. But when she and Traveler had found Kinderbloom destroyed—

Just the memory of it scoured a hollowness into her.

And yet, this place seemed to want to fill the gap. Melanie actually found herself smiling without meaning to.

"Does anyone else feel that?" she called, breaking the quiet.

Traveler turned to her with a worried tilt to his eyes. "Feel what?"

Blitz, however, nodded knowingly. The boy smiled back at her. "Sure do. That's the ley. I'm impressed you can sense it! Maybe my mistress will make *you* her apprentice."

Melanie coughed, glancing awkwardly toward Traveler.

The gearling crossed his arms. "She already has a magical instructor."

Blitz raised his hands. "Sure, sure. And I'll bet you're a real master of empire magic, being made of it and all. But sensitivity to the ley is a rare gift. It'd just be a shame to waste that potential." He cast a sly glance toward Melanie. "You'll be here anyway, right?"

Melanie only just stopped herself from chirping "Right!" She could tell by Traveler's motes that the gearling was flustered. Was he . . . *jealous*?

The Ley Coven were the enemies of the thaumacracy. Each side saw itself as righteous, and the other as evil. Did that mean everyone back at Merrytrails would think *she* was evil too, for taking shelter here? Would Mrs. Harbargain curse the day Melanie had arrived at her door?

The thought was a desolate one, so Melanie set it aside. The fact was, she'd probably never see the other girls again. She'd wished for adventure, and just like that night she'd sought to free Abraxas from the orphanage, her wish had been granted, and it had blown everything apart. She only hoped her friends were safe. Surely the aldermages wouldn't blame them for *her* misdeeds.

Melanie hugged Unicorn a bit tighter. A gift from home, enchanted with love. Every adventurer needed a cloak, Mrs. Harbargain had said.

Light fluttered between the trees—tiny dots, crisp and green.

Melanie gasped. The dots separated themselves from the trees and appeared before her, accumulating in the dark, tumbling playfully together. The lights swelled before Melanie's eyes, cresting like a wave.

Beside her, Blitz sighed contentedly. *"Finally,"* he said.

The air parted.

Melanie had never seen anything like it. The forest itself fluttered open at an invisible seam, the air gathering and folding into diaphanous pleats. And behind this enchanted curtain, tucked into the center of the Black Forest, was a paradise.

The grass was vivid green, and every tree appeared to be in full spring bloom. Pools of clear, glittering water dotted the glade, each surrounded by creatures both mundane and mystical. Rabbits drank beside sleek red foxes, while above them floated beings unlike Melanie had ever encountered. Blitz had said the Hexe of the South was able to conjure spirits from trees, stone, and water, but Melanie couldn't have imagined they'd be so *beautiful*.

Some of the spirits' shapes were long and lithe, their toes pointed like dancers, though they didn't quite touch the ground. Their bodies appeared to be made of swirling air: miniature cyclones that never alighted.

Others rose from the pools themselves. Their shapes were full and hips round. These spirits lifted their liquid hands, letting the clear water pour out of them and back into the pond, like living fountains.

Melanie saw two figures melt out from the trunks of twisted

trees—one a white-barked birch, the other a dark cedar. The figures' bodies mimicked the trees themselves, and each kept a hand attached to their tree as they leaned in to whisper and stare.

In fact, the entire glade seemed to react to their arrival. The spirits and animals all stopped what they were doing, turning toward the opening.

Blitz's face broke into a wide grin. He opened his arms and stepped into the glade.

The boy disappeared, replaced by something very different.

It was more like a sketch of a boy drawn from light, though the sketch was never quite still. Its frame billowed in brilliant ribbons, re-forming moment by moment as the outline redrew itself. It was so strange and wonderful, unlike anything even in this place *full* of the strange and wonderful.

"Ahhh, it feels good to shake off that disguise."

The spirit sounded just like the Blitz Melanie knew, though his voice had an extra something—a sharpness that hadn't been there before. It was the buzz of electricity, the sizzle of static. It was Blitz's fast-talking restlessness distilled to its purest form.

"Where's the mistress?" he asked the glade. "We need to see her right away."

"I'm here, Blitz. Welcome home."

Melanie only noticed the cabin once the woman had stepped out from it. Tucked beneath flowers and foliage, surrounded by what was probably the most mind-boggling menagerie in the thaumacracy, the cabin was a hard pit of normal in the center of this bright, fey fruit.

And smiling warmly from its doorway was a woman whose face Melanie recognized instantly. She'd drawn it a hundred times, in notebooks and on scrap paper. It was a face she could see clearly when she closed her eyes, yet here Melanie was staring right at it with eyes wide open—and growing wider by the moment.

Misty Steppe raised her hand to greet them.

CHAPTER 25

MELANIE glanced around the cozy cottage. After all this time on the road, the simple comfort of it made her eyes sting. She sat at a clean wooden table, in a kitchen full to bursting with herbs, flowers, and vegetables. A fire burned amiably in its hearth, and several hooded lanterns lit the space in gentle tones.

Beyond the kitchen, Melanie could see the indications of a serene, well-kept home: plush seats and wool blankets; the corner of a bed, laid with soft white bedding. It was like Katzy's inn had been dropped into the center of a cursed forest.

Then there was the Hexe herself.

Melanie knew the woman wasn't *the* Misty Steppe. Misty was a book character. She didn't even *have* a face. But she was exactly what Melanie had pictured when she thought of the wayfaring adventurer. Her chestnut hair was short and wavy, her eyes large and curious and expressive. Her pale pink skin was the same shade as Melanie's. The effect was so uncanny, Melanie found herself struck speechless.

The Hexe wore humble clothing—she wouldn't have looked out of place in Hamlen—and her hands were lined with use.

She dried them now on a tea towel as she smiled at her guests.

She was younger than Melanie expected. Traveler had said the Hexe of the South was around for generations, but this woman had a bright, youthful face to match her bright, youthful eyes. She listened patiently as Blitz recounted the story of the procession to Kinderbloom, frowning as he described the aldermage's trap that had ensnared him, and the roar of the battle outside.

Blitz had seen very little of the chaos from his vantage point in the collapsed building. But from what he'd heard, it was clear to Melanie that gryphons had been used in the assault. She shuddered, remembering the three shadows she and Traveler had seen wheeling through the sky as they arrived at Hamlen, bearing south . . . toward . . .

Oh.

Blitz spoke quickly, in his usual breathless bursts. But the boy Melanie had come to recognize was gone, replaced by this buzzing spirit.

She couldn't take her eyes off him. His glowing body crackled and twitched, and when he moved, it was in streaks of almost liquid light, arcing across the table as a gleaming cord. Strangely, the spirit could seem to handle everyday objects with ease. Melanie had expected him to burn anything he touched, but perhaps the conjury that bound him also allowed him a degree of fine control. He even helped the Hexe prepare tea, ferrying an iron kettle across the cottage in a blink.

The Hexe only interrupted Blitz's story once, to ask if there had been other survivors. Here, the elemental spirit finally grew quiet, lowering his beaming eyes.

She closed her eyes too, for a moment, her face tightening in grief. Then she blinked back her sorrow and smiled grimly at Melanie. "Thank you for rescuing my Blitz," she said. "He's the only one of his kind. It turns out that bottling lightning is as difficult as it sounds. Blitz is something of a miracle."

The spirit beamed, literally. His voltaic body glowed with pleasure.

"I didn't do it alone," Melanie said. A whirl of questions clashed inside her, ones she couldn't quite give voice to. "Traveler's the real magician. He's shown me everything I know."

"Not everything." The gearling sat across the table. His glowing motes watched her warmly. "You've wonders all your own."

"I don't doubt it." The Hexe grinned at her, and Melanie felt her mind go all fizzy. What did it mean that she looked just like a woman from Melanie's imagination?

Melanie lowered her gaze to Abraxas, who had deposited himself atop the wooden table to better watch the group. The cat's mismatched eyes were trained on her.

"My name is Ein," said the woman. "I imagine you have questions. I have some for you too, if I'm to offer you sanctuary."

Traveler nodded, crossing his arms. "We'll answer what we can, of course. But you may find there's much we can't."

Ein tugged at a strand of hair. "Let's see how we do. I'll tell you a bit about myself, and then you're welcome to ask your own questions."

She set a cup in front of Melanie that steamed with a delicious aroma. Melanie took a tentative sip: the tea tasted of honey and hibiscus and flavors she had no names for. She'd never drunk anything so complex and wonderful in her life!

"To begin . . ." Ein said as she sat. "Yes, I am *truly* the Hexe of the South. No, I'm not hundreds of years old. I was instructed in the Old Ways by the previous warden of the Zwarte Woud. There have always been eight of us, each warden protecting the ley's eight places of power. It's an honored position, but a solitary one. We are together, but also very, *very* far apart."

Ein smiled wistfully, and her gaze shifted from Traveler to Melanie for a moment. "I was chosen to apprentice as a young girl because of my sensitivity to the ley. And I was *still* a young girl when my mistress died. I inherited this forest and I am indeed bound to it, though that's a bit complicated. I've been alone ever since."

Melanie wondered what Traveler thought of this young Hexe. Ein certainly wasn't the fearful tyrant he'd described. If anything, she seemed a bit sad. Despite the ethereal beauty of the glade, and the serenity of her home, Melanie sensed a glimmer of longing from the witch.

And hadn't she been the same way, back at Merrytrails? Surrounded as Melanie was by love and easefulness, with her best friend ever by her side, she'd still pined for more. For the big wide world outside.

Melanie had at least been able to explore the city now and then! What was it like to be bound to a place from childhood?

"If you've been in the forest all this time, how did you kill the High Enchanter?" Traveler asked, his voice growing serious. "Was the explosion caused by an elemental spirit?"

"No." Ein turned back to him with a grimace. "I *didn't* kill him," she said. "I wish I had."

The mood in the cabin shifted. Traveler's glowing motes narrowed. "Why?"

Ein adjusted herself in her seat, crossing her arms. "Zerend the Red was a terrible man and a fearsomely powerful wizard. We never met in person, but he tested the limits of my magic constantly, trying to discover a gap in the forest's protections. Especially once my mistress passed."

As Ein spoke, Abraxas heaved himself up from the table, then resettled in the Hexe's lap. Melanie remembered Blitz explaining that the ornery cat had come to serve his mistress. She felt a fresh pang of worry for Mrs. Harbargain, who'd have lost her beloved companion twice now. She must be heartbroken.

"Zerend experimented on what spirits of mine he could capture," Ein continued, "all in the hopes of prospecting the ley. As if it were a lode he could mine." The Hexe's mouth curled in disgust. "I thought when he died, the harassment might stop, but *Riquem* has proven worse than his predecessor."

"Blitz mentioned the aldermages stole something from you," Traveler said. "Something important?"

"They . . ." Ein sighed and laughed softly. "That story is even more complicated. Perhaps later."

Melanie took another sip of her tea, sinking into her chair from the pure pleasure of it. The Hexe glanced her way and, seeing Melanie's contentment, winked. Melanie immediately sat up, her face burning.

"Now I have a question for you, automaton," Ein said, turning back to Traveler. "How is it that you live? I've encountered the red wizards' 'gearlings' before. I've even destroyed a few, to be perfectly honest. But none behaved as you do. Is this Riquem's work?"

"Yes, well . . ." Traveler pretended to clear his metal throat, the noise echoing within his mask. "You've come right to the heart of things. To be perfectly honest with you, Mistress Ein, I'm not sure what I am. I'd half hoped you might know. Blitz suggested . . . Well, perhaps I'm a new sort of spirit?"

The Hexe's smile was pitying. She shook her head. "Blitz and his kind are children of the ley. I didn't so much create him as nudge him awake." She rubbed Abraxas's head, her fingers gently kneading the cat's patchy fur. "You, however, are a being of artifice. Thaumacratic magic is powerful, but it's . . . a fabrication. It only *mimics* miracles."

Traveler's glowing eyes narrowed. Melanie doubted that Ein had meant to be cruel, but she'd certainly managed to find the breach in his armor in short order.

"We'll have to agree to disagree," he said. "Just because a miracle is created by people instead of the ley, that doesn't detract from its miraculousness."

"I don't mean to give offense," the Hexe replied. "But only

the ley can create true life. While the metal that makes up your body came from the earth, it contains no trace of the ley."

She leaned forward in her chair. "But let's start at the beginning. What do you first remember?"

"Fire." Traveler's eyes darkened. "I awoke in the blazing ruin of a thaumaturgic laboratory. I don't know where I was, or how I got out. The next thing I *do* remember is wandering the streets of Crossport." Traveler placed his metal hands on the table, curling his fingers. "I used magic to hide for a time, and stole what gold I could. Then I concocted a plan to escape the city and met Melanie here." The gearling's eyes fell to her. "She saved me. Despite my deception, she still joined me. I owe her everything."

Ein tapped her lips thoughtfully. "Didn't Zerend perish in a fire?"

Melanie watched as Traveler's eyes widened, the glowing motes dilating in surprise. The gears in his neck whirred softly as he turned back toward Ein. "Why, *yes*." Traveler's voice was hushed. "But we'd assumed that was *you* . . ."

"And I'm telling you it wasn't," Ein said. "Believe me or don't; it won't change what followed." She let out a slow breath. "Here is what I suspect, gearling, based on what you've told me. I believe that you're a vessel—a record of sorts—of a life that was inscribed upon you, in what must have been a formidable and likely very *illegal* act of empire wizardry. If the red wizards believed this same act of magic killed Zerend, it might explain why they lied about his death." She grimaced. "It's much easier to blame an evil old witch than admit their leader toyed with human souls. And what a convenient excuse to launch a war."

At this, Ein's grimace deepened, carving a scowl into her face. For the first time, she didn't look at all familiar to Melanie. More like the stranger she was.

Just as upsetting was her assessment of Traveler. Melanie realized that it aligned perfectly with Parno's parting shot at the gearling. An outline of a dead man burned into metal . . .

Traveler's eyes fell to his hands on the table. He turned his palms upward. "Am I . . . human?"

"The echo of one." Ein's face softened. She extended her own calloused hand across the wood, touching her fingers to his. "With your permission, I could investigate the spell that binds you to this armor. If I'm correct, I may be able to unlock some of your old memories."

Traveler's head snapped up. "You could do that?" he asked. "How?"

"The process isn't so different from my usual conjury. I'd call to the presence imprinted within you. Use a bit of the ley to coax it out. You are already . . . awakened. But this could open the doors that remain closed."

"I told you my mistress was the best!" Blitz bragged.

Traveler was silent for a spell. Melanie wondered what was going through her friend's mind right then, what doubts he was wrestling with. Doubt is good, he'd said. It proves you're real.

But that didn't mean it was easy.

"Very well," he finally said.

Ein smiled, pulling her hand back. Her eyes flicked briefly to Melanie.

Melanie felt her face flush again. Beneath the uncanny elation of the ley, and the simple comfort of the cabin, something twisted in her stomach. Melanie swallowed. Her head swam and her jaw felt stiff. She had so many questions of her own for Ein, but couldn't seem to grasp hold of one.

"Stand here with me," Ein said, rising from her chair. She set Abraxas atop the wooden table and smoothed out her skirt.

The cat gazed at Melanie the whole time. His eyes bored into her.

Traveler joined the Hexe, his posture loose with excitement. Ein placed her palm to the gearling's armored chest. Her fingers ran over the looping patterns engraved into the metal.

Two eyes watched Melanie. One yellow and one white. One was sharp and clear. The other milky and . . .

Blind.

But they both watched her all the same.

That's not Abraxas, Melanie thought wildly. The realization confused her. What could that mean? And yet, she felt absolutely sure. This was not the cat she'd grown up with.

It was a dubbelganger. An imposter.

She tried to sit up, but found she couldn't. Her back was stiff and unmoving. The cup of tea was still clutched in her hands, but her fingers wouldn't rise to shift it to the table. Her thoughts were a haze.

Something . . . something in the tea!

She looked to Ein and Traveler, where the Hexe's hand still rested on her friend's chest. Melanie tried to shout, but her throat wouldn't cooperate. Her lips trembled but didn't budge. She tried to *open*, to *unlock*, to *free*. But whatever was happening, her power wouldn't work.

Traveler!! Melanie thought as hard as she could at the gearling, just like with the Gossip's Friend charm. She had no idea how the spell worked, but she put all her will into it. *TRAVELER, IT'S A TRAP!*

"What?" To Melanie's astonishment, the gearling began to turn his head toward her. His eyes tilted in confusion.

Ein pushed.

There was a sputter of magic and a sickening crunch as her hand broke through Traveler's breastplate as if it were paper. The metal surrounding her wrist immediately darkened. Veins of rust lanced out from the breach, splitting the gearling's beautiful chassis. All Melanie could do was watch as the lustrous gold corroded with startling speed.

Traveler's head snapped back toward the Hexe. His eyes were bright with alarm. He tried to step backward, but Ein had a grip on something inside the gearling that was impossibly, supernaturally strong. She anchored the automaton in place.

Traveler raised his arm to strike out. Melanie could hear the whirring clockwork inside failing even as he did. His joints stiffened and cracked with the spreading rust. There was a terrible grinding sound—gears shattering—and his arm fell limply aside.

"No!" the gearling shouted. "Let go! Let go of me!"

Melanie looked desperately at her hands, willing them to *Open!*

Nothing happened.

Open! She thought again, putting everything she had into the command. *Open, open, open!*

But her body stayed locked. Whatever the Hexe had given to her, it had muted her ability. Melanie was truly trapped.

"Mistress!" Blitz cried, frantic. "What are you doing?"

Ein said nothing. She simply stared into Traveler's glowing eyes with grim determination. She maintained her grip even as the automaton's legs collapsed beneath him.

"Mistress, *please!*" Blitz screamed. "Don't do this!"

But even if she'd stopped now, it was too late. Melanie could see that. Traveler's glowing motes flickered, the lights failing. They rolled within their mask, angling toward her. Melanie felt a tear trail down her cheek, a scream trapped within her.

I love you, she thought as hard as she could at the gearling. *When you wake, the world will be right.*

But the lights within him had already died.

Darkness hollowed the space behind Traveler's grille, his mask an empty shell. Vagabond—his cloak—slipped off his back, fluttering to the ground. Half a heartbeat later, the rust reached Traveler's helm.

The last of Melanie's friend dissolved before her eyes.

CHAPTER 26

EIN'S hands were shaking.

Melanie watched as the woman wiped rust from her arm, but the stubborn flakes clung to her like dried blood.

Clutched in the Hexe's hand was a yellow crystal. Some sort of gearling power source? A smoky globule of red liquid was suspended in the stone.

Ein set it down on the wooden table, steadying herself against the edge for a moment. Her bright eyes were on Melanie.

"I thought I'd lost you forever," she said, "the day they took you from me."

Somewhere behind Melanie, Blitz was weeping. "I promised . . ." he fizzed. "I promised them safety."

Ein turned, frowning at the spirit. The whimpering abated.

"I'm sorry, Blitz," she said. "But it had to be done." Then her gaze fell back on Melanie. She seemed to register Melanie's own tears for the first time and her eyes softened. "Oh, dearest. Don't cry. Whatever inhabited that thing was already long dead. I simply exorcised its ghost."

Ein sat down at the table with a sigh. "This must be so scary and confusing," she said. "I was confused as well, when you didn't recognize me. Whatever the aldermages did to you, they did it too well. They erased me from you entirely."

Ein's eyes shifted back and forth, searching Melanie's face for something. Some hint of understanding? Of connection?

Well, Melanie had no idea what this murderer was talking about. She dropped her gaze to the pile of desiccated metal on the floor. Vagabond lay discarded and inert among the bits of rust.

"Fine." The Hexe sighed. "I'll explain it to you, then. Whoever you *think* you are, Melanie Gate, it's a lie. A story that others have created for you. You're not an orphan. You aren't even a little girl. You are *me*."

Melanie's eyes shot up. Ein's gaze was cool, her jaw set.

"That's right," she said. "You're a piece of my own soul that I gave shape and sent out from the Zwarte Woud. I was young when my mistress died. Too young. I wasn't ready for the responsibility of the ley . . . or for the isolation. You can't imagine how lonely it was. I was a child whose obligations bound me to this forest. I wasn't ready to have my life consumed by adult concerns. But my gift has always been for conjuration. By tying pieces of this forest to the ley, I can awaken the spirits within them—spirits of earth and water, of air and lightning. And in my desperation, I awoke a spirit unlike any before, using a part of *myself* as the wellspring." The Hexe held out a finger toward Melanie. "That piece became you: a spirit of freedom." Ein's eyes darkened, and the finger turned back around. "*My* freedom."

Spider legs of fear skittered along Melanie's arms. This woman was delusional. What she claimed *couldn't* be possible. Melanie was a girl! She was flesh and blood! She got sick and scraped her knee. She ate meals and slept in a bed and cried real human tears. She was nothing like the spirits of the glade.

And yet . . . she couldn't deny the pull of this place, or the way that Ein had perfectly matched Melanie's inner image of Misty Steppe. As if she'd always been there in the back of Melanie's mind, waiting.

Ein stood again, crossing to where the false Abraxas sat upon the table. She began gently stroking the cat's head.

"I didn't realize what I'd given away in creating you. Without my freedom—without *you*—it wasn't just obligation that kept me in this forest. I was physically trapped here, well and truly. My power was also depleted, a portion carved off in your creation. Still, for a time, all was fine." She chuckled. "More than fine. *Wonderful*. The ley tethered us. I watched through your eyes as you left the wood and journeyed toward Crossport. You were a formless spirit then, able to take whatever shape you chose. Never staying in one for long. You were adventure distilled. A key to open doors. While we were connected, no place was barred to me. Together, we visited Kinderbloom and wandered faraway forests. Soared through the air and swam in the sea. And we spied too. We watched the aldermages in Crossport and noted their plans, laughed at their attempts to infiltrate our place of power. All until the day that *Riquem* caught you."

Ein pulled her hand from the cat, studying it with a hurt, baffled expression.

"I saw it through your eyes," she said. "Zerend's little lackey plucked you from air, incapacitating you before you could escape. And then . . . nothing. You disappeared. From me. From the ley." Her eyes found Melanie's. "I thought you were gone forever. And with you, any sense of freedom I would ever have. Until the night Zerend died."

The wish, Melanie realized. The night she'd exploded the orphanage while freeing Abraxas. Her grief curdled inside her. One night, one mistake—had it all led to this?

"I felt you again for the first time in years," Ein said excitedly. Her bright, lovely eyes were almost raving. "It was just a flicker, and so far away, but it *was* you. I searched for you through every semi-wild creature I could find—searching the spirits of anything that had so much as grazed the ley—until I discovered . . . a cat."

Ein grabbed the false Abraxas by the scruff of his neck. She lifted him into the air, staring into his eyes. Abraxas gazed back placidly, completely calm.

"The thing was so *domesticated,* it's a wonder I reached it at all. But a dalliance with liberty had washed away enough of its urban stink that the ley could touch it. I searched its memories for you. I watched and listened. You left your little group home and I thought I'd lost you again, but then *you* found *me.* Do you remember? Sitting at the table?"

A nagging memory tugged at Melanie. A dream of the

strangest dinner party with seven guests, and one place set just for her.

And a voice . . .

Who is sitting in my chair?

A voice she recognized now.

You!

Seeing Melanie's expression, Ein nodded slowly. "You remember. That was when I had what I needed. For the second time, I pulled a piece from myself. I conjured a *guiding* spirit, and molded it into the shape of the cat, a form you were familiar with. I sent it with Blitz to find you and bring you here."

Ein smiled at the false Abraxas—the dubbelganger created to trap another dubbelganger.

"It was a gamble to part with more of myself, especially after the last time. Each time I did, my power waned. But it paid off. Now, back where you belong, little one."

The false Abraxas began to change. Its fur shifted, the colors blending and churning. Its edges bubbled away and the spirit became a sort of doughy goop that writhed in the Hexe's hand. The ichor thinned, growing watery and insubstantial. It absorbed into her skin like a spill into a rag.

In moments, the cat had disappeared.

Ein stretched her arms with a contented sigh. "That's better," she said. Then she turned toward Melanie, straightening her dress.

"You're safe now, dearest. Safe at home." She smiled indulgently. "You'll live on in me. Everything you've seen, all your adventures, they'll be right here." The Hexe placed a hand against her chest. "The red wizards are burning the world down, but once I've reclaimed the power I so foolishly gave away—once I have my *freedom* back—I can use it to strike against them with a fury that will end this war for good. With your gift—*our* gift—what barrier could stand against me? There can be *peace* again."

Melanie closed herself off. The Hexe kept talking, but she didn't care.

Something cold had dawned within her. A frozen sun crested a blighted horizon.

Everything she'd known about herself was wrong. She'd thought Lady Porta was a fiction—a character she and Traveler had made up.

But Melanie Gate had been the lie the whole time.

You aren't even a little girl.

Then what was she?

A spell.

A story.

A piece of someone else, sent out into the world.

"Please, mistress!" Blitz was saying. "Can't she stay like this? Melanie helped me! She saved me!"

"*I* saved you, Blitz. *I* led her to you. And Melanie is a part of *me*."

Melanie tried to recall her earliest memories, to summon something from her time before Merrytrails. If she could only prove that Ein was wrong. If she could just *remember* something real. But there was nothing. The orphanage had been her whole life. Her friends and Jane and Mrs. Harbargain and even Abraxas—they were all she had.

Them, and Traveler. Beautiful, soulful, one-of-a-kind Traveler. The voice for the voiceless things. Was this what her friend had felt all the time? This gaping void beneath his feet, where years of memory and identity should have formed the solid foundations of his life? How did he survive it?

Doubt.

That's what Traveler had said. *Doubt is good.* Doubt proves you are real, even if everything else is a lie.

Ein claimed that Melanie was just a part of her, like a work of art she'd created, with no mind of its own. She said that Melanie would live on in her, but Melanie wasn't so sure.

Right here, right now, she was alive. She was a thinking, feeling, *doubting* being. She was real. Just as Traveler had been real, before Ein killed him.

And now the Hexe of the South meant to kill Melanie too. Well, she wouldn't let her.

Melanie glared down at her hands, still locked around the poisoned cup of tea.

Open, she demanded.

Her fingers didn't move.

Open! Melanie summoned her will. She searched for the deep core of certainty at the center of the doubt. She was real. She was *real*. She had a life and friends! Jane and Mariana and Baruti and Sun-mi and Helen and even . . .

Take care out there, lock-eater.

Even Agatha.

It's not such a bad name, Traveler had said. *It sounds powerful.*

Melanie had always hated the nickname. It sounded hostile, aggressive. It made her seem like a predator, or a weapon.

Maybe that's why it cut so deep, why she'd held it so far away. Melanie hadn't wanted to think of herself as a force of chaos. But her recklessness had left a path of destruction everywhere she'd traveled. It had brought her to this very moment.

But now that the moment was here, perhaps it was exactly what she needed to be.

Lock-eater.

Melanie closed her eyes. She never left her chair, but she hunted using some inner sense—the part of her that brokered with bonds and persuaded passages. The part that had followed the grouille's rune to its unsettling source. She wasn't even sure what she was searching for. Yet what she found still surprised her.

It was a dinner party.

Melanie sat before a vast wooden table, a slice of wood so round and thick it might have been cut from a single gigantic tree. Other figures were seated at the table—humans and grouille and kassipoi—though each was shrouded in layers of mist like heavy cloaks.

Still, Melanie could tell they were surprised by her arrival. Veiled gazes all snapped toward her; whispers quieted.

It was just like her dream, the one in which Ein had found her. Was this . . . the Ley Coven?

Melanie looked down. In front of her was the same

otherworldly place setting. A knot of vegetation rested inside a black bowl—moss and vines and eerie flowers, all bathed in a broth of churning fog. A gleaming napkin ring was set beside it, engraved with a large *S*.

Melanie didn't know if any of the other figures would try to stop her. She wasn't even sure if they *could*. But she wasn't going to give them the chance.

She took hold of the bowl, gripping its sides and lifting it up. A chorus of gasps and screams rang out—close, but also somehow far away.

This time, she didn't ask or demand or even speak at all.

She swallowed the meal whole.

The table disappeared, swept away like smoke in a gust of wind. Something dark and massive rumbled in the distance.

Melanie opened her eyes. She was back in the cabin.

Ein stood before her, gazing down at her hands, then up at the roof.

"No . . ." she breathed. Her voice was thick with dread. "What . . . what did you *do*?"

Melanie dropped the cup. Tea splattered against the kitchen floor as it shattered. She'd freed herself of Ein's paralysis, but something had shifted. Something big.

Outside, voices began to scream.

"No!" Ein stood, upending her chair. "How did they get here so quickly?" She clawed around the edge of the table, her hands reaching for Melanie. "Come back to me now! Perhaps I can still . . . if I take you back, perhaps the ley—"

Melanie was up as well. She dodged away from the Hexe,

backing through the cottage and staying well clear of her grasp. She remembered the way the false Abraxas had melted to nothing at Ein's touch, and a jolt of panic ran through her.

"What's happened?" Blitz asked numbly. The glittering spirit stared down at his hands. "I feel strange."

"Blitz, help me!" Ein barked. "Grab her, before it's too late!"

The spirit's eyes rose, setting upon Melanie. Uncertainty burned within his shifting expression.

"She *killed* Traveler, Blitz," Melanie said. "Now she'll kill me too."

"She's my mistress," Blitz whimpered.

"GRAB HER," Ein screamed. "NOW!"

"You promised . . ." Melanie said.

There was an arc of light as Blitz moved, interposing himself between Melanie and the Hexe. The spirit held his arms out. "Leave her alone!" he shouted.

Ein snatched him by the neck. Blitz screamed, clawing at his mistress's arm. Lines of electricity spilled through the cottage, lassos of radiance that tied themselves to random objects: the kettle, the iron poker, the crystal on the table.

"Let him go!" Melanie shouted, searching for a weapon to defend the spirit.

"My lightning in a bottle . . ." Ein murmured. A flicker of bright sadness broke through the storm of her fury. The Hexe squeezed.

There was a blinding flash, followed almost immediately by a *BOOM* that shook the whole structure of the cottage.

Spots flared in Melanie's vision. She couldn't hear anything.

But she *could* see the scorch on the cottage floor, right below where Blitz had been standing. It was mirrored by a hole burned into the ceiling; the gap still smoldered.

Melanie ran.

"No!" Ein cried.

Melanie ducked low, narrowly avoiding the swipe of the Hexe's hand, and threw herself toward the cottage door, brushing it with her fingers.

Open! Melanie thought. The door obliged, slamming itself wide just as she burst through and into . . .

A war.

CHAPTER 27

THE peaceful glade had become a nightmare.

Trees were ablaze, and terrified animals wandered the grounds, their eyes wild as they searched for escape. All around the space, strange *doors* were opening into the air, shimmering holes to some other place. Melanie could see a clockwork army on the other side, gearlings of various metallic sheens—silver, bronze, and shiny black. Some lingered inside the apertures, holding their hands out. Fire gushed from the crystals embedded in their palms. Others stepped through and into the glade, where they began attacking spirits indiscriminately. All the automatons' eyes glowed livid red.

But the glade fought back. Bludgeons of water pounded the invaders from the spring, the aqueous spirits crushing them into the earth as soon as they arrived. A boiling figure of yellow fire poured flames into one of the magicked doorways, liquefying the gearlings just beyond and sealing the fissure with a loud *pop!*

Melanie pushed through it all, swallowing the sob that battled for her breath. Her legs trembled and her head was woozy, but she couldn't afford to stop. She imagined Ein's hand reaching for her, saw the false Abraxas liquefy at the Hexe's touch.

The glade was filling with figures—spirits and automatons, along with other curiosities of the forest. They'd emerged to defend the Zwarte Woud. The once-beautiful vegetation that clung to rocks and climbed the walls of the cabin blackened under the gearlings' onslaught. The fresh, clear air that had greeted Melanie just a short time ago now choked in a smoky haze. Even the tall trees that ringed the space seemed to shake with fury. Ein's beautiful cage was burning alive.

But as more and more of the ley creatures arrived, the gearlings soon found themselves overwhelmed. Perhaps the forest could repel them after all.

Melanie bolted for a gap in the battle, unable to plan one step beyond the next. She'd never been so afraid in her life.

Then a new figure entered the glade.

He appeared from a shimmering doorway several yards from the cabin—right in Melanie's path. She scrambled to a stop just as a phalanx of gearlings closed to defend the newcomer's arrival, batting away buzzing elfin sprites that rushed the portal.

The man wore red, just as all aldermages wore red, but his uniform was surprisingly simple. Slacks, a crisp white shirt, a crimson vest—and an intricate gauntlet affixed over his left arm, fashioned after a gearling.

He was thin and unassuming, and he gazed across the chaos with a genial interest.

"Riquem!" Ein's voice lashed out from behind. Melanie snapped around to find the Hexe of the South glaring from just a few yards away. She realized with horror that she was pinned between them.

"You would *dare* to enter this place yourself?" Ein hissed.

Riquem the Red, leader of the aldermages, smiled sheepishly.

"A bit rash, wasn't it?" he called in a reedy voice. "But as it happened, I was searching for someone when your defenses suddenly evaporated. I couldn't pass up the opportunity to see your forest domain firsthand. It's lovely, Ein, truly." The High Enchanter swept his gaze across the space, and a look of sadness touched his expression. "A shame I have to burn it all down."

Then his gaze landed on Melanie.

Riquem's eyes brightened again as her took her in.

"There you are!" he said. "Melanie Gate, you've left quite a trail to follow. I suppose I have you to thank for dispelling the Hexe's wards for me? That's some gift you possess."

"This is your *grave*, Riquem!" Ein raised her hands and the earth around the aldermage's feet began to rumble and split. Rocks snapped together, forming bones of masonry. Soon soil had rushed up, coating them in earthen flesh.

Dozens of muddy hands reached up, dragging the assembled gearlings beneath the ground. Several snatched at Riquem's legs, attempting to pull him under too. But the wizard just raised his own gauntleted hand and the crystal within flared

red. The hands dissolved as quickly as they'd been made, crumbling back to dust.

"A bit lackluster," Riquem said, sounding disappointed. "Did something happen, Ein? I expected more from the fearsome Hexe of the South."

"That was merely a taste," Ein said, a smile playing across her lips. "Now the true meal begins." She closed her eyes and pounded her hands together. Strands of light streaked from the Hexe, a lattice that reached across the glade like a loom, weaving disparate pieces together. A stone was yanked from the earth and water drained from the spring in a glistening skyward spiral. A fire burning near the cottage bled away, lashing together with earth, water, and air.

The clashing elements roared. Fiery eyes burned miserably from within a molten mask. A wail of agony pierced the glade that was parts hiss, burble, and gale. In moments a churning colossus stood before Ein, molded from impossible materials.

"Spirit!" she called. "Destroy the red wizard!"

The chaotic elemental figure lurched forward. Melanie screamed, scrambling from its path. It hurtled toward Riquem with surprising speed, leaving trails of acrid smoke in its wake.

The wizard stepped back with a look of real alarm. He lifted his gauntlet and another portal expanded open behind him. The doorway continued to dilate—growing wider and wider with a stretched, tearing noise. It was so much bigger than any of the others that had appeared.

But the spirit was fast—astonishingly fast. It had crossed the yards that separated them before Riquem could retreat.

Soon it was just above the aldermage, its boiling hand reaching toward him.

Until an enormous metallic piston exploded from the rift, pulverizing the spirit into smoldering fragments in an instant.

A shadow coalesced in the shimmering surface of the portal, huge and looming. With a lumbering movement, it stepped through.

The automaton had the trappings of a gearling. Its armored frame glittered in the fiery light of the glade. Gorgeous looping patterns were engraved onto every surface. But this monster of metal hadn't been fashioned into a humanlike shape. It stood balanced on six mechanical cylinders like the legs of a gigantic insect. At its center, three glowing eyes rolled behind a hissing grille, each swiveling separately. One of those enormous eyes now landed upon Melanie, jolting to a stop. The mote widened, taking her in.

The automaton was larger than even a gryphon. It towered over the aldermage.

"Ein, let me introduce you to the empire's newest thaumechanical wonder," Riquem said, straightening his vest. "I call it the gearetten. I'd brought the prototype with me to deal with a rogue agent, but this will be an even better test. It should be more than enough to obliterate your home."

The Hexe of the South stood dumbfounded, staring at this mountain of metal. The distraction was just what Riquem needed. A gearling was upon her in moments, wrenching the witch's hands behind her and kicking out her feet. Ein fell to her knees.

Melanie decided that now was a good time to run. She shifted to the side, ready to bolt for the tree line.

"Oh, I've brought something for you too, Melanie—don't worry."

A new figure appeared from inside Riquem's enormous portal, one as astonishingly familiar as the gearetten was alien.

Mrs. Harbargain emerged from the shimmering doorway, carrying the real Abraxas in her arms. The cat's fur stood on end, his good eye shooting around in panic. Harbargain was followed by Jane—oh, Jane!—and Agatha and Sun-mi, Baruti and Helen and little Mariana.

And . . . Livia. The tailor emerged with Katzy. Though the two Hamleners were entirely different species, their faces were mirrors of horror as they took in the violence that surrounded them.

The glade was well and truly ablaze now. Seeing the mechanical monster obliterate Ein's powerful elemental spirit with a single blow, ley creatures began retreating into the forest, making for the cover of the trees. Some were burned down by gearlings as they fled, but many more escaped into the Zwarte Woud.

Melanie could only gape. It was like a dream. A terrible, impossible, heart-shattering dream. They couldn't truly all be here, could they? Had Melanie dragged her friends into this danger and chaos?

"Melanie!" Harbargain called through the din. "Oh, my darling!"

The girls all clung to one another, little Mariana hiding her face in Sun-mi's dress. Livia tried to rush toward Melanie, but Katzy held her back, grabbing the girl's wrist with a fearful look.

And Jane. The expression of terror on her best friend's face was more than Melanie could bear.

"I'll offer you this chance once," Riquem said. Though his voice was coaxing—gentle even—his large, dark eyes burned like coals. "Surrender the gearling, or everyone you love dies here."

The girls all gasped, and Mariana let out a shriek.

"You can't be serious!" Harbargain shouted. "You said we were here to *help* Melanie!"

The High Enchanter ignored her. Melanie sensed the man was deadly serious.

There are evil people in the world for whom hurting a child means very little. Often those people wield more power than is right.

What had she gotten all her friends into?

"Lady Porta!" Livia cried. ". . . Melanie!" The girl's colorful braid had come unraveled, and her dress was a tattered mess. So, Melanie's crimes had endangered even her? It seemed everything she touched came to ruin.

Melanie's shoulders slumped. Her eyes stung. The exhaustion that filled her was bone-deep.

"I'm sorry . . ." she said. Her voice was hollow, even to her own ear. "I'm so sorry."

"*Melanie!*" Jane called. The sorrow in her best friend's voice hit her like a physical blow.

"I surrender." Now Melanie's sob finally escaped her chest,

ringing across the ravaged glade. She buried her face in her hands. "Please, I beg you, don't hurt them!"

"Melanie, no!" But Jane hadn't finished speaking. Something in her voice broke through Melanie's misery. She'd never heard her friend so forceful.

She glanced up to find Jane had launched toward the High Enchanter, charging him unexpectedly from behind. "Run!" she shouted. "He'll kill you anyway! He wants the gearling!"

"What are you—?" Riquem began.

Jane grabbed the wizard's gauntlet, attempting to wrench it from his hand. The other girls all began screaming at the same time.

Livia stepped forward, as if to join her, but half a dozen gearlings had already swarmed the group. A silver-colored automaton shoved her back into line.

Jane tugged Riquem's gauntlet, kicking at the wizard for leverage. Inch by inch, it slid across his arm. One good heave, and it would be free.

"*Enough!*" With a swipe of his hand, Riquem knocked Jane to the ground. The High Enchanter's friendly expression had burned away completely, revealing a smoldering rage. He righted the gauntlet in less than a moment, pointing it down toward Jane. His eyes were wide and wild.

"That was very, *very* stupid," he hissed. The gauntlet's crystal flared crimson.

"STOP!" Melanie wailed, rushing forward. "Please, I *surrender!* The gearling is already dead!"

The word rang out like Crossport's third bell, grim and final. Riquem hesitated. His expression fell, the fury smothered.

"Dead . . ." he repeated. The light in his palm slowly faded. "How?"

"I destroyed the automaton," Ein said. The Hexe's ferocity had returned, just as Riquem's was dimming. She grinned joylessly at him. "Though it's not half of what you stole from me, the doll is *dust* now. Along with whatever soul was foolish enough to think they could crawl inside it."

Riquem was quiet for a long moment. His restless eyes tracked mysterious calculations. Finally, he lowered his arm and nodded at Melanie.

"Very well," he said. "I'll let your friends go, so long as they—and you—make no more trouble." He turned back to the Hexe. "Ein . . . I suggest you give up too. If you willingly surrender your piece of the ley to me, I'll even leave this place intact."

Ein's eyes traveled from Riquem to the gearetten. "My *piece*"—she laughed and spat—"cannot be given. Only embraced. You think I don't know your plans, red wizard? Why you started this war? You aren't the first to covet the ley's power, and you won't be the last. It was old when the mountains were young. It has faced countless would-be subjugators. *All* have fallen."

"The ley can join the embrace of the *thaumacracy*," the Third Eye said, "or it can be destroyed. I leave the choice to you."

"There was never a choice." The Hexe braced her legs. She yanked her hands from her gearling captor's grip and held them aloft. Melanie felt a charge as Ein began to conjure. The air grew warm, then hot, then stifling.

Riquem grimaced. "Very well." He lifted his armored hand, and the stone within flashed. "Fire the eldritch canon," he said.

Then his gaze flicked just above Melanie. "Subdue her."

"Yes, operator!" a genteel voice chirped in her ear.

Melanie's head snapped around to find that a gearling stood behind her. The automaton's vacant red gaze was a horrid echo of Traveler's. It pressed something to her arm—Melanie felt a sharp sting and saw a glass tube with a long toothlike needle pull away.

Lethargy tugged at her, as sudden and heavy as a falling curtain. Melanie's legs slumped and she slid downward, caught by the gearling.

The automatons marched her weeping friends through the doorway, while one lifted Jane roughly to her feet. The girl's glassy, defeated stare disappeared behind the shimmering portal.

The last things Melanie saw before unconsciousness took her were the gearetten's three eyes spinning wildly. The motes drew together, forming a single bloody orb that crackled with eerie energy.

The orb brightened, and the world darkened.

Distantly, Melanie heard the Hexe of the South scream.

CHAPTER 28

THE bed was sumptuously soft.

Melanie rolled onto her side, luxuriating in the pleasant give of the mattress. The sheets were silky and freshly laundered. No fewer than half a dozen pillows were piled around her, framing her in an architecture of comfort.

When was the last time she'd slept in a bed? Melanie felt rested. She felt safe. She could hear the gentle patter of rain on the windowsill. Outside, thunder grumbled from far away.

Traveler, crumbling to dust.

Blitz, disappearing with a flash of lightning and a deafening boom.

Jane's defeated face as she was marched away.

Three eyes meeting in a piercing scream.

Melanie's eyes snapped open.

She threw away the pillows and sat up, searching her surroundings. She was lying in an enormous four-poster bed, the frame carved from rich, dark wood. Her bedroom was tidy and fancy; the wallpaper was brocaded in little flowers and embellished with golden threads. A large window filled up nearly the entire far wall, offering an expansive view of a churning sky and glittering city just below.

Her city. Crossport. Though she'd never seen it from this height.

Melanie crawled out of bed. Unicorn and her periwinkle coat hung from pegs by the door, but otherwise she still wore the clothes she'd had on since Hamlen. Melanie tried the door handle. Locked.

Open, she thought. Just a small wish.

The door stood stubbornly closed.

Melanie frowned. She gazed up at Unicorn, taking the edge of the cloak between her fingers. It remained inanimate, hanging heavily from its peg.

Melanie padded toward the window, gazing down. Below her, she could see practically the whole city. Waves crashed against the docks at the harbor. And there was the South Gate, its enormous doors closed for the night. Red roofs sloped elegantly down just beneath her.

The castle. The thought sent a shiver of surprise through her. How many times had she gazed at this very building from the windows of Merrytrails? She tried to pick out the orphanage now, but it was lost amid an ocean of rooftops. How small it must be, compared to the whole of the city. And yet, once it had been her whole world.

Melanie burst into tears.

She couldn't stop them. Here in the quiet and solitude, all the traumas of the past days took hold of her, and they shook her shoulders with a ruthless grip. She couldn't believe that Traveler was gone. And Blitz, who'd only tried to stand up for her. They were her friends and they'd both died because of her. She could only hope the others were safe—that the High Enchanter had kept his word.

Melanie sunk to the floor, collapsing into the rich carpet.

She stayed there for the rest of the night.

CHAPTER 29

IT was past dawn when Riquem came to visit, though the sun was still obscured by the storm outside.

The aldermage carried a tray laden with food—meats and eggs and a bowl of gorgeous, colorful fruit.

He set the tray onto a side table, taking in Melanie's position on the floor.

"Hard night?" he asked. There was a touch of humor in his voice, though the man's eyes were pitying. Still, Melanie had already seen the anger that waited just beneath that placating mask.

She sat up slowly, remaining silent.

"I wanted to thank you personally," the wizard said. He sat against the edge of the bed, sinking into the mattress. "We might *never* have breached Ein's defenses without you. Now, at last, the Hexe of the South is gone. The people of the thaumacracy can sleep soundly."

"What happened to the Zwarte Woud?" Melanie asked. Her throat felt like she'd swallowed a bag of sand.

"Much of the forest remains, though the Hexe's glade was destroyed. What was left of her forces have scattered. We'll hunt down the ones we can, but it's of little concern. Without a warden, the spirits of the Zwarte Woud can't replenish their numbers."

"So the war is over?"

Riquem smiled, but he didn't answer.

Melanie turned away. To hear that the glade too was gone scraped against her already hollow center. Though her short time there had been filled with such misery, it was still a beautiful place. Perhaps one of a kind. Now that sense of deep connection, of belonging, was truly lost.

"I know quite a bit about you, Melanie Gate," Riquem said, breaking the silence, "even though we've never met. Your friends care for you very much. Especially that mousy girl, Jane, hm? It's always the quiet ones who surprise you. A lesson I'll need to remember."

Melanie gasped, glancing back to the wizard. "Jane!"

"Is fine," Riquem said. "Despite her attempted insurrection. They're all back at the orphanage, safe and sound. The Hamlen girls too. I transported us via the castle's thaumaturgic circle. There are only a handful of circles in the empire even *capable* of long-distance teleportation, but naturally we have one here. Still, I'm afraid they had to walk the rest of the way home. With a gearling escort, of course."

Riquem tilted his head, studying her with a bemused expression. "It's clear that most of the people you met on your journey had only small pieces of the puzzle that is Melanie Gate. Orphan, prodigy, con artist—you've worn many hats." He cleared his throat. "The gearling who achieved sentience. It's truly . . . ?"

"Dead," Melanie confirmed. The weight of the word nearly dragged her down to the carpet again.

"Ah," Riquem said after a moment. "That's regrettable."

Melanie couldn't quite decipher the note of emotion in the man's voice. "May I ask *you* a question?" she said.

"You may certainly ask."

She took a deep breath. "Traveler was Zerend . . . wasn't he? The original Third Eye of the Empire? Ein said that Traveler was housing another life, and Parno told us he was some kind of spell gone wrong. The magic that killed Zerend wasn't an attack, was it? It was an accident."

Riquem was quiet for a long beat, his eyes wide as he processed Melanie's guess. Finally, he chuckled and shook his head. "I'm impressed. You are very, *very* close to the truth. And with the evidence you had, how could you come to a better conclusion? But no, your gearling friend wasn't Zerend."

Riquem stood from the bed. "I am."

A jolt of surprise ran through Melanie, accompanied by swelling panic. He . . . what?

"I suppose there's no harm in telling you, since you've figured out the broad strokes on your own. We were working on an immortality spell. I was sick, you see. Dying. Even with the finest helermages at its disposal, a human body can only withstand so much. Mine was failing."

Riquem—*Zerend*—sighed, lifting his arms in a shrug. "It

was highly illegal magic, of course, punishable by death. But I was already dying, and I feared the end. I'm not embarrassed to admit it. You're young yet, but you'll understand one day what it is to look oblivion in the eye."

Melanie knew the feeling better than he realized. She watched this stranger-within-a-stranger warily, his fluid movements and friendly air.

Oh, no. A cold certainly crept over her, subtle and slow as frost.

"I gathered my most trustworthy spellwrights and set them on a new project," Zerend continued. "A secret project. At first, the work had been centered around transferring my consciousness into a form that would never age or wither. Into a gearling. But as we grew closer to a breakthrough, I realized something."

Zerend glanced down at his hands. The palms were smooth and unblemished. "I would never be happy living inside a mechanical shell. I wanted *life,* not just consciousness. So, I changed the trajectory of the work."

"Riquem," Melanie breathed. "The real Riquem. *That* was Traveler. You took his body. And he . . ."

The imposter grimaced, then nodded. "He was my confidant. My friend. I'd always admired him. But more than that, he was hale and cheerful, with a quick grasp of magic. I had my enclave perform the spell, but with a tweak. We . . . lied to him. Betrayed him. Riquem loved me, you see. He never admitted it, of course, but it was perhaps the worst-kept secret in the empire. And it made him easy to manipulate. I lured him to the laboratory, where we quickly disarmed him and extracted him from his body. Then we replaced his consciousness with mine."

Zerend's gaze rose again, and Melanie detected something like sadness in the man's expression.

You loved him too, she thought. *You loved him too, and yet you did that to him.*

He ambled slowly toward the door. "The process went off without a hitch. Then, while the aldermages were cleaning up, I set off the explosion. With time, even trusted allies can become liabilities, you see. Doubtless they would have wanted immortality themselves. The blast destroyed all evidence of the ritual. All except your 'Traveler,' I suppose. Somehow after we'd removed Riquem from his body, a part of him found its way into the gearling, just as I was meant to. Even the most meticulously studied magics occasionally evade our understanding."

The aldermage opened the door and stepped through. "You're a clever girl . . ." Then he turned, frowning at Melanie. "But you aren't really a girl at all, are you? Yes, I've figured that out too. You're a bit of Ein's power, free for the taking. And once I have it, I can begin hunting *all* the Ley Coven down."

Melanie leaped up from the floor with a scream, lunging toward the aldermage. Zerend took a single step to the side and a gearling slid into the doorframe.

It stood between Melanie and Zerend, its red motes burning.

"Meet your chaperone," Zerend said, peering around the

automaton. "You'll be confined to this room for the time being, while I work out the details of how to transfer your connection to the ley to me."

"I don't *have* one!" Melanie pleaded. "Ein did, but I'm not her."

Zerend smiled and shook his head. "You can't feel it because the room is thaumaturgically sealed. Magic won't function within, not even your tremendous gifts. But whatever you did that drained the Hexe's power over the Zwarte Woud, it gave *you* its seed."

With a start, Melanie recalled the dreamy table—and tipping the contents of an impossible supper toward her mouth. Another brash decision, made in panic. For a brief moment, she'd become the lock-eater she always feared, and look what had resulted.

"You're the ley's newest vessel," Zerend said. "One that I need emptied. I *will* have it, Melanie."

The wizard turned his back on her, disappearing into the hall while the gearling gently closed the door.

The last thing she heard was Riquem's voice calling back, "Enjoy the view! The docks are lovely this time of morning."

CHAPTER 30

MELANIE paced the small bedroom for the rest of the day.

She thought about Traveler and Riquem, and wondered if the gearling would have been glad to know his origins. Melanie's had brought her no joy.

She thought of the girls at Merrytrails, who were heart-breakingly close—just across the city!—and wondered if they had any idea she was watching *them* from the castle.

She thought of Livia, and wondered if the clever, funny shopgirl would spare a thought from time to time for "Lady Porta" and her enchanted needles. Would Hamlen keep making gryphons even after Parno's death? It seemed likely. Would some other aldermage take up the responsibility of the aerie? Did Princess-Electa Maximillia hate Melanie for destroying her beautiful chateau? Would the grouille continue to protect Hagalaz, even if Zerend wrestled control over the ley?

She thought: *Open.* She thought this word many times, in many different ways. She even tried reaching out with her senses, finding her way back to the Ley Coven and their otherworldly table.

It never made a difference. The room was a prison even she couldn't escape.

That was all that happened on that day, however.

CHAPTER 31

WELL, perhaps one more thing.

As the wind turned outside, and Melanie paced inside, the storm over Crossport grew fiercer—rattling even the thick castle windows. It was almost dusk, though Melanie couldn't tell how she knew. The sky had been dark all day, and there wasn't a single clock present in the room.

Fingers of lightning jabbed at the air, as if hoping to dig something from the clouds. With every flash, the cracks grew faster and louder—the thunder rolling closer.

Finally, unnerved by the storm's intensity, Melanie decided to close the curtains. She padded to the window and drew them shut. The sheer cloth billowed prettily.

A blinding flare illuminated the fabric as lightning struck close by. Not even a moment passed before the thunder followed, rattling the whole room. Melanie took a step back from the curtain, her mouth agape.

She shook her head. Impossible.

For a moment, it had looked like a figure floated behind the curtain—the shape of a boy, sketched in lightning.

Melanie's hand shook as she lifted it to the curtain. She tried not to hope. She begged herself not to hope.

She threw open the fabric.

There, floating in midair, was Blitz. He looked like a human again—a drenched boy somehow riding the storm like a kite.

Blitz took one look at her and his face split into a wide smile. Melanie slapped her hands over her mouth, just capturing a sob before it escaped. The spirit pressed his hand against the window and began talking. Though his lips moved with their usual enthusiasm, Melanie could barely hear him. Between the storm and the thick glass, his voice was too muffled.

Melanie shook her head. "I can't hear you!" she mouthed.

Blitz rolled his eyes in frustration. He reached into his pocket and pulled out a yellow stone, holding it before the glass. Melanie squinted. She recognized it.

Traveler. Ein had pried the crystal from the gearling's chest when she destroyed him. Melanie could just make out the thread of crimson suspended within, like a ribbon of blood.

Melanie searched for a way to open the window. There was nothing she could see—no latch or handle. And even if there had been one, she wasn't sure what a room sealed against magic might do to a living spell.

She pressed her hands to the glass in a circle, then placed her mouth inside her palms.

"Merrytrails Orphanage!" she shouted as loudly as she dared. "Go to Merrytrails! Give my love to Abraxas!" It was a desperate ploy, but it was all she had. Mrs. Harbargain had told Melanie to use the secret phrase if she was in trouble. If Blitz told Harbargain where Melanie was, and he knew the phrase, then perhaps . . . ?

The spirit made a confused face. Was it because of the odd message, or because he hadn't heard her?

"Go to Merrytrails and give my love to Abraxas!" she shouted again into the glass.

The door slammed open behind her. Melanie wheeled around to find the gearling guard watching with its bright red eyes.

"This one warns Melanie Gate not to make a commotion," it said. "The operator has instructed this one to punish you, should you misbehave."

Melanie nodded, her back pressed against the window. "S-sorry," she said. "I'll be good."

"Have a pleasant evening," the gearling said. It closed the door.

Melanie swallowed, then she turned slowly back around, glancing toward the glass.

Outside, only the storm gazed back.

CHAPTER 32

MIDNIGHT came and went.

Melanie slept fitfully. She ate only crumbs. The storm abated and the sky cleared. An uneventful night was followed by an extremely eventful morning, but in order to understand how that story unfolds, a brief interlude is needed. We must pull away from Melanie and her pillowy prison.

Past the gearling sentry, staring blankly forward with its crimson eyes.

Past Zerend the Red, who lived on in his assistant's body, as he pushed a quill to paper. He was working on the mystery of how to transfer a magical bequest from one person to another. He thought he was close. It wasn't so different from removing a soul from a body, after all.

Though it would certainly kill Melanie Gate.

We move through the upper floors of a red-roofed tower full of aldermages, each busy in their research. None knew of Zerend's true identity, or his true plan—to take control of the ley and build an army of gearlings and spirits answerable only to himself. Once he'd done that, he would storm Ultrest and the

Donjon with these twin forces, deposing both the monarchy and the prime minister in one swoop.

Soon, the thaumacracy's flag would bear only a single eye.

We breeze through the lower floors of the castle. Past bustling servants and haughty aldermages. Through echoing hallways full of stately paintings.

And finally, out the front doors, where two guards stood, facing a small squad of orphans, a shopgirl and an innkeeper, and their frazzled matron.

"Th-there must be some mistake!" Mrs. Harbargain protested. "We were told to arrive promptly this morning for our . . . well, for our *tour!* The girls were absolutely beside themselves with excitement."

"I've always wanted to see the castle!" Agatha chimed in, adding a touch of flair to Harbargain's shaky performance. Jane nodded her agreement.

"Oh, me *too!*" Livia agreed, taking each girl's arm. "I wonder if the High Enchanter is inside."

The first guard looked to the second. They were the same men who had let a young witch and her stolen gearling through the South Gate, and they were not inclined to draw the anger of the High Enchanter again for neglecting procedure.

"You hear anything about this?" the first guard asked.

"Not a peep," said the second.

"I'm sorry, madam, but who did you say you spoke with?"

"Felidae Seagreen. The enchantress."

In her panic, Mrs. Harbargain blurted the first name that

came to mind—the one the gearling had used to steal Melanie away from Merrytrails. She barely understood what she was doing here, risking herself and the children. Not to mention Abraxas, who was stuffed unhappily into the picnic basket she now clutched to her.

Once Riquem had returned the girls to Merrytrails under gearling sentry, he disappeared with Melanie, offering no explanation about what would happen to her . . . or how to return the Hamleners to their homes. The children were devastated, and Harbargain had been sick with worry. She'd never felt so powerless to protect one of her girls. She'd written petitions to the king and prime minister, and even several to that horrid High Enchanter himself, begging for leniency on Melanie's behalf. She'd also sent letters along to Hamlen, alerting Livia's and Katzy's parents to the girls' whereabouts.

Then, a strange boy had arrived during the previous night's storm—yet another mysterious midnight visitor. And he told the most incredible story.

When little Mariana announced that there was a boy at the window—no, *not* the door but the upstairs window, precisely where Melanie had let Abraxas out just a month ago—none of the girls believed her.

"Boys arrive through the front door, sweetheart," Mrs. Harbargain had told her. "At least in *this* house they will."

"Is he on a ladder?" Baruti asked, looking up from her book on grouille history. "Out in the storm?"

Little Mariana shook her head, her hair fluttering. "Not a ladder," she said. "He's FLYING!"

Katzy purred with laughter. She was assembling an old puzzle of the girls' on the dining room table, her tail flicking with concentration. "Foundling prodigies and flying boys," she muttered. "Seems this orphanage is full of fibbing kittens."

Mariana huffed and crossed her arms. She decided *not* to tell the kassipoi about the puzzle's three missing pieces.

Livia glanced over from the window, where she was in the process of anxiously darning every frayed or threadbare piece of fabric she could get her hands on. Shirts, socks, and nightgowns lay all around her, their holes patched in wild, mismatched colors.

Livia had grown especially somber since the horrors in the Zwarte Woud and Melanie's arrest; she no longer peppered the foundlings with questions about their friend. Jane found she missed the flurry. The other girls' funny and fervent memories had kept her feeling close to Melanie.

Jane sat with Livia now, marveling at the enchanted needles that worked their way through cloth as naturally as worms through soil. Apparently, the needles had been a gift from "Lady Porta." Livia seemed to treasure them.

The tailor was adamant that Melanie had enchanted the needles herself. Whatever had happened on her journeys—

whatever the rogue gearling, "Traveler," had been to her—it was clear that Melanie had picked up a few tricks along the way. The girl that Jane had found in that strange, enchanted glade was deeply changed.

And in deep trouble.

Jane had no doubt that Riquem's plans for her friend were dire. Mrs. Harbargain could write all the letters she liked; if they didn't *do* something, she was sure they'd never hear from Melanie again.

"Is it possible you saw something that only *looked* like a boy?" Livia asked Mariana, glancing up from her work. She pulled a needle out from the corner of a homespun blanket, careful of its wriggling point. "Sometimes, if it's dark and stormy, I imagine the mannequins in my family's shop move when I turn my head. I'm still half convinced they talk about me behind my back."

Mariana rolled her eyes. "I *know* the difference between real and pretend," she said. "It was a *flying boy*."

"Boys don't fly," Agatha muttered from her upside-down position on the sofa. Though her feet were pointed up in the air and her head toward the floor, Mrs. Harbargain apparently didn't have the energy to reprimand her.

But when Sun-mi shrieked in surprise from the upstairs hallway shortly after, the girls all scrambled up to find the hall window wide open, and Sun-mi tending to a drenched and exhausted-looking boy on the landing.

Blitz, as the boy introduced himself, looked like the storm itself had carried him there. He said he was a friend of Melanie's, and that he knew where Riquem had trapped her. And Blitz had even known the secret phrase—the one Harbargain had told only Melanie, to use in case she needed help.

"She says . . ." he panted, "to give her loaf to a brass axe."

Well, it was close enough.

Blitz confirmed that Melanie was in trouble—*big* trouble. Somehow the red wizards had caged the girl who couldn't be caged.

"But what can we do?" Sun-mi said, wrapping a blanket around the boy. "We're foundlings! We don't have spells or gearlings. We can't magically open doors."

"Yes, we can."

The foundlings and Mrs. Harbargain all turned to regard Jane, who was standing at the end of the hall.

"Jane? What do you mean, sweetheart?" Harbargain said.

And so she told them what she meant.

Together with her friends, Jane spent the night concocting an irrational, unbelievable, completely absurd plan to rescue one girl from the grip of the most powerful wizard in the thaumacracy.

Which brought them to this moment.

The two guards looked at each other again.

"Seagreen, Seagreen . . . Does that name sound familiar to you?" the second asked the first.

The first guard pressed a finger to his lips. "Now that you mention it . . ." He shrugged. "Nope."

"Sorry, madam. But no one gets in without a formal-like invite."

Beside Mrs. Harbargain, little Mariana Porch began to cry. She wrapped her arms around the woman's leg, her large black eyes flooding with tears.

"There, there, sweetheart," Harbargain said softly. "It will be all right. Palaces aren't for foundlings, I suppose. I'm sorry I got your hopes up."

The second guard grimaced, taking in the weeping orphan.

"Foundlings, you said?"

"That's right," Harbargain replied with a resigned sigh. "On our very first trip to the castle. What a treat it would have been for these girls, who've made do with so little all their lives. But it can't be helped. Best they understand the world will always be cruel to the likes of them."

"This Seagreen lady. She said she'd meet you inside?"

Harbargain nodded. "She's arrived fairly recently. A noble witch from . . . elsewhere. I suppose she didn't know the proper procedure for visitors. Formal paperwork can be such a bother."

The guard groaned. He turned and pulled the door open. "Oh, hurry up, then," he muttered.

One by one, the girls filed inside. Mariana gave the guard a big, long hug as she did. They were followed by a single boy, strangely dressed, like some wandering hunter. When Mrs. Harbargain had finally made her way in amid a profusion of thank-yous and bless-yous, the guard closed the door and stood at attention once more.

"You're a sap, you know that?" the first one said to him.

"I'm a foundling, is what I am," the second replied.

Jane, Mrs. Harbargain, and the others ascended the castle floor by floor, taking one obstacle at a time, just as they'd planned. Here, Harbargain played the part of tour guide, instructing the girls about the palace and its history—all of it completely made up.

"And this, girls, is where Lord Sassafras wrote his famous ode to his love, Lady Marmalade."

The foundlings all *Oooh*'d and *Ahhh*'d theatrically, Baruti diligently scribbling the nonsense into her notebook.

When confronted by the palace servants, Sun-mi Church-yard presented them with her homemade dumplings, garnished with a sprinkle of cricket legs. The staff were so pleased by the savory treats, they waved the foundlings on.

It was Jane herself who determined how to handle the palace's absent-minded aldermages . . . by walking right past them. She found that when grown-ups were busy with their own preoccupations, sometimes the easiest way past them was just to leave them be.

Finding a disused door that unlocked from her side, she opened a passage for the rest of the girls to enter through—completely bypassing the wizards' offices.

Katzy's keen senses alerted the group to Adrianus, now

freshly returned from Hamlen. She stalked the apprentice through the palace halls with feline grace, Livia following just behind. The Hamleners prepared to bind and gag the boy with a skein of yarn Mrs. Harbargain had lent Livia. Then they'd stuff him into whatever supply closet was handy—preferably a cramped one.

That *was* the plan, until the boy had suddenly snapped around.

"I know you're there," he said, glaring at the Hamleners. Katzy froze mid-crouch, while Livia brandished a knitting needle like a dagger.

"I never liked you," Katzy said with a swish of her tail.

"I never cared if you did," Adrianus scoffed, though his tan cheeks pinked a little. "You're here for that *girl*, aren't you? Lady Porta? Riquem says the top floor is off limits, but my new mentor saw him take her to the containment suite. He won't tell anyone where he's been or what happened to Parno."

The boy stepped forward and the girls flinched. Livia raised her needle higher.

"Stay back!" she hissed, just as he said, "Let me help you."

Both Hamleners stared in surprise.

"Help us?" Katzy finally asked. Her vertical pupils narrowed suspiciously. "Why?"

"I owe her," the boy muttered. "*Yes*, I know what you think of me. You've made that perfectly clear. But Lady Porta saved me from . . ." Adrianus swallowed. "From whatever punishment

Parno had in mind. My new mentor, Saanvi, is an idealistic fool, but at least she's not a sadist. If I help Lady Porta now, we can call it even."

Katzy remained skeptical. She didn't take her eyes off the boy, and kept her posture tight, ready to pounce.

But Livia's face softened. She glanced back down the hall, to where six foundlings, their matron, and a strange forest boy peeked around the corner.

"How can you help?" she asked, turning back.

"The containment suite muffles all kinds of spellwork, but there's a way to dispel the antimagic wards. If you do, Lady Porta can use her magic again. I'll tell you how, then my mentor and I will clear out the lower floors so you can escape. We'll say there was a thaumaturgical accident."

"You're sure she'd aid us?"

Adrianus nodded impatiently. "Saanvi *hates* Riquem. Or she does now, anyway. I guess they used to be close, but Riquem changed after Zerend died. He demoted her and the other reformers who'd objected to the war against the Ley Coven— all his former friends." The boy shrugged. "Whatever Riquem plans for Lady Porta, it isn't good. Trust me, you'll need my help. And I promise I will give it."

"I *still* don't like the aldermage kitten," Katzy said. Her fur bristled with disdain. "But I believe what he says."

Livia chewed her lip. She shook her head and lowered the needle. "Fine," she said. "Tell us how to stop the wards. But if you're lying, Adrianus, just know that we'll find you—and any punishment of Parno's will seem like a Night of Gold gift in comparison."

When they reached the topmost floor, Baruti Harbor discovered how to open the lock to the tower. It was a complicated mechanical thing with four spinning dials instead of keyholes—each dial featuring a column of ten numbers, zero through nine. Only a single combination would spring the lock, and Baruti calculated that there were 9,999 different combinations available.

The correct combination was 1-2-3-4.

And Agatha Chickencoop, the steely actress, walked right up to the door of Zerend's office.

Wizard and girl both stared at each other for a tick, confusion knotting Zerend's stolen face.

"What—?" he said.

"I've reconsidered," Agatha informed him. "Your gauntlet is tacky."

"Stop right there!" Zerend exploded up from his desk just as the girl turned around, bolting in the direction she'd come from. He was out in a moment, but was shocked to see the shadow of a child already bounding down the tower stairs. How had she moved so quickly?

And why was his hair standing on end?

He took off after the intruder, screaming for the gearlings to apprehend her as he went.

When he was gone, a bulging tapestry on the far wall began to writhe. One by one, Mrs. Harbargain, the foundlings, and the Hamleners scurried out from behind the heavy weave,

Agatha appearing last. Livia snatched a set of keys from the High Enchanter's desk, while Helen Stables covertly pocketed a handsome horse statuette from one of the bookshelves. They pressed on, determined not to waste the head start Blitz had given them.

Which brings us back to Melanie.

She was lying on the carpet again, staring up at the ceiling and very much *not* imagining that her friends were currently storming the palace to rescue her, when she heard a commotion outside. Voices were raised in alarm—voices she recognized.

"This one demands you halt!" The gearling's metallic voice echoed through the heavy door.

"*Maow!*"

"Abraxas, no!" Mrs. Harbargain wailed.

Melanie leaped to her feet, rushing to the door. "Mrs. Harbargain?" she called. "Mrs. Harbargain!" Melanie began pounding against the wood. "Let me out!"

She heard a frantic jingle of keys, then the familiar sound of a lock turning. Only this time, someone else was doing the unlocking.

The door swung open, and Melanie stood face-to-face with Livia. The girl wasn't wearing her usual lively patterns. In fact, Melanie recognized the simple dress as Baruti's. But the sight of her still managed to stupefy Melanie, just as it had the morning of their first meeting.

Melanie's mouth fell open. "You . . ." she said thickly. "You're not . . ."

"I think the cat may be in trouble," Livia said, pointing down the hall.

Melanie turned to see her gearling sentry several yards down the corridor, swiping at a blur of gray as it clawed its way across the automaton's back. Farther down, Mrs. Harbargain and the other girls from Merrytrails were all shouting.

"Oh! The ward!" Livia turned to a portrait at the end of the hall, of a stately woman waving the thaumacracy's three-eyed flag triumphantly. Livia lifted an enormous needle (had she been *knitting* on the way here?) and stabbed it into the flag's bright red eye.

The world shifted. A rush of *something* sent Melanie sprawling to her knees. The hallway dilated, then exploded into streams of light and color. Ahead, she saw Abraxas illuminate like a toverlicht, a core of light igniting within the cat.

That brilliant core extended down as a lustrous thread— through the castle, through the city and the stone beneath it—until it connected to . . .

Ah, something that was not quite a voice but very like one whispered in her ear. *There you are, young Hexe of the South. Welcome to the Ley Coven.*

Melanie glanced down at her own chest. A core burned within her too, though several times as brightly as Abraxas. It connected her to the same immense *thing* she'd felt when she touched the Lotus Gate's lock—a presence so colossal as to be unfathomable. She sensed it shift, and a ponderous gaze fell upon her. She was so miniscule beneath its scrutiny.

The ley.

Traveler had once said it was alive, or something close to it. But he couldn't have known . . . . It seemed almost to be many lives, many minds, all working in tandem.

And then, for just a moment, Melanie was somewhere else.

She sat at a large wooden table with eight place settings, one made up just for her. Melanie was dimly aware of other figures at the table, eyes that were far away, yet also deceptively close. The diners were made of mist, and they watched Melanie from the north, east, and west, northeast and northwest, southeast and southwest.

All were there to greet their newest member.

The bowl in front of Melanie no longer contained a dense knot of vegetation. That, Melanie knew, was long gone. But in its place, a single sproutling twisted upward, spring green and covered in dew. A purple-blue flower glistened atop the sprig, barely more than a bud. Melanie didn't have to guess at the blossom.

Periwinkle, she thought sadly.

So noisy in this city, the voice that was not a voice said. *Come back to the forest. We'll speak more. There's work to do.*

My friends, Melanie told the voice. *I have to help them.*

Then help them, the ley replied.

You aren't angry with me? It's my fault that Ein is dead. Her glade was destroyed because of me.

Could the ley laugh? It seemed to. Melanie knew so little of what it actually was.

All things are destroyed in time, it said without saying. *And the new grows over the old. Ein made her choices and you will make yours, each according to your natures. I won't define you, Hexe of the South. Even that name is yours to set aside. I just ask that you don't hate your predecessor too much. She was very tangled . . . and very lonely.*

Or do, it added. *That too is your choice. But it's still too noisy here. Good-bye now, Melanie Gate.*

"Melanie!" Livia's voice blared in her ear. "Melanie! Are you all right?"

Then, suddenly, she was back in the castle hallway. The misty watchers had vanished, along with the presence of the ley. As its influence waned, the colors dimmed, and the shimmering lights went with it.

Melanie discovered she'd fallen to the floor. Livia kneeled beside her, her eyes wide with concern. Melanie saw the gearling advancing upon her friends. Its livid red eyes glowed balefully. Abraxas clawed futilely at its mask.

Melanie leaped to her feet, stepping behind the gearling. She pressed her palm against the back of its armored chassis.

The gearling swiveled its head with an audible whir, just as she thought at it, *Open.*

All the complicated machinery that made up the automaton's body suddenly unfastened, and the gearling's head fell backward. Its chest split along a hidden seam, the panes of armor sliding apart. Steam billowed out from within as the gearling's inner workings presented themselves.

The girls stopped screaming, but they still looked terrified. Melanie peeked from behind the exploded clockwork figure.

"You came," she said to Jane.

"No magic could keep me away," her friend confirmed. Melanie burst forward, wrapping her arms around the girl, who pulled her into a ferocious hug of her own. Then all the girls swept in, hooking their arms together, and were enveloped by Mrs. Harbargain in a bone-cracking embrace.

For the first time in days, Melanie felt safe.

Jane pulled away, wiping a tear from her eye. "Your friend Blitz is keeping Riquem busy. We should hurry, but he said to give this to you right away. He said . . . he said 'Traveler is still inside.' Do you know what that means?"

Jane pressed something hard and cold into Melanie's hand. She looked down to find a yellow stone resting in her palm, with a crimson cordon at its center.

"Still . . . inside?"

Slowly, Melanie turned, facing the disassembled gearling. Fastened in the automaton's exposed chest was a second yellow crystal, identical to the one Melanie held.

Except this stone was empty. No ribbon of red swam within.

Melanie took a tentative step forward. Then another. Her hand trembled as she carefully removed the yellow crystal from the sentry's chest. Then she replaced it with Traveler's, the stone sliding easily into place.

But the gearling remained inert.

Disappointment lanced through her. It hadn't worked. Why hadn't it worked? She took the crystal out, readjusted it. Nothing.

Melanie slammed her hand against the gearling's chassis.

"Come back!" she said, her voice thick with emotion. "Please . . ."

It wasn't fair. Blitz had said Traveler was still in there, but how did she reach him? Was he trapped somehow? Melanie pressed her hand to the gearling's chest.

Open, she thought. *Open now!*

But if Traveler truly was inside, he was beyond her reach. Melanie pressed her forehead to the metal breastplate.

Jane gently touched her shoulder, wrapping her arm around Melanie. Melanie leaned into her friend, thankful to have her near again, to share the burden of this heartache. Though Jane hadn't known Traveler, she knew Melanie. They were family, and family bolstered one another when their loads became too much.

Even submerged in her sorrow, Melanie was buoyed by gratitude. These people had risked everything for her. What a difference it might have made to have them with her on her journey.

Is that all you want? the gearling had asked her once. *Adventure?*

Is there something bigger for you? The want beneath the want?

Melanie hadn't known how to answer him then, but she did

now. She wished she could tell Traveler that freedom was nothing without ties. Without family. Ein's isolation had twisted and embittered her, but Melanie had been lucky. She'd *had* a family her whole life—Jane and Mrs. Harbargain and the others. And Traveler too. She'd been *surrounded* by love.

If you ever figure it out, you let me know. I'll do everything in my power to help you get it.

"I know now," she whispered to the metal. A hot tear seared her cheek.

And what's the final *ingredient?*

"Please," Melanie said, grasping at her new connection to the ley. She took the gearling's hand in hers, pouring as much love as she could into the wish. *"Open."*

And it did.

CHAPTER 33

THE walls of the palace seemed to blast away, careening into oblivion. Before she knew what was happening, Melanie found herself tumbling through a milky sky filled with endless twinkling stars.

It felt like she was floating through the pocket dimension Traveler had conjured for Parno, only this time Melanie was making the voyage alone. Jane and Livia and the others, even the unlocked gearling, had all disappeared, replaced by an empty skyscape.

"*Hello?*" she cried out into the void. "Is anyone there?" But with nothing to absorb them, the words simply sailed away. Melanie floated too, aimless in the expanse. She felt the familiar dread of loneliness creep in. The cold and smothering dark between the stars swelled.

She took a deep breath. Melanie let the feeling run through her. She let herself feel it without fear or fervor—and then, when she was ready, she let it go.

She wasn't alone. This wasn't even real. Her friends were still with her. They'd come to save her. This illusion of isolation wasn't hers at all—it was *his*.

"I'm here," she said. "Traveler? I'm here!"

Slowly, the cosmos shifted.

All around her, the sparkling motes brightened and grew, the stars' edges opening like windows. And inside each porthole there waited a moment, little scenes of life that were dazzling in their intensity.

In some, Melanie caught glimpses of her Traveler, the gentle automaton she'd come to cherish. But in others there swam a stranger. A trim man in a red vest appeared again and again, going about a life that was utterly new to her. It was Riquem—the real Riquem.

Here he was as a boy in a uniform very much like Adrianus's. Beside him, another boy just a year or so older was also clad in apprentice's garb. The two were attempting some kind of spell, but it blew up in their faces, painting them both in bright purple goo. The boys collapsed together in a fit of laughter.

In another memory, the boy Riquem, now a young man, watched as his friend accepted a gauntlet of office. He'd just been selected as the new High Enchanter, and it seemed like Riquem's chest might burst with pride for Zerend the Red.

A thousand voices crashed together, a jumble of memories that were not Melanie's own—drowning out her thoughts. The memories' brightness flared, overwhelming her. She shut her eyes against the blinding light.

And then, just as suddenly as they'd risen, the voices went silent. Melanie opened her eyes.

She stood in a long hallway lined with closed doors.

Impossibly high white ceilings stretched to brocaded walls that wound and wove their way to glistening floorboards. It was the Crossport palace, but exaggerated to impossible scale. For such a grand space, the room was totally empty. All except for Melanie and . . .

"Oh!" a voice called out in surprise, echoing in the surreal hall. "Hello there!"

Melanie gaped.

Riquem stood before her. She wasn't sure how she knew, but this was not the same man who'd trapped her in the palace. He had the same unassuming air, the same sheepish smile, but this Riquem wore no glittering gauntlet. And he looked a bit confused, his expression vague but friendly.

"Are you lost too?" he said. "I can't seem to find my way out. None of the doors will open. I'm Riquem."

Melanie nodded slowly. This shade, or memory, or whatever-he-was of Riquem didn't seem to recognize her. "Melanie . . ." she said. "I'm Melanie Gate."

"Melanie." Riquem smiled, his eyes growing distant. "How funny. I've always liked that name." He looked around. "You're the first person I've seen in . . . well, I'm not really *sure* how long. Do you know a way out of here?"

Melanie glanced toward the nearest doorway. She remembered something Traveler had once said, of his memory being like a wide chamber filled with closed doors. Was he somewhere inside here too?

"Probably," she said. "I mean, yes. We could go together, if you like, but . . . I don't know exactly what's beyond here."

Riquem grinned at her, his expression befuddled. "You seem like a good person, Melanie. I trust you."

Melanie took a deep breath. She walked to the nearby door, her footsteps clicking in the empty hall. She pressed her palm against the wood and thought gently, *Open*.

With a soft creak, the door swung inward.

Melanie turned, extended her hand. "You can still go alone if you want," she said. "You're . . . you're not a prisoner here. You get a choice."

The wizard gazed at the now-open door apprehensively. His eyes were wide. "You know . . ." He swallowed. "I can't say why, but I have this feeling it may be important for us to go together. Isn't that strange? Have we met before?"

Melanie smiled sadly. "Maybe once."

Riquem stepped toward her and accepted her waiting palm. They walked through, hand in hand.

They arrived in a room not so different from the one where Zerend had imprisoned her—though a good deal smaller. Melanie could smell the salt on the sea air as it wafted through the room's open windows.

Another Riquem, years younger, sat at a large escritoire desk, absently picking at a spell. Beside him, a complicated piece of machinery was pointed toward the sky. A telescope, Melanie realized. This younger Riquem turned to it, stooping toward the eyepiece, then pulled back and adjusted the spell. An illusion of a purple-blue orb spun lazily between his fingers.

Suddenly his face shot up, his eyes lancing toward Melanie and the older Riquem beside her.

Melanie gasped. She stepped back in surprise, but the Riquem beside her gave her hand a reassuring squeeze.

This was a moment that had already come to pass. They were merely invisible witnesses. This memory of Riquem wasn't looking *at* them—he was gazing past them, toward . . .

His hand lashed out and a bubble appeared in the room's far windowsill, trapping a small fluttering shape inside. Melanie recognized the spell—it was the same transparent barrier Traveler had used to shield her from the rain their first night outside the city.

She turned, studying the imprisoned creature. A tiny yellow bird blinked its black eyes in alarm.

No . . . in a moment the avian shape had melted away, transforming into a butterfly. Then the butterfly shivered, and its wings brightened and blurred, until it too was replaced by a mote of sunlight. The beam stretched and hardened, becoming a long, white rat.

"What is it?" Melanie whispered in awe.

"I . . ." The Riquem beside her swallowed. For some reason, he wouldn't meet her eyes.

The memory of Riquem stood from his desk, leaving the telescope behind. He cautiously approached the bubble. All the while, the shape inside kept changing, fighting against the barrier. It was a spider, a serpent, a toverlicht. It was a pixie, an alligator, a wasp.

You were a formless spirit then. Ein's voice cut through her memory, sour as rot on the warm sea air. *Able to take whatever shape you chose. Never staying in one for long.*

"No." Melanie exhaled the word, pushing it from her lungs. She shook her head. "No, it can't be."

All until the day that Riquem caught you.

"Are you . . . a ley spirit?" the memory of Riquem asked the shifting creature. "I've never seen one in person. Oh, it was very foolish of you to come here, little one."

Muffled voices rose outside the door. A deep baritone bellowed from the hallway. "Riquem! You're needed in the laboratory!"

Riquem winced. "*Very* foolish," he muttered. "If Zerend finds you here, he'll . . ."

The man grimaced. But as he gazed at the tiny sparrow beating against its prison, watched it change into a bright green lizard before his eyes, Riquem's face softened.

"Sleep now," he said, passing his hand over the bubble. Inside, the spirit melted into a hedgehog, which curled into a ball. For the first time since Melanie had laid eyes on it, it was utterly still.

Riquem guided the bubble into his wardrobe, burying it behind the cloaks and coats within. And as he closed it, the door to the room burst open.

Zerend the Red stepped inside, wearing the ornate gauntlet that marked him as High Enchanter. Now a full-grown adult, he was tall and broad, with a dark, trim beard that made his frown all the more severe. But there was also a wanness to his face that deepened every cleft and shadow. Melanie remembered Zerend mention he was ill when he took Riquem's body. Dying, even. Was this the first sign of his ailment?

"Didn't you hear me?" Zerend asked, his tone clipped. "I said I need you, Riq. The project is almost . . ." The High Enchanter glanced toward Riquem's desk, where the purple-blue globe still hovered gently beside the telescope.

"Not this again," he said with a sigh. He brought his hand up, pinching the bridge of his nose. "Enough with the romantic pet projects. I need your focus *here*, Riquem, on *this* world. Not out in the cosmos, seeking planes you'll never visit."

"I might someday," Riquem said defensively. He moved to the desk, covering the slowly rotating spell under a glass bell jar.

Only now did Melanie recognize it. It was the very world Traveler had taken her and Parno to during their illusory jaunt through the stars, but rendered in miniature. A strange place full of marvelous alien life.

"The magic isn't there yet," he said. "But it could be someday. Perhaps if we focused less on defense, and more on exploratory pursuits . . . Don't you ever want to see what's beyond the thaumacracy?"

Zerend narrowed his eyes. "We *are* the thaumacracy. Wherever we go, we bring it with us. There is no *beyond*. And we have too many enemies to stretch ourselves thin with sentimental diversions."

Riquem sighed, leaning back against the desk. "Perhaps seeing enemies everywhere is what creates them."

"And perhaps pretending they *don't* exist—or won't—is exactly what allows them to win." The man turned and stepped through the door, casting one last look behind him. "The laboratory, Riq—*five* minutes."

As he left, Riquem gazed nervously toward the wardrobe.

The vision shifted, darkness blotting the cheery sunlight pouring through the windows. Night fell, and the walls of the palace fell with it; a long stone road slithered into the distance like a gray serpent.

Melanie and Riquem stood side by side, watching as a cloaked wizard approached the South Gate from that road. In his hands was a tiny sleeping hedgehog, still curled into a ball. The younger Riquem glanced down the Wonderstraat, making sure there were no errant travelers approaching.

He set the hedgehog down on a tuft of grass.

"It's not a perfect plan," he said to the spirit. "But it's a chance. Forgive me, little one, but I can't have you returning home to your mistress."

Riquem held his hands over the hedgehog and began to cast. The spirit yawned and stretched, and its shape changed. Pale fur yielded to smooth pink skin. Its legs and arms elongated, and locks of chestnut curls burst from its head. In a moment, a young toddler stood before the wizard, clothed in a peasant dress and blinking curiously at him.

It was Melanie. Her curls bounced. Her bright, curious eyes were the same ones she saw in the mirror every morning. And it was Ein too. A younger version, yes, but Melanie could clearly see the resemblance now.

The memory of Riquem gave an astonished laugh. "I wasn't

totally sure that would work," he said. "Transmutation can be tricky magic, but you helped me, didn't you? By choosing this form yourself. It's very cute." He squatted low, eye level with her. "Now, let's set the mold." He tapped the girl on her nose. She giggled, and a light flared from the tip, spreading over her face and hair and across her whole body. Then the radiance slowly faded, casting the road in darkness again.

"There. I'm sorry, little one, but you'll need to stay in this shape for a while longer. It's not all bad being human, though. You'll still change, just more slowly than you're used to. And you'll be freer in some ways than you were before. There's an orphanage in the city. They say the matron is very kind and will take good care of you. And I'll be nearby. Someday I'll check in on you, but for the moment it's probably safest if I don't. Ah, before I forget!"

Riquem pulled a small scrap of cloth from a pocket in his cloak. It was a scene of a town surrounded by tulips. Below the tableau were the words *Kinderbloom, the Garden Village*.

"It's not the Zwarte Woud," he said as he smiled down at the embroidered flowers, "but it's as close as I can point you. Someday, when you're older and want answers . . . Well, hopefully it will be in a better world." He pressed the cloth into the front pocket of the girl's dress. "Let's try our best to make it one, all right?"

The girl smiled up at him, reaching for his dangling earring.

Riquem sighed. He pulled a second item from his pocket, a hastily dashed note bequeathing the name *Melanie*. This too he tucked into the dress pocket.

"It was my mother's name," a metallic voice echoed beside her.

Melanie glanced up in surprise. The Riquem she'd been standing beside had disappeared, replaced by a gleaming gearling with two bright motes for eyes.

Traveler gazed at the scene before them.

"It was the only memento I felt comfortable leaving behind." Now the gearling turned to her, his glowing eyes wide with some indecipherable emotion. "Oh, Melanie . . ." he rasped. "I'm so sorry."

Melanie laughed and shook her head, wiping away a tear. "I forgive you," she said. "And I forgive him too."

"Blast!" the memory of Riquem cried. The South Gate had begun to swing shut. "No, no, no, no, no!"

He scrambled toward the door, hefting the toddler in his arms. But the ponderous hatches were already being pushed closed from the other side, the charge of their protective spells crackling in the night air. It was too late.

The toddler placed her hand against one of the doors. There was a shriek of metal and a loud POP; the shifting gate ground to a halt. Shouts of alarm rang out from the other side.

Riquem gazed down at the young Melanie with his mouth agape.

"Well!" he said softly. "It seems there's still a bit of spirit to you after all." He set the girl down beside the gate and backed away, his hands raised in a pacifying gesture. The toddler watched him go with a perplexed expression. The clamor within the city grew noisier.

"Be brave, Melanie!" the memory of Riquem whispered back to her. "I'll see you soon, in a better world!"

Then he melted into the shadows

And the vision melted with him.

Melanie opened her eyes with a gasp. Inside the gearling's chest, the stone that was Traveler radiated a warm, honeyed light. At its center, the ribbon of red billowed prettily, no longer frozen like a bug in amber.

All this time, it was Riquem who . . .

Who'd saved her. Who'd given her a life and a name. And a chance.

It was almost too much to bear. Melanie's heart felt like it might burst at the slightest strain, expelling all that love and loss. Her hand was still in the gearling's metal grip.

Now, she thought. *Close.*

Melanie had never tried to use her power to close things before. It simply hadn't occurred to her. But as soon as she thought the word, the automaton's clockwork began to click and clack. Gears swiveled in synchronized circles. The armored breastplate folded shut, and the gearling's head lifted.

Behind its mask, those two red motes blinked awake. After a moment, they paled to gentle white orbs.

"Melanie?"

Traveler glanced down at her. His eyes were tilted in confusion. "What happened? I had a . . . a *dream*. I was someone else. And you were there too."

Melanie burst into tears. She let them fall, flinging her arms around the gearling.

"You're awake," she said. "The world is right."

CHAPTER 34

TRAVELER'S glowing motes shifted as they moved, taking in the severe stone castle. The palace hallways were empty, and their footsteps echoed against the tiles. They walked in a line—foundlings, gearling, matron, and Hamleners—all pressed against the wall.

"I know this place," Traveler said. "I remember everything . . ."

"Oh, I have so much to tell you, though!" Melanie said. "Ein and the glade are gone. Zerend destroyed them, but before he did—"

"I really must insist that we be quiet," Mrs. Harbargain gently chided. "At least until we've made it out of the castle, but possibly until we've safely relocated to another kingdom."

"I can hide our escape," Traveler said. He glanced around a corner, then turned back to the others. "But we'll need to stay close together. Everyone take the hand of the person next to them."

The girls all did as asked, clasping their palms. Melanie took Jane's hand with her left, and Mrs. Harbargain's into her right. She heard Unicorn honk affectionately at the matron. The fabric stretched out to nuzzle her. Once Melanie had retrieved her cloak from the room, it came alive again, as if waking from a long sleep. Did the cloak recognize its former owner?

"Oh! Um, hello, there." Harbargain chuckled. "Good to see you again too. Now hush, dear. We're trying to be sneaky."

Traveler's eyes narrowed in concentration, the motes dimming.

"There's too many of us," the gearling said finally. "I'll need everyone's help. Think of a secret—something you've never told another living soul. Hold the secret fresh in your thoughts. Good, I can feel the magic moving. Now, I need you all to confess your secrets."

"*What?*" Melanie blurted.

"Secrets hold power, and divulging them releases that power. The sympathetic magic of revealing a hidden thing can then be rechanneled to hide *us*." The gearling glanced nervously down the hall. "I'll go first. I'm desperately jealous that I can't eat food. Taste and smell—I *remember* them. It breaks my heart that I'll never know that pleasure again." Traveler's glowing motes landed upon Melanie. "Now you."

Melanie balked. She didn't—! But she . . .

Only one secret stood fresh in her mind. She searched her thoughts for another less embarrassing confession, but Melanie knew this was the one that was needed. She could feel it.

"I have a crush on Livia," she blurted. Oh, lords and ladies, she'd said it. "I think . . . maybe . . . I like girls."

Several smiles slipped out among the foundlings, a cozy ring of recognition. Melanie's face burned. She felt the seamstress's eyes on her, though she kept her own gaze grimly forward.

"Well . . ." Livia cleared her throat. "This is awkward." The girl sighed. "I have the same secret. Should one of us change ours?"

Melanie's eyes shot up to where Livia was grinning at her, also blushing furiously.

"Oh, Melanie!" Mrs. Harbargain said as she pulled her into a hug. "How wonderful. You're growing up, my darling."

"I *know*," Melanie grumbled. But her face burned even brighter with embarrassment.

In the end, everyone made their confessions. Mrs. Harbargain loved dogs but she was allergic, so she'd settled on Abraxas. "I am so pleased with my choice, though!" she said, lifting the flap of the basket to reassure him. Abraxas turned sleepily in his carrier, presenting his rear end.

Mariana Porch envied Melanie for getting chosen to become a witch, while Baruti Harbor found the whole *concept* of magic somewhat ridiculous. Helen Stables had never met a horse before last week, and Katzy had snuck away for a nap after giving Lady Porta her list of chores. Sun-mi Churchyard pulled at her dress as she revealed her own crush on *Blitz*, the dashing stranger who'd arrived by night and smelled of forest rainstorms.

"I'm sorry for calling you lock-eater," Agatha told Melanie. She grimaced. "Even when I knew you didn't like it. The truth is, I *was* jealous. You had this amazing talent, something none of us could do. I knew that someday you'd get your adventure—and when you did, we'd be left behind."

Melanie was flabbergasted. Yet all the foundlings looked at one another with expressions that said much the same.

"The entire journey," Melanie began slowly, "Merrytrails was always in my thoughts. There were moments I wouldn't have *survived* without conjuring something from each of you." She shook her head. "I needed you all, more than I can say. You're my family, and no adventure is worth having if you're not with me."

Traveler nodded appreciatively. The air quavered between the gearling's hands. "It's working," he said. "The magic is reacting, but it's not quite there. Does anyone else have a secret? *Anything* they can spare?"

Jane Alley stepped forward.

"I do," she said, her voice resonating with a boldness that surprised the other girls. She took a deep breath. "Everyone thinks I'm shy, but I'm not. I'm quiet, but that's not the same. The world loves people who are loud and exciting and talk a lot. It believes quiet people like me won't make a mark. But I—I'm a troublemaker and a soothsayer. I'm wise and confident and thoughtful, and I see things others don't. That's the real me. I'm not going to change who I am, but I will let you in on a secret. Jane Alley is the name I was given. But it *isn't* my name. It's a cocoon. And I'm breaking free of it."

"I *like* this one," Katzy whispered.

Melanie's eyes were wide as she watched her best friend. She squeezed the hand of the person who was not Jane Alley, remembering all the times she'd supported Melanie in the same way.

"My name is Jae Jetblack. And I'm going to be a *magician*." She looked at Melanie. "A remarkable one."

Melanie nodded, her smile stretching into a grin. An idea was growing with it—a small caprice, but sharp and clear. It was the kind of idea Misty Steppe would approve of. Melanie hoped Jae would too.

First, however, they had to make it out of the castle.

The spell in Traveler's hands ballooned, the edges of the magic stretching near to breaking. The gearling struggled to contain it.

"The proclamation of a true name . . ." He chuckled. "Well, that will certainly do it! Everyone—hold on to each other!"

Traveler let go of the spell, grabbing Mrs. Harbargain's hand as he did. An undulation of energy crested over the girls. Then, one by one, Traveler, Harbargain, Melanie, Jae, and the others all popped out of sight. The hall was suddenly empty.

"We're invisible!" Melanie heard Mariana exclaim.

"Don't let go of each other's hands," Traveler warned. "We're all using the same spell. If one link in the chain breaks, the whole enchantment will fray and fall apart."

They moved slowly and methodically. Melanie found it surprisingly difficult to climb down a staircase without seeing her own feet. Holding hands only made it harder. Once, Baruti tripped, nearly spilling down the stairs, but Agatha yanked her back into place, holding her steady as she found her balance.

As they reached the lower floors, it became clear that Adrianus had honored his word. Rooms that had been occupied by aldermages were all emptied out. In the quiet, the palace took on an eerie, haunted quality.

Finally, they reached the bottom. The grand entrance hall sprawled before them, lustrous and clean. The vestibule was empty—the front doors sealed. Despite their invisibility, Melanie could hear the group's footsteps clomping noisily against the marble floors, and the ever-present whir of Traveler's clockwork ligaments as he moved. Perhaps they should have considered a *silence* spell too.

"Melanie, when I say so, I want you to open every door and window you can," Traveler's voice buzzed. "Then all of you make a break for it. There are bound to be guards and aldermages outside. I'll hold them off while you escape. We'll meet back at Merrytrails."

"I'm staying with you!" Melanie protested.

"No. We've been lucky so far, but the aldermages could return at any moment. Or even Zerend himself. We shouldn't underestimate him. He's an extremely powerful wizard."

"Riquem, how kind of you to say."

There was a quaver in the air as Zerend popped into existence, standing in the middle of the entrance hall.

His armored hand was wrapped about Blitz's neck. The boy-spirit hung limply from his grip.

"You may as well drop the illusion," Zerend said. His eyes—Riquem's eyes—glinted with an uncanny sheen. "I can see you all as clear as day. Hello, girls. How far you've come from your orphanage, and after such a long journey." His shimmering eyes narrowed. "I'm afraid it was a very dire mistake."

"An Owl's Oath charm," Traveler hissed. The veil fell away from the group. Melanie and the others shimmered back into view.

Zerend nodded, smiling. "Good for peering through magical artifice. If I'm honest, I only cast it for *this* little rascal." The wizard lifted Blitz roughly by the neck. "I sensed he was more than what he seemed, but when I discovered an *elemental spirit* had come to visit the castle, I knew Melanie must be involved." Zerend lowered his arm, dropping Blitz to the floor. The boy just lay there, and Melanie felt a jolt fear. She lunged toward him, but Jae gripped her hand, holding her in place.

"Riquem, I . . ." A beat of quiet sounded between the wizard and the gearling. Zerend swallowed. He crossed his arms, his bare fingers tapped restlessly against the metallic gauntlet. "I'm glad you're alive. That must sound ridiculous, but it's the truth."

Traveler watched the man. "If that's so," he said slowly, "then why is there a siege engine pointed at us?"

The wizard made a pained expression. He waved his hand. With the movement, it seemed as if all the air in the space folded aside, like a stage curtain being drawn open. An invisibility spell as large as a house cascaded away, revealing the enormous gearetten looming behind Zerend, along with a platoon of crimson-eyed gearlings.

Melanie's friends all screamed, clinging to one another. The gearetten's three glowing orbs rolled behind their mesh, watching them with insectlike vacuity. It was even larger than Melanie remembered, and it completely blocked their exit.

"Secrets . . ." Zerend muttered. "I had so many to choose from for this spell." He sighed ruefully. "I can't let these girls leave, Riquem. There's too much at stake. Even *one* of the things they know would ruin me, and none of them knows half of what I've been up to." The wizard set his jaw. "I'm afraid that's how it has to be . . . for them."

Zerend took a tentative step forward. "But not for you," he said. "I made a mistake. I see that now. In my paranoia, I created enemies out of my closest friends. Even you. Especially you. But we have another chance, Riq. By some miracle, you survived! You were a dearer companion than I deserved. Let me give back what I took from you and more."

Zerend threw his arms open.

"You can have your old body!" he said. "I can do that. Now that I know how, we can take any bodies we please. We could be *immortal,* together."

Melanie scowled. "Traveler would never—"

"Be *silent!*" Zerend lifted his gauntleted hand and the gearetten's three eyes clouded to a gory red. It stomped an enormous piston leg, rumbling the entire receiving hall. "I was not speaking to you." The wizard's face was bright with rage, but when his eyes flicked back to Traveler, his expression softened again—clouds rolling over the furious sun.

"Or to 'Traveler,' or whatever you're calling yourself," he said. "I'm asking *you*, Riq. Begging you. Come back. We can travel the cosmos together! See what's beyond the thaumacracy."

There was a whir as Traveler gazed down at his metallic hand. He flexed his fingers, each buzzing with complicated internal machinery.

"I remember . . ." the gearling said. "Thanks to Melanie, I remember everything. This place, the aldermages, they were his whole world. *You* were." Traveler's glowing motes rose. "But Riquem is dead, Zerend. You killed him, just as you've destroyed countless others. The more I remember, the more I understand. The gryphons. Kinderbloom. The Hexe of the South. You *are* the thaumacracy, and everywhere you go, you bring its burning three-eyed gaze with you. Riquem saw you preparing for war and he *let* you do it."

Traveler extended his arm protectively in front of Melanie and the other Merrytrails girls. "*I* won't. I'm not him. I'm something new, built from the salvage of Riquem's tragedy."

Zerend squeezed his eyes shut. "And yet you sound just like him," the man said. His voice was husky. Tired. He lowered his gauntleted hand and the gearetten's orbs dimmed. All around the wizard, the assembled gearlings eased their ready stances, their red eyes blanching white. "Perhaps . . . perhaps you're right. Perhaps there's another way through this. Riquem would have wanted that, I think."

Melanie noticed a flurry of movement behind Zerend's back. Fingers contorting, braiding together with the frantic grace of a pianist.

"He's casting a spell!" she shouted.

Traveler's response was dismal. "I know."

And as Zerend's curse went off, time seemed to stretch—the instant turning slowly like the page of a book. The wizard extended his unarmored hand. His fingers pulled at the air, which shivered with heat. A glowing dart streaked outward, aimed at Melanie and the others.

The dart didn't get far.

It was caught by a gigantic bubble, having apparently been floating unseen between them the whole time. Traveler's favorite charm, Melanie thought. And *of course* it was. Blithe and buoyant and deceptively tough—the protective barrier was a bit like the gearling himself. Its edges glistened in the glare of the burning dart.

As the missile passed through, the bubble wobbled serenely. The dart skidded along the globule's inner perimeter, twirling with circular elegance, emerging back on the side it had entered from.

Pointed straight toward Zerend.

The wizard's eyes widened. "What—?"

Traveler raised his hands. Blitz's body snapped toward them, spilling through the air. Traveler cast a second shimmering barrier just as he caught the boy. It hovered over the group, spinning gently.

And that was all Melanie saw before the explosion.

As the dart struck Zerend, it bloomed like a flower. Or a star.

Even through the protection of the barrier, Melanie could feel the blast's heat. She lifted her hand to shield her eyes: five fingers outlined in flame. In front of her, Traveler did the same. From Melanie's perspective, their hands intersected—metal and flesh, empire and ley. Beyond, a fiery orb spun in the distance.

The flames died almost as quickly as they'd been born. The long shadows cast by the glare retreated, and the room went from very bright to very dark. Traveler waited a moment longer, then made a gesture with his hand. The bubble surrounding them popped.

There was nothing left of Riquem's body, though Zerend's ornate armor survived as a gnarled lump of metal. The floor was covered in a black smear, the smoking remains of the gauntlet resting at the very center of it. It was surrounded by a molten army of scorched and twisted gearlings.

Melanie stepped forward, standing beside Traveler. "Is he all right?" she asked, nodding to Blitz.

The gearling kept his eyes forward. "He's alive," he said.

"And *you*?" she asked.

Now Traveler turned. At first, his glowing motes were carefully blank. He looked like any other gearling—stiff, genteel, unfeeling. Then something in the expression changed. His eyes tilted. They warmed. The shift was subtle, but effective. Even after all their time together, it still amazed Melanie how communicative Traveler could be with just two little dots.

"I'm alive too," he said.

"Even if everything else is a lie," Melanie agreed.

The gearetten had been scorched. Its three eyes were dark behind the mesh, and it sat in a tilt, pushed back by the force of the explosion. It still blocked their way out, but it also blocked the guards from swarming *in*.

Melanie could hear a great clamor of voices from the other side of the doors, likely responding to the blast. In the distance, a bell began to ring—*once, twice*. A citywide emergency was being declared.

"We'll have to find another way out," Melanie said. She gazed across the entrance hall. All the other doors led inward, and the windows were too high to climb through. "Maybe if we double back, we'll find other exits . . . some kind of service door or secret passage."

She felt a rumble behind her. The guards must be trying to push the door open.

The second rumble was even stronger.

"What are they *doing* out there?" Melanie frowned, turning. The other girls were all backing away from the doors with alarmed expressions.

No, not the doors, Melanie realized.

From the gearetten.

Three glowing dots ignited.

"w W-Hat?"

An odd voice echoed out of the machine. The white motes swirled behind their grille, moving in confused rotations.

"W-w wHEre aM I?" The gearetten lifted itself heavily

from its prostrate position, looming even higher. Its enormous metal legs droned with the sounds of heavy machinery.

"Oh," Melanie gasped. "Oh, no." Her words rang through the hall like the tones of a bell.

"I I I I c-cAN't Fee e l aNYthInG. RR rriQ?"

Traveler's eyes were bright with shock. "That spell was the same one Zerend used to destroy the evidence of his work. The same explosion that created *me* . . ."

Traveler pressed forward, his hands raised. "Zerend, stay calm," he said. "You're alive. That's the most important—"

"nO."

"Zerend, *please*. Listen to my voice."

"No nO NO NO NONONO. nO-T liKE THI I I I IS." The gearetten's piston legs began to churn. Steam sprayed from valves all over its body. Its three eyes jerked wildly—the color clouding from white to bloody red.

"MM m E L aaNeeeee GaTe."

Melanie's eyes widened. A chill climbed up her back. "Run." She turned to Mrs. Harbargain. "Get the others inside! Somewhere deep. Go now!"

Mrs. Harbargain scooped Blitz from Traveler, then herded Melanie's friends inward, back toward the castle's interior. The matron brought up the rear, carrying Blitz in her arms. She turned when she realized Melanie hadn't followed. "Come with us," she called.

"I'll be right behind you!"

Harbargain's face crumpled. "You won't," she said. "I let you go once. I was a fool then. What would I be now?"

"Yyy-y OUr f-faULT! mmEL a NEe!"

The gearetten's front leg swiped out, obliterating a castle column in a single movement. The entire hall shook. Dust rained down from the ceiling.

"You'd be the woman who stormed a castle to save my life," Melanie said. "Now go, please! Protect the others!"

Harbargain glanced behind her to where Melanie's friends had disappeared into the castle. When she looked back her face was resolute. "I love you, Melanie Gate. Take care, my little wonder."

Melanie nodded, fighting back tears.

Another crash. The building shook with even more violence. She turned just in time to see one of the gearetten's three eyes center upon her. The red pupil expanded.

"MM EL A N EE!"

The automaton lurched forward. One of its enormous mechanical legs lifted upward and came punching toward her with frightening speed. Traveler lifted his hand and conjured a glittering globule. The bubble repelled the blow, but burst in the process, dissolving to nothing.

"We have to get you out of here!" Traveler buzzed, raising another barrier. "He'll bring down the whole palace."

"The whole city!" Melanie said. She could hear the dread thick in her own voice. "This thing *destroyed* Ein's glade with some kind of weapon . . . he called it an eldritch canon!"

Zerend's voice shrieked out of the automaton's metal grille. The gearetten shifted its weight onto its back four legs and struck downward with the other two at the same time. Traveler shouted in alarm. He pulled his arms wide and the bubble flattened and stretched, shielding a broader area. The legs bounded off just as the spell shattered.

"Jump onto my back!"

Melanie did as she was told, climbing onto the gearling. Once she was on, Traveler burst forward, loping beneath the gearetten.

The entrance to the castle was still fastened shut, but now that the obstruction blocking their path had moved away from it, rising up to kill her, it meant she could . . .

OPEN! she commanded, pressing her hand to one of the enormous doors.

They burst apart, revealing a small army on the other side. At first the city guards looked frightened to see a gearling bounding through the suddenly open entryway. Then, as they caught sight of the enormous mechanical monstrosity behind it, they looked truly terrified.

"Run!"

"The machines have gone mad!"

Guards fell over themselves attempting to retreat, creating a mass of fleeing bodies.

"Hold on!" Traveler crouched low, then took a flying leap over the crowd. He landed on the other side with a hiss of steam.

The guards were still scrambling out of the way when the gearetten burst through the castle's facade, obliterating what was left of the entrance.

"y-yOUR FAU-lt ME L L L L an EEEE!"

"We're in the heart of the city!" Traveler rasped. "There's no way to lead it out without people dying."

Melanie remembered the smell of seawater in Riquem's vision. "The docks!" she cried. "They're just west of the castle."

Traveler skidded into a turn, bounding westward. Melanie glanced behind her to see the gearetten charging after them. Its six insectlike legs pumped furiously, each step shattering the stones beneath them.

It was morning in Crossport, but the emergency bells meant most civilians were required to take shelter in their homes or nearby businesses. Even so, some people still milled about in the streets. Curious bystanders gaped toward the commotion, and a stubborn few ignored the alarms entirely to go about their business.

Melanie saw a kassipoi merchant hurriedly clearing his table of merchandise as he noticed the chaos barreling toward him. The kassipoi yowled, his fur standing on end. He scrambled out of the way as Traveler and Melanie sprinted past, only narrowly avoiding the gearetten's pulverizing legs.

Ahead, Melanie could see the harbor juddering between the last two buildings of the avenue. Merchant ships rocked gently against the docks. Now that the storm had passed, the sea was unnervingly calm. She tried to think. How could they lead Zerend to the water? She doubted that enormous metal body was much good for swimming. Perhaps if he was angry and disoriented enough, she could—

A thunderous crack erupted from behind her. The sky dimmed, darkness swallowing the avenue. Then morning returned, and the hulking shape of the gearetten crashed upon the harbor—right in front them.

Melanie screamed as Traveler skidded to a halt.

The gearetten's three motes clicked into a monstrous synchronization. They began to spin, the lights drawing together. Soon they'd formed a single blood-red eye. Energy crackled from the orb, lines of red lightning snaking across its metal body.

"This . . ." Melanie gasped. Her last memory of Ein's glade snapped into focus. "This is the eldritch canon! He'll kill everyone!"

Traveler's face turned down toward Melanie's. His eyes were despondent. "It's too strong," the gearling said. "We have to run."

"No."

Melanie was tired of running.

Ein had told her she was a spirit of freedom—a key to open doors. And true enough, all during her journey Melanie had been bursting through barriers, usually to flee.

But she was also more than what Ein had meant for her to be. She was a foundling, a prodigy, and a con artist. A witch, a rebel, and a friend. She was a girl and a spirit and whatever else she chose. She was a lock-eater.

I won't define you, Hexe of the South. Even that name is yours to set aside, if you choose.

She was the Hexe of the South—but on *her* terms.

She was a key to open doors.

And, apparently, to shut them.

"Get me closer," Melanie said. "I need . . . I think I need to touch it."

Traveler's eyes tilted doubtfully, but a moment later he nodded. "Very well."

The gearling burst forward, skittering agilely across the street—and then the wooden planks of the harbor. Zerend shrieked unintelligibly. The gearetten punched its legs at them, attempting to pin them against the docks. Its glowing eye brightened, growing almost as intense as the morning sun.

A leg shot out toward them. Traveler only just dodged the thrust. The second one Traveler buffeted away with a glittering bubble. The gearling crouched and pivoted, leaping toward the automaton's enormous scorched abdomen.

He was too slow for the third strike.

Traveler tried to leap over the sweeping limb, but the blow caught his legs, sending them both spinning through the air. Melanie felt the shock of impact as she landed, saw bright spots burst before her eyes. She reached out blindly, finally grasping . . . metal.

"*Melanie!*" Traveler's voice sounded so far away.

"**D I EEEEE.**"

In contrast, Zerend's voice was everywhere, rumbling through her entire body. Her eyes focused. She was directly beneath the gearetten.

"*CLOSE!*" Melanie screamed.

It was a brief wish, but a strong one, and it passed right

through her hand where she'd pressed it against the gearetten's armor. The metal heard her, and it did its very best to grant such a potent wish.

It imploded.

Once, Melanie had witnessed a ship sinking, when an old merchant vessel gave way just outside the harbor. The wood sang as it collapsed, in a mournful hymn. The sound Melanie heard now was similar. There was a sharp crunch of metal, then a high warped chime.

"W w w h-ha t?"

Melanie lurched suddenly backward, flying through the air. She landed against a floating bubble that Traveler had thrown her way. The gearling quickly helped her down, and the two of them stood side by side as they watched the enormous mechanical monster folding in upon itself.

"R rr riQum! N o!"

Another high screech, but this was from the glowing eye. The lines of electricity grew more intense, crawling across the shrinking metal sphere.

Traveler raised his hand and the stone inside his palm flared. Then one last billowing bubble appeared, swallowing the gearetten and yanking it backward.

Zerend fell into the sea. The surface of the water hissed and boiled on contact, but it wasn't long before all that densely packed metal plummeted downward. There was a dull, startling *BOOF* that shook the docks. Then, after a few churning waves, the water quieted.

The morning was silent again.

They stayed there for a time, listening to the lapping water. Finally, Melanie turned to Traveler. "I'm sorry," she said softly. She took his hand in hers. "He was . . ."

How to put it into words? *He was your friend. He was so much more than your friend. He was a life, and I know what it cost you to end it.*

"He was a murderer," Traveler finished for her. The gearling let out a little sigh that echoed within his mask. "We should find the others," he said. "I doubt staying in Crossport would be wise. For us *or* your friends."

Melanie nodded. "I know a place," she said. "One we can make our own."

The gearling turned his gaze toward her. His glowing eyes tilted hopefully.

"Lead the way."

CHAPTER 35

NEARLY everyone at the Merrytrails School for Magic agreed: Abraxas was a good cat.

Not the kindest. Or the most beautiful. Or the most entertaining, or agile, or sweet-smelling. But deep down he was *good*.

Which was why they were throwing him a nameday party.

No one was quite sure exactly how old the cat was, of course. Not even Mrs. Harbargain. But when you're a family of foundlings, you don't get too caught up in the details.

Abraxas had acquiesced to a miniature party hat for exactly seventeen seconds. He now batted at what was left of the unfortunate headgear, on the ground in shreds.

Melanie the Periwinkle, the First Hexe of the South, began the speeches. She held Mrs. Harbargain's hand in her own as she recalled the day a year ago when she'd accidentally released Abraxas from their orphanage . . . *also* accidentally exploding the building in the process. The South Coven all smiled at one another, remembering that night.

Agatha the Cardinal, the Third Hexe, reminded Melanie that she'd snuck a fire iron into the room. The Fifth Hexe, Sun-mi the Celadon, recalled that she'd even given a little speech!

Sun-mi set Abraxas's birthday cake in front him, drawing the cat's attention away from the clawed-up strips of party hat. The loaf was baked from eggs, fragrant cheese, and fish scraps, and topped with a generous helping of fried crickets. It smelled *awful,* but a more conventional cake awaited the girls inside. Sun-mi had only used a few crickets in that one.

"What was it you said we'd have to rename the orphanage?" she asked, pressing a finger to her lips. Beside her, Blitz's shining face split into an expectant grin. He hadn't heard this part of the story.

"The Merrytrails Asylum for Cat Killers!" cried Baruti the Zaffre, the Fourth Hexe, and all the girls cackled with laughter.

Melanie flushed. "I never said that."

"You DID!" insisted the Sixth Hexe, Mariana the Pearl. "And you got in so much trouble!"

"Well, in any case, this isn't about me," Melanie said primly. "It's about *Abraxas.*"

"Wasn't that what *started* the whole thing with Traveler?" asked Jae Jetblack, the Second Hexe, turning to the gearling. "Abraxas escaped, but then he brought you to Melanie. To *us.*" She looped her arm through Traveler's, leaning affectionately into him. The two had become fast friends in the past year, and Jae was easily the most apt of his students. In her black coat with lacy sleeves (designed by Livia) she looked every bit the magical prodigy she'd proven herself to be.

Traveler the Gold's glowing eyes rose to meet Melanie's, the dots two mirthful crescent moons. "Technically Melanie found *me* first," he said. "In a different life. But that's right . . .

I was alone in Crossport, desperately seeking a way out of the city. I knew of an orphanage, and had heard about its *unusual* accident. But on my way, I got lost in the storm. I had no idea which building was yours. Then I saw a poor creature huddled beneath a windowsill. He was soaked to the bone. And he was just outside Merrytrails."

"You rescued each other!" exclaimed Helen Sunglow-Stables, the Seventh Hexe. "So we have Abraxas to thank for all of this."

"To Abraxas!" Jae shouted.

"To Abraxas!" Blitz's body flared, sending sparkling arcs across the glade. Several of the water spirits cried out, splashing the witches in protest with glittering droplets.

Melanie smiled as her friends all screamed and laughed, shielding themselves from the spray with minor protection spells. Abraxas hissed at the spirits, retreating from his birthday feast. It was probably for the best, Melanie thought. A cake that fragrant combined with a cat that gassy was asking for trouble.

Still, in that moment, she was nearly overcome by the debt she owed the mean old tom.

It had taken a year to build their little school in the woods.

A year, and toil, and no small amount of luck. The aldermages had followed them, of course. In the days following Zerend's destruction, it seemed like the entire thaumacracy was after their heads. But with Traveler's help, the girls had escaped the city and made it to Hamlen, where Katzy's and Livia's grateful families hid them for a time.

Thankfully, it wasn't long before the truth of Zerend's treachery was revealed. His notes on the body-stealing spell were discovered, along with several detailed prospective strategies for a coup against the king and prime minister.

With such a wealth of evidence pointing to the empire's highest ranking magical mind being both a murderer and seditionist, the remaining two heads of state agreed there was only one reasonable course of action.

They quietly pretended the whole thing had never happened.

Not that there weren't changes. A new high enchanter was chosen, and it turned out that Adrianus's mentor, Saanvi, had been selected for the job. She began a sweep of reforms, including ending all hostilities against the Ley Coven and a systematic purge of corrupt aldermages. She even loosened restrictions on the Imperial Census of Spellwrights, allowing grouille royalty to practice magic for the first time since the Wizard War.

Many fought back against Saanvi the Red's new policies, but with the king and prime minister behind her, there was little her rivals could do to stand in her way. It wasn't perfect, but it was a chance.

Melanie and the girls were able to journey to the Zwarte Woud unthreatened, where they found Ein's glade a burned-out ruin. The spirits were scattered. The forest denizens in hiding.

But the power of the ley was strong in those woods, and it was pleased that Melanie had returned. Together, they set to work. The girls journeyed back and forth between Hamlen and the woods, trading with the villagers.

In the wake of High Enchanter Saanvi's reforms, Hamlen's aerie was shuttered—a hard blow for the village that had reshaped itself around rearing the beasts. Some of the Hamleners returned to shepherding, while others were set on a new project. Saanvi established a sanctuary not just for gryphons, but *any* creatures, from chimeras to cockatrice, created by thaumaturgic means for the purpose of warfare. She tasked her apprentice, Adrianus, with its administration. The Hamleners who'd taken a shine to the gryphons now dedicated themselves to caring for them—ensuring the animals lived out their lives in comfort.

All except for the one that had killed Parno, which was never caught. Rumors still reached the girls of a great golden raptor that made its home in the Albes Mountains.

Melanie was pleased to get to know Katzy better in Hamlen—but spent most of her time there with Livia, who'd enthusiastically agreed to outfit the girls in the chosen colors of their new Ley Coven personas. The two had grown close in the last year, much to Melanie's astonished delight. Livia even tried to convince Melanie to die her *hair* periwinkle as part of her new look, though Melanie had declined.

Mostly.

She *did* allow the girl to color a single streak. And after gazing at herself in the mirror and tucking the purple-blue lock behind her ear, the two had shared a first bashful kiss.

Together, the foundlings built a new home. They learned to cast spells, taught by Traveler and empowered by Melanie's newfound connection to the ley. Melanie had promised herself she would accept the title of Hexe of the South on her own terms—and that was exactly what she did, sharing both the power and responsibility with her family. No one was trapped in this forest, and none were forced to shoulder its obligations alone.

And if the other wardens of the ley disagreed with Melanie's choice to divide her power? Well, they were simply outvoted.

When the nearby villages began to hear stories of a kindly new coven who'd appeared in the Zwarte Woud, it wasn't long before pilgrims arrived at the forest, hoping to apprentice under them.

At first, Melanie had balked. Magic had caused *so much* harm; she'd been a horrified witness to the atrocities that it could wreak in the wrong hands.

But Traveler calmed her worries.

Magic would exist, with or without them. It was always there, and it was always dangerous—both a weapon *and* a tool.

So they taught peace, as well as spellwork. They instructed their students to build, heal, and grow. To fill their spells with love. They took any students who came to them. Girls and boys and those who were neither or both. Humans and kassipois and grouille, and spirits that were utterly unlike anything Melanie had ever seen before.

The foundlings even received some unexpected financial help in Princess-Electa Maximillia, who had apparently forgiven Melanie for accidentally destroying her castle. The princess proposed to invest in their new school, on the condition that her tadpole nephew be allowed to attend, once he'd grown a suitable pair of arms.

Melanie and the others had only one condition of their own. To work together with the Grouille Principality, exploring a safe method of destroying Hagalaz for good. It was a requirement Maximillia was more than happy to oblige. After years of hiding their doomsday spell, the grouille welcomed the opportunity to rid themselves of their secret burden.

The girls still missed Merrytrails from time to time. Their hasty retreat from Crossport meant the orphanage had passed along to a new matron, a young woman named Ms. Blithepact. Mrs. Harbargain had checked in on the orphanage once, during a covert trip to Crossport. She seemed pleased by the state of things, and even left a generous donation for the burgeoning orphanage—a gift from one Felidae Seagreen.

The place had been full of so many important memories . . . but it was still just a place.

People made a house into a home; it was a magic even the ley couldn't reproduce.

Melanie glanced across the glade at her family, all of them gathered to celebrate their old friend Abraxas. Her eyes met Traveler's, and the gearling nodded. He always seemed to know just what she was thinking.

Somehow, by some miracle, they had both awakened.

And found the world was right.

ACKNOWLEDGMENTS

THIS novel is my "solo" debut, but the truth is that it's benefitted from the enthusiasm and expertise of so many kind, patient, brilliant people. I'm immensely grateful to everyone who's had a hand in getting this story into shape, and into the world.

First, to my editor, Jessica Dandino Garrison . . . How to adequately thank you? You took a chance on this story, and pushed me to make it all it could possibly be. Your grace and kindness during the editorial process kept me buoyed even when I felt like I was floundering. You're a genius, and I'm so appreciative that you shared some of that genius with me.

Thanks to my agent, Ammi-Joan Paquett, who has always been a steadfast champion. I'm immensely lucky you took me on as a client.

Thanks to everyone at Dial and Penguin Random House who have so much as looked at this. Every book is bolstered by countless unsung heroes of various departments —managing editors, copyeditors, and proofreaders; finance, production, and planning; the rights, sales, marketing, and publicity teams. Thank you, Nancy Mercado and Lauri Hornik of Dial, who were among the first to see the initial chapters.

Thanks to early readers Jennifer Ridgway, Shanta Newlin, Doni Kay, and Lauren Festa. Special thanks to Rosie Ahmed for her keen insights, and to our great expert reader, Sharifa Love, and copyeditor, Regina Castillo.

Also thank you to Super Designer, Jessica Jenkins, interior designer Cerise Steel, and to artists Fiona Hsieh and Julia Iredale for sharing your jaw-dropping artistic talents with us in the development of the book's cover package. I'm honestly in awe of your abilities.

Thank you to my writing group, the Afictionados—Preeti Chhibber and Rafi Mittlefehldt—who had such sage observations about the concept and early chapters. And thank you to the small army of friends who have offered advice and words of encouragement: Andrew Eliopulos, Nick Eliopulos, Tate Geborkoff, Laura Heston, David Levithan, Jack Lienke, Nico Medina, Billy Merrell, Sarah Miller, Tony Sarkees, and Seth Sklar-Heyn.

Thank you to my family: Matthew Collin Clark, Latham Zearfoss, Terry Clark, and my mom, Melanie Clark, who is Melanie Gate's namesake. I'm so fortunate to have a caring, supportive clan who've always fostered my love of storytelling. And thanks to my amazing in-laws, Richard Lewis, Joan Sapinsley, Sam Lewis, and Christian Lopez, for welcoming me into your family with open arms.

Lastly, thank you to Zack Lewis. As of this writing, you're my fiancé, but when the book publishes, you'll be my husband!

Thank you for adventuring with me, for patiently listening to my anxieties, and for being the very first person to offer encouragement on this project. I love you.